THE LETTERS OF WILKIE COLLINS

Portrait of Wilkie Collins (1850) by Sir John Everett Millais (*reproduced by courtesy of the National Portrait Gallery*)

The Letters of Wilkie Collins

Volume 1
1838–1865

Edited by

William Baker

and

William M. Clarke

First published in Great Britain 1999 by
MACMILLAN PRESS LTD
Houndmills, Basingstoke, Hampshire RG21 6XS and London
Companies and representatives throughout the world

A catalogue record for this book is available from the British Library.

ISBN 0–333–67466–9 Volume 1: 1838–1865
ISBN 0–333–73246–4 Volume 2: 1866–1889
ISBN 0–333–73247–2 two-volume set

First published in the United States of America 1999 by
ST. MARTIN'S PRESS, INC.,
Scholarly and Reference Division,
175 Fifth Avenue, New York, N.Y. 10010

ISBN 0–312–22343–9 Volume 1: 1838–1865
ISBN 0–312–22344–7 Volume 2: 1866–1889

Library of Congress Cataloging-in-Publication Data
Collins, Wilkie, 1824–1889.
[Correspondence.   Selections]
The letters of Wilkie Collins / edited by William Baker and
William M. Clarke.
p.   cm.
Includes bibliographical references and index.
Contents: v. 1. 1838–1865 — v. 2. 1866–1889.
ISBN 0–312–22343–9 (v. 1). — ISBN 0–312–22344–7 (v. 2)
1. Collins, Wilkie, 1824–1889—Correspondence.   2. Novelists,
English—19th century—Correspondence.   I. Baker, William, 1944–
.   II. Clarke, William M. (William Malpas)   III. Title.
PR4496.A4   1999
823'.8—dc21
                                                99–19642
                                                CIP

This book is printed on paper suitable for recycling and made from fully managed and
sustained forest sources.

10   9   8   7   6   5   4   3   2   1
08   07   06   05   04   03   02   01   00   99

Printed and bound in Great Britain by
Antony Rowe Ltd, Chippenham, Wiltshire

For our wives

Contents

The Index of Correspondents and Subject Index are printed at the end of Volume 2

List of Illustrations

Volume 1

Plates 1 and 2   William and Harriet Collins, Wilkie's parents, by John Linnell. (Faith Clarke)

Plate 3   Charles and Wilkie as children by Alexander Geddes. (Horace Pym Collection)

Plate 4   Wilkie as a baby by William Collins. (Faith Clarke)

Plate 5   Charles Collins, Wilkie's brother and son-in-law to Charles Dickens.

Plate 6   Charles Collins with Dickens and other members of the family at Gad's Hill.

Plate 7   Wilkie Collins by Herbert Watkins in 1864.

Plate 8   Caroline Graves in the 1870s. (From *The Secret Life of Wilkie Collins* by William Clarke)

Volume 2

Plate 9   Martha Rudd.

Plate 10   Wilkie Collins with Martha Rudd. (Faith Clarke)

Plate 11   The cover of *The Bookman*, June 1912.

Plate 12   A Christmas card featuring titles by Wilkie Collins, actual size.

Plate 13   F.W. Waddy's caricature of Collins, 1872.

Plate 14   "I am dying old friend." Plate 15   "I am too muddled to write. They are driving me mad by forbidding the [Hypodermic] Come for God's sake." The last letters Wilkie Collins wrote to his doctor. (Princeton University Library)

Preface

This edition of the letters of Wilkie Collins will shed light on the life and activities of one of the few remaining major Victorian creative personalities whose letters and papers remain uncollected and unpublished. Although Collins has been the subject of recent biographies, these works only quote brief extracts from the limited correspondence already available to biographers. One of the reasons there has been no edition is the reluctance of his heirs to expose to public scrutiny the author's unconventional lifestyle. Collins had at least two common law wives and the stigma of illegitimacy has haunted the resulting children and their descendants even into the latter half of the twentieth century. Now that permission has been given to examine and publish the long-hidden correspondence – one of the editors, William Clarke, is the husband of Collins' great-granddaughter and author of the revealing biography of Collins *The Secret Life of Wilkie Collins* (1988, 1996) – the edition will illuminate an extraordinarily rich and varied Victorian life. It will shed light on Victorian literature and publishing, music, art and many other areas of intellectual, cultural and artistic endeavour.

There are two main sources for Collins letters: those which survive in institutional holdings or in private hands, and those which have disappeared but survive in printed form. In *Letters of Charles Dickens to Wilkie Collins*, published by Harper Brothers in New York in 1892, Laurence Hutton collected the letters Dickens sent to his close friend Collins. In his preface to *Wilkie Collins* (1952) Robert Ashley wrote of "the huge bonfire at Gad's Hill to which, irritated at the invasion of his privacy by the press, Dickens consigned the whole of his correspondence". Consequently, he concluded, "although we have many of the letters Dickens wrote to Collins, we have none of those which Collins wrote to Dickens". Ashley also noted that "another loss was occasioned when Collins himself burnt the greater part of his correspondence before moving from Gloucester Place to Wimpole Street in the closing years of his life".

Kenneth Robinson's biography *Wilkie Collins* appeared in the same year as Ashley's work. Robinson drew upon unpublished letters and other materials then in the possession of John Lehmann, Frank H. Arnold, the Morrish L. Parrish Collection at Princeton, and letters in the possession of A.P. Watt & Son, the London literary agents. Since 1952 many of these letters have moved across the Atlantic to Princeton, or have remained in private hands. Another biographer to utilize institutional holdings to cite brief extracts from the letters was Nuel Pharr Davis in his *The Life of Wilkie Collins* (1956). In his doctoral dissertation "The University of Texas Collection of the Letters of Wilkie Collins, Victorian Novelist", (the University of Texas at Austin 1975), William Rollin Coleman presented an edition of 262 letters from the holograph manuscripts, transcriptions and photocopies at the University of Texas. Subsequently the University of Texas has added to its Collins holdings, especially with its acquisition of the Robert Lee Wolff collection of Victorian novelists.

Two biographies have drawn upon some of the many extant letters throughout the world in university libraries and private collections. William Clarke's intention in his biography is to unravel the secrets of Collins' complicated private life. Clarke's pioneering research revealed the identity of Collins' copyright holder and identified 18 institutions whose libraries held Collins' letters and the names of some private holders. Catherine Peters in her *The King of Inventors: A Life of Wilkie Collins* (1991), building upon Clarke's foundation, interweaves Collins' complicated life with her subject's literary achievements. Clarke's biography prompted Sir John Lawrence to reveal the existence of letters sent by the ageing Collins in the last years of his life to an eleven-year-old girl and her mother. The bulk of the letters to "Nannie" are published in full here for the first time.

The largest institutional collections of Collins letters are to be found at the Pierpont Morgan Library in New York, the Parrish Collection at Princeton and at the University of Texas. The Pierpont Morgan has over 300 Collins letters. These include 117 revealing letters to his mother, 86 to his close friend Charles Ward, and letters to publishers such as Harper and Brothers and William Henry Wills (1810–1880) the general manager and proprietor of *Household Words* and *All the Year Round*. There are also many letters, not included here, by other members of Collins' family – his mother, his father and his brother Charles. The Parrish Collection has upwards of 250 letters including those to Collins' close friends the Lehmanns, to his physician Dr Frank Beard, his various publishers and a host of other correspondents. The University of Texas has been adding to its Collins holdings edited by Coleman in the 1970s and now has just under 300 letters.

These three repositories alone yield upwards of 850 letters. There are also significant Collins holdings at the Berg Collection, New York Public Library, including letters to the publishers George Bentley (94), and George Smith (21), at Harvard, the Huntington Library, the University of Illinois at Urbana, the Beinecke Library, Yale University, and elsewhere including Kansas and Stanford. Interestingly there are fewer Collins letters in institutional holdings in the British Isles. The largest of these, over 140 letters to Collins' solicitor W.F. Tindell, are at the Mitchell Library in Glasgow. There are smaller collections at the British Library, the National Library of

Scotland, the National Art Library (the "V and A"), the Bodleian Library, Oxford, the John Rylands University Library of Manchester, the Manx National Heritage Museum and elsewhere. These holdings numerically do not compare with those in the United States.

The most extensive collections of Collins' letters (more than 300) in the United Kingdom are in private hands, owned by his descendants or by private collectors who inherited them or purchased the letters at auction. Thanks to the generosity of these collectors, some of whom wish to remain anonymous, we have been able to utilize their holdings. Collins' letters are emerging almost daily at auction and in dealers' catalogues. A worldwide search reveals Collins letters on three continents including Australia.

There are Collins letters scattered in printed sources, many of which belong to the last years of the nineteenth century and the early years of the twentieth. Various memoirs by actresses such as Kate Field and Mary Anderson; actors such as Frank Archer, and Squire Bancroft; literary figures such as William Winter and publishers such as Bernhard Tauchnitz, included lengthy and interesting Collins letters. C.K. Hyder's article "Collins in America", published as a festschrift from the University of Kansas in 1940, contained lengthy extracts written during Collins' stay in North America during the winter of 1873–74. *Six Letters of Wilkie Collins ... at Stanford University Library* (1957) contains reproductions of the letters with transcripts. The letters "form a sort of vignette of the personality, pre-occupations and temperament of" their writer. T.D. Clareson's "Wilkie Collins to Charles Reade: Some Unpublished Letters", published in *Victorian Essays: A Symposium*, edited by W.D. Anderson and T. Clareson (1967), reveals just a few of the many letters Collins wrote to his fellow novelist – who also enjoyed a non-conventional lifestyle. Some of Collins' letters to Reade are published in full, others are given in summary form. The particularly helpful catalogue of the *Parrish Collection of Wilkie Collins and Charles Reade* (1940) includes important early letters Collins wrote to the American novelist Richard Henry Dana Jr (1815–1882), author of *Two Years Before the Mast* (1840), and a friend of Collins' father. Letters of a business and a professional rather than of a personal nature are found in Desmond Flower's "Authors and Copyright in the Nineteenth Century, with Unpublished Letters from Wilkie Collins". *The Book-Collector's Quarterly*, No.VII (July–September 1952), publishes lengthy letters Collins wrote to publishers and editors in order to protect his copyrights and on behalf of other authors on the question of protecting their interests on matters of international copyright.

Collins' letters are scattered throughout the world and found in diverse locations and sources. So it is hardly surprising that an edition of his letters has never been published. There were huge gaps in his correspondence, and – unlike Charles Dickens, George Eliot and Anthony Trollope (to mention but three of his contemporaries whose letters have been collected together and published) – there was no substantial edifice to build upon.

In the first volume of *The Letters of Rudyard Kipling*, Thomas Pinney observed that "though it aims to be generous and fully representative, this is a selected, not a 'complete', *Letters*". He went on, "When I began my work I began with the intention of publishing everything that I could find, but it did not take long to modify that intention." We have encountered the same problem. Our researches have uncovered upwards of 2,000 letters written by Collins in institutional and private holdings. Some of these letters are social notes – Collins was invariably polite – for instance declining invitations to dine. Others are brief notes to his publishers or business letters. Some repeat what has been previously written – for instance to his agent A.P. Watt. Some letters are polite responses to people he doesn't know who for one reason or another have made contact with him. Others are of importance and contain details of his personal or artistic life, political, religious, or other opinions. Some are found only in summarized form.

Pinney finally concluded "It can certainly be argued that for the sake of the record, and for the sake of the detail that only completeness can provide, everything available ought to be published. But, while admitting the force of the argument, I conclude in favour of selection over completeness." We have done the same. We have decided to publish transcriptions of 591 important Collins letters, with annotations and linking commentary. Pressures of space have forced us to summarize 127 of those letters. The summaries retain the flavour of the originals while omitting redundant matter. In addition, in the interests of future researchers and biographers, we have also appended to each volume a list of letters, in date order, not given in full or even summarized. Each is given one line indicating recipient, date, topic discussed and, above all, the present source. These amount to a further 1,632 letters. We hope that in this way these two volumes will provide researchers with a comprehensive guide to contents and show the diverse nature of Collins' letters.

Acknowledgements

Many people and institutions are to be thanked for helping us prepare this edition of the letters of Wilkie Collins. Faith Clarke (née Dawson), the great-granddaughter of Wilkie Collins and Martha Rudd, has been most generous with permissions, allowing publication of hitherto unpublished Wilkie Collins letters and other materials. Andrew Gasson, Chairman of The Wilkie Collins Society and author of *Wilkie Collins: An Illustrated Guide*, who placed his extensive knowledge of Wilkie Collins, his life and writings, at our disposal, has been most helpful.

Our debts are many, and thanks are also due to the following libraries, institutions and individuals for assistance and permission to consult and quote from manuscripts in their holdings: Dr Dianna Vitanza and the Armstrong Browning Library, Baylor University, Waco, Texas; Vincent Giroud, Curator of Modern Books and Manuscripts, Beinecke Library, Yale University; Department of Manuscripts, British Library; the Bodleian Library, Oxford; T.K. Campbell, Archivist, Bolton Metro Libraries; A.C. Smith, Editor in Chief, *Bolton Evening News* (*Bolton Evening News Archive* [ZBEN]); Roberta Zonghi, Curator of Rare Books, Boston Public Library; Christopher Sheppard, Brotherton Collection, Leeds University Library; William H. Loos, Curator, Grosvenor Rare Book Room, Buffalo and Erie County Public Library, the Keeper of Manuscripts, Cambridge University Library; Columbia University Library; the Curator, the Dickens House Museum, London; the Archivist, Enthoven Collection, British Theatre Museum, London; the Mistress and Fellows, Kate Perry, Archivist, Girton College, Cambridge; Marvin S. Taylor, Fales Librarian, the Fales Library, New York University; the Folger Shakespeare Library, Washington; Linda Burke, the Mitchell Library, Glasgow City Council Libraries Department; the Trustees, Harrowby Manuscript Trust, Sandon, Staffordshire; the Archivist, Hertfordshire County Record Office, Hertford; Leslie A. Morris, Curator of Manuscripts, Jennie Rathbun, Emily C. Walhout, the Houghton Library, Harvard University, Harvard; Cathy Henderson, Research Librarian, and her colleagues at the Harry Ransom Humanities Research Center, University of Texas at Austin; Sara S. Hodson, Curator of Literary Manuscripts, Department of Manuscripts, Laura Stalker, Henry E. Huntington Library, San Marino, California; Robert A. McCown, Special Collections and Manuscripts Librarian, the University Libraries, the University of Iowa, Iowa City; Amy Presser, Special Collections, Johns Hopkins University; William Brockman, Nancy L. Romero, Rare Books and Special Collections Library, University of Illinois at Urbana-Champaign; Ann Hyde, Curator of Manuscripts, Kenneth Spencer Research Library, University of Kansas, Lawrence, Kansas; the University of Kentucky Library; David Goodes, and the Walpole Librarian, the King's School, Canterbury; B. Jackson, County Archivist, Lancashire Record Office, Preston, Lancs.; Alice L. Birney, Manuscript Division, Library of Congress, Washington, DC; the Archivist, Liverpool City Libraries, Liverpool; the Archivist, Manchester Central Library, Manchester, England; Roger M.C. Sims, Librarian Archivist, Manx National Heritage Museum, Douglas, Isle of Man; Dr Iain G. Brown, Assistant Keeper of Manuscripts, National Library of Scotland; the Board of Trustees, National Art Library, Victoria and Albert Museum, London; Francis Mattson, W. Furman, the Berg Collection, and Special Collections, Research Libraries, the New York Public Library; Timothy Pyatt, Curator of Manuscripts, University of North Carolina at Chapel Hill; the Archivist, The Northumberland Record Office, Gosforth; the Archivist, Nottinghamshire Archive, Nottingham; the Librarian, the Historical Society of Pennsylvania, Philadelphia, Pennsylvania; Alexander D.Wainwright, Curator, the M.L. Parrish Collection, Mary Ann Jensen, Curator, William Seymour Theatre Collection, Jean F. Preston, Princeton University Library; Robert E. Parks, Robert H. Taylor, Curator of Autograph Manuscripts, Anna L. Ashby and colleagues, the Pierpont Morgan Library, New York; Portsmouth Central Library; Preston Harris Museum and Art Gallery, Preston, Lancs; the University of Queensland Library, Queensland, Australia; Reading University Library; Nigel Cross, Archivist, the Royal Literary Fund; Dr Peter McNiven, the John Rylands University Library of Manchester; the Scottish Record Office, Edinburgh, Scotland; the Shakespeare Birthplace Trust, Shakespeare Centre, Stratford upon Avon; Stanford University Libraries, Stanford University; State Library of New South Wales, Sydney, Australia; State Library of Victoria, Melbourne, Australia; David McKitterick, Librarian, and the Master and Fellows of Trinity College, Cambridge; Christine Penney, University Archivist, the Department of Special Collections, University of Birmingham Library, Birmingham, England; Department of Special Collections, University of California at Los Angeles; Richard A. Schrader, Reference Archivist, Manuscripts Department, University of North Carolina at Chapel Hill; the University of Waseda, Japan; Curator, the Townshend Collection, the Wisbech and Fenland Museum, Wisbech, Cambridgeshire.

Our other debts are many. Thanks are due to many colleagues at Northern Illinois University, and to its Information Delivery Services Department in the University Libraries, and to Professors Jitka Hurych, Heinz D. Osterle, and Gustaaf Van Cromphout who have been assidious with their assistance with languages unknown to us. Professors Neal R. Norrick, M.S. Schriber, Graduate Director, and Professors James I. Miller, Heather Hardy, Chairs of the English Department, were ever supportive –

for example in finding graduate assistance with word-processing. Special thanks must go to Janet Engstrom, Mark O'Connor, and especially Jayne Higgins who in good humour not only put up with William Baker's moods but transformed an unwieldy text into an excellent finished project, manipulating what seemed like a myriad of disks into manageable order. Dr Nancy Cervetti of Avila College, Kansas, Professor Peter Edwards of the University of Queensland, Glen Horowitz the indefatigable New York book seller, Dr Graham Law of Waseda University, Paul Lewis of the Wilkie Collins Society, London, Professor Norman Page, Arthur Pinnington of Waseda University, Professor Ira D. Nadel of the University of British Columbia, Vancouver, Professor Lillian Nayder of Bates College, Maine, Mrs Juliet Noel (née Reade), John Pym, Dr Judy McKenzie of the University of Queensland, Dr Alexis Weedon of the University of Luton, Philipp Scofield of the Wellcome Unit for the History of Medicine, Oxford and John Wilson of John Wilson Autographs, provided most valuable assistance. Thanks to Vivien Allen, in the Isle of Man, for allowing us to use her summaries of letters from Collins to Hall Caine, which emerged from her research for her recent biography of Hall Caine, and to Roger Sims, the librarian archivist at the Manx Museum and National Trust, of the Manx National Heritage for permission to publish them. Also of especial value has been the assistance and advice of Professor Donald Hawes of the University of Westminster, London, Catherine Peters of Oxford University (Wilkie Collins' biographer), Professor Joseph Wiesenfarth of the University of Wisconsin, Madison, and Professor Kenneth A. Womack of Penn State Altoona College. William and Faith Clarke, Judy and Tony van den Brook, Avril and Charles Gilmour were splendid hosts during William Baker's lengthy London visits.

The English Department, Northern Illinois University and the University Libraries, Northern Illinois University granted William Baker a study leave of absence for the Spring semester, 1997 to work on this edition of the letters of Wilkie Collins. The Dean of the Graduate School at Northern Illinois University, Professor Jerrold H. Zar, the Dean of the College of Liberal Arts and Sciences, Professor Frederick L. Kitterle and the Director of the University Libraries, Professor Arthur P. Young, provided research funding for the purchase of photocopies and microfilms, travel funds, and other generous assistance. Dr Young granted valuable research time release and moreover located a scarce copy of Laurence Hutton's *Letters of Charles Dickens to Wilkie Collins* (1892).

Research for this edition has been aided by a grant to William Baker from the American Philosophical Society. Our commissioning editors at Macmillan, Charmian Hearne and Julian Honer, must be thanked for their belief in this project, their good humour, wisdom and patience.

This edition of *The Letters of Wilkie Collins* is dedicated to our wives without whom it would not have been possible.

Editorial Principles

With two exceptions, Collins' letters appear in the order of their composition. A letter that can be dated only approximately is placed at the earliest date on which the editors believe it could have been written. Letters with the same date are printed in alphabetical order of the addresses, unless the contents dictate an alternative order. Letters to which it has not been possible to assign a day or month are placed at the end of the year. We have made an exception to our chronological order in the case of Collins' correspondence with Nannie Wynne, which extended from 1885 to 1888, because it forms such a unique exception to all his other letters. We have therefore put these particular letters in a separate section of their own.

As well as being arranged in a general chronological order, the letters have also been divided into ten groups that reflect major stages in Collins' life. Each of these sections is introduced by a brief summary overview which also gives background sketches of crucial events for the benefit of those who wish to read the letters sequentially. Readers interested in particular correspondents or subjects treated in the letters can find access through the various indexes. Each letter is preceded by a brief head-note that identifies the addressee, the date, the manuscript location, or other source for the text that follows, and other pertinent information.

Collins' often difficult to read letters have been transcribed literally for the sake of fidelity to the originals and in the interest of keeping their special flavour as cultural and historical documents. Nevertheless some minor regularizations have been made. This is a diplomatic transcription: for instance, Collins' punctuation is very inconsistent and has been regularized. We therefore indicate below exactly which editorial procedures have been followed in preparing this edition.

1. Ampersands, cancellations, abbreviations, and Collins' often idio-syncratic spelling, *are retained*. Uncertain readings, textual cruxes, and material cancelled by Collins but still legible, and other editorial insertions, appear in square brackets. Collins' word spacing and line division are not reproduced, but to conserve space, line divisions in addresses, headings, and complimentary closes are indicated by a vertical rule (|).

2. Paragraphs are sometimes not clearly indicated in the letters. Collins at times marked a change of subject by leaving a somewhat larger space than usual between sentences; sometimes Collins started a fresh line. In both of these cases, a new paragraph is started in the transcription.

3. Collins' signature is conveyed in its various forms. It has not been practical, however, to reproduce his inconsistent underlinings of his name. Sometimes Collins signed his letters with his initials "WC", and the "C" of his final name is often much longer than his "W": it has not been possible to reproduce such flourishes. Collins extensively underlined words or parts of words, including his name, sometimes using a single line, or double or treble underlining. Double and treble underlining is noted in the explanatory notes, as is marginal lining when conceivably useful to the reader.

4. Collins often uses both single and double quotation marks inconsistently within the same letter. Here, double quotation marks are used throughout, and punctuation at the conclusion of quotations follows current conventions.

5. Return addresses at the top of each letter are taken from the letter itself. If Collins did not write an address, then wherever possible it has been supplied in square brackets. Complimentary closes are brought to the right-hand margin; names of recipients, when Collins wrote them in, appear after his signature. WC used a variety of printed stationery. In order not to confuse the reader a standard address style has been used.

6. Less familiar foreign words and phrases are translated, in square brackets, within the text of the letters. Explanatory notes, which for convenience follow the text of each letter, briefly identify references, whether these be personal, historical or contextual. We have tried to identify every person or title mentioned, usually at the first occurrence. The sources of quotations and literary allusions have similarly been given when possible. Many names, titles, and allusions have, however, eluded us, and we shall be grateful to readers for suggestions and corrections. In reference to printed books, when no place of publication is given, London is understood as the place of publication.

7. Postmarks and watermarks have been recorded when conceivably useful in any way; for example when they are evidence for the date or address of the letter.

Abbreviations

[ ]	Matter supplied by the editors
|	Indicates line division in manuscript
...	Omitted passage
BL	British Library
Beinecke	The Beinecke Rare Book and Manuscript Library, Yale University
Boase	Frederic Boase, *Modern English Biography*, 6 vols. Truro: Netherton, 1892–1921
Bodleian	The Bodleian Library, Oxford
Clarke	William M. Clarke, *The Secret Life of Wilkie Collins*. Far Thrupp, Stroud, Gloucestershire: Alan Sutton Publishing Limited, 1996
Clareson	Thomas D. Clareson, "Wilkie Collins to Charles Reade: Some Unpublished Letters," *Victorian Essays, A Symposium*, ed. Warren D. Anderson and Thomas D. Clareson, pp. 107–24
Coleman	William Rollin Coleman, "The University of Texas Collection of the Letters of Wilkie Collins, Victorian Novelist". PhD diss. University of Texas at Austin, 1975
DAB	*Dictionary of American Biography*, ed. A. Johnson, et al. New York: Charles Scribner, 1927
Davis	Nuel Pharr Davis, *The Life of Wilkie Collins*. Urbana: University of Illinois Press, 1956
Dickens,	*The Letters of Charles Dickens.* [*The Pilgrim Edition*], ed. Madeline House
Letters	Graham Storey, Kathleen Tillotson and others. Oxford: The Clarendon Press, 1965
DNB	*Dictionary of National Biography*, ed. Leslie Stephen and Sidney Lee. 22 vols. Rpt. Oxford: Oxford University Press, 1959–1960
Fales Collection, NYU	The Fales Collection, New York University
Gasson	Andrew Gasson, *Wilkie Collins – An Illustrated Guide*. Oxford: Oxford University Press, 1997
Glasgow	The Mitchell Collection, Glasgow Public Library
Harrowby	Harrowby MSS Trust, Sandon, Staffordshire

Houghton, Harvard	The Houghton Library, Harvard University
Huntington	The Henry E. Huntington Library and Art Gallery, San Marino, California
MS, MSS	Manuscript, manuscripts
NLS	National Library of Scotland
NYPL (Berg)	The Berg Collection, New York Public Library
NYU	New York University
PM	The Pierpont Morgan Library, New York
Parrish	M.R. Parrish with E.V. Miller, *Wilkie Collins and Charles Reade: First Editions Described with Notes*. London: Constable, 1940; reprinted New York: Burt Franklin, 1968
Peters	Catherine Peters, *The King of Inventors: A Life of Wilkie Collins*. Princeton, New Jersey: Princeton UP, 1993
Princeton	Princeton University Libraries
Robinson	*Wilkie Collins: A Biography*. New York: Macmillan, 1952
Smith and Terry	N. Smith, R.C. Terry, eds, *Wilkie Collins to the Forefront: Some Reassessments*. New York: AMS Press, 1995
Sutherland	John Sutherland, *The Stanford Companion to Victorian Fiction*. Stanford, CA: Stanford UP, 1989
TL/copy	Carbon-copy of a typed letter; no signature
Texas	The Harry Ransom Humanities Research Center, University of Texas at Austin
Todd and Bowden	*Tauchnitz International Editions in English, 1841–1955: A Bibliographical History*. New York: Bibliographical Society of America, 1988
WC	Wilkie Collins
Weedon	Alexis Weedon, "Watch This Space: Wilkie Collins and New Strategies in Victorian Publishing in the 1890s", *Victorian Identities*, ed., R. Robbins, J. Wolfreys. London: Macmillan, 1996, pp. 163–83
Wolff	Robert Lee Wolff, *Nineteenth-Century Fiction: A Bibliographical Catalogue Based on the Collection Formed by Robert Lee Wolff*. 5 vols, in 2. New York: Garland Publishing, 1981

Introduction

Wilkie Collins' letters, brought together here for the first time, cover most of his life. They range from a typical schoolboy's letters home, at the age of 13, to his final plea to his doctor ("I am dying old friend") at the age of 65. Together with his 30-odd novels, collections of short stories, a biography of his father and a travel book, and the biographical comments of his literary and artistic friends, they are the foundation for any outline of his life and any judgment of the kind of man he was. His novels can be searched for hidden meaning and depths; the pattern of his life put under a microscope; and his cluster of relationships sifted for clues. Like his novels, the letters are the substance of the man himself – his own words. Yet they still both reveal and hide what we are all seeking: who it was who wrote some of the most compellingly readable books of the nineteenth century.

For the main events and major turning-points in his life, they remain the essential framework. His friendship, good humour, social graces, candour, lack of pomposity, shrewd judgment, his capacity for work, play and high living, as well as his constant battle with ill-health, shine through them. His views on politics, art and religion are not hidden, when a stimulus is given.

Here is a man one longs to know better, from the characterizations he has given, with such assured touches, to Count Fosco and Marian Halcombe in *The Woman in White*, Rosanna Spearman in *Armadale*, Gabriel Betheridge and Miss Clack in *The Moonstone* and Captain Wragge and Magdalen Vanstone in *No Name*. In his correspondence, he occasionally explains how he writes, or rather how he prepares for the writing of, his books. He dwells on the lengthy preparation, the building up of his complex plots, the formation of the main characters and how they are deliberately meant to inter-relate, how the story-line is developed, and the fact that before he writes a word he already knows who will live, who will die and how the plot will be resolved. Yet why and how he came to be attracted to the atmosphere he builds up or to the personalities he uses, and their peculiar characteristics, he rarely dwells on.

Although we now know far more than we did about his colourful private life and his tense relations with his father, as well as being far more aware of the demons driving his curiosity in building up such strange and compelling plots, there is a limit to what he wishes to reveal.

I

By the age of 13 he had had the guiding hand of his mother, an occasional tutor, a year at a day school for boys, as well as trips to the French coast and two years on an eye-opening visit to Italy. All this was before he went as a boarder to a private school in Highbury, in north London. In later life he often dwelt on his experiences at the Maida Hill Academy, off the Edgware Road, his first school, and Highbury School, where he was sent on his return from Italy. And it is from Highbury that we first meet his early letters home – a not unknown combination of tasks set by the headmaster and the exuberance of a lively, even self-assertive, schoolboy.

It is not hard to guess what may have irked his fellow students: he thought it stemmed from the prize he won one year, but who knows what resentment he caused with his new-found facility with languages and his apparent familiarity with snippets of foreign literature. As for his contretemps with the headmaster at Highbury and especially his wife, who must have had the measure of him, Wilkie was clearly feeling the stern hand of real authority for the first time and, in contrast to the stern outward morality and soft-centre of his father, hardly relishing his teachers' firmness.

Little wonder that, at one stage, he deliberately broke into fluent, though hardly polished, Italian, to report his real feelings to his mother. This independent streak, which was to give him such strength of conviction in later life, was showing itself early, though he obviously had the good sense not to show much independent resistance to his father's somewhat rigid moral views, preferring to hide behind a teasing banter in his letters to his mother.

Although we have his own letters written as a schoolboy, we often have to rely on later descriptions, in his writings, to fill in essential details of his early life. This applies both to his recollections of bullying school friends, as well as some of the pleasures of youth. In one unexpected enthusiasm for skating, in a letter to Holman Hunt at least a quarter of a century after the event, he outlines his prowess on the ice: "I hear you took up the noble art of skating, last frost. If there is any more ice this winter, let us meet, and tumble in company. The whole secret of skating consists in not being afraid of perpetual sprawling at full length" [2 February 1861].

By the time his father secured him the job in Antrobus's tea-merchanting firm in the Strand, in central London, at the age of 17, Collins was already turning his spare time (even in the office) to writing short articles and literary pieces of all kinds. The stimulus to do so was all around him. At that time the west end of the Strand was a hub of magazine publishers and no doubt he got as many rejection slips as most young writers. His first success, at least under his name, did not come until his second year at

Antrobus's when *The Illustrated Magazine* published his short story "The Last Stage Coachman".

This was the period when his father and mother began to move about with more freedom. His father, elected to the Royal Academy, already a fashionable painter of country scenes and the English coastline, continued his visits to wealthy art patrons, while his mother, Harriet, was at last able to accompany her husband or, more often, strike out on her own among her sisters and other friends from her youth. Wilkie and his younger brother Charles were increasingly left on their own in London: hence the number of letters we still have of Wilkie's reports to his parents, mainly his mother, of affairs at home.

These family letters not only reveal the different relationships Wilkie had with his two parents but also, as he reached his twentieth year, a bantering style and an almost deliberately provocative reportage that can hardly have appealed to his father. Whether his father blamed his elder son or the influence of the young friends he attracted, he continually frowned on their escapades in London, and especially on their early trips to Paris.

Wilkie's letters home from Paris in the mid-1840s bring out, for the first time, many of his later interests: his deep love of the French capital; the freedom it gave him; his genuine interest in, and continuing fascination with, art and contemporary artists (later fully recognized by Holman Hunt); his growing love of the theatre, good and bad; his attraction to the morbid (twice describing bodies he had seen in the Paris Morgue, one a dead soldier laid out "like an unsaleable codfish" [4 September 1844], another a young girl, just fished out of the Seine); his appetite for good food and drink and, above all, his zest for life, high and low.

Many of the letters are written with an almost forced raciness, as though designed to annoy his father, who duly responded by recommending good books and plain food and an end to the escapades he and Charles Ward were getting up to. At least Wilkie had the good sense to reply by way of letters to his understanding mother, though the teasing tone remained. On one occasion he tells his mother: "Considering that he is a lamb of Dodsworth's flock, Mr Collins evinces a most unchurchmanlike disposition to scandalise other people. Heap coals of fire upon his head by giving him my love in return for his fabrications" [16 September 1845]. On another he is even blunter: "Give my love to the Governor and tell him that I will eat plain food (when I come back to England) and read Duncan's *Logic* and Butler's *Analogy* (whenever I have no chance of getting anything else to peruse)" [13 September 1845].

One not unexpected theme runs through his correspondence from Paris, and later Brussels: his need for extra cash and often extra leave from his job at the tea-merchants. Having been employed in tea-merchanting through the friendly relations of his parents with Edward Antrobus, Wilkie plainly had few scruples about using their influence on his boss in trying to get him a longer stay in Paris. It was rarely successful, unlike his requests for extra cheques, which were invariably made out from his father's account at Coutts Bank, though usually the result of Harriet's pleas on his behalf.

Unsurprisingly, it is in his requests for extra money that we get the first reference to his first novel *Ioláni*, the manuscript of which must have loomed large in the Collins household, persuading Wilkie at least to assume that publishers Chapman and Hall, in their wisdom, would quickly accept it and as quickly put him in funds [13 September 1845]. It was not to be. The novel was rejected (its manuscript surfacing some 150 years later in New York) and Wilkie was again dependent on family support for his travelling expenditure, on one occasion having run out of money for the journey back.

II

He had begun his Continental travels early, spending two years in France and Italy when he was 12 and 13, after earlier visits to the French coast. When he finally threw off parental control, in the visits to Paris with Charles Ward, he quickly established the kind of freedom he was to enjoy there some years later with Charles Dickens. He was at home in the French capital, cultivating the same people, the same habits and the same hotel (the Hotel des Tuilleries on the Rue de Rivoli, his "favourite hostelry"). And Paris was always "this earthly paradise" or "the Capital of Europe" to him. Even knowing his father's disapproval, he still refused to curb his enthusiasm for Paris and its distractions in his letters home. "We are now thoroughly settled here", he told his mother in an early missive, "and are dissipating fearfully – gardens, theatres and Cafés being the conglomerate parts of the Parisian Paradise we are most inhabiting" [4 September 1844]. No doubt other, less salubrious, places too.

He missed little when walking the streets, remembering how things had been some eight years earlier and noting how little both people and their habits had changed since their last visit. "The men stick to their [beards], their arguments, and their sugar and water, as usual", he reported to his mother. "And the women eat as many bonbons, wear as many 'bustles' & make as many speeches, as ever" [13 September 1845].

It was an atmosphere he thrived on: the anonymity; the lack of what he regarded as British hypocrisy; the chance to get up when he wanted to and go to bed when it suited him; the opportunity to indulge his sense of the strange, foreign, unusual, even bizarre; the temptation to encourage his growing addiction to good food, sauces and fine wines; in other words, the ability to do as he pleased, without either hiding it or flaunting it. It was an attitude reflected in his later life in London and fully explained why Charles Dickens found him such a fascinating companion.

In effect Collins' twenties saw his transition from a young man, still living at home with his mother and brother, with no clear career ahead of him, apart from a natural interest in art induced by his father, to a young writer with an active social life, a growing group of lively friends and a close friendship with Charles Dickens. As he explained later, his father slowly realized that the art school he had assumed would be Wilkie's first step in a path he himself had trodden with such profit had no attractions for him; nor did the tea trade or, later, the legal profession, where at least he succeeeded in being called to the bar. The "scribblings" he confessed to having undertaken while in the tea merchant's office slowly brought their reward, from occasional published articles, along with the inevitable rejections and setbacks.

Several early articles, even poems, never saw the light of day. A complete novel, *Ioláni*, to his consternation, was rejected outright. His second novel *Antonina* was only a third finished when his father died, and he was forced to turn his talents to a two-volume biography of William Collins. It turned out to be the stimulus, and success, he needed, even though it was initially touch and go whether he would attract enough subscriptions to help pay for the printing costs he and his mother had had to meet themselves. The effort brought him to the attention of the literary world, opened up new friendships and, with the encouragement of his mother, who became a remarkable hostess to her two sons in Hanover Terrace, led to the combination of writing and the theatre that occupied so much of his life.

His correspondence in these early days was naturally confined to his mother, when he was travelling, and to close friends and literary colleagues, such as Charles and Edward Ward and Edward Pigott. Other acquaintances featured in the letters reflect the kind of life he was leading, and the things that occupied him as he began to carve out a literary career, while still earning essential income from journalism. Early correspondents included such august names as Sir Robert Peel and Benjamin Disraeli, as well as American writers such as R.H. Dana, author of *Two Years Before the Mast*, as he either coaxed information for his biography from his father's old friends or subscriptions from his father's eminent patrons.

It was not always his writing that confirmed or sometimes initiated some of these early friendships. Dickens sought him out, through Augustus Egg the painter, to join them in amateur theatricals. He and Edward Pigott, who edited *The Leader*, were as relaxed with each other's company under sail as they were in the office. Yachting became a way of life they both enjoyed. And Wilkie, who could hardly be described as an athletic person, though he immersed himself in all the habits of athletes and boxers for a later novel, was never so happy as under sail in a strong sea. He entered into every trip with the enthusiasm of the expert: "Now about the yacht trip" he once enthused to Pigott. "Everything very jolly, *except* the tremendous consideration of the *Equinox*. I find by my Almanack that it begins on the 23rd September ... And as for returning in an Equinoctial Gale ... had we not better make a brief burst upon the Welsh coast, and get back before Boreas can overtake us?" [4 September 1855]. Sailing, good food, lively company and travel kept them all entertained.

Having begun early with his family's trips to France and Italy, Collins continued to travel throughout his youth when he could afford it; sometimes when he couldn't. He sought his own pleasures where he could, though never failing to provide his mother with a censored version of his activities, local gossip, news of the latest fashions, and descriptive passages of people and places that were soon to be put to more lucrative purposes.

The letters he sent back from what were still the wilds of Cornwall to his mother and friends, quickly became the basis of an illustrated travel book, the burden of which he shared with an artist friend, Henry Brandling. They did up to 14 miles a day with knapsacks on their backs, a sight hardly ever seen in the lanes of the Duchy and an exertion he was rarely to be capable of again, even alongside the striding Dickens. His enthusiasm for the sights, the physical wonders of the Lizard, the people, their oddities and the local food poured into his letters home and to his friends in London. Having surveyed Kynance Cove and the sea smashing against the rocks, he could hardly restrain his prose. "Oh Ward! Ward! I have seen such rocks! Rocks like pyramids – rocks like crouching lions" [15 August 1850].

Of equal interest were the landladies and chambermaids who looked after their creature comforts: some jolly, some curious, one "a nasty thin woman in black with a bilious complexion and a crocodile grin", another "unpleasantly addicted to perpetual perspiration on the forehead". His favourites were a fat landlady and chambermaid in Looe "who coddled us in comfortable beds and fuddled us with comfortable ale, and stuffed us to bursting with good pies and puddings and sweet cakes and then sent us into the garden of the Inn, to keep us out of mischief like children" [29 July 1850].

What had begun during earlier visits to Brussels, Paris and parts of Normandy, was continued from his different ports of call in Cornwall, his mother again receiving a running description of the local sights – churches, old houses, festivals and local customs and characters, along with outlines of the countryside – on the surface and down the mines. *Rambles Beyond Railways* was the final result, a chatty amusing travel book, with illustrations, and an account of life beyond the civilization of modern travel.

Yet one gets the strong feeling that he was only in Cornwall for the experience, to seek out the unusual, to see how the other half lives. Despite his enthusiasm for what he found, he knew he would be returning to the metropolis. Even "one of the most beautiful and most romantic counties in England", as he liked to call it, could not replace the lure and attractions of

London or Paris. When detained too long in the country, as he once remarked after a spell in rural Surrey, he quickly got bored with "a cursed confused chirping of birds – an unnecessarily large supply of fresh air – and an [odd] absence of cabs, omnibuses, circulating libraries, public houses, newspaper offices, pastry cook shops, [with] other articles of civilisation" [19 March 1850]. Wilkie remained a confirmed townie.

Although he had already made a clean break from his father's original ambitions for him in the art world, the habit of sketching, visiting art galleries, and having views about individual artists never left him. Through his younger brother, Charles, who had continued in the steps of his father at the Royal Academy school, most of the early members of the Pre-Raphaelite Brotherhood were close friends. John Millais was subsequently to provide the introductory sketch for *No Name,* and was one of the threesome (with Charles Collins) when Wilkie made the legendary rescue of Caroline Graves, Collins' first mistress, outside a villa close to Regents Park in North London, said by Millais' son to be the basis of the similar episode at the beginning of *The Woman in White.*

Wilkie's own efforts at sketching were often described in letters to his mother on his foreign trips, and he always kept close to artistic gossip of the day. As he shows in the biography of his father, *Memoirs of the Life of William Collins R.A.,* he had a firm grasp of the techniques of painting and an ability to describe the intentions and achievement of individual artists, apart from his father. Following the publication of the first volumes of *Modern Painters,* starting in 1843, he summed up John Ruskin to R.H. Dana, the American novelist, as "a vigorous and dashing writer, who had studied the Art with genuine enthusiasm, but with doubtful judgment" [12 January 1849], and added that the second volume was better than the first. Little wonder that Dickens, who had hardly the same interest, found the artistic discussions between Collins and Augustus Egg on their long visit to Italy a trifle tiresome.

It was during this particular trip to Italy in the early 1850s that he sent back to his mother his personal assessment of the Florentine and Venetian schools: "I am more struck than I could have imagined possible, with a sense of the superiority of the Venetian painters – and especially of Tintoretto, to my mind the chief and greatest of them all ... These Venetians, employed as they almost always were, to represent conventional subjects, are the most *original* race of painters that the world has yet seen" [25 November 1853].

III

Introduced initially to Dickens through Augustus Egg, simply to play a small part in one of Dickens' many amateur theatrical productions at home,

Collins found their friendship growing through a number of similar interests and activities. Both were keen to get behind the footlights, Dickens dominating most things he appeared in, Collins perhaps showing more enthusiasm and willingness than acting ability. One was already an established writer, the other still making his way. Both soon proved to have a journalistic talent in common too.

They were soon touring the provinces together, prompting a flow of letters from Collins about their theatrical successes in the provinces, following a Royal Command performance before Queen Victoria. "We filled the Philharmonic Hall at Liverpool" he boasted from the North of England "two nights following – Jenny Lind in the height of her vogue in the provinces was afraid to try what we have accomplished. *King Public* is a good thing for Literature and Art!" [16 February 1852]. It was not long before Dickens, the highly successful editor of *Household Words*, found he could use Collins' flexible talents on the magazine and within a year of their introduction he was staying with Dickens at his house in Boulogne and sharing accommodation with him in Dover, where Dickens finished *Bleak House* and Collins worked on his second novel, *Basil*. Dickens later said it was this novel that convinced him of Collins' undoubted talent.

Before long, they had discovered that they could relax together too, Dickens depending on Collins to provide the right kind of entertainment, while keeping a discreet silence about Dickens' growing infatuation with Ellen Ternan. Some of their later escapades, and particularly Dickens' proposals for nights out in London or Paris, have emerged from Dickens' own letters, but Wilkie's replies and encouragements to Dickens, sadly for us, literally went up in smoke on a bonfire at Gad's Hill on 3 September 1860, when Dickens destroyed what he described as "the accumulated letters and papers of twenty years". He even followed this up a year before his death with the destruction of "all the letters he had kept from everyone" [Georgina Hogarth to Lady Lytton, 20 March 1900, Dickens *Letters*, I].

We are left to surmise what Collins conjured up, whether in Paris, London or even Brighton, for their joint amusement. But at least we can be in little doubt what Dickens had in mind from letters he sent to Wilkie on different occasions and that survived the original censoring of his daughter and sister-in-law, Mamie Dickens and Georgina Hogarth, (as well as that of Wilkie himself). They speak for themselves:

"If you are free on Wednesday" he wrote to Collins on one occasion " ... I shall be happy to start on any Haroun Alraschid expedition."

"On Wednesday, Sir, on Wednesday if the mind can devise anything sufficiently in the style of sybarite Rome in the days of its culminating voluptuousness I am your man. I don't care what it is. I give (for that night only) restraint to the Winds."

"Any mad proposal you please will find a wildly insane response in – yours ever."

Had Dickens not put all his received correspondence on the two bonfires at Gadshill, we might have got Collins' colourful replies and a truer picture of the loose life Dickens only hinted at in the letters left to us. Even on his own in Paris, Dickens felt compelled to report and share with his lively companion what he had found in what he called "the strange places I glide into". In one dance hall, Dickens explained, there were "some pretty faces, but all of two classes – wicked coldly calculating, or haggard and wretched in their warm beauty". His eye had fallen on one in particular, he told Wilkie, "handsome, regardless, brooding, and yet with some nobler qualities in her forehead. I mean to walk about tonight and look for her" (Clarke, pp. 80–3). One is left wondering with who else of Dickens' closest friends but Collins would Dickens have shared such thoughts.

As he reached the threshold of his thirties, freed from the influence of his father and encouraged by his mother, Wilkie Collins had already established himself as a young writer to watch. *Basil* had been followed by *Hide and Seek* and his growing collaborations with Dickens on *Household Words* had produced a stream of articles and short stories, some of which were later published in separate books, such as *After Dark* and *The Queen of Hearts*.

By this time it was becoming clear how far Wilkie differed from his younger brother, Charles. Charles was as handsome as his father and, oddly enough, as Wilkie's own son later, whereas Wilkie, with his deep forehead and smaller stature, could hardly be described as immediately attractive to women. Yet Wilkie's charm, self-confidence, teasing correspondence and sheer personality plainly won over most of the women he met. Wilkie rarely lacked conviction: his brother was inclined to dither. And while Charles almost dutifully followed his father's wishes, following him into the art world and reflecting his religious outlook in outbursts of High Church mania, even religious fads such as fasting, Wilkie was determined to lead an independent life, carve out a writing career and think for himself.

Another early acquaintance, Edward Pigott, who later became a close friend and sailing companion, also began to use Wilkie's journalistic talents. They had been fellow students at Lincoln's Inn and were called to the bar together, both moving away from legal affairs towards the literary and, in Pigott's case, the political as well. Even Wilkie showed a wider interest in current affairs – political and religious – than has been generally assumed, in his early collaboration with Pigott on *The Leader*, a magazine that Pigott edited and later owned.

Like many young enthusiastic writers, Collins was finding that writing to a daily or monthly deadline, with payments attached, had both immediate cash rewards and intellectual stimuli. He had a flexible enough mind to allow it to turn in a variety of directions, reviewing books in one issue, and attending theatrical first nights for another, while generally commenting on the issues of the day. Nor, eventually, did Wilkie stint in giving Pigott his considered and surprisingly clear-cut views on the make-up of the magazine and an assessment of what would attract readers.

It was in his regular correspondence with Pigott that Collins' early views on religion occasionally had free rein and where one can grasp how far he had moved away from the rigidity, even priggishness, of his father's beliefs. One issue that prompted an outpouring of his religious stance to Pigott was the proclamation by Pope Pius IX of the Immaculate Conception in 1854. Collins felt strongly enough to write a separate note: "Does not every good Papist who will not let his butcher, baker, wife, or children, rob him of one particle of his common sense if he can help it, voluntarily hand that common sense over altogether to the keeping of his Priest whenever his Priest asks him for it? ... What is there in the Immaculate Conception to outrage millions of people who believe (if one may abuse the word by using it in such a sense) – who believe in 'the real presence'? – when Smith, a lay Papist, believes that if he gives money to Jones a clerical Papist to pray his soul out of Purgatory, Jones will succeed if Jones prays fairly up to his terms, what in Heaven's name is there in the Immaculate Conception to stagger Smith?" [December 1854].

Otherwise his thoughts on religion were rarely prominent. He never followed the strict beliefs of his father, bringing a flexible, liberal approach to his Christian background, allowing faith to override reason only in a particularly narrow area. The Sermon on the Mount, as a guide to living, meant more to him than the intricacies of theology. "I am neither a Protestant, Catholic – or a Dissenter" he once confessed to Pigott. "I do not desire to discuss this or that particular creed; but I believe Jesus Christ to be the Son of God."

Yet he had still retained strong views about the place of religion and its discussion in a political forum such as *The Leader*. He was convinced that a literary, political journal was not the place to openly discuss such convictions. He was quite adamant both in discussion and in correspondence with Pigott on the issue: "In regard to your mixing up of the name of Jesus Christ with the current politics of the day", he warned him on one occasion, "I am against you – against you with all my heart and soul" [20 February 1852]. And on another occasion, he went on: "As to what is 'irreligious' or what is 'heterodoxy', or what is the 'immensity' of the distance between them, you and I differ; and it is useless to broach the subject. Nothing will ever persuade me that a system which permits the introduction of the private religious, or irreligious, or heterodoxical opinions of contributors to a newspaper into the articles on politics or general news which they write for it, is a wise or good system – either in itself, or in its effect in the various writers whom you employ. It is for this reason only that I don't desire to be 'one of you' – simply because a common respect for my own religious convictions prevents me from wishing to – but writing on this subject is of no use. I hate controversies on paper, almost more than I hate controversies in talk – I'll explain myself as fully as you desire, when we next meet; and there's an end of it!" [16 February 1852].

The result of the clash of opinions was typical of Collins. He expressed his views clearly and with firmness and came to a swift decision: he would no longer contribute, under his own name, to that section of the journal that mixed religion with politics. Yet he continued on friendly terms with Pigott both in the office (writing in other sections of the journal), in social life and, especially, under sail for many years to come. Collins was a man of candour, with little capacity for bearing grudges.

One of the features of Collins' writings is his command of scenic descriptions and his ability to paint atmosphere into them, as essential adjuncts to his plots. Many of his early letters to his mother and close friends bring out this combination of a journalist's eye for detail and an artistic eye, with an almost brooding attraction for the significant, sometimes even bizarre. His early visits to Cornwall, and to Paris, Rome and Naples provided ample opportunity.

His travels through Cornwall brought vivid images: "Old tottering grey sign posts stand like spectres in lonely criss-cross roads, [plus] strange Druidical stones, and black grand rocks, piled fantastically one upon another" [29 July 1850]. And again: "the raging sea seemed to shake us on our pinnacles – where the water was spurted in our faces from fifty feet off, through hidden holes and slicks, followed by roaring blasts of wind, as loud as if the devil himself was blowing his bellows at the fires of Hell" [14 August 1850].

Rome and Naples provided colourful snapshots: "I saw the same Bishops, in purple stockings, followed by servants in gaudy liveries – the same importunately impudent beggars – the same men with pointed hats and women with red petticoats and tightly swaddled babies that I remembered so well in England since 1837 and 1838" [13 November 1853]. A decade later he writes: "Naples is not much changed ... The hideous deformed beggars are still in the streets ... vagabond cabmen drive after you go where you may, grinning and shouting and insisting on your getting into their mangy – little vehicles – no two members of the populace can meet in the street and talk about anything without screeching at the tops of their voices, with their noses close together and their hands gesticulating madly about their heads" [13 November 1863].

Nor was he averse to a little nostalgia and sentiment: "There was an old blind fiddler in the boat, who sang some Italian national songs ... I never felt nearer astonishing everybody by bursting out crying (!!!) than I did while we were ferrying over the river and listening to the blind fiddler's Italian songs" [28 October 1853].

IV

The three most conspicuous gaps in the list of Collins' many correspondents are his father (only a few letters survive) and his two mistresses, Caroline Graves and Martha Rudd (none have surfaced). Just as William Collins always included admonishments and, occasionally, encouragements directed at Wilkie and Charles in his letters home to Harriet, Wilkie himself, as he grew up, also adopted the habit of responding to his father through his mother. He could hardly be as jocular in direct correspondence with William as he was, indirectly, in his letters to Harriet. It often means that we have to infer the relationship between father and son, which is hardly difficult, though still unsatisfactory, rather than consult direct evidence.

In the case of Caroline and Martha, the absence of letters is partly the result of reticence and natural discretion and partly, especially in the case of Martha, a reflection of class differences. While Caroline is mentioned by name in several of Wilkie's letters to his friends, beginning in the second half of the 1850s, when he was openly living with her in New Cavendish Street, Martha is only referred to by name to his solicitor and indirectly (in references to his "morganatic family") in correpondence with some of his closest friends. Although there are a number of letters from Caroline to various of his literary contacts, before and after his death, when both she and later her daughter acted as his secretary, any letters she sent to him were no doubt discreetly destroyed. Martha's too.

Caroline had come on the scene just as Wilkie's literary reputation was beginning to gather momentum. He already had a biography, a travel book, four novels and, possibly, a book of short stories to his credit when they met. How, and exactly when, they met is still difficult to pinpoint. But Wilkie himself liked others to believe that he had run across her, literally, as he, his brother and John Millais were passing a villa near Regents Park, late one summer evening in the mid-1850s. At least that is what Millais told his son. Whether embroidered or not, the story has it that Caroline ran screaming from the villa, and was immediately followed by Wilkie, who rescued her and, next day, told his brother and Millais that she had been captive in the villa and was a young girl of good birth and position.

That a similar episode occurs at the beginning of *The Woman in White*, written some five or six years after the reported rescue, has simply added lustre to the story. As we now know, Caroline had a quite different background from the one painted by Wilkie. She was not the daughter of a gentleman and the widow of an Army captain, as she hinted in more than one official document; her father was a carpenter from a small village near Cheltenham and, after her young husband had died from tuberculosis, she had been living with her late husband's mother in London, along with a twelve-month-old child, Harriet.

While the first references to Caroline occur in 1859, the year when Collins began to write the *Woman in White* at a rented cottage on the outskirts of Broadstairs, they had already been living together at three different addresses in or near Marylebone. In one letter she is referred to as "Mrs Collins". In the first Census after he met her she was described as his wife and he became "a barrister and author of works of fiction". Then, finally, she appears in the rate book of succeeding houses as "Mrs Graves". In Wilkie's letters to friends, mainly his men friends, she is either "Mrs Graves" or "Caroline".

One of the early letters referring to Caroline makes it clear that she is already acting as his hostess to his men friends. "I have today got a ticket sent me (for tomorrow night) to my friend Mr Townshend's box at Covent Garden" he writes to his friend Charles Ward. "You won't mind my going away at eight o'clock – will you? – and leaving the engagement between us two on every other respect *exactly the same*. Dine at six – cigar afterwards – tea – I slip off – Caroline keeps you company and makes your Grog – and you stay as long as you feel inclined" [May 1859]. The kind of relaxed arrangements that his friends had grown used to, though hardly their wives.

Collins' later meeting with Martha Rudd, who was 15 years younger than Caroline, has been narrowed down to the mid-1860s, when he was making preparations for *Armadale* and visited the Norfolk broads and coastline. Martha was born to a poor family living in Winterton and making a living from work on the land, though other members of the Rudd family, before and since, were members of the local sea-going community. She was only 19 when she met Collins, probably at a hotel in Great Yarmouth, south of Winterton.

She was first detected in London some four years later, in 1868, the year Collins' mother died and as he was completing *The Moonstone.* The novel was finished that summer and Caroline suddenly decided to leave him and marry a young man named Joseph Charles Clow. Then within twelve months Martha had his first child – Marian – not far away in Bolsover Street and, within a couple of years, Caroline had left her young husband and had returned to live with Collins and he (and Martha) were expecting their second child.

None of these complications emerge from the letters. The first references to Martha arose when Collins was writing to his solicitor before and during his American visit in 1873–74, reminding him of the need to look after "Mrs Dawson" in his absence. She is also referred to, briefly, in later correspondence relating either to his will, or to insurance policies taken out to protect

Martha and their children – Marian, Constance Harriet, and William Charles. And, on one occasion, he mentions that he is on holiday with his morganatic family and has become "William Dawson, barrister at law". But that is all.

Why he never married either woman, or anyone within his own social group, remains a matter of conjecture. Several of his novels, including one of his earliest, *Basil*, suggest that the difference in class was not the main impediment. And the letters, here and there, offer other clues. On the eve of John Millais' wedding, he joked: "May he consummate successfully! And have the best cause in the world to *lie late on Wednesday* morning! (You see I am like that excellent parson and bulwark of the church, who married George) – I can't resist *Priapian* jesting on the marriages of my friends. It is such a dreadfully serious thing afterwards, that we ought to joke about it so long as one can" [2 July 1855]. And he continued to express his fear of being left, like so many of his friends, a middle-aged married man with a growing paunch and little freedom. It became a constant theme.

The tone of his letters is basically calm, peppered occasionally with a kindly banter. The exceptions are when he believes he has been swindled or let down, as when he realized that some of the money he had paid to an insurance agent in Boston had been pocketed rather than passed to the insurance company. But most of his rage was reserved for the continuous attempts to deprive him of legitimate income by the pirating of his books and plays. The battle went on most of his life. He suffered in most countries – France, Holland, the United States and to a lesser extent Germany, as well as his own. Sometimes, as on one occasion with a provincial theatrical group, his anger was mollified when he was persuaded they had acted out of ignorance.

His problems began early and he quickly realized the basic problem: "The whole question of protection of the interests of authors as well as artists in their own works" he wrote to an artist friend in the mid-1850s, "is coming before the public – in connection with the taking off of the Newspaper Stamp, which will enable any scoundrel who starts a low paper to steal articles from good papers – or whole books with perfect impunity, as the act now stands – just in fact as the scoundrel stole your name and sold his copy of your picture with it" [20 March 1855].

When he was faced with an outright attempt to publish one of his books in Holland, without paying him a penny, he reacted by writing to them and then exposing them in the English press in the following forceful terms: "I declare any publisher who takes my book from me, with a view to selling it in any form for his own benefit – without my permission and without giving me a share in his profits – to be guilty of theft, to be morally, if not legally, an outlaw and a pest among honest men" [18 November 1869].

He never doubted where the solution lay. "The remedy rests with the [House of] Commons. If Disraeli's books were dramatic enough to be stolen for the stage I should recommend (quite secretly!) an immediate adaptation of one of them, without asking his leave. If he could be made to move in this matter, something might be done" [25 February 1873].

His main battles, however, were with American publishers, who simply stole his text from excerpts serialized in magazines, or from his legitimate publishers in New York, and remained unpunished by the absence of any international copyright agreement by the United States Congress. Although he managed to curb the worst excesses by deliberately publishing versions earlier in the United States, occasionally before those at home, he was never fully protected.

V

The 1860s and early 1870s were the years of Collins' greatest literary successes and stage triumphs but also a period of domestic distress and turmoil. His almost perpetual sufferings from gout and rheumatism reached a peak, as did his reliance on laudanum to assuage the pain. And personally he had to cope with the death of his mother and the departure and return of Caroline to Gloucester Place. The birth of his own children, by Martha, not far away, brought him joy, but also greater responsibility. His letters reflect these changing fortunes and do not hide his continual battle with ill-health.

One of the most stressful peaks was reached in the early part of 1868 when his mother was dying, when he was still trying to complete *The Moonstone* for serialization (which had already started), and he was so ill he could not write and had difficulty in finding a secretary able to ignore his pain. The result was inevitable. He took more and more laudanum, until his doctor finally persuaded him to try and cut down his dependence on it. One of his letters in February, 1869, brings out the full details:

"My doctor is trying to break me of the habit of drinking laudanum. I am stabbed every night at ten with a sharp-pointed syringe which injects morphia under my skin – and gets me a night's rest without any of the drawbacks of taking opium internally. If I only persevere with this, I am told I shall be able, before long, gradually to diminish the quantity of morphia and the number of the nightly stabbings – and so emancipate myself from opium altogether" [26 February 1869].

He was unsuccessful, largely because of the continuation of his gout attacks. As the 1870s wore on these bouts of illness hardly subsided. He had a welcome respite from gout and rheumatism when he was in the United States in 1872–73 and, occasionally, when the weather in England was dry and cold. Otherwise the symptoms persisted: first, bloodshot eyes, followed by rheumatic pain spreading to the rest of his body, usually ending in his knees. His spells of incarceration in Gloucester Place increased, either because the outside air affected his sight or the pain in his knees made it difficult (sometimes impossible) to walk without a stick. His correspondence was rarely free from references to his illnesses, not from any seeking of sympathy (he usually made light of his afflictions) but rather as reasons for refusing, or cancelling an earlier acceptance of, outside invitations. For the rest, he told Fred Lehmann, "Work, Walk. Visit to my morganatic family – such is life" [26 April 1876].

It is now widely assumed, correctly in our view, that his writing reached its peak between 1860 and 1868 with *The Woman in White, No Name, Armadale,* and *The Moonstone.* There is also a strong body of opinion that stresses that he never reached such heights again, because of the growing impact of laudanum on his writing abilities and his recurrent illnesses on his stamina. Some have painted a picture of a bachelor recluse, beginning to shun the outside world, attempting to relive past glories and slowly failing. It was not so simple.

There is certainly evidence of the effects of opium on his imagination and on his ability to convey atmosphere, through visual descriptions, one critic maintaining that *The Haunted Hotel,* written in the late 1870s, could easily have taken place in a station hotel in Wigan, rather than a luxury hotel in Venice. He himself was well aware of opium's impact on the body. As he told a friend who had taken laudanum on his advice, the dose should have had two effects: a stimulus first, leading to a clarity of mind, and a sedative reaction to follow. Whether this secondary effect dulled the mind and the imagination he did not say.

Although he had later successes with *Heart and Science, The Haunted Hotel,* and *The Black Robe,* the high literary level of the 1860s was hardly repeated. Whether this was the result of opium or simply the wearing down of his constitution by his continuing illness, and the way he wrote his novels – under intense, almost feverish pressure – is well worth considering. His letters in the last 15 years of his life provide ample clues as well as a puzzling contradiction. In contrast to some of his later literary efforts, they remain as lively and stimulating as ever.

These later years were a strange mixture. Close on a half of the letters refer to his illnesses, beginning with what was clearly inherited gout and rheumatism, which afflicted his eyes, face and legs, sometimes producing bloodshot eyes and the need for eye patches and sometimes an inability to walk, along with persistent pain. On one occasion he declared, wrongly, that gout "had attacked his brain" [24 September 1864]. Later he plainly suffered from what he described to several correspondents as a "weak heart", most probably angina. He finally had a stroke. Against this background, his methods of plotting and writing his novels hardly helped.

He explained his methods on several occasions in his letters, especially in relation to *The Woman in White* and *Armadale*: "Neither *The Woman In White*, nor any other of my Serial Stories," he told one enquirer, "were completed in Manuscript, before their periodical publication. I was consequently obliged to know every step of my way from beginning to end, before I started on my journey ... In the story I am now writing, [*Armadale*], the last number is to be published several months hence – and the whole close of the story is still unwritten. But I know at this moment who is to live and who is to die – and I see the main events which lead to the end as plainly as I see the pen now in my hand – as plainly as I see the ground laid, months since, in the published part of the story, for what (if I am spared to finish it) you will read months hence" [5 October 1865].

In effect he might spend up to a year or more putting up what he often described as "the scaffolding" of the novel and then began to write, against a serialization deadline, in a feverish haste. It was hardly the best way to conserve his health. As he explained on more than one occasion, the result left him completely exhausted: "The last ten or twelve chapters of *I Say No* were written without rest – or intermission (except when I was eating or sleeping). And when the effort was over a more prostrate wretch could hardly have been found in all this great city than your friend" [16 July 1884].

His conclusion was clear: " Is there any fatigue in this weary world" he asked, "which is equal to the fatigue that comes of daily working of the brains for hours together? George Sand thought all other fatigues unimportant by comparison – and I agree with George S" [January 1881]. It can be argued that his method of writing and his persistent bouts of gout and rheumatism had as great an impact on the quality of his later novels as the huge quanties of laudanum he took. The combination was certainly lethal.

The freshness of his later letters, in contrast, reflect a period of domestic contentment and the stimulation of a growing number of theatrical and literary friends, both in this country and the United States, written no doubt in more leisurely fashion between the feverish bouts of his literary work. At home he had settled down to the established, albeit somewhat bizarre, combination of a former mistress (Caroline) acting as his housekeeper and hostess in Gloucester Place, and later Wimpole Street, and the mother of his morganatic family (Martha) living a few streets away with his two daughters and son. And he sometimes had the added joys of a combined family, Martha's children and Caroline's grandchildren, mingling together in London and on holiday in Ramsgate.

At the same time a lifetime of social and literary successes, along with an engaging personality, had brought an enviable range of friends and correspondents. He encouraged them to the full, developing contacts in his later years with prominent actors and actresses, following his stage successes in London and on Broadway. The full flavour of his experience of writing and of stage craft emerge from these later letters to such varied friends as Lillie Langtry, Mary Anderson, the Bancrofts, Charles Reade and Anthony Trollope. And right to the end he maintained a warm, lively, welcoming, often optimistic, response, amid all his afflictions.

Chronology of William Wilkie Collins' Life

1824	Born 8 January, at 11, New Cavendish Street, Marylebone.
1826	Brother, Charles Allston Collins, born.
1830–36	Family moved to 30, Porchester Terrace, Bayswater.
1835	13 January: first day at Maida Hill Academy.
1836	19 September: departure of family for Italy.
1837	7 January: arrival in Rome.
1838	Autumn: return to London. New house at 20, Avenue Road, St John's Wood. Collins attends Highbury School.
1840	Family moved to Oxford Terrace in London.
1841	Joined tea merchants, Antrobus & Co.
1843	First article published ("The Last Stage Coachman") in *Illustrated Magazine*.
1846	Entered Lincoln's Inn as law student. Reader's ticket at British Museum.
1846–47	First novel, *Ioláni*, turned down by publishers.
1846	Family moved to Devonport Street.
1847	February: death of his father, William Collins.
1848	Published *Memoirs of the Life of William Collins*. Family (mother and two sons) moved to 38, Blandford Square.
1850	Family moved to 17, Hanover Terrace, Regents Park. Visits Cornwall.
1851	Published *Rambles Beyond Railways*. Met Dickens. Took part in play *Not So Bad As We Seem* with Charles Dickens. Published *Mr Wray's Cash Box*.
1852	Published *Basil*. First contribution to Household Words: "A Terribly Strange Bed".
1853–54	Toured Italy with Charles Dickens and Augustus Egg.
1854	*Hide and Seek* published.
1855	*The Lighthouse* produced at Tavistock House.
1854–56?	Met Caroline Graves.
1856	Temporary lodgings in Howland Place.
1857	*The Dead Secret* published. *The Frozen Deep* produced at Tavistock House. Visits Cumberland, Lancashire and Yorkshire with Charles Dickens. Mother moved to 2, Harley Place, New Road, Marylebone.

1858	Wilkie (and Caroline) moved to 124, Albany Street. Later to 2a, New Cavendish Street.
1859	Mother moved to 2, Clarence Terrace.
1860	Published *The Woman in White*. Opened bank account at Coutts Bank in the Strand. Moved to 12, Harley Street.
1861	Put Caroline down in Census as his "wife" and himself as a "married lodger", a barrister and an author.
1862	Published *No Name*.
1863	Visited Rome with Caroline and her daughter Harriet.
1864	Met Martha Rudd in Norfolk. Caroline and Wilkie moved to 9, Melcombe Place.
1866	*Armadale* published.
1867	*No Thoroughfare* produced at the Adelphi Theatre.
1868	His mother died. Published *The Moonstone*. Caroline left Collins to marry Joseph Clow.
1869	*Black and White* produced at Adelphi Theatre. Martha Rudd's first daughter, Marian, born.
1870	*Man and Wife* published.
1871	Martha's second daughter, Constance Harriet, born. Caroline returned to Gloucester Place.
1872	*Poor Miss Finch* published.
1873	Death of brother, Charles Allston Collins. *The New Magdalen* published.
1873–74	Visit to United States and Canada.
1874	Martha Rudd's third child, William Charles, born.
1875	*The Law and the Lady* published.
1876	*The Two Destinies* published.
1877	Wilkie and Caroline visited Venice.
1878	*The Haunted Hotel* published. Harriet, Caroline's daughter, married to Henry Powell Bartley, Wilkie's solicitor.
1879	*The Fallen Leaves* published.
1880	*Jezebel's Daughter* published
1881	*The Black Robe* published.
1883	*Rank and Riches* produced at Adelphi Theatre. *Heart and Science* published.
1884	*"I Say No"* published.
1886	*The Evil Genius* published.
1887	*The Guilty River* published.
1888	Moved to 82, Wimpole Street.
1889	Death on 23 September, Funeral at Kensal Green cemetery.
1890	*Blind Love* (finished by Walter Besant) published.
1895	Caroline died. Buried with Collins in Kensal Green cemetery.
1919	Martha died in Southend.

FAMILY TREES
Wilkie Collins, Caroline Graves and Martha Rudd (Dawson)

CAROLINE ELIZABETH GRAVES

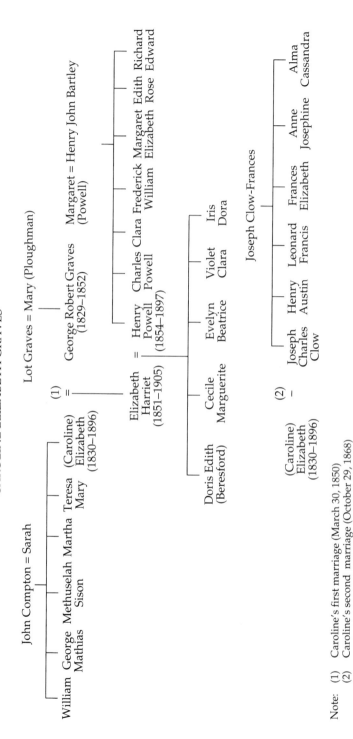

Note: (1) Caroline's first marriage (March 30, 1850)
(2) Caroline's second marriage (October 29, 1868)

MARTHA (RUDD) DAWSON

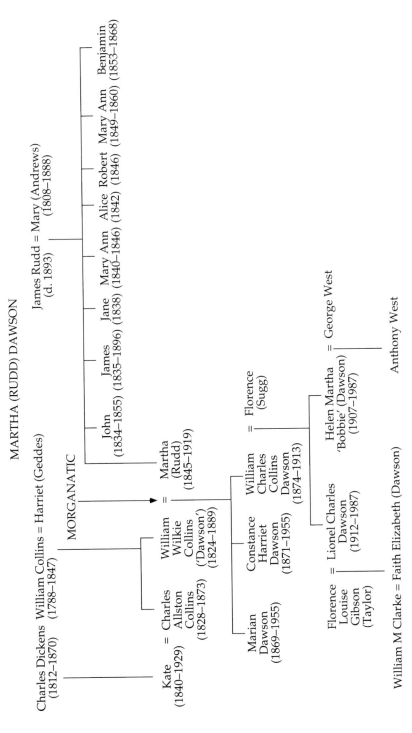

James Rudd = Mary (Andrews)
(d. 1893)   (1808–1888)

Charles Dickens   William Collins = Harriet (Geddes)
(1812–1870)   (1788–1847)

MORGANATIC

John   James   Jane   Mary Ann   Alice Robert Mary Ann   Benjamin
(1834–1855) (1835–1896) (1838) (1840–1846) (1842) (1846) (1849–1860) (1853–1868)

Martha
(Rudd)
(1845–1919)

Kate   = Charles   William
(1840–1929) Allston   Wilkie
             Collins   Collins
             (1828–1873)   ('Dawson')
                            (1824–1889)

Marian   Constance   William   = Florence
Dawson   Harriet   Charles   (Sugg)
(1869–1955)   Dawson   Collins
                    (1871–1955)   Dawson
                                     (1874–1913)

Florence = Lionel Charles   Helen Martha   = George West
Louise   Dawson   'Bobbie' (Dawson)
Gibson   (1912–1987)   (1907–1987)
(Taylor)

                                                  Anthony West

William M Clarke = Faith Elizabeth (Dawson)

Sources: William Clarke, *The Secret Life of Wilkie Collins* and David Higgins, West Minch, Norfolk.

Plates 1 and 2 William and Harriet Collins, Wilkie's parents, by John Linnell.

Plate 3 Charles and Wilkie as children by Alexander Geddes.

Plate 4 Wilkie as a baby by William Collins.

Plate 6 Charles Collins with Dickens and other members of the family at Gad's Hill.

Plate 5 Charles Collins, Wilkie's brother and son-in-law to Charles Dickens.

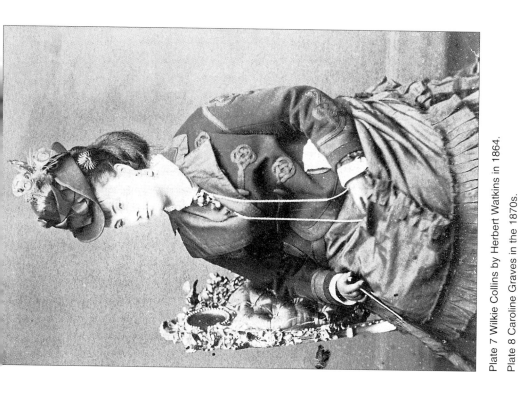

Plate 7 Wilkie Collins by Herbert Watkins in 1864.

Plate 8 Caroline Graves in the 1870s.

Part I
Youth

1838–1846

YOUTH 1838–1846

This first group of letters illustrates Wilkie Collins' relationships with his parents and his brother. Those at the beginning are written from school at Highbury, where he demonstrates his early independence by writing in Italian and rather shows off his knowledge of Virgil. He arrives late for school, slides in the frost, comments on the cold weather, enjoys making boats, and suggests to us that his teachers employ the carrot and stick method of teaching [1 December 1838]. Later ones [18 September and 28 September 1839] show Wilkie engaged in a schoolboy exercise, in copperplate hand, on benevolent despots and in a letter to his father [28 September 1839] he succinctly describes the Siege of Troy. Two letters in Italian [September and October 1839] to his "Mama" reveal what are to be constant concerns in his letters: the state of his eyes; his relationships with the opposite sex (in this instance he is merely "looking at little girls"); his health; and his love of food ("delectably luscious" cake). A rare letter to his "Papa" [December 1838] tackles a subject which was to occupy him greatly in subsequent years – the state of his brother's health.

Lengthy letters to his mother written from Paris [August and September 1844, September and October 1845] and from Antwerp and Brussels [July and August 1846] reveal a mature descriptive style, an obsession with food, the theatre, fashion and women. He writes that his brother "Charley is a Scribe" and that he is "a Pharisee". He is "triumphantly Commercial" and Charlie is as "intensely pictorial as ever". Though he seems uninhibited in writing to his mother, confessing to "dissipating fearfully" in Paris, he spares her much of the detail. The first of a series of letters home when staying at the Hôtel des Tuileries with Charles Ward, refers to visits to theatres, galleries, cafes, the opera, even the morgue [28 August 1844]. He sees Rahel at the Theatre Français [21 September 1844] and tells his mother [13 September 1845] that he had oysters and cutlets for breakfast.

In a lengthy letter, when he was working at Antrobus's tea office in the Strand [30 July 1844], he is at once hyperbolic and not afraid to send his mother sexually suggestive rhyming couplets and in another he speaks of a "seraglio of women". His future career emerges in a letter [13 September 1845], in which he mentions a manuscript (probably *Ioláni*) being considered – and later rejected – by Chapman and Hall. By the summer of 1846 Wilkie is no longer an exuberant youth, but a perceptive descriptive writer. In Belgium he finds the country is "a great flat damp grim meadow, speckled with church spires like pepper-boxes and dwellings like over-coloured baby-houses. I find the people possessed of immense physical energies – little intelligence and enormous seats to their breeches. The posterior portion of our Ostend waiter's trousers would have clothed a whole family of destitutes in St Giles's."

To Mrs Harriet Collins,[1] 1 December 1838
MS: PM[2]

My Dear Mama/

As my last contained the History and Design only of the Æneid of Virgil, I shall now proceed, as I promised, to give you the Arrangement of that celebrated Poem.

The Arrangement is:

Virgil divides his Poem into twelve books. He begins, like all other Epic poets, by stating, in the first few lines, what the subject of his Poem is, he then mentions the causes of Juno's anger against the Trojans. Then he describes Æneas, in the seventh and last year of his voyage, just about to land on the shores of Italy: when Juno, enraged at this, begs Æolus to raise a storm, by which the fleet of Æneas is dispersed. Neptune stills the tempest, and Æneas, with seven ships out of thirteen, is driven on the coast of Africa.

This is as far as my class have read. I shall give you further descriptions of this great Poem, in future letters.

Mr Cole[3] desires me to say, that we separate, for the Christmas Vacation, on Wednesday December the 19th; and return to our studies on Wednesday January the 30th, 1839.

I remain, dear Mama, | Your dutiful son, | William Collins.
39 Highbury Place, | December 1st, 1838.

Notes

1. Harriet Collins, née Geddes (1790–1868), WC's mother.
2. Letter written in copperplate hand.
3. Rev. Henry Cole to whose school at 39 Highbury Place WC was sent in 1838 after two years abroad.

To Mrs Harriet Collins, 11 March 1839
MS: PM[1]

My Dear Mama

As I thought you would like to hear from me in about a week after my arrival here, I now sit down to tell all the news I can collect. I arrived here about 2 minutes before prayer time which was sooner than I expected as we did not get the omnibus directly. We have had several long walks, and some sliding, in the frost wich began here Thursday morning and has been colder I think than it was in the holidays. Tell Charlie[2] with my love that we have made the boat and it sails very well. I hope his lessons are not so difficult as they were when I was last at home. I suppose when I see you again at Easter Papa's[3] pictures will be almost ready for the exibition. I hope he is not prevented by headachs from going on with them. The boys here do Themes three times a week and Mr Cole has hinted at the probability of the senior boys of our class beginning after Midsummer holidays. Some of the boys in our class have begun to write down the sermon and I suppose it will not be long before I have to do the same. I suppose Charlie has had some sliding but has I hope had no mis-fortune with his [b]reeks. On Sunday the frost was so severe that the ponds in the neighbourhood were covered with boys sliding. I think I have now exhausted all my news and remain with love to all at home

> Dear Mama your affet^c. son | William Wilkie Collins
> 39 Highbury Place | March 11th 1839.

Notes

1. Letter written in copperplate hand.
2. Charles Allston Collins (1828–73), WC's younger brother.
3. William John Thomas Collins, R.A. (1788–1847), WC's father, celebrated portrait and landscape painter.

To [Mrs Harriet Collins], 18 September 1839
MS: PM[1]

Θὐχ ἀγαδὸν ωολυχουρανίη
Homer

Proposition What a profitable lesson may be drawn from this maxim of the Grecian poet: "The government of many is not good"!

Reason. Because, different men have different sentiments on systems of government; and if they were all to enforce their own opinions, nothing but confusion and every evil would ensue.

Confirmation – How many kingdoms, after having prospered under the government of one, have been exposed to the horrors of anarchy and revolution, through the government of many.

Argument. The happiness of a nation depends on the government of the state; diverse nations require different forms of government; but the most perfect and most happy form of government has generally been found to be a wise and good monarchy.

Comparison. As the calmness of a river is diminished by its [mixing] with many and different streams: so is the calmness of a state disturbed by many and various rulers.

Example. When the Roman Empire was attempted to be governed by the great Triumvirate, it was distracted by their destructive dissentions.

Testimony – Our poet is supported, in this wise sentiment, by Bias, one of the Seven Sages of Greece, whose maxim was: "Θι πλαιους κακοι" too many are bad.

Conclusion. Nations, armies, and societies, have most painfully proved the truth of this assertion of the immortal bard.

William Collins
39 Highbury Place,
September 18th 1839

Note

1. Letter written in copperplate hand.

To William Collins, R.A., 28 September 1839
MS: PM[1]

My dear Papa

It is my intention in this letter to commence describing the 2nd Book of the Æneid of Virgil having finished the description of the 1st Book in former letters

My last left Æneas finishing with Dido to whom he now relates the fall of Troy and his adventures from that period to the time of his now being in her presence. The Grecians who had been besieging the city for ten years now pretended flight but hid themselves behind the island of Tenedos and left a wooden horse which was internally filled with soldiers in the camp. In the mean time Sinon undertakes to accomplish the stratagem. He presents himself to the Trojans as having escaped from the Greeks and is led into Troy with his hands bound behind him. He relates a false history of his life in order that he might persuade the Trojans to bring into their city the wooden horse by the introduction of which Troy is burnt sacked and finally destroyed.

I remain my dear Papa | Your dutiful son | William Collins
39. Highbury Place | September 28th 1839

Note

1. Letter written in black ink copperplate hand.

To Mrs Harriet Collins, [? September 1839]
MS: PM

Piazza di Highbury | Venredi nella matina.

Cara mia madre

Credendo farvi una piacere, vi ho scritto questa biglietta Italiana per mostrarvi che non l'ho dimenticato affatto. Cominciava le mie studie Giovedi, é le mie occhie stanno benissimo ché vi assicuro mi da molto piacere perché era una cosa horrible di aver niente á fare é di sedere tutto il giorno guardando le piccole ragazze. Spero ché la povera papa sta assai recovrato e che addesso continua le tavole da lo il mio amore, e dite lo che spero che non dimentica la sua gran parola Italiana, "<u>Comé Sechiama</u>"! Ero molto dispiaciuto di udir dell novelli tante male di Carlo e spero quando vedrei lei ancora di saper che e recovrato. Elizzabetta veniva, e mi portó delle deliziosissime fiche. Non ho veramenté piu dire é colla amore mio a tutto, é la speranza per la saluta di tutti,

Sono La sua affettuosa figlo. | Gugliegmo Collini.[1]

Note

1. Translation:

Highbury Place (Piazza)
Friday morning

My dear Mother,
  Believing it will give you pleasure, I have written this note in Italian to show you that I have not at all forgotten it. I started my studies on Thursday and my eyes are fine, which I assure you gives me great pleasure, because it was horrible to have nothing to do and to sit down all day looking at the little girls. I hope poor papa is very well recovered and that now he is continuing[with] the tables [tablets?]. Give him my love and tell him that I hope he will not forget his great Italian phrase "COMÉ SECHIAMÁ" [what's it called]. I was very sorry to hear the bad news of Carlo and I hope when I see him again to know that he has recovered. Elizabeth came and brought me some delicious figs. I have really got no more to say and with my love to all and hopes for everyone's health,

I am your affectionate son, | Guglielmo Collini

To Mrs Harriet Collins, 12 October 1839
MS: PM

My dear Mama/

  I did not write until I had tasted the cake, as I thought you would like to know that it was most <u>delectably luscious</u>. The whole parcel arrived quite safely, and I am very much pleased with the trousers, I think they are the nicest pair I ever had. You cannot think how delighted I was to hear such a good account of Papa, I suppose when I see you on Saturday the 26th he will be hard at work making up for lost time as the coachman says. I suppose as you [are : erased] say nothing of yourself and <u>Charles Allston</u> – that you are both quite [bobbish]; I am happy to say that I have never felt the least ill since I last saw you.

I am afraid that I shall not be able to fill this side, as I really have no news at all here and must therefore make a virtue of necessity, and conclude with best love to all at home.

Dear Mama | Yr affec Son | W W Collins

P.S. Charlie[']s letter amused me very much, it looked exactly like the autograph of a great man!!! —

39 Highbury Place Oct 12th 1839.

To Mrs Harriet Collins, 14 October [1839]
MS: PM

Piazza di Highbury | Le 14th Ottobre

Cara mia madre

Ho avuto da fare quella pena di "writing out" é cosi non ho potuto scrivere mia lettera piu tosto. Non c'è stato niente di nuovo qui con eccetta questa cosa la bella é amabile moglie del governatore di questo castello mi ha detto colla sua propria bocca ché posso dire una <u>bugia</u>! con molta bellezza. E poco sogetta poverina alla colera. vi dico piu, quando saro a casa nostra ancora. Spero che il visagio di Carlo sta meglio. Fa i miei complimenti alla piccola gata e comprate una cosa per la colla sua. Avete trovato "The tales for an idler," spero di si saro inconsolabilé se no – Ho scritto questa lettera con un calmajo cattivissimo credo che non e possibile leggerla. Da la mia amore al padre, spero che non ha preso freddo la sera di Domenica. Non posso da vero dir piu adesso in questo loco maladetto non si puo avere dei novelli – scrivemi presta e credemi

Cara mia madre | tuo figlio amantissimo | Gulielmo Wilkie Collini[1]

Note

1. Translation:

Highbury Place [Square]
14th October

My dear Mother,

I have had to do that penalty of "writing out", so I have not been able to write a letter before now. There has been nothing new here except this: the beautiful and amiable wife of the governor of this castle [prison?, establishment] told me with her own lips that I can tell a <u>lie</u>!

beautifully. She is a bit inclined, poor dear to anger. I will tell you more when I am at home again. I hope Charlie's face is better. Give my compliments to the little she-cat and buy her something for her neck. Have you found "The Tales for an Idler", I hope so, otherwise I shall be inconsolable. I have written this letter in terrible ink. I think you will not be able to read it. Give my love to father, I hope he didn't take cold on Sunday night. I cannot really say any more now. In this cursed place one cannot get any news. Write soon and believe me, dear mother,

your most loving son | Guglielmo Wilkie Collini

To Charles Collins, [6 December 1839]

MS: PM

[39 Highbury Place | Highbury | 6 December 1839]

My dear Charlie,

You really cannot imagine how vividly I can [depicture] your agonizing yells "<u>de chi de noche</u>", and also poor Mama's anxiety on your account, which I can judge of as I was a witness of it at Naples,[1] when your vocal (I will not say <u>musical</u> powers) were exercised on that memorable night, but I am what the boys here would call <u>bullying</u> you, and therefore will immediately close the subject but I assure you, not withstanding all this nonsense, I felt the greatest pity for you. I must now conclude from want of room to expand my ideas!!!

And remain your affectionate brother, | W W Collins

Note

1. "A reference to the occasion towards the end of the family's stay in Naples, when Charles had his arm broken by being pushed off a wall. The episode is described in Harriet Collins' diary now in the Victoria and Albert Museum, London: 'His pain increased all the evening. We got to bed soon after eleven but no sleep. Scarcely all night. Poor Charlie screaming with pain'" (Clarke pp. 39–40).

To Mrs Harriet Collins, 6 December 1839

MS: PM

[39 Highbury Place | Highbury | 6 December 1839] | Friday aft-

My dear Mama/

I was very much pleased to receive your letter, as I was exceedingly anxious to know how you all were, particularly as the account I received from Colin Campbell was not very consoling. Poor Charlie's ear ach was sad news indeed, I [too: erased] know that it is the hardest of all pains to bear, having felt it myself: between them both I really wonder how you keep as well as you do especially with Master Charles [Co] [four? indecipherable letters] [&c] whom we all know is not very easily [erased word] pacified; but I must not however send any messages to him, as I intend to devote a separate portion of this epistle for his benefit. When I see you on the 18th which you mention as the day on which we are to meet, I really hope that [we: erased] I shall see Poor Papa "himself again", for our holidays would be most miserable if he was as unwell then, as he was last Midsummer. Give him my best love and tell him that I hope he will be able to pass his opinion upon a whole host of <u>works of art, fecit his son</u>.[1] With <u>best</u> wishes for the health of all and earnest wishes for the holidays.

I remain dear Mama | Your affectionate Son | W W Collins

Note

1. The first two letters of "son" are doubly underlined.

To Mrs Harriet Collins, 13 June 1842
MS: Private Possession

Tait's Hotel, Princes Street, Edinburgh | 13 June 1842

My dear Mama,

We[1] set off this morning for Melrose and on Friday (in consequence of information we have this day received from Mr Cadell)[2] depart by steamer for Wick.

I think these five lines have put you, or ought to put you, in perfect possession of our plans so I will proceed at once to tell you through the medium of a bad pen, worse ink, a man covered in perspiration eating a hot breakfast and a "stuffy" coffee room, what I think of – "Edina Scotia's darling seat".

I am beyond all measure delighted with the country and the old Town, but <u>tremendously disgusted</u> with the melancholy, grass-grown, ill-paved covered – all – over – with – large – squares – part of the city, denominated "the New Town". It is infallibly, and inexpressibly, <u>good for nothing</u>.

I climbed Arthur's Seat, at the imminent hazard of falling headlong down, in consequence of taking a path of my own to ascend by, instead of the orthodox mode of progression. View <u>inexpressible</u> on one sheet of paper.

I've seen Rizzio's blood, Queen Mary's work basket, the Calton Hill, dirty children, filthy fish wives, slovenly men, dropsical women, Salisbury Crags, ill managed drains, Grassmarket, Presbyterian chapels, the hill people, a sea "darkly [indecipherable word] beautifully blue", a dog (Mr Smith's) delicious, a fellow traveller dyspeptic, a – pho! I'm out of breath and so will you be if you read this description through once, so just gasp out at the end, if you please "What a deal the boy seen!"

William Wilkie Collins[3]

Notes

1. William Collins took his son, the 18-year-old WC, with him on his trip to Scotland.
2. Possibly a member of the Edinburgh publishing firm.
3. Note added from his father, William Collins : "I think I am mending – not yet strong, but hopeful. When we return tomorrow I hope to find a letter for me at Mrs Smith's – I had a long and interesting conversation last night with Miss Smith the elder. She is full of love for you – so am I ... Kind regards to Miss Otter – I have written to her brother in answer to his letter; ... tell her that we hope to see her brother next week." The Otters from Southsea were old family friends.

To Mrs Harriet Collins, [before 2 July 1842]
MS: PM

Dear[1] Mother

I am sorry I can't be with you[2] but I write to you without <u>any cand</u>le at <u>mid-night</u> – as light as evening.

We are quite safe and well here and as I want to go to bed I have only time to tell you that we think of going to the Orkneys by the end of this week and [when] our plans [are] more settled we will write again –

Best remembrances to Charlie and all at Oxford [indecipherable word] and believe me

Your <u>luminous</u> | and affectionate son | <u>William Wilkie Collins</u>[3]

Notes

1. At the top of the letter WC writes: "Thurso | 1/4 past 12 | at night".
2. These words are printed.
3. WC's letter is followed by a note from his father.

To Mrs Harriet Collins, 2 July 1842
MS: PM

Lerwick | Shetland | July 2nd 1842

My dear Mother/

Most of the spare moments that I have wanted during our journey have made their appearances here, so that I am able to give you a detailed account of our present proceedings.

"The principal features of this place" (to borrow Mr Pickwick's phrase) are, Dutchmen, Peat bogs, Ragged Ponies, Beggars, and Fine Scenery – One of our first excursions here, was on ponies to Scalloway a fishing town about 8 miles from Lerwick, the Governor's sketch will give you a better idea of the scenery than my pen and I will therefore merely tell you that we were entertained there on politics oatcake and whisky by a shoemaker whose hand nose and mouth are one of the sights of the place my verdict upon them is – <u>monstrous</u>! and dirty.

We have made another tour to Sumburgh head (mentioned by Scott in the Pirate) it is 30 miles from head quarters. After we had ridden as far as [N]ighton (20 miles)

Mr Bruce who lives there insisted upon our walking in and taking tea with him. While discussing fowl and ham and the charms of the scenery it began to rain as if all the water in the world was being emptied on the elevated roof that sheltered us. Mr Bruce declared we must <u>sleep there</u> so sleep we did after talking till 12 oClock. After breakfast Mr B– accompanied us half the way to Sumburgh and there bade us a hearty adieu. This is the usual practice here and the best bed room in every Zetland House is always kept for the use of strangers. That day we rode 40 miles and " Il padrone" was very tired.

Correct information is a quality undiscoverable in the common people here they have the most lofty disregard of elementary distances and the most extraordinary spirit of inquisitiveness I ever saw. If a common labourer meets you he lingers to converse thus – "Good morning Sir" (a pause). "If you please Sir you'll just be staying at Lerwick – Where do you come from if you please Sir? Your name is no Henderson is it? You'll be from London" && – All this without the least idea that this curiosity is at all disagreeable –

The paper I write to you on was purchased of an old gentleman most awfully drunk after wringing both our hands with the tears in eyes asking us to his house and almost falling back with astonishment at the likeness between your carospizo and myself he began to talk about you.¹ Taking my hand in both his and detaining me with what the fashionable novels call "a gentle force" he wheezed forth in a sentimental and sickly tone of voice

"Ha! Ha! Ha! Ho! Ho! Ho! you'll be able to swear Ha! Ha! that your mother is a most amiable most delightful most accomplished most splendid woman Ha! Ha! Ho! Ho! Ho! Ha –" I [assured] him most devoutly that I could and left him with his hands outstretched for another shake and a sweet smile irradiating his venerable countenance.

We start on Monday evening for Wick on our homeward route but of the precise time we shall be "sur le chemin" I am at present ignorant. I hope you have prepared Mr A for our prolonged stay as directed in our last letter. Give my love to Charlie when you write to him. Remember me to Miss Otter. I hope we shall find on our return that you have accompanied her to Portsmouth and believe me

Your affectionate son | <u>William Wilkie Collins</u>[2]

Notes

1. The word is underlined twice.
2. Following WC's letter there is a note from his father. The rest of which, and an account of WC's Shetland visit, may be found in WC's *The Life of William Collins, Esq. R.A.* (1978 reprint), II, 210–25.

To William Collins, R.A., 24 August 1842
MS: PM

Strand | 24th August 1842

My dear Father/
    True to my agreement, I hasten to tell you that no material change has as yet taken place in the constitutions of Charlie, Margaret, Susan, The House, or your humble servant. Last night, on my return from M[rs] Gray's,[1] I examined it myself, I put a head into the drawing room, a nose into the parlour, and a hand on every available window lock that I came to, and went to bed with a horrible-foreboding, that something would certainly happen, on account of this my third attempt at universal carefulness – The two former as <u>Mama</u> will recollect proved abortive, but this as far as I have been able to discover, is as effective as you could possibly wish.
    Pray write and let me know whether that abominable engine of destruction in which you yesterday mentioned yourself, has deposited you uninjured at Southsea – I assure you I am positively nervous this morning, about that, and everything else, in consequence of the conversations at Mrs G's. It turned (it generally somehow does whenever I [erased words] am in her company) upon literature, and I sat with my back to the window, and my hand in my pocket freezing my horrified auditors by a varied

recital of the most terrible portions of the Monk and Frankenstein – Every sentence that fell from my lips, was followed in rapid succession by – "Lord!" – "Oh!" "Ah!" "He! He!" "Good Gracious!" —

None of our country relations I am sure ever encountered in their whole lives before such a hash of diablerie, demonology, & massacre with their Souchong and bread and butter. I intend to give them another [erased word] course, emphasizing, the Ancient Mariner, Jack the Giant Killer, The Mysteries of Udolpho and an enquiry into the life and actions (when they were little girls) of the witches in Macbeth.

The news this morning is Lord Auckland's[2] arrival in London, and a deluge of attacks upon his Government in India – The Scotch are speculating upon how cheaply they can dress at the Queen's drawing room in Edinburgh. The ladies – Saving creatures! – won't get court dresses, so they go in bonnets; and the Gentlemen citizens, shudder at the idea of all appearing in blue coats and bright buttons, an idea that must have been started by two or three prodigal Englishmen I fear – There is a little stealing, a little suicide, a little rioting, a little "dropping down dead suddenly", a litle larceny, and a great deal of twaddle in the people besides – but nothing worthy of "my Grey Goose Quill" – or of your perusal.

My letter, is as usual, rambling and ill written; however the best of it to you, is at the first, and the worst of it, is comprised in the three little capital letters at the end. Give my love to Mama and tell her Charlie caught by the blandishments of Davis is going to have a new pair of[3] Make my Kindest remembrances to Miss Otter, Mrs Otter, Miss Musgrave, and any other numbers of the "Clan", that may be at Gloucester Place,

And believe me | Your affectionate Son | W.W.C.

Notes

1. i.e., WC's aunt, Catherine Gray.
2. George Eden, Earl of Auckland (1784–1849: *DNB*), governor-general of India. Held responsible for disaster of November 1841, when the British Afghan garrison was overrun, and recalled by Peel, forced to resign from office.
3. WC draws what appear to be a pair of breeches, 2 cm in length, following the word "of".

To Mrs Harriet Collins, [1842]
MS: PM

Monday morning

My dear Mama,

We are all going on very well at home. I have had a letter from my Aunt-Christy which was put in for you, it made us all laugh much. George putting a message in your letter that he was a monkey. You are very kind to think of trying to get such baskets for us, it is very pleasant to be near chain pier as that, which we were obliged to ride. I hope you have not the trouble of paying that place. Papa and I think of going to Gravesend if the winter does not come too soon. We hope to see you come home quite well and in good health. I am very sorry you do not get any walks on the beach for rain.

Your most affectionate son. | ^{Will} W. Collins.

To Mrs Harriet Collins, [1842]
MS: PM.

Southsea | Portsmouth

My dear Mama/
    I really don't know what to do. On mentioning Brighton to Miss Otter she said she thought I should [indecipherable words] and that place – by myself and thought I had better stop by Southsea, only she was afraid I should find no amusements there. I of course (and with a very safe conscience) declared I had been much entertained during my stay, but was fearful of becoming a bore and there the affair has dropped for the present; and I acknowledge myself perfectly unable to determine what I ought to do; I think I am much better here – , but then a month seems a long time to billet myself upon friends.
    Tell Charlie I am riding upon a splendid black mare just bought by Mr Otter as [free] as the wind yet withal as Gentle as a lamb, rowing in the "dingy" till my arms are almost off whenever the weather permits, and contemplating should the detestable rain and wind now prevailingly disappear a tour to the Isle of Wight.
    I suppose this will be deemed a most unsatisfactory letter. Probably it is so, but I have stated the facts exactly as they are, and must leave your maturer[1] judgement to determine as it best may.
    I am delighted to learn so good an account of the Governor – remember me kindly to <u>all</u> in Oxford Terrace and believe me dear Mama

Your <u>undecided</u> Son, | William Wilkie Collins

Note

1. The word is doubly underlined.

To Mrs Harriet Collins, 13 January 1844
MS : Private Possession

The Strand | 13 January 1844

Summary:

"My dear Madam,
    I've been in such a halo of commercial enterprise since I received your letter of 'advice gratis' that this is my first opportunity of telling you that I feel the spirit of 'maturity' strong upon me, having been in a 'state of grace' ever since the 8th of this month[1] as regards my mental faculties; and in a state of deplorable feebleness as regards my bodily. The <u>parties</u> have knocked me up – I've made two <u>speeches</u> at supper and drunk so much of the juice of the grape that (to use the impassioned language of Elihu the Buzzite a <u>comforter</u> of Job) – 'My belly is as wine.' We got home last night after one of the festive scenes at 10 minutes past 4 <u>A.M.</u> Charlie was so horrified at hearing the cock crow that he showed a disposition to whimper and said that people out late as we were not in a <u>fit state to die</u>.
    We've had some curiously bad dinners and Charity has made some ponderously heavy stuff in substance like putty and sugar enclosed in boiled mahogany. Your husband being an imaginative person says its home-made <u>bread</u>![2] So we eat it, and I make a mental apology to my stomach for every morsel I put into my mouth.
    Don't hurry your departure – work out the Doctor's Bill in sea air. Don't eat any rumpsteaks. Give me your opinion of the Portsmouth Tarts (mine is favourable) and [indecipherable word] for Wm Collins Esqre R.A. who will eat no pudding and swears that everything is poison but mutton and bread. He says he laid my case before the <u>Galens</u>[3] of Southampton. If they are to be believed – by the time you return I shall have no stomach at all. Vive la Gastronomie! 'which being interpreted' means Damn Digestion!
    I've no particular messages – beyond Loves from Devonport Street – we are all well. I wish I could say the same of the Antrobus' family.[4] Poor little Ellen is laid up on an invalid couch in consequence of a weakness in the hip which Mr [R] Brodie seems to think requires great care.
    Make my modest remembrances to Mrs Otter, Miss Smallridge and Miss Otter and any other of my friends at Portsmouth."

Notes

1. 8 January 1844, his twentieth birthday.
2. WC doubly underlines "read" of "bread".
3. Galen (Claudius Galenus), Greek physician to Marcus Aurelius. Wilkie's nickname for the Bullars, their doctor friends.
4. Edward Antrobus (1806–1886) was a prominent tea-merchant, whose children had been painted by William Collins. As a friend of the family he gave Wilkie his first job at his office close to Coutts at the western end of the Strand.

To Mrs Harriet Collins, 30 July 1844
MS: PM

44[b]– Strand West– | July 30th 1844

My dear Madam

Charlie is a <u>Scribe</u> and I am a <u>Pharisee</u>: for <u>he</u> pays you real attention, while I only talk about it. However I mean to take my turn at the employment epistolary, now; and by way of quieting your anxiety about us, I will <u>begin</u> by assuring you that I am as triumphantly Commercial and Charlie as intensely pictorial as ever.

Miss Thompson arrived yesterday evening – Susan, [Miss] Brandling "Brother and self"[1] welcomed her – Currant pie, drawing room sofa and captains biscuit awaited her – moral conversation soothed her – Bed and washing-stand refreshed her – Breakfast settled her – She is well – "[Saluberius est]" [very healthy].

An invitation came a few days ago from [Leslie] for you two and your humble servant – I went – met Miss Macready[2] – very nice woman – wish her husband wasn't a Radical.

Tomorrow the Horticultural Society have a fête for those who did not use their tickets in the day when "the hurrican[ors] spouted". I shall go – Six military Bands and the Duke of Devonshire's grounds open.

Charlie goes to day to settle with Hogarth[3] about the pictures being removed. There is a report that the Academy will allow two rooms to be open for the Art – Unionites[4] to choose pictures from. In my own part, I don't believe it. The Exhibition closed as usual on Saturday and I doubt their opening it again for anybody. However, in case of such a thing taking place, would the governor like the much-imposed but unalterably benignant "[Patuisch]" to take his chance with the rest?

Mrs Gray made us a present a little while ago of half a bread and butter pudding which we had tasted at dinner at her house, and most delicious it was – Strange woman that sister of yours!

No letters of consequence have come. The Newtonian epistle of expostulation Charlie says he sent you a day or two back. Has he told you my having the other night to answer the bell "at one oClock in" <u>the morning</u>? Never had such fun in my life – called out "who's there?" – before I opened the door – Sepulchral voice answered – "Phelps".[5] – Vague thought came across my mind that it was the wretched paper-monger of Edinburgh, who having failed in Commerce as well as in Engraving had come to sponge upon <u>us</u> – Answered – "no Phelps here" – voice returned – "Susan [Gellire]" "All right" says I, "Susan's up stairs taking a snooze." "She's sleeping with my wife" says he. "Good Heavens" says I – "She's got the Ring of my house." – "<u>Has</u> she?" says I – "Will you wake her?" says he – "With pleasure" says I – "I've been from Putney to Chelsea" says he – "Indeed" says I – "And from Chelsea here" says he –

Well, Madam, I let him in; seeing how it was at last. <u>Martha</u> (<u>not</u> the sister of Mary) had been visiting Susan with her [brats] – her husband had not come to fetch her as he promised. She had given him up for that night and (taking the Ring of their house with her) had gone to sleep at a neighbours, not being able to carry the [brats] to Chelsea by herself. This I did not find out till I had woke Susan.

    I knocked at their (the servant's) door, and: –

    The virgin, She lept from her bed,
As Solemn as usual, (confound her!)
    With her nose looking devilish red,
And chemises by dozens around her,
      Cries she, "what's the matter?" – Says I,
"Mister Phelps you're unable to chouse[indecipherable letters]
    "In the passage he's piping his eye,
"Cause you've taken the key of his house"
        Fol de roll!
"I've not got it" says she – "Pon my life"
    Says I, "you're o'erdoing the spree!
You may cheat the man out of his wife,
    But damn it Maam! give him his key;
You'll find him, I think, in the hall;
    I leave you my blessing and candle;
Ere you seek him just put on a shawl,
    Or I swear I won't answer for scandal."
        Fol de roll!

Well, she went down and sent off the unhappy Phelps without his Ring – What he did, whether he slept anywhere, or took it out in walking the Streets, I don't know. Susan, of course looked very foolish and made a good many apologies the next morning. I was not surprised at the mess they had all got into, knowing, as I do, what a set of apes the lower orders are in this country.

If you'll stay till I come back from Paris, I'll visit you at Ventnor – Shall you. Either if you be in London before I go?

Now, will you answer <u>this</u> question and the other about the Patriarch? It generally takes <u>three</u> letters <u>to make</u> you answer <u>one</u> [interogatory] – witness the difficulty we had to get you to reply to us about [Caulton] The Bigamist.

I've only seen Romeo Ward[6] once, for [erased word] the last fortnight. He's so taken up with Juliet Chips that he's as impossible to be seen as a picture in the Octagon Room.[7]

Everybody sends regards and felicitations. The longer you keep Mr Collins in the country the better he'll be.

Don't let him come up on <u>our</u> account. We <u>look into rooms in the dark</u> – Peep about at bars and fastenings – Get up early in the morning – don't drink anything like a glass of wine in a day – and are upon tremendously affable terms with the domestics.

Upon taking the effect of this letter at a distance it strikes me as being of Bob: Leslie dimensions, so I pull up for the present in the character of yours, my dear Madam,

Very affectionately | Wilkie Collins

Mrs Collins | Mrs Brasiers Poplar Cottage | Ventnor | Isle of Wight

Charlie is in great tribulation about what he is to say to Crocker[8] who came for the order to remove the pictures as usual. Why is he cut out by Hogarth?

Notes

1. Susan Brandling, the sister of Henry Brandling, a young artist who was to illustrate Collins' <u>Rambles Beyond Railways</u>, 1851.
2. Catherine Macready (?1806–1852), née Atkins, wife of William Charles Macready (1793–1873), the great actor-manager.
3. Possibly an allusion to the great painter and caricaturist William Hogarth (1697–1764).
4. Probably a reference to Royal Academy politics.
5. Doubly underlined.
6. Charles James Ward (1814–1883), close friend of WC, who married his favourite cousin, Jane Carpenter, in February 1845.
7. "The Octagon Room at the Royal Academy was considered the 'den' – the worst place to have a picture hung in the annual Exhibition" (Peters, p. 63).
8. Unidentified.

To Mrs Harriet Collins, [July 1844]
MS: PM

Dear Mama

The enclosed letter from Miss Clarkson is unspeakable agitating for me. I have placed the house at her disposal – expect the three ladies to come of course – and have asked Marian Gray (!) to meet them, and help me to put them to bed, and "let down their back hair", and tuck them up, and so forth. What in the devil's name, am I to do with this seraglio of women? (<u>six</u>, including the servants). Shall I get the garret for Marian Gray – Charley's room for one Miss Clarkson – your room for the other – the large bedroom for the Mama? Have we towels, sheets, soap, enough, in the house? Oh Lord! Oh Lord! What shall I do? Write quickly and tell me!

I suppose I have done right in asking Marian Gray to come – A woman is wanted in the house isn't she? – It was Mrs Charles Wards' idea – I intended to have asked one of Charley's "sluts"[1] to come and help me

Good God, suppose they should want a change of chemises!

I send some Prospectuses. Get me some subscribers. Mrs Bullar is at Southampton, I have forwarded your letter, Spend money at the Sale of [courts].

Kind regards to all Southsea —

Yours affectionately | W. W. C.

PS. Don't think of doing anything so foolish as to come back on account of the guests. If you give me some directions, I shall manage well enough. I don't feel much about anything but the chemises.[2]

Notes

1. The word is underlined twice. Peters explicates it as "presumably artists' models" (p. 63).
2. The word is underlined three times.

To Mrs Harriet Collins, 8 August 1844

MS: Private Possession

Strand | 8 August 1844

Summary:

"My dear Madam,

I enclose a letter from Robertson the Miniature Painter[1] which I think requires an answer.

With regard to the Carpet Bag, if there is nothing else for me, I suppose I must take it though I hate Carpet Bags with a great and bitter hatred. They don't protect your linen from damp, your brushes from [breaking] and your waistcoats from crumpling as a Portmanteau does. People sit upon a Carpet Bag because it is soft. Trunks tumble upon it for the same reason. There is not an accident to which luggage is liable that a Carpet Bag does not fall victim to. It never was meant for anything but a few shirts and stockings that may be knocked about anyhow. It is the most disagreeable machine to pack – the most troublesome to unpack – the most impractical to carry that human science ever invented: and yet in spite of all these objections I must take it I suppose because I can't get anything else ... I shall pack it myself. That infernal fool Susan will spoil everything if she attempts it. I lectured her the other day upon inhumanity. In her zeal for science or for her kitchen (I don't know which) she attempted to re-introduce by the kitten's nose that which the innocent animal had just previously expelled as worthless from an opposite and inferior portion of its body. Charlie tried <u>rage</u> upon the subject with the cook. I tried philosophy with the housemaid. He failed. <u>I</u> succeeded – Purified is the nose of Snooks.

I am very much obliged for the permission to bleed the Estate. I shall take my money in £5 notes. They change them <u>in Paris</u> at an advantage to the English. Charles Ward will recommend me to the man he employed for this purpose.

I will see that ... Callcott[2] is inquired after immediately.

Leigh Hunt's son's wife has been at it again. Charlie commiserated and that <u>was all</u>. Let me only catch any of these hangers on that Mr Collins's <u>No.12</u>[3] has brought about the house! They would not trouble us again I suspect till the governor returns. – If that great man Malthus had been attended to we should have had no beggars by this time.

No other letters of any importance have come – the carpenters are at Hampton Court.

I though you had cut Marshall [Clanton].[4] He'll borrow money of you if you don't mind. MacKay[5] you won't be troubled with long. He's just the man to tumble off a high rock during his geological researches. Or you might frighten him to death by one of your vocal performances. He's easily got rid of – poor Devil!

Oh those frescoes! Upon my honor I can fancy the spirit of Raffael wandering round the Hall at night and weeping for shame and sorrow as he looks at them. Maclise[6] is the only man there is any hope of. He seems to understand his material at least.

Of course you have heard that the Queen has Duke of Yorked us.

'The confederate' will lend me his box. So is there any harm in taking that instead of the Carpet Bag ?

We are going to follow the footsteps of Sterne – from London to Calais – Calais to [Montreuil] – &c."

Notes

1. Andrew Robertson (1977–1845), Scottish-born minaturist and landscape painter.
2. Sir August Ward Callcott, R.A., (1799-1844: *DNB*), landscape painter.
3. "No. 12" doubly underlined. The precise allusion to "Leigh Hunt's son's wife" eludes us.
4. Unidentified.
5. Unidentified.
6. Daniel Maclise (?1806–1870: *DNB*), painter, friend of Charles Dickens.

To Mrs Harriet Collins, 28 August 1844
MS: PM[1]

Hotel de Tours | Place de la Bourse | Paris

My dear Mother

We[2] have just arrived after a journey of four and twenty consecutive hours at the above house of call for man and beast. I am so horribly hot, tired and hungry that this letter must be merely a warranty that we are both hitherto "sound in wind and limb". The voyage was remarkably calm and the journey by Diligence favoured with the loveliest weather – the situation here is the most "central" in Paris – within a few minutes walk of the Palais Royal The Louvre &c

You shall, in a few days, have a more extended account of our non-adventures[3] and some idea of our future plans. Answer this as soon as possible for I want to know where you are and whether those infernal domestics have got their "governor" or not – Ward sends remembrances – and I love and apologies for the shortness of this letter.

Yours affectionately | Wilkie Collins
Mrs Collins | 1 Devonport Street | Hyde Park Gardens | Augt 28th 1844

Notes

1. Postmark: "L | AU-31 | 1844".
2. i.e., WC and Charles Ward.
3. WC doubly underlines the letters "non-ventures": "ad" is singly underlined.

To Mrs Harriet Collins, 4 September 1844
MS: PM

Hotel de Tours | Place de la Bourse | Sept 4th, 1844

My dear Mother

On our return from St Denis where I had been thinking about the death of the Kings of France (who are all buried there) I received your intimation of the lives of my relations – a much more satisfactory subject for reflection.

We are now thoroughly settled here – and are dissipating fearfully – gardens – theatres and Cafés being the conglomerate parts of the Parisian Paradise we are most inhabiting. Last Sunday we went to Versailles. Quantity of Pictures there tremendous. Quality exactly the contrary – about half a dozen seemed to me exquisitely beautiful; but the rest (being those pictorial abominations called "Battle pieces") I could not appreciate. The

Louvre we have visited several times. "The Judgment of Brutus" and "the Wreck of the Medusa" are worth the Journey to Paris alone. The first I think the very finest historical picture of modern times. The Luxembourg Gallery we have yet to penetrate.

I saw yesterday a glorious subject for Charlie – a dead soldier laid out naked at the Morgue; like an unsaleable cod fish – all by himself upon the slab. He was a fine muscular old fellow who had popped into the water in the night and was exposed to be recognised by his friends.

We breakfast out – dine out – read out and do everything in fact in the open air but sleeping. Ward was most horrifically bedbugged on the first night of our sojourn but has changed his room and escaped further nocturnal visitation. I have seen nothing of the kind yet. The exertion of getting into my bed (which is as high as an elephant's back and as soft as the Slough of Despond) being quite sufficient for me without the further trouble of noticing live stock.

Will you write to Mr Antrobus when he returns (about the middle of this month) to ascertain the utmost extension of leave of absence that he will allow me. I should like to know it before the End of Sept in order to settle my plans. Will he give me the first week in October? or <u>more</u>? or less? or what?

The weather is delicious not too hot any more. You shall have a further bulletin of our adventures in a few days. While this fine weather lasts, I find great difficulty in saving time for anything but sight-seeing. Finishing this letter today is impossible Ward being outrageous for his dinner and I being interrupted by mortality's most important visitation – clothes from the wash –

12 o'Clock

I have just got home from the Opera (Othello). The music most monotonously dismal and Duprez most grievously hoarse. It is a noble Theatre, however; and its Wardrobe (judging by tonight's performance) is superb.

Talking about Wardrobes – Mr Collins ought to go to Calais – The Costumes of the people are so admirably characteristic. Upon second thoughts, though, I recollect hearing him [erased word] speak about the place himself – so I may as well spare my enthusiasm on this head, as, under existing circumstances, it may turn out a bore.

Our journey to Paris was pleasant enough while it was day; but at night 'twas rather disagreeable. We could only get places in the banquette (a kind of pigeon house among the luggage at the top of the carriage). We were – three dogs and three passengers besides the conductor. The defence [erased word] against the night air was an ill-fitting glass above, and a leather apron below. What with the fidgetting of the dogs behind me, the howling of the driver to his horses, the melancholy parody upon snoring executed by Ward – the grunting of the fellow passengers and the indefatigable cigar smoking of the conductor I found sleeping impracticable and took it out in nocturnal meditation upon "everything in general and nothing in particular" –.

We got to Paris at 12 oClock the next day having raced the whole distance with a rival vehicle. The contending drivers [two erased words] swearing "three Volumes – Post-Octavo" – full of oaths at each other at every opportunity.

I am delighted to hear of Mr Otter's promotion and of the smooth current of affairs at Devonport Street. When you write again let it be to the same direction as before. Ward has gone to bed after desiring his remembrances and I must do the same after sending love to all.

ever yours | Wilkie Collins

P.S.

Let me hear again soon.[erased word] When all your plans are definitely settled "haste me to know it", for they will, of course, rather influence mine. You say you will leave Miss Otter's before we come – you had better stay there I think (they are sure to ask you) and we can be stowed away anywhere – Of this, however, here after –

To Mrs Harriet Collins, 21 September 1844
MS: PM

Hotel des Tuileries | Rue de Rivoli | Sept 21/44 | Saturday

My dear Mother

We have at last settled our plans – We start for Rouen on Wednesday next – stay there a day and then proceed to Havre and Southampton: so as to be at Miss Otter's either the 28th, 29th, or 30th. (on which of these days we shall arrive I cannot say for certain) Thus I shall easily be able to begin my official duties on the morning of October 3rd –

I have just returned from the Tour of the Churches – nothing but weddings going on – great mass of the people here always splice each other on Saturday because the night's ball does not interfere with the next day's work; when that next day is Sunday – Don't take much interest in Matrimony – so can't tell you anything more about the ceremony of marriage here than that the bridegrooms looked foolish and wore ill-cut coats and that the Priests looked sulky and had generally speaking red noses.

Going tonight (as a duty) to the Theatre Français – to see Rachel in Les Horaces.[1] Know by bitter experience what a boor it will be – men in buff coloured blankets with fuzzy heads growling about their beloved country through five long acts with porticos ad libitum behind them for scenery – Have taken care to secure comfortable seats with Spring cushions, so as to go to sleep with dignity – Shall lie furiously about it in England – say it was superb &&& to gain credit for a classical taste.

How shall I be able to stand the Tea & coffee breakfasts at home I don't know! Lambert[2] and I take to the dejéuner à la fourchette regularly – Oysters and Chablis – omlettes and radishes much better than that infernal charity-boy-cum-servant-maid-compound commonly called bread and butter – Yesterday we had some fish that <u>literally</u> made Ward bilious to look at it – afraid I shall be as fat as a pig if I stay here much longer – do nothing but eat and Drink – very wrong I know – shall [feast] upon leg of Mutton and rice-pudding when I get home.

Ward has bought the hog tools – he says they are capital. Three dozen is the quantity he has procured.

There will be no time I am afraid for you to write to me again before I leave Paris – your next letter had better be directed to Eastlands.

I was indeed – and am still very much shocked to hear of poor Mr [Tweedell's] death. He was [erased word] a really clever-fellow and a most admirable companion. [several heavily erased words] It is a most unfortunate commencement for the surveying labours of our friends in the north.

The weather with us is breaking fast – For the last two or three days it has been [erased word] chilly and cloudy and I am afraid our homeward journey will be a very rainy one – However we have no reason to complain – Three weeks of sunshine being enough to satisfy everybody but British Agriculturists.

Give my Kindest remembrances to the party at Eastlands and with love to you all believe me yours affectionately | Wilkie Collins

Notes

1. The great French actress Rachel (Élisa Félix, 1820–1858) made her Théâtre Français debut on 12 June 1838 as Camille in Corneille's *Horace* (*Les Horaces*).
2. Unidentified.

To Mrs Harriet Collins, [9 September 1845]
MS: PM

Tuesday evening | Hotel des Tuileries | Rue de Rivoli | Paris

My dear Madam

I arrived at this place (<u>without</u> my baggage) this evening. The infernal boobies who govern the station at Rouen must have forgotten to put it (my portmanteau) in the luggage car. I made a tremendous disturbance about their negligence at the station here; the result of which has been a promise to recover "my effects" by tomorrow. As I saw my luggage <u>safely</u> delivered to the railway porter, I have no doubt that I shall find it on application, tomorrow afternoon.

On the passage across, there were only <u>three</u> people well enough to sit at the dinner table; of which trio, the heir of your late father's estates made a voracious and most important unit. As, (like "Marlow")[1] "I generally make my father's son welcome wherever he goes" I made acquaintance with every soul in the ship, from a good-natured <u>negro</u> who told me he was a student in <u>philosophy</u>! to a man with a blood-spotted nose, who knew all the works, of all the artists, ancient and modern, all over the world. Ere, however, I reached Paris "my very good friends" vanished into thin air; with the exception of a very agreeable family party, who visit this earthly paradise for the first time and whose good graces I may yet cultivate. Like young Rapid I have "kept moving" ever since my arrival; having shaken hands with every soul in this, my beloved hostelry, taken a bath, [indecipherable word] boots, eaten a dinner, changed a sovereign, smoked cigars imbibed coffee and procured one of the chambermaid's neck-handkerchief, as an impromptu nightcap, within a couple of hours after my first setting foot in "the capital of Europe".

As for Rouen, it is very fine indeed; I got a man in a blue blouse to take me all over the place in two hours – Gothic architecture, painted windows, palace of Justice, Joan of Arc, Chateau de Bellefort – by the powers, I saw them all!

Tell Charley (in case he comes home first) that the <u>keys</u> are in the cabinet drawer. Mr Hall sent the letter of introduction the <u>evening before</u>, I <u>set off</u>. It is (with the M. S.) in the same berth as the keys.

I am so horrifically sleepy, that I am incapable of writing another line: beyond – yours affectionately | W. W. C

Wednesday morning–

Write as soon as receive this, telling me how the Governor goes on and what you mean to do about Torquay – How is Charley? Have you heard from him again?

News about my luggage must come in my next. I do not go to recover it till after post-time.

Note

1. Goldsmith's Marlow in *She Stoops to Conquer* is "attracted by a supposed barmaid, but stutters to a halt in the presence of a lady" (Peters, p. 66).

To Mrs Harriet Collins, 13 September 1845
MS: PM

Saturday Sept 13th 1845– | Hotel des Tuileries | Rue de Rivoli

My dear Mother/[1]

The day after I wrote my last letter, I recovered the baggage, by dint of "apostrophising" everybody at the station in the most forcible expressions I could muster up.

I am so weak with last night's laughter (at "Le Medicin malgré lui")[2] and so crammed with this morning's breakfast (oysters and cutlets) that writing this letter is by no means an employment of ease. I have scarcely been "all alone by myself" an hour at a time since my arrival. Yesterday, in sweating through the Louvre (with the travelling companions I told you of in my last) I [erased word] met – Solomon Alexander Hart. R.A.[3] and the day before drove past William Hookham Carpenter[4] in the Place Vendôme. An addition to these meetings with the British will arrive, next week, in the person of Charles Lambert[5] and three ladies.

Doctor [Bullar's][6] letter of introduction, I have not yet presented. Mr [Chovunk's] note I delivered when I applied for my monies; but the individual indicated [thereon], was not in the office to [greet] the individual indicated therein. I shall use him when I apply for my next remittance.

I have got some [boxes] of boots in the newest Parisian fashion, which is:- Toes, broader than any other part – a freak of dandyism most delightful to people with "corns, bunnions and [callosities]".

They have made a play, here, of the Whirlwind at Rouen, which I saw the other night. It began with a chorus of manufacturers (sung out of tune) and ended with thunder lightning, fire from Heaven, smoking ruins, and a fat woman in tights and muslin petticoats who said she was Charity. It was evidently intended to be very impressive and, as the audience laughed prodigiously, I suppose it was.

Paris is twice as full as it was last year. The Palais Royal is now encased in denser clouds of tobacco smoke and more crammed with heterogenous crowd of people, every evening, than ever I saw it before. The children who assemble there are worth the journey from England, alone. An evening or two since, a creature (whether "masculine, feminine or neuter", I know not) bowled his hoop against the toe of my boot and made me an apology (he seemed just able to walk and talk) so elaborately civil that I was perfectly astounded and took off my hat to him "in the impulse of the moment". The men stick to their [beards], their arguments, and their sugar and water, as usual; and the women eat as many bonbons, wear as many "bustles" & make as many speeches, as ever. The [gutters] hold their rights unimpinged, the churches rejoice in their accustomed emptiness, the organ plumes still glitter in gorgeous indelicacy of design, each shopkeeper leaves his business to his wife and each grisette is redolent of sentiment and prodigal of smiles, as in the days of Sterne – in short (saving that it is more [desecrated] than usual by the presence of the beef-eating British) Paris flourishes its "flesh pots of Egypt" and nourishes "the old man Adam" with the serious industry and perseverance of former days.

Why the deuce don't you come over here instead of vegetating among the [desines] of Devonshire? My family (I put them down as my family, to save trouble, in the books of the Louvre!) want me to go to Nice with them. Could you not send me £100, upon the strength of my M. S. and Chapman and Hall?[7] Or could you not make up your minds to take the journey yourselves and stay at Nice (think of the Protestant Church and the "resident English" [heavily erased word]!) While I conveyed the younger branches of "my family" to – what Plummer the portly calls – "Cara Italia"? Life is short – we should enjoy it. I am your affectionate son W. Wilkie Collins – you should humour me! –

P.S.

Give my love to the Governor and tell him that I will eat "plain food" (when I come back to England) and read Duncan's Logic and Butler's Analogy (when I have no chance of getting anything else to peruse).

Notes

1. WC writes at the top of the letter: "Pray find out, whenever you think it Politic to do so, the utmost extent of leave that I can obtain from Mr A. I left London the 7th of this month, I ought to have my liberty extended to the 15th or 20th of October – at least." WC uses an elongated slash mark following his salutation to his mother.
2. A three-act prose comedy by Molière.
3. S.A. Hart, R.A. (1806–1881), Anglo-Jewish painter.
4. William Hookham Carpenter (1792–1866), Keeper of Prints and Drawings at the British Museum: husband of WC's aunt.
5. Unidentified.
6. The Bullars in Southampton were old friends of the Collins family. Dr Joseph Bullar was consulted during William Collins' last illness. John Bullar was executor of William's will. And Henry Bullar, a barrister on the western curcuit, became one of WC's close friends.
7. A reference to WC's first novel *Ioláni, or Tahiti as it was: A Romance*, which was turned down by Chapman and Hall and was then "lost" for nearly a century and a half. WC's father

submitted the manuscript on 25 January 1845 to Longmans who, despite a favourable reader's report, rejected the novel on financial grounds. They were prepared to publish it if WC's father would pay the entire cost. Collins senior, in a letter of 8 March 1845 (now at the British Library, Add. Mss. 42575 f158) declined. The fair copy of the novel finally turned up in New York in 1991 and is being published by Princeton University Press (edited by Ira B. Nadel).

To Mrs Harriet Collins, 16 September 1845
MS: PM

Hotel de Tuileries | Rue de Rivoli | Sept 16th 1845 | Thursday

My dear Madam

I was agreeably impressed by the appearance of your letter this morning, as [two erased words] I had given up all hopes of further epistolary communication on y<u>our</u> part, having received Ward's answer to my first missive on <u>Mond</u>ay last.

"The Evil One" (whom you mention with somewhat unladylike want of courtesy at the close of your letter) is such an exceedingly gentlemanlike dog in this city, with his theatres and his kitchens, that I find it rather difficult to "cut his commission". I have bought an Opera Glass, so I must, of necessity, go to the Play to use it. I have got a box of Soda Powders, so I must, in common justice, deliver myself to Gastronomy, to test their correcting powers, [erased word] on my digestory organization. In short, "I sticks" to the "pomps and vanities" – ne'er an [Evangelical] of the lot of 'em can accuse me of being "a spiritual rebel", now.

I have seen no sights – the pictures and your sister's spouse excepted – I kept the mighty hunter of prints away from his dinner till the landlady of the Hotel positively came in to remonstrate! But as he had the audacity to tell me that he considered that he was journeying hard "in the capacity of a public servant" (!) <u>my</u> bowels had no compassion for <u>his</u>, and I stuck to my seat and my conversation to the very last.

It has rained pretty [pertinaciously] with us, for the last four or five days; so, I have subscribed to Galignani's Library to keep off ennui. Harrison Ainsworth[1] was there today, sitting, as usual, in the positions of his different portraits. Hart, too, is here – I met him at the Louvre.

I have just come from the Exhibition of the rising landscape painters in France. The worst Suffolk street landscape is superior to the best picture of this precious collection, which is worth a visit, as affording an example of a very rare human attainment – the <u>perfection</u> of incapacity – Skies, trees, grass – colour – composition, drawing – all are equally bad. Not a square inch of any of the canvasses is respectable even by accident. Yet these daubs have received twice the criticism bestowed upon the whole Royal Academy with us, and have produced twice the sensation every[one] felt in England on the opening of the Exhibition! The s<u>tart</u> of a [young: erased] new man in Literature or Art is a matter of intense moment to every educated individual in this city. If the Governor sent a sea-piece to the Louvre, he would be deified in the papers and ho<u>t-pressed</u> in every salon of Paris. [erased word] Money is to [be] obtained, too, as well as admiration. The average amount yearly of the remuneration to the Dramatists only of this place, [erased word] is from £70,000 to £80,000!

I suppose you have heard [that: erased] of the death of poor [erased word] [Mrs] Ward. It happened about a week or a fortnight ago.

Doctor Bullar's letter of introduction still remains in my pocket-book. I am leading so thoroughly free and easy a life that I feel immensely disinclined to the bore of making a new acquaintance – I must, however, present my "credentials" I suppose, or I shall give offence to the "Medico" – You say nothing about Charley, so, I suppose he is just as pleased with his disgustingly pastoral pursuits as you are.

If you want anything in the way of spectacles &c &c, this is the place for them. An opera glass in London costs £4 – – here it comes to £2 – 4 – – Every other specimen of the Opticians craft is equally cheap –

I always read your letters <u>through</u>. Considering that he is a lamb of Mr Dodsworth's[2] flock, Mr Collins evinces a most unchurchmanlike disposition to scandalise other people. Heap coals of fire upon his head by giving him my love in return for his fabrications and believe me | affectionately yours | W. Wilkie Collins

Remember me very kindly to the Antrobus' and Strong and everybody at Torquay but [Mrs] Travers, who has rather too much of "the leaven of hypocrisy", as Moses observes, for my taste –

Notes

1. Harrison Ainsworth (1805–1882), prolific novelist.
2. A reference to the Tractarian William Dodsworth whose church William and Harriet Collins had joined in the 1840s.

To Mrs Harriet Collins, 23, 24, September 1845
MS: PM

Hotel de Tuileries | Rue de Rivoli | Sept 23rd 1845

My dear Mother

The weather, here today, is again admirably adapted for letter-writing. It has been raining furiously the whole morning and as a matter of course I have been reduced to reading furiously at Galignani's Library by way of adapting myself philosophically to the changes of the [weather: erased] sky.

I am much obliged [for]¹ your information about my return. I shall give up the Belgium plan and come back the shortest way – by Boulogne and Folkestone. Paris is the same to me, with, or without, sun; but travelling in rainy weather (and I see no chance of a change) is detestable.

The [erased word] old characteristic and indiscriminate regard for "the small sweet courtesies of life" withstands the innovations of the new school of melodramatic rudeness more slowly than I supposed. There are <u>some</u> Frenchmen, still, who possess the polite[ness] that once enchanted Sterne. A gentleman, covered with roses, who sat in the next stall to me at the play, the other night, made me two bows and begged my pardon for taking the liberty of removing the <u>tail</u> of <u>my coat</u> (which had obtruded itself on his seat) to get at his opera glasses. This was tolerably delightful; but, an adventure that happened to me yesterday, eclipsed the gentleman with the [ouders], completely.

I was just passing the "cuisine" of this hotel in my way to the Café where I breakfast when I was stopped by a loud cry of Monsieur Collins! I turned round and confronted the Kitchen maid with an immense pan of some boiling ingredient, which in her hurry, she had forgotten to lay aside – [commsut]? "Virginia,² desires her kindest remembrances to you, Monsieur" said she – and [here] the Kitchen maid put down the boiling ingredient and wiped a "black" off her nose with the end of her apron. "I am extremely obliged to Virginia", said I, "but who is she?" – "What! Monsieur has forgotten Virginia", said she; "Oh Heavens! this is very <u>desolating</u>" – (I translate <u>literally</u>).

"She had my place, that poor Virginia and bearing on a visit to the landlady, that you were here, she could not refrain from charging me with the kindest remembrances." By this time I discovered that Virginia was <u>last year's</u> Kitchen-maid; but I had not <u>then</u> and have not now a clear recollection of her – However, I told a lie and said I had, for fear of hurting Virginia's feelings. Is not this deliciously <u>French</u>? Fancy the astonishment of a thoroughbred Englishman at hearing that a Kitchen-maid named Virginia(!) whom he scarcely recollected and whom he never fed with money, had sent him her kindest remembrances when she heard he was again in the Hotel where she had once served! – You might rummage the world over without finding such a set of originals as the people at this place. They all attempt to talk English and all fail in the most ludicrous manner. I had scarce put my head out my bedroom door, this morning, when the waiter approached me swinging his arms, opening his mouth, and making an indistinct cackling noise in which the word "Omeberellaw" played a prominent part. I screamed with laughter and (after he had <u>cackled</u> for a short time longer) so did he. He had been learning (from the master I suppose) to address me in English about the necessity of taking an umbrella as it was raining dreadfully; but such a horrible mess did he make of his harangue that not one word of it was intelligible except – O<u>meberellaw</u>. It was really and truly exactly like the "<u>cackling</u>" of a goose.

It is too late today to send this; I must (like Caliban) "to dinner"; and finish my epistle tomorrow –

Sept 24th

I have just seen the Historical Exhibition of pictures by the rising men. There is more respectability in this show than in the last I told you of – but the works of the young frenchmen in history are still ineffably below those of the Royal Academy students –

On returning from the Beaux Arts I looked in at the Morgue. A body of a young girl had just been fished out of the river. As her bosom was "black and blue" I suppose she had been beaten into a state of insensibility and then flung into the Seine. The spectators of this wretched sight were, for the most part, w<u>omen and chil</u>dren.

I conclude by your letter that you are not likely to be in London before November. Hart leaves Paris today. He hopes the governor has found some sa<u>ndbanks</u> to paint as he is in the field as a purchaser. (This was his message, what it means I know not).

Doctor Bullar's friend is, I suppose, not in Paris. They knew nothing about him at the address indicated on my letter of introduction.

As I [erased word] do not pester myself with sight-seeing, I cannot oblige Mr Collins by <u>making notes</u>; but, I will do the next best thing – I will go to the Opera [Comique] tonight and <u>hear</u> them.

Love to the governor and kindest regards to the Antrobi –

Affectionately yours | W. Wilkie Collins

The name of the family with whom I became acquainted on the journey is – Cormick. They have left "this earthly, sensual, and devilish city".

Notes

1. "[for]" is our assumed reading for what looks like WC's shorthand.
2. The word is doubly underlined.

To Mrs Harriet Collins, [30 September 1845]
MS: PM

Hotel de Tuileries | Rue de Rivoli

My dear Madam

Either my two last letters have been lost or you have parted with the faculty of memory. The "mysterious" letter you refer to was the answer to the <u>first</u> I received here; and has been followed by two others – answers to your subsequent epistles. [What should: erased] [erased word] Why you should [to: erased] refer, in your present communication, to my second letter ex<u>clusively</u>, at the expense of my third and fourth, I do not know – unless, as I have hinted above, both my latter answers have been lost.

If you complain of my former epistles, you will be furious at this – It contains no impiety and it attempts no jokes – [erased word] It is devoted to a statement of my approaching INSOLVENGY.[1]

My "monies and [indecipherable word]" will last in for my miscellaneous expenses here; but will not pay, either my bi<u>ll</u>, or my passage home. A cheque for £10 – –, crossed with Ward's name, or with "Messrs Coutts & Co", and enclosed in a letter directing the said Ward to pay the said cheque into the hands of Messrs Lafitte, Paris, will have the effect – weather permitting – of returning me to Devonport Street.

Should Mr Collins vow that he will pay no attention to the above modest, and, I may be permitted to say, [erased word] luminous suggestion, do not be in the least alarmed or put out of the way. I can live here a long time upon my <u>credit</u>, and when that is exhausted I can go into a "spunging house" without disgracing myself by any ungentlemanlike violence of behaviour to "my opposing creditors" – the actual difference between imprisonment at Paris and imprisonment at the Strand being too inconsequential to be worth ascertaining to a nicety.

My joke about Mr Collins's scandalising propensities was an answer to one of yours of the same nature – referring to his [comment: erased] statement that I did not care about your letters; but it shall be [the: erased] my last witticism. People who live in the country and eat beefsteaks are not to be joked at with impunity.

The weather is as bad as it can be. I told you in one of my missing epistles that I should return by the direct way – i.e. Boulogne; and I see no reason – from the continuance of the rain and cold – to alter my determination, at present.

Hart left last Thursday. I have met no one since that I know. Doctor Bullar's friend is not in Paris and Charley Lambert has not yet dawned in "this pestilential city". Thus, to the great benefit of my French, my confabulations are all in the native language; and are held with all sorts and classes of the population except the representations of the Jeune France; who are noisy, dirty, brainless fellows and whose near neighbourhood I cannot abide.

I am very sorry to hear of [Brissy's] death; but I certainly disagree with you about the unworthiness of the world, for good people. The proof that you are wrong, is in the existence of such individuals as Mrs Collins in "this habitable globe" – (Don't forget the £10 – –). Excellence such as your's – my dear Madam – cannot exist independant of usefulness, and would not be useful were people altogether unworthy of its softening and humanising influence. (The cheque must be crossed "Messrs Coutts & Co") Therefore, I am inclined to conclude; that as long as you are in the world, the world must, logically and absolutely, be worthy of everybody and everything in it. (A letter must accompany the cheque directing Ward to forward it to Lafitte & Co Paris.)

The weather has, hitherto, prevented my journey to Versailles to see Vernet's last great picture. Everybody is in extasies about it, here.

I am sorry to hear that the governor's cough is again making its appearance. He must take care not to follow my example and catch cold. I have been snorting and sniffing for the last three days with very disagreeable regularity.

I shall be in the Strand the 14<u>th</u>, or 15<u>th</u>, I hope without fail. You need not be much alarmed about weather, as far as I am concerned. I shall take a place in the coupé; and I bought a coat at Edgington's, before I left London, as thick as a hearth-rug and as warm as a vapour bath.

With love to the governor, affectionately yours | W. Wilkie Collins

Your account of Charley is very unsatisfactory. He seems [erased word] to have more chance of becoming a member of the Royal Academy of Dancing at Paris, than of the Royal Academy of Arts at London –

Remember that I have not disobeyed your parting injunctions about economy. You said you hoped I should make my Cheque last for my <u>trip</u>. It <u>has</u> lasted for my <u>trip</u> but not for my <u>return</u>.

Note

1. WC uses decorated block capitals.

To Mrs Harriet Collins, 6 October 1845
MS: PM

Hotel de Tuileries | Rue de Rivoli | Oct: 6th 1845

I have just received – my excellent present – your delightful communication of the 2<u>nd</u> inst – Many thanks for your expressions of affection and your announcement of the departure of the cheque.

It is raining in torrents today. My landlady in giving me your note assured me that she was shocked at the want of complaisance in the weather and that she could only account for it by imagining that "le bon Dieu" had been "dreadfully" offended by some "[maladupe]" on the part of somebody, and that the human family at large was "[superstitious]" on that somebody's account!

Yesterday however the human family had a respite from "la [pénitence]", which I took advantage of to go to Versailles and see Horace Vernet's last great [erased word] painting "The taking of Smalah".[1] I know of no picture – except Michael Angelo's Last Judgment – in Ancient or Modern Art, so triumphantly successful as this wonderful work. Difficulties of the most stupendous nature, in drawing and composition, extending over a space of upward of two hundred feet, and varying in complexity at every succeeding foot of canvas, are overcome by Vernet – positively – in every instance. [erased word] The Arab palanquins, the squadron of French cavalry galloping out[2] of the picture – the frantic [indecipherable word] pursued by an infuriated herd of cattle – the overthrown tents – the fainting women – the scared antelopes – the sand hills in the background – the slaughtered and slaughtering Arabs – these, and a hundred other objects incident to the terrible occasion, are all treated with <u>equal</u> fidelity and <u>equal</u> skill. How long I stood before the picture, I know not. It [erased word] raised my [erased words] belief in the power of painting to a pitch I could never have imagined possible before. It stands alone among the productions of Modern Historical Art – above all expression and beyond all criticism.

I have definitely fixed to depart by the 2 oClock (P.M.) Diligence for Boulogne, on the 13<u>th</u> – and hope to be in Devonport Street on the evening of the 14<u>th</u>. My official labours will, therefore, commence on the morning of the 15<u>th</u> -. By this plan, I attain the utmost extension possible of my stay in Paris – a very pleasant and necessary achievement, considering that the Italian Opera has begun and that "Pâtés de Foies Gras" are daily expected at the principal Restaurants.

You need cherish no feelings of commiseration for my solitary state. The privilege of being able to consult my own tastes and inclinations without the slightest reference to any one else, quite counterbalances the inconvenience of my being – like a late royal Solomon – "all alone by myself". My time has never hung heavy upon my hands since my arrival; and, with the exception of an occasional sigh – physically necessary and morally natural – when I am more than usually sensible of the increasing tightness of the waistband of my br-ch-s, a serene cheerfulness has pervaded my mental temperament here, from my first pinch of snuff in the morning to my last at night.

If you think the air of Devonshire too [irritating] for the governor you will do quite right to quit Beacon Terrace as soon as possible. Nevertheless, I must say, [erased word] I am horribly afraid that he will catch another severe cold if he winters in London. I should strongly recommend him to <u>write</u> to Doctor Chambers, and ask his advice upon his future movements, before he makes up his mind to brave the November fogs in the Great Metropolis.

I <u>thought</u> I saw Mr Dodsworth the other day at Galignani's. The [Lauriers] I have not met with anywhere; but I may see them tonight at the Opera as all the Paris world is to "assist" at the "début" of Moriani in Lucia de Lammermoor.[3]

With love to the governor, affectionately yours | W. Wilkie Collins

I have just come from Lafittes. The £10 – <u>has ar</u>rived, and I am grateful – <u>Wednes</u>day morning –

Notes

1. Horace Vernet's (1789–1863) "The Taking of Smalah d'Abd-el-Kader al Taguim" depicts the events of May 1843 when a force headed by the duc d'Aumale "surprised and defeated the zmala", or the household of about 30,000 people of the Amir Abd al Qadir. See John Ruedy, *Modern Algeria* (Bloomington: Indiana UP, 1992) p. 64.
2. Doubly underlined.
3. Napoleone Mariani (1808–1878), Italian tenor made his Paris debut in October 1845 at the Théâtre-Italien, in the revival of Donizetti's "Lucia de Lammermoor".

To Mrs Harriet Collins, 31 July 1846
MS: PM

Hotel de St Antoine | Antwerp | July 31/46

My dear Mother

The heat in this place is of a superior degree of intensity to the temperature of Timbucto. I write this, <u>literally</u> in a <u>reeking</u> state. Ward arrived – all dust and perspiration – at 4 o'clock this afternoon at the above direction.

I accompanied Ward in the second class, after all the impression the hard benches made upon my personal [superficies] can never be effaced. As if labouring under insanity, I continued his companion, and therefore part of the Steamer at 3 o'clock in the morning and got wet through with the spray – Ward vibrated between the bilious and the sick the whole voyage – I was perfectly well.

On our arrival at Ostend reason returned to me and I [inveigled] my beloved friend into a first class train – after perspiring for five torrid hours, we reached Antwerp in a state of [fusion].

My observations on this country, like Adam's first essays on ploughing, have been made by "the <u>sweat of the brow</u>". I find the country a great flat damp grim meadow speckled with church spires like pepper–boxes and dwellings like over-coloured baby–houses. I find the people possessed of immense physical energies – little intelligence and enormous <u>seats</u> to their breeches – The posterior portion of our Ostend waiter's trousers would have clothed a whole family of destitutes in St Giles's.

I would continue my "revelations of" Belgium were I not, at the moment, overpowered by the heat and at a loss for time and paper – you shall have some more buffoonery on my next letter (if you can read this).

Write to me by return of post, letting me know how you go on at Iver, and, with love to Mr Collins, believe me

Affectionately yours | W. W. Collins

To Mrs Harriet Collins, 6 August 1846
MS: PM

Hotel de Flandre | Brussels | Aug^t, 6th 1846

My dear Mother[1]

Finding Antwerp [dull] – after its antiquities had been exhausted – by no means a disagreeable residence for idle men, we removed to this place a day or two since, having directed my letters that might arrive after our departure from Brussels, to be forwarded to the above address. We have neither of us received any epistolary considerations from the bosoms of our respective families up to this morning.

I cannot ask you to answer this as we shall be en route for Bruges tomorrow – Ward refuses to extend his tour out of consideration for the suffering of his bereaved wife during his absence. He sports domestic – talks about his moral duties – tells me that I am a profligate and vows that he will be in London by Monday next. As I have no great pleasure in travelling by myself I shall return with him, and probably use my travels by an expedition to Iver the day after our arrival at Devonport Street.

Although Antwerp is essentially a dull town although its inhabitants are a [miserable] compound of the worst parts of the Dutch and French character, the pictures that are [indecipherable word] there make it worth a visit, were the transit from [London] ten times more difficult and expensive than it is now as I never knew of what the [genius] of Rubens was really capable till I saw the Descent from the Cross and the marriage of St Catherine. These two works are of such character of colour and composition, that I felt as I looked at them, the [justice] of Sir J. Reynolds's remark "that it is difficult for the most sober judgment to name the superior of Rubens" in the art of painting on first beholding his works at Antwerp. We were admitted to see a private collection containing some of his smaller pictures among which I noticed a portrait of a fat [dignitary] in the church with a large jowl, blear eyes, and a sensual expression [which] was the finest piece of picturesque and natural portrait painting that I have ever beheld.

Last Sunday the streets of Antwerp were decorated with large strips of white linen numerous enough to have covered miles & tied on to young fir spars planted artifically in the pavement, [three erased words] inscriptions, gaily-coloured floats and portraits of Saints rose imposingly above this deluge of spotless calicos. Crowds of phlegmatic Belgians sauntered through the streets – pictured themselves in the windows and sat at their doors in chairs placed in perilous propinquity to the kennels. This mighty preparation was intended to greet a procession carrying a new relic box of [silver], which was expected to appear every moment. We mixed with the crowd (who to use the words of Don Quixote – "smelt of anything rather than amber") and awaited the [solitary] [advent] of the sacred box with considerable impatience. After a long interval <u>four</u> soldiers loomed dimly visible through the masses of the crowd, and were followed by a troop of dirty-looking men carrying filthy tallow candles and every now and then turning round and bowing indefatigably to a gang of priests in tawdry dresses who bore aloft a Britan[n]ia – metal – and – decidedly – second-hand-looking cross between a gigantic snuff-box and an old woman's tea caddy; stuck on the shoulders of four corpulent copper angels endowed with an imposing amplitude of wing and gifted with singular sedateness of expression. These celestial gentlemen were [tattoed] for the occasion with leaves of flowers cast on them by several devout old women among the crowd. After being carried through the different streets in the manner I have just described, this honorable box was deposited in a church; where it was to be sung to and prayed over for <u>fifteen</u> days! So much for the piety of the good people of Antwerp!

The old city seems in many instances to have changed but little from its former self. The children still look as if they had just stepped out of one of [Teniris']² pictures, the drinking Vessels at the public houses have not varied in form since the days of OStade,³ and the houses and the Churches present the same picturesque variety of architectural combinations as in the distant days of the persecution of Alva and the commercial glories of the merchants of Antwerp.

At Brussels, with the exception of a few old houses, everything looks clean new and modern. People have called it an imitation of Paris. I can see no resemblance between the two cities. There is none of the all-pervading gaiety of the French metropolis about this place. The spirit that animates the Boulevards and Cafés of Paris is wanting to the Boulevards and Cafés of Brussels. There is little in it to interest and less to amuse.

I have much more to write about-but-my physical energies – so awful is the intensity of the heat – completely fail me – My strength will carry me no further than the bottom of this page. Give my love to Mr Collins and believe me

Affectionately yours | W. Wilkie Collins

Notes

1. WC's letter paper is heavily smudged and blotted – a reflection of the heat!
2. Probably a reference to David Teniers, the younger (1610–1690), Antwerp-born realist and genre painter.
3. Adriaen van Ostrade (1610–1685), painted genre scenes.

Part II
Early Writing: Dickens

1847–1854

EARLY WRITING: DICKENS 1847–1854

The late 1840s witnessed Wilkie preoccupied with his efforts to find patrons for his biographical tribute to his father. Letters to George Richmond, Robert Peel, Benjamin Disraeli, Alaric A. Watts and William Etty, among others, are chiefly concerned with this object. An important, lengthy letter [17 June 1850] to his father's close American friend, the author R.H. Dana, ranges over a variety of topics such as the state of England, the lack of leadership in the country, Landseer's popularity, Macaulay's profits and reminiscences of earlier family tours to Italy and Wordsworth's fear of cholera.

Wilkie's letters to his mother, from his excursions in Paris, Normandy, Cornwall and elsewhere, continue to contain passages at once humorous and descriptive. Two other correspondents with whom letters are to continue over the years now emerge. His letters to Charles Ward demonstrate a pattern of using Ward as an intermediary between himself and his mother over his almost continuous youthful overspending. Letters to his fellow law student, Edward Pigott, are concerned with Wilkie's journalism, his involvement with *The Leader*, and his views on religion and politics. By the early 1850s theatrical activities, with Wilkie involved in provincial repertory, become a focus of interest. The presence of Dickens emerges during Wilkie's annual summer visits. On 20 November 1851 he is called to the bar with Pigott. A remark in a letter to his mother written from Dover [9 September 1852], where he is staying with Dickens is prophetic: "The sea air acts on me as if it was all distilled from laudanum."

The beginning of 1853 sees Wilkie in a flurry of activity, reviewing plays and novels for *The Leader*. He writes of friendships with such artists as Millais, the success of his novel *Basil* and of French interest in his writings. However, one letter [25 June 1853] begins a recurring pattern in his letters of personal sickness and worry about his health; already he seems afflicted with a somewhat mysterious illness. He is "not strong enough to do more than 'toddle' out for no more than half an hour at a time with a stick" and his illness and long confinement "muddles [his] brain dreadfully".

For the remainder of 1853 in letters written to his mother, Charles Ward, his brother and Edward Pigott, Wilkie is part of the Dickens circle. He writes of the pleasures of Dickens' rented house in Boulogne and expostulates on the delights of being a sailor and sea voyages ("everyone is sick" on the Channel voyage, except Wilkie). Wilkie's letters from Boulogne, Amiens, Switzerland and Italy complement Dickens' letters written during the same period. His letters, especially to his mother, are exceedingly lengthy and contain detailed descriptions of places, people, scenery and events. Swiss people living in the mountain valleys are full of aberrations, "disease and deformity" and "many people [are] born idiots". Material used in letters to his mother (for instance the crossing of the Simplon) are creatively transformed to resurface subsequently in fictional form in, for instance, *Armadale*.

He writes to Ward [31 October 1853] from Genoa and Milan not only of methods to evade robbery, but of his artistic reactions too. Leonardo da Vinci's *Last Supper* is "not a picture. It is the utter ruin of something that once was a picture" and is "painted over in the most infamous manner by modern restorers". La Scala is "miserably lighted, wretchedly dirty, mournfully empty and desecrated by some of the very worst singers" he has ever heard. The Pope, methods of travel, an excursion to Vesuvius, and people from the past are just some of the concerns of letters to his mother and brother in November 1853.

The year 1854 sees the publication of *Hide and Seek* and the development of a maelstrom of literary activities which are subsequently to engage him. He is writing reviews of books and of exhibitions, the literature section for *The Leader* and also contributing to *Household Words* and *Frasers*. A note to Ward [15 March 1854] reveals a strain of radicalism with his "sentiments on the approaching Russian War" and "disinterested feelings of patriotism". Wilkie opposes the Crimean war and sides with Bright. Late summers are now spent with Dickens in Boulogne.

To Mrs Harriet Collins, 2 August 1847
MS: PM

Hotel du Grand Cerf | Aux Andelys, Normandie | August 2nd 1847

My dear Mother/
   The date of this letter will be geographically speaking – a mystery to you – Let me therefore tell you that we are still in Normandy at a place an hour and a half distant (in a railway point of view) from Rouen. Our hotel was built in the [9th] century and has remained to this day uncontaminated by the "hod" of the bricklayer of Modern times. At a short distance from a ruined castle and on a mighty crag which overlooks the Seine – opposite to us is a church built like this house in the year 1200 and ornamented with grand old painted glass windows [crisscrossed] with effigies of queer [saints] – incomprehensible emblems and unimaginative [verdure]. Around us are picturesque old women sun burnt with an Indian red – large sheep dogs. (I have already made acquaintance with one of them) [gentle] tortois shell cats (uncommunicative to strangers) and fierce young gentlemen with dirty faces blue blouses and beards whose [explaintive] [hairiness] might put [indecipherable word] himself to the blush – to say that we look out on all sides on toppling – dirty old houses deeply suggestive of vermin and three [indecipherable letters: ered] woman's only to tell you what you already know – that we are in an old [indecipherable word] towards and to achieve that I mean to sketch [furiously] at all points [until] under any circumstances is only to inform you that I intend to make some use of a useful article of my luggage – of my cherished painting box – which with infinite "toil and vexation of spirit" I have always carried at my back wherever Ward and I have turned our exploring steps.
   Apropos of the painting box – I had made three sketches – the first <u>two</u> are failures – the third is exceedingly good, and a most elaborate undertaking – for it occupied three days of my time – But as I said before it is exceedingly good and the hours of my youth have therefore not been wasted upon it.
   As to Rouen – I am glad we have left it – A more ghostly set of people than <u>Rouenuese</u> it has never been my misfortune to meet with. When you have seen the old churches (in which by the bye there is not a picture or a statue worth five minutes contemplation). When you have seen the place where Joan of Arc was burned (I don't believe in Joan of Arc at all for my own part) you have seen all that Rouen can afford to interest you. The people are all sordid trades people who sit behind their counters all day and lounge silently about the Exchange all the evening – Last Saturday night we went to a (so-called) Fête given at some public [garden] near the city. The profits of the festivities to be [delivered] to the poor. When we got

into the gardens the air smelt damp and earthy as if we had descended into a catacomb – A few lamps – enclosed had [dirty camoas] and half expiring – the [indecipherable word] beau ideal of the illuminations of an applewoman's stall – were all that brightened the darkness of the night – We found swings and roundabouts rotting direfully in sharp unfragmented walks – women varying in ugliness [from] the simply plain to the utterly repulsive – and [men] [game] as peacocks – silent as boarding school [myself] at [their] first ball and restless as condemned spirits in the [vastness] of the ancients – After a mournful interval we were "bidden into" an open air theatre – where we found an [orchestra] composed of <u>one</u> fiddle and a dramatic personae of three <u>amateurs</u> – Anything more dismally wretched than the acting of this histrionic trio or more hopelessly unintelligible than the play they performed [indecipherable word] – After the theatre came some dancing – in which the [two indecipherable words] stood in the same relation to the spectators as three to three hundred – or a [indecipherable word] wherry to a three decker. After the dancing came a display of fireworks which lasted <u>five</u> minutes and accomplished – nothing – After the fireworks Ward and I got too intensely miserable to do anything but depart for our hotel. How long the townspeople continued their funereal Saturnalia I known not. The papers advertised that the Entertainment was to begin at eight of the clock in the evening and to end at five of the clock in the morning!

We have made two or three country excursions from Rouen. <u>One</u> was the Ancient Abbey of St George Bosherville[1] – We started at 6.A.M. by steamboat (without breakfast) got put ashore on the banks of the Seine at eight o'clock – walked (still without breakfast) – <u>eight miles</u> – arrived at last at St George &c and breakfasted at a "cabaret", where the hostess (a woman five feet broad by three feet long) asked us, as she laid the cloth, whether we had our own knives with us (!) – This excellent woman had no milk in the house, so we breakfasted a la [fourchette] on wine, meat, omelette &c &c – which gave Ward a violent headache and made me very sleepy and [unideal] – After our meal we started to see the Abbey Church but the Beadle was practising agriculture – i.e. labouring in the fields, so we went into a pine wood to wait his return. There, Ward fell asleep and I made a sketch – One of the <u>failures</u> already alluded to. When <u>I</u> had finished my failure and Ward had finished his nap we returned – but the agricultural fervour still possessed the beadle – the villain was still pastoralising in the fields – and though I penetrated into the priests' garden and asked everybody I met to let us into the Church – and "drummed" at the Church doors, and so forth, we could not get in, after all. So we returned to the (<u>Cabaret</u>) and got a <u>huc[k]ter's</u> cart to take us back to Rouen – or rather to the entrance of Rouen; for Ward was proud and refused to drive up to the Hotel in our excellent but humble and uneasy vehicle –

Soon after this we drove out to a country chateau inhabited by a rich Frenchman – a [erased word] ci-devant merchant. Our Phaeton drove up to this gentleman's <u>private</u> grounds as if we had arrived by invitation – we were met in [descending] [indecipheral word] our [indecipheral word] by the owner, who asked us into his house and showed us all over it himself. He was a very polite old gentleman – a batchelor and an admire[r] of the Arts. His rooms were decorated in the Classical Pompeian style – His walls were covered with choice engravings from Wilkie Turner[2] and all the old masters – His halls and staircase were adorned with beautiful bronzes and magnificent copies of the Apollo Belvidere – the [indecipherable word] de Medici[3] and other irreproachable antiquities. His library was excellently provided with the works of English authors as well as French and Latin and one of his rooms was stocked with the finest collection of [of] stuffed tropical birds I ever beheld. But the greatest treat we derived from our visit was from the view from the Chateau – The Park commanded the whole panorama of the Seine, with its wooded islands, its rugged cliffs – its undulating forests and its rich pasture lands; and the complete extent of the distant city – of Rouen – the cathedral spires of which rose before us through the hot golden mist of a cloudless summer day – We stood upwards to two hours at the gentleman's abode and returned, coveting our neighbour's house, in inexpressible forgetfulness of [erased word] the patriarchal requisites of the tenth commandment.

I received your letters with great satisfaction. The news about my excellent "Snooks" was perfectly gratifying.

As I am ignorant of the length of our stay here and of our next destination – I cannot tell you where to write to should you feel inclined to answer this – Ward talks of returning to London next Saturday.

It is getting late – and we are to rise at six o clock tomorrow-morning – so with love to Charley and blessings for Snooks and the rest of the domestic circle – I get me into my comfortable but <u>verminous</u>-looking bed, and remain | Yours affectionately | W. Wilkie Collins

Notes

1. In one of his earliest publications, "A Pictorial Tour of St George Bosherville", <u>Bentley's Miscellany</u>, 29 (1851), 493–508, WC describes his visit to St George Bosherville. Ward becomes "his travelling companion and friend, Mr Scumble". WC is "Tired of Rouen!" (p. 493). The hostess, where at last they had breakfast, "was a corpulent woman; she had evidently never gone without her breakfast as long as we had, in the whole course of her life" (p. 499). However, apart from one or two other details such as the absence of "the beadle who kept the keys" (p. 500), the <u>Bentley's</u> account is much longer and very different from that given in the letter: The visit to "the polite old gentleman" is omitted completely.
2. i.e., Joseph Mallard William Turner (1775–1851).
3. The Apollo Belvedere statue, probably fourth century B.C., was discovered at the end of the fifteenth century. The Medici family were great Renaissance patrons of the Arts.

To Mrs Harriet Collins, [early August 1847]
MS: PM

Paris!!!! | Hotel des Tuileries | Rue de Rivoli | Monday afternoon

My dear Mother,

Are you not disgusted? Would you not give-up a week's walking in Kensington Gardens to be able to express to me, viva voce, the feelings aroused by the date of this letter? Let me first tell you then that I have money enough to keep me here three or four days and to pay my journey back. You see therefore that I have not been extravagant at other places and do not intend to be so here. We have come to Paris because we have exhausted all the best views of Normandy and find provincial cities insupportably oppressive to our mercurial characters. The fact is that the scenery in Normandy has been very much exagerated. It is very pretty of its kind but exceedingly monotonous – and the castle at the place whence I last wrote to you, which the guide books informed us was a magnificent view and which as we thought (on seeing it under the shades of evening) was deserving of its reputation – turned out on inspection at broad day light to be by no means so picturesque an object as we had thought it. So we made sketches of it and then finding nothing more in the neighbourhood that was unusually attractive and having wandered about [Rouen] and its neighbourhood till we had exhausted both we determined to say farewell to France at its Capital – where we are going to take great care of our health and stay only a short time.

Will you write to me here to let me know whether Charley and Henry Bullar[1] have settled everything about Cumberland – and if you have a spare five pound note by you ("I thought it would come to that"!) you may send it through Coutts's to W. Wilkie Collins at Paris <u>as soon as possible after you receive this letter</u> – telling Coutts that it is "for the use of W. Wilkie Collins at Paris" –

If it is not convenient for you to send me this money, <u>do not do it</u> – As I said before I have money enough to keep me here and take me back – I ask for the five pound note because I shall want both boots and [glasses] when I come back, and can (if I have some extra money) get them cheaper and better here than London. Consider the subject – stifle your indignation – and believe me affectionately Yours | W. Wilkie Collins

Note

1. Henry Bullar (1815–1870), barrister on the western circuit and lifelong friend of WC.

To Charles Ward, 10 August [1847]
MS: PM[1]

Hotel des Tuileries – Rue de Rivoli | Tuesday morning: –

My dear Ward

Up to this moment I have received no communication – monetary or epistolary – from England, and I now write to you, with eight francs in my pocket – and in debt for two pair of boots, to ascertain whether I am to expect any remittances at all – before I become bankrupt – an event which I have my suspicions will take place tomorrow.

On the day you left me I made a calculation of my resources – including the five pounds I expected from England – and found to my horror and astonishment that if I paid for my boots – my bill here and my journey back, like an honest man I could not stay more than two days longer at Paris, at the furthest –. I made up my mind therefore to start for London to<u>day</u> rather than spend a single farthing more money – but on Saturday no money arrived – on Sunday no money arrived – on Monday no money arrived – and today – this present Tuesday – "par le sang bleu"! I have changed my last "Nap" and have not a banker at Paris to go to for any more!

I suppose Mrs Collins is determined to punish me for going to Paris at all – by keeping me there as long as she pleases in a state of <u>pauperism</u> – This may seem at the first glance – a monstrous good joke – but it will be found on closer inspection to be rather an expensive one. – Every day I stay here enlarges my bill in the Hotel and increases my current expenses – which – carefully as I watch them – grow upon me as fast as moss on an old house or pimples on a drunkard's face.

I breakfast for a franc and a half – I dine for three francs and a half. I have never entered a hackney coach since I have been at Paris – I have missed the Theatre o<u>ne</u> wh<u>ole</u> night – I occupy myself all day in painting and taking salubrious walks – I have had three glorious bowel complaints since I saw you which have done my stomach a world of good and made my complexion as pure as milk of roses – Can anything be more economical – more salubrious – more virtuous than such a mode of life as this?

Have the goodness to show (or send) this letter to Mrs Collins – directing her attention particularly to the above paragraph and also to the statement of my assets and liabilities exposed beneath –

Liabilities – (supposing that W.W.C. departs from Paris in a solvent state on Saturday next [from Paris: erased]. N.B. this is only allowing proper time for securing my place in the Diligence and getting the money from London)

Assets
Frs
Probable amount of [erasure] Lodging – Washing – Candles – Servants 8

or in two words – "Hotel Bill" –   40
Journey back (Cheapest way)   65
Bill for boots   68
(This bill for boots includes two new | pair at 50 frs.
(charged £3– in London) | and new fronting an old pair the leathers |
and soles of which have burst – at 18 frs – | charged £1- in London)
Board and pocket money for five | days at 10 frs. a day
(i.e. 15 | frs. <u>less</u> than I spent at Paris per <u>diem</u>, | on my last visit   50
Total   223
                                                                                     8
Liabilities   215 frs or £8..12..6[2]

This will doubtless appear very horrifying to Mrs Collins, but it is not
entirely my fault – I have spent £2–15 on boots in Paris – because I must
have spent in the course of the year – £4 – for the same articles of clothing
but less lasting in London – if the £5 – – had arrived on Saturday morning
– I should have set off today and not have wanted a farthing more –

If you have already forwarded five pounds to Lafitte's – forward another
five immediately[3] on the receipt of this – without waiting to get it from Mrs
Collins. I will settle with you on my return – If you have not remitted me
a "<u>rap</u>" (Mrs Collins being unpropitious) ask her boldly for £10 – at "one
fell swoop" and send the money with all possible despatch to Lafitte's. If
Mrs Collins refuses to touch the estimate let me know by return of post. –
It will then be time to pawn my watch and coat at the Mont de Píeté and
try my fortune with the proceeds at a table of Rouge et Noir (Horror!
Horror!!)

Above all things be speedy (and excuse the trouble I am giving you) "Je
[soutiendrai] ["] pugnis et [calcibus]"[4] that I have not thrown away a
farthing of money in this business and that I have been very ill-used by the
Devonport Street dynasty – to which however in a fine spirit of Christian
piety I extend my forgiveness and desire my love.

How did you get home? How did you find Jane and [progeny]?[5] Write
and tell me all about <u>my</u> pecuniary and <u>my</u> domestic affairs – D— me! I
<u>must</u> have a letter from Somebody!

I have finished my view of Chateau [Gaillard] – It is if possible a more
sunny little bit of nature than my representation of Dieppe [D'H] – the
foreground is exquisitely luxurious – full of [dui-oscura] – and suffused in
airy freshness.

I have also bought as much writing paper <u>as I can afford</u> (3 Penny-worth)
and intend to write something – It is to be a farce or a sermon – I have not
yet decided which.

"le Vine d'Eau" was admirably played at the Francais – the night you left
– Brindeau made a brilliant and gentlemanlike Bolingbroke – In mentioning

however "Swift, Prior, and Atterbury" as his newspaper colleagues – he pronounced the names of these British worthies a little obscurely – as thus: –

Shwiffhs – Preeore – Auttorboorey –

The actress who played Queen Anne acted with an ease grace and dignity delightful to look at – she [erased word] is a particularly ladylike and elegant woman and is named (I think) [Mddle Denain] – The piece played before the comedy was one of the most original and interesting I ever saw – It was called "The Chef d'[oeuvre] inconnu" – and treated of <u>one</u> Act – Michael Angelo being one of the characters.

It is time to leave off – or I shall miss today's post – Don't forget my monies and [indecipherable word] – for I am anxious to get back to my work at home and am not particularly enamoured of an e<u>conomical</u> sojourn in Paris –

Ever truly yours | W Wilkie Collins

C.J. Ward Esq | Messrs Coutts Co

Mrs Collins may say – that I gave her "the option" of lending me the £5 – or <u>not</u> – but surely I had a right to be told by return of post what I was to await [erased word] – how could I otherwise be expected to arrange any plan – economical or [otherwise: erased] the contrary? – This epistolary silence is most unaccountable – Can anything have happened?

Notes

1. Postmark: "PARIS | 10 | AOUT | 12 | (60)".
2. WC doubly underlines "£8–12–6", and draws a slanted line between the "8" in his total and the "8" in his assets.
3. Doubly underlined, apart from the first letter "i".
4. i.e., "I maintain with strength and cunning".
5. i.e., Jane Ward née Carpenter, WC's cousin and wife of Charles Ward whom he married on 4 February 1845.

To R.H. Dana,[1] 15 November 1848
MS: Princeton. Parrish, pp. 7–8

38, Blandford Square | London | November 15th 1848

My dear Sir

I have allowed so long a time to elapse since I last had the pleasure of communicating with you that I am afraid you will have almost forgotten both me and my book. During the last two months I have had little time to devote my attention to anything not connected with the printing of the

Memoirs of my father's Life; and I was unwilling to write to you again until I could inform you definitely of the period of the publication of my work – in which you have taken so kind an interest, and to which you have contributed so much information giving interest to that portion of it referring to Mr Allston's[2] character and genius.

Many causes connected with delay in engraving the illustrations to the book and with changing the arrangement of parts of the Mss. have contributed to put off the publication of my work – It will, however, be "out" <u>at last,</u> in about a week or ten days hence. It occupies two volumes, is dedicated by permission to Sir Robert Peel,[3] and will be published by Messrs Longman. What chances of success can be predicted for a book devoted to so peaceful a subject as the Art, amid the vital and varied interests of home politics and foreign revolutions now attracting everybody's attention in England, it is impossible to say. I resign myself philosophically to await the event of my experiment – hoping little and foreboding less.

One of my objects in writing to you, is to ascertain the safest and easiest method of sending you a copy of my work; which I hope you will accept as some small return for your kindness in enabling me to give so many valuable particulars respecting Mr Allston's death and character from your own letter to my father. I hope you will think that I have done justice to this part of my subject when you see the Memoir, which shall be forwarded to you as you may direct.

As regards matters of Art generally, our most important event, here, has been the presentation by Mr Vernon[4] of his magnificent gallery of modern pictures to the nation. Of this you have most probably heard, and perhaps also of the place to which this splendid bequest has been consigned – the dark ground-floor rooms (never intended for pictures) of our ugly and inconvenient National Gallery. Considering the legislative carelessness about most public buildings, peculiar to this country, I think it doubtful whether money enough will ever be granted to build a fitting receptacle for this collection of the finest works of the English school. If any hope is to be entertained on the subject, it can only exist in the chance that the effect of our new Houses of Parliament (which are really magnificent buildings) may be powerful enough to excite the government, at some future time, to attempt the reformations and additions which are so much wanted in so many of our other Public Edifices.

Trusting to hear from you soon, I remain

Dear Sir, very faithfully yours | W. Wilkie Collins

To, R.H. Dana Esqre

Notes

1. Richard Henry Dana, Jr, (1812–1882), author of, amongst other works, *Two Years Before the Mast* (1840).
2. Washington Allston, American painter (1779–1843).
3. Sir Robert Peel (1788–1850: *DNB*), Prime Minister 1841–46: patron of the arts.
4. Robert Vernon (1774–1849) presented a collection of 157 paintings to the nation on 22 December 1847.

To R.H. Dana, 12 January 1849
MS: Princeton. Parrish, pp. 8–10

38, Blandford Square | London | January 12th 1849

To | R.H. Dana, Esqre
My dear Sir,
    On Saturday the 30th December last, I gave Messrs Longman directions to send a copy of my Memoirs of my late father's Life to their Boston Correspondents – Little & Brown, addressed to you. They assured me that the parcel should be despatched at the first opportunity – I hope you will receive it with as little delay as possible.
    The book has hitherto succeeded very satisfactorily. It has been received with much greater indulgence, and reviewed at much greater length, by the Press, here, than I had ventured to anticipate. More than half the edition of 750 copies is already sold; and this success thus far, trifling as is its importance in itself, is a matter of some gratification to me – not merely as showing that I have not entirely failed in my undertaking – but also as relieving me from some pecuniary responsibility; for the Memoirs are my own speculation, and by the sale of the larger half of the edition, the somewhat heavy expenses connected with their publication are already <u>more than paid</u>. I sincerely hope that you may be led to form a favourable opinion of the work, on perusal.
    You ask what is the opinion among artists here of Ruskin's Modern Painters.[1] Although I do not follow my father's profession, (being a student of Lincoln's Inn; and only painting in leisure moments, in humble <u>amateur-fashion</u>, for my own amusement) I live very much in the society of artists, and can therefore tell you something of the impression made by Ruskin's work. The violent paradoxes in the First volume, had the effect which violent paradoxes, when cleverly argued, usually produce: – they amused some, displeased others, and startled everybody. It was pretty generally admitted that the author was a vigorous and dashing writer, who had studied the Art with genuine enthusiasm, but with doubtful judgment. On the other hand, however, the greater part of his readers (with whom I came

in contact) while doing justice to his capacities, thought him woefully misdirected; and considered him as a man, who having determined to say something new on every subject that he touched, resolutely overlooked or dogmatically contradicted, any received and tested principle of intellectual or critical truth that came in his way; and fancied that he had achieved originality when in many cases he merely succeeded in producing what was eccentric or absurd. His book had its small circle of resolute admirers – but it made a sensation, and <u>only</u> a sensation, among the larger class of readers – artists and amateurs.

His <u>second Volume</u>, published some time after his first, and containing an expression of regret for the arrogance of manner in his preceding publication, has, however, raised him immensely in the estimation of cultivated and thinking readers. I have merely looked into it myself, but I have heard it spoken of by artists who have read it carefully as a work of very unusual power, exhibiting a deep sympathy with the highest purposes of Art – poetical observation of Nature – and profound critical appreciation of many of the works of the "Old Masters". Some paradoxical opinions it might contain, in common with the preceding volume; but they were urged in a different spirit, and were amply compensated by the general intention of the book, and the real good to be gained from it – philosophically as well as pictorially – by attentive readers. Such is the general opinion of this second volume, so far as it has reached me.

All <u>literary</u> London is now astir however, about a work of a very different order – Macaulay's History of England.[2] It is regarded everywhere, as a really great achievement, and as tending to found a new school of Historical writing. The first edition of three thousand copies was out of print in a fortnight. This is indeed a great age for great authors. Dickens told a friend of mine, that he had made <u>four thousand guineas</u> by his last year's Christmas book – (The Battle of Life) – a five shilling publication,(!) which everybody abused, and which, nevertheless, everybody read. Eighteen thousand copies of his present Christmas book (The Haunted Man) were "subscribed for" by the booksellers, before publication.

I quite agree with you, that it is a matter of importance, that Mr Allston's portrait of Coleridge, should be engraved with the next edition of his works. I do not know any of the members of Coleridge's family, myself; but I know those who are acquainted with them; and will mention the subject to these friends of mine, at the earliest opportunity. To interest the Poet's <u>son</u> in the matter, is now unhappily out of the question – Hartley Coleridge's death having appeared in the papers of a few days since.

It has been one of the greatest sources of gratification to me, since the publication of my work, that the Memoirs have gained the favourable opinion of Sir Robert Peel; whose long and kind friendship with my father, and whose well-known judgment in matters of Literature and Art, concurred to give the highest importance to any criticism of his, on my undertaking. I had the pleasure of visiting him, by invitation, at his country seat, to receive his personal congratulations; and enjoyed the privilege of seeing in his gallery (for the first time) two of the largest and finest pictures my father ever produced – both painted some twenty years since, and both exhibiting those high and genuine qualities of Art, which will preserve them as "classics of the English School of Painting" – whatever the alterations of style which that School may hereafter adopt. You will find them, in the Memoirs, described by me from my Mother's recollections, under the titles of "A Frost Scene" and "The Morning after a Storm".

I remain, My dear Sir, | Very faithfully yours | W. Wilkie Collins.

Notes

1. Volume one published in 1843, volume two in 1846.
2. The first two volumes published in 1848.

To E.M. Ward,[1] 28 June [1849 or 1850]

MS: Texas: Coleman

17, Hanover Terrace | Wednesday | 28 June [1849]

My dear Edward,

I called at Slough on my way back to London from Maidenhead, about two hours before your return as I conjecture. Mrs Birch[2] was at home, however, and told me all I wanted to know about Mrs Ward. The Carter Halls[3] gave such contradictory accounts that I had no clear notion of what had been the matter with her, until I heard from Mrs Birch the good news of her recovery.

Have you <u>fixed</u> the Christening party for next Wednesday – July 5th?[4] And if you have, at what hour do the orgies begin? And which train ought one to travel to Slough by? Is it a morning or evening party? Will the male guests be in black, as to their breeches, or in general colours? I have promised to communicate these particulars, except about the breeches, to Egg,[5] to answer at your earliest convenience.

An awful crowd at the Mayor's last Thursday. Stewards with names of distinguished individuals on private printed lists – charged to make civil speeches to all authors and artists – made hideous mistakes indeed – Cardwell[6] taken for Bulwer[7] – your humble servant taken for a P.R.B.[8] and asked whether the author of <u>Antonina</u>[9] was there that night – gallons of cider-cup in a vessel like a gold slop-pail, out of which the company drank like horses out of a trough – seedy next morning and miserably unfit to be in the house of a virtuous man whose servant had never heard of Brandy and Soda Water in the whole course of his life.

Ta-Ta, | WWC

I met Bulwer at a party on Monday night. He is looking bright and plump. Now is the time to take his portrait.

Notes

1. Edward M. Ward (1816-1879: *DNB*), artist and close friend of Wilkie Collins. His wife Henrietta, also an artist, her *Memories of Ninety Years* (1924), has anecdotes about the Wards and their friends.
2. The Wards' housekeeper?
3. Samuel Carter Hall (1800–1889: *DNB*), editor, writer, and journalist. Mrs Carter Hall (Anna Maria Fielding) (1800–1881: *DNB*) was a prolific writer. "By general consent Mrs Hall was the more agreeable of the two" (Dickens, *Letters*, I, 481, n.4.)
4. For details, see Robinson p. 52.
5. Augustus Egg (1816-1863: *DNB*), artist, theatrical enthusiast.
6. Viscount Edward Cardwell (1813–1886: *DNB*), politician.
7. Edward George Earle Bulwer-Lytton (1803–1873: *DNB*), novelist dramatist, editor, social critic.
8. i.e., Pre-Raphaelite Brotherhood.
9. Reference to <u>Antonina</u> suggests that the letter should be dated 1850, not 1849.

To Richard Bentley,[1] 30 August 1849
MS: NYPL (Berg)

Private[2]

38, Blandford Square | August 30th 1849

Sir,

Having nearly completed an Historical Romance in three volumes, illustrative of the events of the first siege of Rome by Alaric, and of Gothic and Italian character in the fifth century, I have thought it probable that such a work might not inappropriately be offered for your inspection, while recent occurrences continue to direct public attention particularly on Roman affairs. I now write therefore to say, that it will give me great pleasure to forward it to New Burlington Street, upon hearing that such an arrangement meets with your approval.

Without now entering into detail, (which I shall be happy to do, if you think an interview desirable) I may merely observe that the subject, as far as I know, has the merit of being an original one; and that, while I have spared no pains to collect all the historical information connected with the period of the Romance, I have not forgotten that it was important to present that information – as far as lay in my favour – in the graphic form most likely to be attractive to the taste of readers of the present day.

I can only mention to you, as an introduction, my work published at the close of last year: – "Memoirs of William Collins R.A." – the success of which has encouraged me to enter on another literary undertaking.

It is perhaps hardly necessary for me to add, that you will much oblige me by considering this offer – in case you should not be willing to entertain it – as stri<u>ctly confidentia</u>l.

I remain, Sir, | Your obedient servant | W.Wilkie Collins

P.S.
Two volumes and a half of the MSs are ready for Press.
To Richard Bentley Esqre

Notes

1. Richard Bentley (1794–1871), founder of the publishing house and publisher of *Bentley's Miscellany*, specializing in novel serialization. Published *Antonina* in three volumes on 27 February 1850. See Gasson.
2. WC doubly underlines "rivate" of "Private".

To Mrs Harriet Collins, 8 October 1849
MS: Private Possession

[38, Blandford Square]

Summary
"Miss Elwin [1] ... has been suffering with the face-ache; but is now much better. Her sole piece of domestic intelligence is: – that the woman who roasted flesh and punches dough into bad pie-crust for us, is about to leave for her new place on Wednesday next. We confidently expect that our creature-comforts will be improved in the matter of confection, from the day of her departure – as the kitchen will then be turned into a Republic – Miss Elwin taking the post of Minister of the <u>Interior</u>; and Emma[2] that of Public Works.

I returned from Brighton full ten days since, 'sick and sorry'; but was speedily restored by the air of London from the effects of the noxious sea breezes of the Sussex coast. On this day week (Saturday) Charles Ward and I propose setting forth at about half-past eleven at night to embark at London for Boulogne – 'en route' to Paris, Tours, Fontainebleau, Orléons, and whatever other places in the neighbourhood we can find worth seeing – we return in a fortnight.

Two volumes of my book are in Bentley's hands. I wrote a civil letter offering them on trial, received a civil answer accepting them on trial; and expect, in process of time, a second curt answer, refusing them on trial. After this, I suppose it will be time to try if Newby[3] will let my 'little book' puff out on its brief trial trip to the terminus of Popularity, along the same publishing line as the Curate of Wildmere.[4] If Newby declines (I shall begin to feel grievous doubts about the quality of the book if he accepts) it will be time, I suppose to see about publishing it myself. In the meantime nearly 200 pages of Volume 3rd are ready for press, and the remaining hundred so chalked out 'in the rough' that I could get them 'executed', like the country orders of advertising tradespeople, 'on the shortest notice'.

So much for the Literature of one of your sons. As to the Art of the other, he is now filling in his design for his large picture; and is so engaged in that, and some other pictorial matters, as to be unable to leave home, on any visits whatever, for some time to come ....

You were told ... of the visit of the excellent Lady Chantrey,[5] bearing a bandbox filled with clouds of musty and indefinite white muslin, destined to encircle your head in such a halo of airy elegance as never floated around it before ..."

Notes

1. Unidentified member of the Blandford Square domestic staff.
2. *Ibid*.
3. Thomas Cautley Newby (?1798–1882) "without doubt, the most notorious publisher of fiction in the Victorian period" (Sutherland, p. 461).
4. Probably one of Newby's publishing ventures.
5. *Antonina* dedicated to Lady Chantrey, the wife of Sir Francis Legatt Chantrey (1791–1841), sculptor and friend of WC's father. See Gasson.

To Richard Bentley, 22 November 1849
MS: University of Illinois, Urbana

38, Blandford Square | November 22nd 1849

My dear Sir,

I hope there is no doubt of our coming to an arrangement satisfactory to both, as regards the publication of "Antonina".

I think I shall best show my frankness in stating my views, by telling you what consideration guided me in calculating [erased letters] the amount of remuneration which I should ask for the MSs. I felt, in the first place, that I had no right to mention, or to think of, any price which might adequately reward me for the time and pains that I have bestowed on the book in writing it, and shall still bestow in correcting it for press, because – although it [was: erased] is not my first work – it is my first novel; an experiment on the public, of which you are willing to take whatever risk there may be, and in the profits of which, if successful, you are therefore justly entitled to have the largest share. You see I state the case against me, candidly, just as I feel it.

At the same time, I reflected on the other side of the question, that the book was likely – in virtue only of its historical information (much of which remains to be put into notes) to appeal to a wider class of readers than general novel readers, in these times when history is so much in vogue; and that the modern taste for present times and the horrible, having been somewhat surfeited of late, a work appealing to other sympathies, would on that very account have, as a novelty, a considerable chance.

I was further guided in forming my views, by the profit I made on the "Memoirs" of my father's Life, and by what I had heard of the prices given to men of great reputation as novelists. Calculating on these, considerably <u>downwards</u> from the <u>last</u>, as you will see, I came to the conclusion that if I [erased word] mention two hundred pounds, as the consideration on which I should be willing to part with my MSs, I should be proposing an amount of remuneration, which I candidly assure you I cannot but think rather <u>under</u> than <u>over</u> what anyone else in my peculiar situation would ask.

And now, my dear Sir, having frankly placed my offer and the reasons which lead me to make it, before you; and while I await your answer, which I know will be as fair and friendly as your letter now in my hands – I can only repeat that it will not be <u>my</u> fault if Antonina does not make her appearance in the world under your protection. And, sanguine as I may be, I cannot help hoping that the connection between us, thus begun, may so continue that we may have no reason to regret it; and may both feel the same inclination to renew it at future periods.

Very faithfully yours | W.Wilkie Collins

PS
I should have answered your letter by return of post, but I felt that a day of consideration was due to it, before I replied.

To Charles Ward, 19 March 1850
MS: Private Possession[1]

Albury | Near Guildford | March 19th 1850

Dear Ward,

Bentley was out of town for the day when I called yesterday at New Burlington Street and you were lunching (you always are lunching) when I dropped in at The Strand. I saw Bayfield,[2] and gave him a message to you – concerning the newspaper of the 14th ultimo, which contains the review quoted from [indecipherable word] the advertisements.[3]

One of Bentleys myrmidons told me that there would be a review in the "Dublin University" for next month – but you will see the advertisement of all the magazines, and you will buy those which notice "[mein schönen buke]" and you will apply to Mamma Collins for payment of your charges – and Mamma Collins will reimburse and read.

There is nothing particular here – very few leaves on the trees – very little grass on the fields no political changes in the village – a cursed confused chirping of birds – an unnecessarily large supply of fresh air – and an [odd] absence of cabs, omnibuses, circulating libraries, public houses, newspaper offices, pastry cooks shops, [with] other articles of civilisation.

Kindest regards to Jane, and the new infant too, whenever it is foolish enough to poke its innocent head into this nasty vicious world.

Believe the assurance of your Collins.

Don't forget to send me down any new reviews and the papers.

To Charles Ward Esq

And see glimpses of light in the gloom of despair

Which we all must exist in, while [looped] in the [square][4]

Notes

1. On the first leaf of the letter WC draws a face with beams radiating from it.
2. Unidentified.
3. Probably a reference to advertisements for WC's *Antonina*, published in three volumes by Richard Bentley, 27 February 1850.
4. Verse at end of the letter.

To R.H. Dana, 17 June 1850

MS: Present whereabouts unknown.[1] Published R.L. Wolff, *Nineteenth Century-Fiction: A Bibliographic Catalogue* (New York: 1981), I, 255–6.

38, Blandford Square, London | June 17th 1850

My dear Sir,

As I consider myself quite inexcusable for having so long delayed answering your kind letter in acknowledgment of the receipt of my biographical work,[2] I shall not venture to make any apologies – but rather trust entirely to your good nature to pardon my "shortcomings", and still to preserve some faith in my regularity as a correspondent for the future.

I called at Chapman's[3] on Saturday, and heard that he had received Mr Allston's Lectures, and had forwarded them to Longman, I shall no doubt have the book, either today, or tomorrow. Pray accept my best thanks for it – I need hardly tell you that I anticipate no small amounts of instructions and pleasure from the perusal of the welcome addition to my library with which you have kindly provided me.[4]

I shall be most happy to make your son's acquaintance. If I can be of any use to him in London, I hope he will not scruple to employ my services in any way that he thinks proper. I wish I could look forward to the pleasure of seeing <u>you</u> here, as well. We have still great men and great institutions enough left, to make the Old Country worth a visit. There is certainly an absence of any leading Great Man in England – but does not this "absence" extend to other nations as well? I think it is the tendency of the present times to make greatness more of a <u>Republic</u>, and less of a <u>Monarchy</u>, than it was. The vast spread of education and knowledge, the hot competition existing in all branches of human acquirement, seems to be placing clever men upon an intellectual <u>level</u> – and, I am sanguine enough to think, a very high one. It appears to me, that what was well done before (in statesmanship, for instance) by o<u>ne</u> man, is now as well or better done by <u>many</u>. There is less honour acquired collectively by the m<u>any</u> <u>men</u>, than was formerly acquired by <u>one</u>; but the advantage derived by the world is the same – nay, it is in one respect, perhaps, greater, as regards England. For I cannot forget that under our great men, we engaged in some long, bloody, and not very creditable wars, and I cannot help suspecting that under a Chatham, or a Pitt – under any leading man like these, who influenced all things by his own individual Genius, and naturally referred all things, more or less, to his own individual feelings – we might have had a recurrence of War, on more than one matter of provocation within the last ten, or twelve years. <u>Now</u>, whatever diplomatic difficulties we involve ourselves in, we don't fight about them – we don't go to war with France about the Greek affair[5] – the rule of the <u>lesser</u> men who now govern, is with all its faults, a rule of

Peace – and surely this is some compensation for the loss of those great men, whose rule was a rule of <u>war</u> –

However, enough of Politics! I suspect I am writing more <u>hopefully</u> than <u>wisely</u> about them – but like all young men, I look at "the bright side of things", and believe in all our national changes, as, in the main, changes for good.

I have little news to tell you. There is rather a lull here, just at present in the world of Literature – we have nothing to talk about, but the two forthcoming Volumes of Macaulay's History. In reference to this book, I was told upon good authority, that the <u>profit</u> derived from the sale of the two volumes first published, was £20,000! Such is the sum that a popular book will produce in a short period! – and [the same: erased] it is much the same with a popular picture. Landseer's "Duke of Wellington re-visiting the field of Waterloo" (one of the prominent attractions of this year's Royal Academy Exhibition) is to be engraved: and the sum of £<u>3000</u>, has been given to the painter, for the mere right of [three erased words] making a print of it, by the publisher who has entered on the speculation. Truly, there is no want of encouragement among us, for good Literature and good Art!

Even in my own small way, I have succeeded beyond what I had ventured to anticipate. A second edition of my Romance[6] has been called for – I completed, a day or two since the revisal of the last sheet. I confess I had my misgivings about the book, when it was first published. The story, I feared, was laid at too remote a period (the fifth century), and illustrated too remote an event, (the first seige of Rome by the Goths, under Alaric). However, it seems to have satisfied the critics and pleased novel-readers, here; and this is some encouragement to go on, and do better, if I can. I believe the publisher (Mr Bentley) sent some copies of the first edition to America.

I don't know who the article on the biography, in Blackwood, was written by.[7] I have read "Two Years before the Mast", and read it with great delight – it is a most entertaining and most original book; and is deservedly popular in England, among all classes of readers.

Wordsworth's death was, I believe, not unexpected by those who knew him – his health had been seriously impaired for a long period. I well recollect being introduced to him, by my father, on the Pincian Hill, at Rome. I was a boy then, (in 1837) and was much struck by the remarkable mildness and kindness of his manners. He seemed as little fitted, as any man I ever saw, to bear (much less to <u>enjoy</u>) the bustle and constant change of a travelling life – he looked, to use the common phrase, "quite out of his element", in a foreign land, and among foreign people. The "Cholera" was then, beginning its ravages in Italy – Wordsworth was bound for Naples, like ourselves; but the reports that the pestilence had broken out in that city "gave him pause". I remember being quite astonished at the earnestness with which he entreated my father to do as <u>he</u> intended to do, and not only abandon all idea of going to Naples, but leave Rome at once for England. My father tried in vain to combat his apprehensions – the very idea of the Cholera seemed to fill him with horror – he left Italy, as he had determined to leave it, and <u>we</u> went on, as <u>we</u> had determined. I never saw him any more; but he wrote me a very kind letter[8] about the Life of my father. He was a good man and a great man – greater, I think, as a moral teacher than as a poet.

I am at present residing at the address, at the head of this letter; but it is very possible that I may move before long. Your son will, however, be sure to find me out, wherever I may be, on application to my publisher, Mr Bentley of New Burlington Street.

Believe me, to remain, My dear Sir | Most faithfully yours | W. Wilkie Collins
To | R.H.Dana, Esqre.

Notes

1. Text of the letter transcribed from a microfilm now at the Hyder Collection, University of Kansas Libraries at Lawrence.
2. *Memoirs of the Life of William Collins*.
3. The publishers.
4. WC writes in *Memoirs* of the friendship between Allston and his father "while Allston was studying and painting in England" (I,134). Allston was Charles Allston Collins's godfather, and brother-in-law of the elder Dana. A copy of his *Lectures*, published in 1850, doesn't appear amongst the lists of books in WC's possession at his death.
5. See [George Finlay], "Greece again", *Blackwood*, 67 (May 1850), 526–39.
6. *Antonina*.
7. Probably a reference to John Eagles, "Memoir of W. Collins, R.A.", *Blackwood*, 67 (February 1850), 192–207.
8. See *The Letters of William and Dorothy Wordsworth*, 2nd ed., VII. *The Later Years: Part IV, 1840–1853*, ed., Alan G. Hill (Oxford: Clarendon 1988), 882: 10 December 1848. Letter now at PM.

To Mrs Harriet Collins, 29 July 1850
MS: PM

Fowey | July 29<u>th</u> 1850

My dear Mother/
We are now fairly in Cornwall. I date this letter from a sea-port town on the South Coast – the most uninteresting place we have yet met with – All before Fowey has, however, been wonderful. The scenery in the valleys is amazingly fertile and beautiful. Trees forming natural arches over the lanes – ferns and grapes in the hedges, of an almost tropical size and luxuriance.

Then, when you rise to the ridges of the great hills which run through the middle of Cornwall, the whole prospect changes – vast, solemn moors stretch out on all sides – generally over shadowed [with: erased] by black clouds – you see your road winding in before you till it looks like a white thread in the far distance. Old tottering grey sign posts [start: erased] stand like spectres in lonely cross roads + strange Druidical stones, and black grand rocks, piled fantastically one upon another, meet you at one place; and picturesque little farm-houses, pleasant cornfields, and holy wells with ruined chapels and sturdy Saxon crosses near them, present themselves at another. Cornwall is, in short, what I always thought it, one of the most beautiful and most romantic counties in England.

We are not idle in <u>preparing</u>, at least, for a book of some kind. Brandling sketches and I journalize diligently – What we shall yet do remains to be seen. We shall bring home some materials at any rate.

You can trace out our route on the large map of England, if you like. From Plymouth we went to St Germans (in Cornwall) by a b<u>oat</u> (a pleasant way of beginning a <u>pedestrian</u> excursion!). We had a lovely little voyage by moonlight – and met with some adventures, which you shall hear when we return. From St Germans we journeyed to Looe (on the coast) by land. This was our first start on foot with our knapsacks. The weight of the knapsack was anything but contemptible for the first mile or two, which was all u<u>phill</u>. But "poor human nature" gradually accustoms itself to all things – and during the latter part of our walk (a ten mile one) the knapsacks became as familiar and as comfortable as natural humpbacks.

We found Looe a snug cosy primitive old place, with a nice old bridge, and toppling old houses with two or three doors each, leading into two or three zigzag, labyrinth-like old streets. There was also a fat landlady at the Inn, and a fat chambermaid who coddled us in comfortable beds, and fuddled us with comfortable ale, and stuffed us to bursting with good pies and puddings and sweetcakes, and then sent us into the garden of the Inn, to keep us out of mischief, like children; and to digest our feast in harmony and peace – Leaving Looe, and leaving all the best and purest affections of our – <u>stomachs</u>, with the landlady and the chambermaid, we walked to <u>Liskeard</u> to see the Druidical remains and curious rocks in the neighbour-hood – At the Inn here, there was an awful change – The landlady was a nasty thin woman in black, with a bilious complexion and a crocodile grin – the chambermaid was unpleasantly addicted to perpetual perspiration on the forehead, and was shod in [an awful: erased] a mighty pair of boots that creaked and clanked all over the house without interruption – there was nothing good to eat, and nothing good to drink – so we changed this Inn for another in the Town, where we again found a nice landlady, who said she liked us for being such nice strong young Englishmen, who walked about independently and didn't mind the weight of our knapsacks – "<u>We</u>

were not effeminate dandies, and she liked us for it, and bid God Bless us with all her heart"! From Liskeard we journeyed to Lostwithiel – a little town in a valley; full of Methodists ranting and singing (on Sunday morning) through their noses discordantly enough to set all the teeth of all the angels in Heaven on edge. We went to the Church; and heard a sermon of the old school from a nice harmless old parson, which edified us considerably, and strengthened us in our generation [indecipherable word] as it out. From Lostwithiel we walked here today; and from this place we intend starting for [St Austell] tomorrow.

Direct your next letter (and write me a long one) to "Post Office, Falmouth, Cornwall". If you do anything about a house in Fitzroy Square – mind the drains – have a surveyor to examine them particularly – Some of the houses are badly drained. Is [Gould] to help you to move? Write to Charley and ascertain distinctly when he is coming home – he must be able to settle some time – give him my love – ever yours affectionately | W W Collins | Brandling sends his love –

To Charles Ward, 1 August 1850
MS: Harrowby Mss Trust

[St Austell,] Cornwall | Augt 1st 1850

My dear Ward

I have not written to you before this, because I wished to gain experience enough of Cornwall to be able to give you a fair, full and trustworthy report of the country. If you look at a large map of England, you will see that, at [St Austell's,] we are about half way down the Southern coast, on our way at the Land's End – or rather to Penzance, our headquarters for the Land's End. At Penzance you can meet us easily, if you will, and you really ought to see Cornwall – more varied, picturesque, and romantic scenery, than this, I have not often beheld, anywhere – and I am yet in what is considered the least interesting part of the country.

If you like old churches, here they are in abundance, Brandling is now sketching the tower of [St Austell's] Church – a fine specimen of Gothic architecture of the 14th century – studded all over with quaint images of Saints, and stone faces of ladies and gentlemen in purgatory, grinning horribly upon you at every corner – Churches of this sort abound all over Cornwall – Besides this, there are holy wells dedicated to old Cornish saints, with little ruined chapels, and curious stone crosses near them. If such things as these, are not interesting ecclesiastical remains – what things are? – Then, the scenery. In the valleys, it is fertile to the utmost degree of fertility. Ferns and grasses in the hedges almost as tall as I am – trees of all varieties, in full verdure – long undulating cornfields – pleasant little streams – and snug little farm houses, all built of solid granite with chimneys of bright red brick. On the hills, you see half over Cornwall – immense moors roll as [if here] one over the other, to the far horizon – with [masses] of cloud blown up from the Atlantic, grandly overshadowing them! The rain from these clouds is confined to certain spots on the highest ridges, and seldom reaches you on the roads and footpaths lower down. I only recollect <u>two</u> showers since we entered Cornwall – nothing could be finer than the weather has been hitherto.

Our way of travelling is the most independent and delightful that can be imagined – We start at our own hour – walk where we please – stop where we please. After you have had it on for the first half hour, the weight of the knapsack ceases to be felt as an encumbrance of any importance – and the [privilege] pleasure of having all one's luggage on one's back and caring nothing for whole legions of porters, is hardly to be described. The people in Cornwall are a remarkably civil and orderly race. We have only met with <u>one</u> beggar; as yet throughout our travels; and he was evidently "a tramper" from some other part of the country. The living at the Inns is remarkably cheap, and generally speaking remarkably <u>good</u>. We have had but <u>one</u> bad dinner since we left. Beds vary in price from <u>one</u> shilling to <u>two</u> (generally <u>one</u>); and breakfasts and dinners are proportionally low in price.

I am keeping my journal very regularly; and I have some hope of finding enough in it, when I get back to London, to make a book – we have already met with some adventures, have seen some curious people, and have visited some remarkable places – the granite rocks, Druidical monuments, and bog wells in the neighbourhood of Liskeard being among the most surprising of the Cornish sights that we have yet beheld – we have asked in <u>vain</u>, at all the towns, for a guide book – so there is at any rate, [an opening] ground enough "to let" on literary "building leases", in the county of Cornwall.

Now, does what I have already written [to] tempt you to join us, or does it not? If it does, you can [join] meet us comfortably by the middle of August, at Penzance – And you must proceed thus:

Take a passage on the Cork Steamer (from Margate Wharf: Office 25, Mincing Lane) either to Plymouth or Falm[outh] To Plymouth costs 12/6; to Falmouth £1 – (Stewards' Fee included) The steamer stops all night at Plymouth on the way to Falmouth, so perhaps you may prefer going the shortest voyage to Plymouth only. In this case, you will have to get coach conveyance to Falmouth (plenty of coaches run along the Southern coast). You will get every information at Radmore's <u>Globe</u> Hotel, Plymouth where we have left our heavy coats till our return. I have just this moment heard, here, that the mail runs from Plymouth to Truro direct – and then from Truro to Penzance or you can travel thus, easily and expeditiously enough – To go straight by sea at Falmouth and then by coach from Falmouth to Penzance would be the cheapest plan – but the <u>shorter</u> the voyage, in <u>your</u> case the better, I suppose–

By this plan you would see all the best part of Cornwall with us – Meeting at Penzance we should visit all the wonders of the Lands End, and return by the Northern Coast and the mining districts to Plymouth in time for you to give Jane a week at the end of your holydays – As for luggage, you can buy a mackintosh knapsack for £1 -0- or a <u>leather</u> one for £1[...5[...] – or if you don't like this expense, a small carpet-bag strapped onto your back, will do as well as any knapsack.

Write as soon as possible and let me know whether you will come or not[1] (directing your letter to "Post Office, Falmouth, Cornwall"). If you will come, set off if possible, the very first day of your holydays (the steamers go Monday – one company; and Thursday – another –) Tell me the day when you set off, and then write again from Plymouth to Post Office, Penzance and there will be no fear of our not meeting – I will send you any fresh directions you may want.

How is Jane? and how are the children? I heard they had the measles – but as this is generally [supposed] considered to be an excellent thing in young families I suppose I ought rather to congratulate than to condole with you – I only hope Copsey & Compy are having the <u>infantine</u> <u>epidemic</u> favourably – at any rate, they couldn't have it at a better time.

Is my second edition out yet, or not?[2] I wrote yesterday to Mrs Collins; but forgot to tell her to forward me any letters that come to my address. Perhaps you will be kind enough to give her a message to this effect, with my love.

If Charley comes back before you leave London, bring him to Cornwall with you.

Give my kind remembrances to Jane – tell her to keep up her spirits about the children – think <u>yourself</u> how much good the measles will have done them, <u>after the measles have gone</u>, and believe me

Ever truly yours | W. Wilkie Collins

Notes

1. Charles Ward didn't join Collins and his friend the artist Henry C. Brandling in Cornwall.
2. The second edition of Collins' *Antonina* appeared at the end of May 1850.

To Mrs Harriet Collins, [3 August 1850]
MS: PM

Falmouth | Saturday

My dear Mother,[1]

   Although I have the greatest contempt for <u>money</u>, myself, I find that the people of Cornwall regard gold and silver in a very different light. It is actually a fact that we cannot get on here without <u>money</u>; and it is, <u>as</u> actually a fact too, that my money is slipping out of my purse in a most unaccountable manner – I have just 30 Shillings left. Under these circumstances, I beg you will have the goodness to send me £10 – – forthwith – in two Post Office Orders for £5 – – each. Have them made out in the name of "William Wilkie Collins" (the name in full) – and let them be made payable at the Post Office, Helstone,[2] Cornwall. Pray send them immediately.

   Brandling wants the same sum, sent in the same way, to the same place – Will you let Miss Emma Brandling know this <u>at once</u>, at Fitzroy Square. Brandling left the key of his desk with Miss <u>K. Howard</u> so Miss Howard will be perhaps the best person to apply to.

   I don't know whether you think this extravagant, or not. It certainly is not. By the time the remittance reaches us – £10 – each, will have lasted us <u>three weeks</u>! £5 – you still owe me on our account – and £5 – I must borrow of you – Mind the name of the place (Helston) is spelt right.

   I resign myself to Hanover Terrace (and to the Queen's Bench afterwards) But I do not feel quite resigned to leaving you to "move" by yourself – If you want me back, write and tell me so, and I will come back at once – Write moreover to advise me of the departure of the P.O. order – in a separate letter – dated[3] properly.

   I wrote to Charles Ward, the day after I last wrote to you – But have received no answer yet. If he has not written in reply before you receive this, he had better direct his letter to Helston instead of Falmouth (as I told him). I sent him full directions for joining us, which I hope he will do.

   There is no more news to tell of our journey. We walked 14 miles from St Austells to Truro – and took a boat down the river from Truro to Falmouth. Neither Truro, nor Falmouth are interesting places. The first is a large market town, exactly like all market towns – with the usual allowance of dull streets, dull shops, and dull people. And Falmouth is as dirty and struggling as most seaport towns are.

   If I was dropped in it blindfold I could not tell it from Portsmouth – and on the same plan, I could not tell either from Plymouth. The weather goes on very fine and very hot – a most debilitating heat – but with bathing in the sea and walking on the land, I continue to defy all atmospheric influences.

Helston, to which we go tomorrow, is, the point where all the fine scenery of the Land's End begins – continuing from that place all up the Northern coast. We look to these parts as the material of the book. As for my letters, they are about as fit for print, as your washerwoman's bills, or as this present business-letter, which you will not find particularly interesting – and which I must abruptly conclude to save post – | ever affectionately yours W W Collins

Love to Charley – glad he knows a brace of Lords – hope they will do something for him – I have no time before post to write direct to Miss Brandling – and Henry can't – for he is suffering (unlucky wretch!) from a violent fit of toothache. Tell Miss Brandling also, that he received the two letters sent to Fowey.

Notes

1. Envelope postmarked: "FALMOUTH | AU 3 | 1850 | B".
2. "elston" of "Helstone" are doubly underlined.
3. "ate" of "dated" are doubly underlined.

To Mrs Harriet Collins, 14 August 1850
MS: PM

Penzance | August 14 th 1850

My dear Mother/

Seeing sights, noting down recollections of them in my Journal, walking, eating, drinking, and sleeping, leave me very few opportunities for writing letters with a degree of regularity. I can only find [erased word] an opportunity to indite the present "missive", by cribbing half an hour from my bed time.

We have seen the rocks and precipices of the "Lizard", since I last wrote, and have stood on the Southernmost promontory of England and beheld the Atlantic itself [foaming: erased] at our feet. [three? erased words] The cliffs that gird the land east and west of the Lizard are really sublime – they reach their climax at a place called Kynance Cove. Fancy an amphitheatre of separate rocks two hundred feet high – some rising like pyramids and steeples – some stretched longitudinally on the sand and pierced with great black caverns – some crowned with wild asparagus at the top, and tunnelled with holes at the bottom, in which the sea roars and boils with the thunder of a whole park of artillery – fancy the first sight of these rocks, from a precipitous cliff 300 feet high, wrapped in a mist which exagerated their size twofold, with thousands on thousands of [sea: erased] gulls flying screaming round them, with the white foam of the sea leaping-up their black sides, and flying over them in long clouds of spray – fancy, finally, these same rocks, when the weather cleared, and the sun shone out of them, sparkling with splendid colours – deep red and rich brown and green and yellow and silver [gilding] – as bright as polished marble, with the sea suddenly changed to a <u>Mediterranean blue</u> and the sky covered with minute driving, fleecy clouds; and you will have as good an idea as I can give you of Kynance Cove. Most of the rocks I climbed with a guide, and looked down into hideous black tunnels, where the raging sea seemed to shake us on our pinnacles – where the water was spurted in our faces from fifty feet off, through hidden holes and slicks, followed by [a: erased] roaring blasts of wind, as loud as if the devil himself was blowing his bellows at the fires of Hell. Then the caves, – we w<u>riggled</u> ourselves into them on our bellies, like snakes, where they were blocked up by rocks – and groped our way along their sides in pitch darkness where they rose, again to their full-height, the guide telling me stories of drownings and smugglings and shipwrecks which harmonized admirably with the wild features of the scene. The visit to Kynance Cove was of itself alone worth the Journey from London.

We have had our comic adventures too. When we entered the kitchen of the Inn at Lizard Town, we found it literally crammed by 15 or 20 babies, and 15 or 20 Mamas. The local doctor had got a supply of "fine fresh matter from London". (as the landlady said) and was vaccinating all the babies by wholesale. Perhaps, as a mother yourself, you can imagine the noise these babies made – I can't describe it – There were two pigs a flock of geese, and an assembly of little boys – all looking into the Kitchen at our heels; but the noise they made was of no consequence at all, compared to the noise of the 15 or 20 babies and the 15 or 20 Mamas.

At this place Brandling immortalized himself by making an <u>omelette</u> – Six eggs, a tea-cupful of clotted cream, new milk, an onion, and chopped parsley, made the ingredients! We gave the fat landlady a bit. She was a hugely fat, good natured soul, who was obliged to prop herself up against a wall or a door, whenever she came into the parlour to speak to us – As for the omelette, she smacked her lips; declared it was the most delicious thing she had ever tasted – and vowed that she would make one herself "please God as soon as she got out of bed tomorrow morning"!

I hear from Charles Ward that you are going to Southsea – and am very glad to hear it – But who is to forward my letters, if any come? And how is this letter to get to you, if you are gone before it arrives? I suppose Miss Elwin is to be "locum tenens" [temporary guardian of the place].

If you answer this directly, address your letter to "Post Office, St Ives, Cornwall". We go to the Land's End tomorrow, or next day – then round to St Ives, then to <u>Redruth</u> – to which place the next letter must be directed. Thomas Price has given us a letter of introduction to a gentleman here, who is the most good natured and hospitable of men. We almost live at his house – and have been driving about in his gig all day [erased word].

You may as well tell me in your next letter what is the <u>number</u> of the house in Hanover Terrace – or when I get home, I shall not be properly qualified to find out where my house is. By the bye, don't forget that there will be something <u>considerable</u> to pay annually for keeping up the <u>inclosure</u> in the Park and that this must be settled somehow with Mr Gibbons.

Tell me any news of Charley. Ward says he is "busily engaged in painting a fly's eye with lashes to match" – for Heaven's sake take care of my unfortunate papers[1] – and believe me |

Ever your affectionately | W. Wilkie Collins

Note

1. Word underlined with "ape" doubly underlined.

To Charles Ward, 15 August 1850
MS: Private Possession.

Penzance | August 1850 | (I don't know what day of the month or week)[1]

My dear Ward,

I have received and read your two letters, on my arrival at Penzance. I am inexpressively shocked by your sentiments in reference to your native country. It will be three weeks or a month before I am able to leave Cornwall – I have no money to spend at Paris, and I shall have a Cornish [indecipherable word] to write (not a guide book or handbook) as soon as I get home. So, if you will go to France – and will not come here – you must be left to your own evil ways. I know France from Boulogne to Marseilles – there is no scenery in the country worth a d–n, compared to Cornish scenery. And as for eating, "stap my vitals", if I have eaten chop or steak more than once, since I have been here. <u>Here</u>, Sir, we live on Ducks, Geese, Chickens, tongue, pickled pilchards, curried Lobster – Clotted cream – jam tarts, fruit tarts – custards – cakes, <u>red mullet</u>, conger eels, – salmon trout – and fifty other succulent dishes. I have almost forgotten the table of joints – we have nothing to do with them.

Oh Ward! Ward! I have seen such rocks ! Rocks like pyramids – rocks like crouching lions – rocks toppling, as if they would fall on your head, (three hundred feet high) – rocks pierced with mighty and measureless caverns – rocks covered with the most exquisite natural mosaic-work in all colours – rocks crowned by mist at one hour, and brightened by sunshine at another – rocks whose indescribable grandeur I might go on attempting to describe for the next two pages, if I thought it was any use – but I am writing to a prejudiced Anglo-Misanthrope, and I may as well save my pains and my paper. No descriptions of the "Lizard" rocks and precipices will ever affect you – you won't come here and you will go to France which I know to heart already. Oh Ward! Ward! This is bitter mockery to a man who admires Nature, and is bent on making a book of Cornish Nature – and has not yet seen the Land's End, and has the wonders of the North Coast still to explore.

I thank you heartily for your information about my second edition (which God speed) and I condole with you still more heartily on your family troubles – but remember your numerous compensations – you have a very excellent wife (my love to Mrs C.J. Ward), you are a British Father (my respects to your Social Title) and you have begotten, and are begetting and will beget many British Babies (smack their bottoms in my name, and for my sake!). What are measles, and tumblings out of bed compared to such blessed privileges as these ? Ah ! "Got-for-Dam", I wish I was married, and had a family and a respectable pot-belly, and a position in the country as a householder and ratepayer – but this is not to be. By all the napkins of all the babies of England, I begin to fear that I am little better than a vagabond – only fit to wander about Cornwall, and be very sorry that I can't divide myself in two and wander about France at the same time, with C.J. Ward, who detests my manner but whose very affectionate friend Wilkie Collins – I nevertheless remain.

Will you give my love to dear Mama, and say that I will write in a day or two – I have not had 5 minutes to myself for the last three days, or I would have written before. We start for the Land's End tomorrow or next day.

Note

1. Letter postmarked: "16 AU... | 1850".

To Richard Bentley, [23 October 1851][1]
MS: University of Illinois, Urbana. Davis, pp.105–6.

17, Hanover Terrace | Regents Park | Friday evening

My dear Sir,

Mr Marsh[2] has, I dare say, told you that an idea for a <u>Christmas Story</u> made a morning call in my brain the other day. The sort of book I propose would be a 5/- affair, running to about <u>130 pages</u> – a sort of tragi-Comedy in the form of a Story – and the title (of course we keep this strictly <u>entre nous</u>)

The <u>Mask of Shake</u>speare.[3]

The story would be of <u>Modern</u> date, [for: erased] starting from a curious <u>fact</u>[4], which I should mention in the Preface.

Now I feel pretty certain of getting this book done by, [the:erased] or before the 15th of December – so that it could be published by the <u>20</u>th – If you like the notion of a Christmas Story by me – and like the MS. – I have no doubt we can easily arrange about terms. The pressing part of the business is the Illustration part – <u>that</u> ought to be settled at once if we are to have Illustrations – and I think we ought.

My idea is that a Frontispiece Vignette and Tail Piece would be quite enough – <u>well</u> done – ordinary mediocre work won't do – work by the famous men is only to be had at a high price; and, as far as my knowledge of the great names goes, not even <u>then</u> to be had in time. I should propose that the three illustrations should be done by three young gentlemen who have lately been making an immense stir in the world of Art, and earned the distinction of being attacked by the Times (any notice <u>there</u> is a distinction) – and defended in a special pamphlet by Ruskin[5] – the redoubtable <u>Pre-Raphael-Brotherhood</u>!!

One of these "Brothers" happens to be <u>my</u> brother as well – the other two Millais[6] and Hunt[7] are intimate friends. For <u>my</u> sake as well as their own they would work their best – and do something striking, no matter on how small a scale – I could be constantly at their elbows, and get them to be [erased word] ready as soon as I should. Should you be willing to try them? – and give them <u>some</u> renumeration ? – the amt of which I could easily settle between you and them.

Will you let me know what you think of the scheme – and whether you care to engage in it? I will come to New Burlington Street and speak to you on the Subject, at any time you may appoint. If I ask for an <u>early</u> time, it is only because I must know at once what my position is with respect to you and the book.

In great haste | Very truly yours | W Wilkie Collins

Notes

1. "Wilkie's way of referring to the *Times* suggests the letter was written shortly after the review there on October 23, of his travel book" (Davis, p. 315, n.39).
2. J. Marsh, Bentley's office manager.
3. WC underlines "Mask of Shake" once, and "Mask of Shakesp" twice.
4. WC doubly underlines "act" of "fact".
5. *The Times* attacked Millais and Hunt's work at the Royal Academy on 7 May, 1851: Ruskin replied in two letters to *The Times*, 13 May, 30 May 1851. Cf. Peters, pp. 102–3.
6. John Everett Millais (1829–1896), painter, founding member of the Pre-Raphaelite Brotherhood, and close friend of WC and Charles Collins.
7. William Holman Hunt (1827–1910 *DNB*), painter, founding member of the Pre-Raphaelite Brotherhood, and close friend of WC and Charles Collins.

To Edward Pigott,[1] [Autumn 1851]
MS: Huntington

17, Hanover Terrace | Regents Park | Sunday evening

My dear Edward/

On Friday morning last, an idea came into my head for a <u>Christmas Book</u> – I tell it you, mind, as a <u>profound</u> secret – don't say a word about it to <u>anybody</u>. If I am to put this new notion into shape and form <u>this</u> year, I must work night and day; and I mean to do so.

I want you, if you will, to give me a helping hand in this way.

The pivot on which my projected story turns is the <u>taking a plaster cast from a Bust</u>.[2] I am nothing like so well acquainted with the process of doing this, as I ought to be. I want to know all about <u>moulds</u>, <u>plaster of</u> Paris, and so forth – and I must apply to some sculptor. Gibson[3] is the only sculptor I know at all intimately – and I have not the slightest idea where he is. Can you manage a meeting at your rooms between a friend of the [call]-party, Mr Durham,[4] and me? I would come in the evening – any evening you appoint. Information I must have from somebody – and that at the very earliest opportunity possible.[5]

It would be enough to tell Mr Durham that I am writing something with which mould for plaster casts have to do.

Can you manage what I want, without inconvenience? Pray let me know <u>immediately</u>.

Ever yours | W.W.C.

Where does Mr Durham live? The shortest way would be to go to his Studio if <u>you</u> can & spare the time. – Could you manage a morning visit to him on <u>Tuesday</u>? A quarter of an hours talk would set me all right, and leave me more leisure for writing than an evening interview would. Can we make an appointment for Tuesday <u>morning</u>? or <u>afternoon</u>?

Don't fear <u>my</u> being engaged – I have <u>cut</u> every evening engagement for the present. Could you make it Tuesday evening?

Notes

1. Edward Frederick Smyth Pigott (1824–1895 *DNB*), connected with the *Leader*, close friend of WC with whom he studied at Lincoln Inn.
2. A reference to *Mr Wray's Cash Box*, published by Bentley, 17 December 1851.
3. John Gibson, sculptor (1790–1866: *DNB*), He had helped to arrange the Collins family visit in Rome in 1837.
4. Joseph Durham (1814–1877), prolific sculptor.
5. The last four words are doubly underlined.

To Charles Dickens, 2 November 1851
MS: PM

The Grove | Weston-super-Mare | Novr 2 | 51

Summary:
Delighted at sale of tickets at Bristol[1] and that a second performance is to take place. "A day more or less in the country in the middle of November, is of no consequence." He is "always ready to support the whole weight of the <u>fourth-Act</u>" on his own shoulders.

Note

1. See WC to Pigott, 11 November 1851, n.1.

To Edward Pigott, 11 November 1851
MS: Huntington

Tuesday morning | [11 November 1851]

My dear Edward,
  The performance last night "drew" magnificently. Every place was filled, in a much larger room than the Hanover Square Room. I can't say as much for the <u>quality</u> of the audience, as the quantity. There was immense attention to the Comedy; but the applause was scanty. The Bath people were evidently determined to understand Bulwer's story;[1] and, what is still more extraordinary they <u>did</u> understand it! – and applauded the <u>dénouement</u> vehemently after having missed almost every point in the first three acts. We had to speak so distinctly from the giant size of the room, and its bad capabilities for conveying s<u>poken</u> sounds, that the performance took longer than usual – It began at $\frac{1}{2}$ past seven, and was not over much before $\frac{1}{2}$ past 12! – the farce went well as a matter of course.
  I have no time to write more – We start for the Bath Hotel Clifton, immediately –

Always truly yours | W.W.C.

Note

1. WC played in *Not So Bad as We Seem*, a comedy written for Charles Dickens's company at the Assembly Rooms, Bath, on Monday 10 November 1851.

To Thomas Joseph Henry,[1] [17 November 1851]
MS: Princeton

17, Hanover Terrace | Regents Park | Monday Evening |
[17 November 1851]

Dear Henry,

The affecting national ceremony of calling me to the Bar,[2] will take place on Friday next (the 21st). If you don't mind Lincoln's Inn wine, and have no better engagement, it will give me great pleasure to see you at the Cab Party.

Very faithfully yours | W. Wilkie Collins

Notes

1. Sir Thomas Henry (1807–1876), barrister and magistrate, 1840–76.
2. WC entered Lincoln's Inn on 18 May 1846 and he and Pigott were called to the Bar on 20 November 1851.

To Edward Pigott, [22 November 1851]
MS: Huntington

Saturday morning | 17, Hanover Terrace

My dear Edward,

Look over the proof and see whether it will do for Press now.

What a night! What speeches! What songs! I carried away much clarets and am rather a seedy barrister this morning. I think it must have been the oaths that disagreed with me!

We'll talk it over next week. Today I go to [Price's][1] and return on Monday morning.

Always yours | W. Wilkie Collins

Will you dine with us on Tuesday next at 6, punctually?[2] You will meet a Lincoln Inn man – Charles Otter – just one old friend; and no one else.

Notes

1. Possibly James Price (1804–1879), landscape painter.
2. "unctually" underlined three times.

To Richard Bentley, [6 December 1851]
MS: NYPL (Berg). Extract Davis, pp. 108–9.[1]

17, Hanover Terrace | Saturday morning

My dear Sir,

There are three damnable mistakes in the one advertisement of my Xmas Book, in this morning's Times!

First, the artist's name is spelt is spelt Willais – It ought to be Millais.[2]

Secondly, the work is advertised as Mr Wray's Cash-Book. It ought to be Cash-Box.[3]

Thirdly, after my names comes "Author of Antonini".[4]

I once wrote a book called Antonina. If it means that it's a very bad imitation of the meaning.

I have never yet had a book advertised right for the first time; but this tops everything! Pray get it immediately set right; and give the printer over (in my name) to the devil and all his "angels" at the same time. If we put the public, at the outset, in the way of making mistakes about our title, they will never know it afterwards – Make it a Cash Box (as the ear) to the miserable printer, | and believe me | yours faithfully | W. Wilkie Collins

I have had no proofs yet from Bradbury & Evans. Mr [S] Bentley sends me proofs of the new ed: of Rambles,[5] which I send back to Bearer for press, so no time is lost.

Notes

1. Davis dates the letter 6 December 1851.
2. WC underlines "Millais" three times. Millais' first-ever book illustration was for *Mr Wray's Cash-Box; or The Mask and the Mystery: A Christmas Sketch*, published by Bentley, 17 December 1851. Cf. Gasson.
3. WC underlines "Box" three times.
4. WC underlines the final "i" of "Antonini" twice.
5. Second edition of *Rambles* published 9 January 1852. See Gasson.

To J. Marsh,[1] [14 December 1851][2]
MS: University of Illinois, Urbana.

17, Hanover Terrace | Sunday evening

My dear Sir,

My ten copies of "Mr Wray's Cash Box" did not arrive on Saturday evening. I am obliged to ask you to be particular in sending them by tomorrow (Monday), because I wish to send two copies, on that day, to a certain friend, whose good offices, will be of <u>very great importance</u> to the future of the book.

I think the binding (judging from the copies my brother brought home with him) very neat and pretty. As, however, we have adopted a less elaborate (and therefore I conclude) a <u>cheaper</u> cover than was at first proposed, it now becomes a question on whether we may not spare money enough to indulge, at the eleventh hour,in the luxury of <u>gilt edges</u> – gilt edges certainly make the book look more costly, and more fit for a present; but if they are to lead us into any <u>important</u> additional expense, let us abandon them by all means – We must beware of cutting down our profits from <u>this</u> book! –

And now about the <u>lettering</u> of the Plate – Have the <u>present</u> lettering <u>stamped out</u>, the moment it is possible to do – and substitute my lettering: – "T<u>he New Neckcloth</u>".

I think a title is better than a mere reference to the page. As for the present title, then my two friends to whom I have hitherto shown the book have both asked me, what "Mr Wray's Cash box" has got to do with the picture? – the public will ask the same question I suspect.

Mind the new lettering is kept as <u>faint</u> as the old.

Here, I think, my budget of petitions may fairly end. I would have made them in person; but doctor's orders forbid me to busy myself by going out to look after my affairs on Monday – and on Tuesday I depart for a week of rest and restoration in the country.

Very faithfully yours | W. Wilkie Collins

To | J. Marsh Eqre

Notes

1. Employed by Bentley.
2. Davis' dating, see pp. 109–10 and p. 316, n.7.

To Edward Pigott, 12 January 1852
MS: Huntington

17, Hanover Terrace | January 12th 1852

My dear Edward,

I am about to write down, hap-hazard, as you desired, One or two suggestions for altering the arrangement of the "Leader".

In the first place, starting from the News of the Week, and leaving it (as one of the admirable features of the paper) where it is, and <u>what</u> it is – I think the leading articles in Public Affairs, ought to be placed immediately after the weekly summary. These articles, might, I think, properly follow the summary, because they are in nine cases, out of ten suggested by it – they are the thoughts of thinking men on the news of the week, and might therefore be naturally connected as a matter of arrangement with that news. Thus the most important political part of the paper, would at once present itself to the reader, as he turned over the first leaf.

Literature, the Portfolio, the Drama &c, I would keep where they are, at the end of the paper. Thus the two <u>special</u> [numbers] of the Leader (the Political and the Literary) would have the two prominent places; and the whole space between them would be left free for general contributions and general news, topic after topic following in due order of classification without a single <u>break</u>.

If the "making up" of the paper would allow of it, I should like to see this said "General news" arranged as much as possible under different stated "heads". I will refer to last Saturday's number to explain what I mean,

<u>"The Continent"</u>

Under this head, the letters from Paris – the "continental notes" – and all other foreign intelligence from Europe.

The Colonies[1] – The Cape – Everything about India, New Zealand, Australia &c &c

America[2] –

The Army[3] –

The Navy[4] (the interesting journal you are publishing might come under this head)

Home News[5] – the Ministerial [hubroglio], the Revenue, the case of the Engineers, National School Association – Omnibus grievances.

This sort of heading and arrangement, would keep the same topics together in the same place. I should like to see Law[6], made another division, and more attended to in the Leader. Abstracts of the results of the week's "cases", both civil and criminal, are wanted – They might be the merest abstracts, and still be of use. Important cases might have a pretty <u>stout</u> paragraph now and then accorded to them – And legal anomalies and corruptions might be thoroughly [lashed] from time to time, in leading articles – Legal abuse is a subject on which even your mild Protestant "Church and State" man, can feel and talk furiously. King Public would go with us with all his soul, quote us, praise us, learn us by heart, on such a subject as Law Reform, I find no articles in the Times and the Examiner so highly praised by all parties, and so constantly reproduced second hand in conversation, as the Law Articles. Let us then, from time to time as opportunity offers, <u>politely</u> d–m Magistrates, and spit in the face of Juries. A birch-rod for the backside of old Mother "Justice", is a weapon for which people are beginning to feel a household sympathy. Lay it on, Mr Editor! Lay it on thick!

If we made the <u>Fine Arts</u> a Special Subject, we should penetrate into the Studios. There is no occasion to take up much room with this topic – except in such cases, as the Royal Academy Exhibition. Notices of new prints, for instance, might bring print-selling advertisements. What do you say to a circular, sent round to the print-sellers – to say, that the beginning of a new year, and a change in the Proprietorship, were good opportunites for mentioning some extension which was contemplated in the sphere of the paper. Part of this extension, to be more attention shown to the Fine Arts – notices of New Prints and new Art-Publications, written in the same spirit of impartiality, and with the same due deference to due claims, which have distinguished the literary notices.

Nothing more occurs to me just now. I only throw out these suggestions for your experienced men to use them as you like. Indeed, I should hardly have ventured to write them at all, if <u>you</u> had not asked me. One thing I know – the present <u>arrangement</u> of the paper is objected to, as confused, not mind, by our enemies, but by our <u>friends</u>. You and the Editors are the men to set this right – <u>I</u> only jog your elbows to try and make you do it.

I hope you will be able to make out this miserable letter. I write it, under the benign influence of gin and water.

Ever yours | W. Wilkie Collins

I think I shall be able to do something amusing for you, about the Pre-Raphaelites painting School in the country. John Millais (entre nous) is going to lend me his diary – He is cut up in last week's Athenaeum, along with me – They have [poked] the Christmas Book into their "Library Table", and mauled it about,[7] rather more maliciously than usual. The fiend receive their souls therefore!

Notes

1. This is doubly underlined.
2. *Ibid.*
3. *Ibid.*
4. *Ibid.*
5. *Ibid.*
6. This is doubly underlined.
7. The *Athenaeum*, 10 January 1852, p. 50, damned W.C.'s "Christmas Book", *Mr Wray's Cash-Box* published 17 December 1851 "with faint praise" (Davis, p. 112).

To Mrs H. Collins, [13 February 1852]

MS: Private Possession

Adelphi Hotel Liverpool | Friday morning

Summary:
"Our triumph in Manchester was worth all our other triumphs put together. Two thousand, seven hundred people composed our audience – and such an audience! They never missed a single 'point' in the play[1] – and applauded incessantly. My part, you will be glad to hear, was played without a single mistake – and played so as to produce some very warm congratulations from my Manager, and indeed from the whole company. The dress and wig made me (everybody said) look about <u>sixteen</u>. The first sight of the audience, when I peeped at them through the curtain ... was something sublime – nothing but faces from the <u>floor</u> to the <u>ceiling</u>. I did not feel in the slightest degree nervous, and was not 'thrown off my balance' by a round of applause which greeted my first appearance on the stage. When the curtain fell on Dickens and your dutiful son, at the end of the first act, the audience were all rolling about like a great sea, and roaring with laughter at the tops of their voices."

Charles Dickens made a speech at the end. I shall never forget the sight of the audience just as he spoke the last word – they were all on their legs; the women waving their handkerchiefs, and the men their hats, with roar after roar of applause, continuing for some minutes after the curtain had fallen –

Yesterday we dined <u>here</u>, with the Mayor. A real banquet in rooms in the most magnificent Hall – Sixty or seventy people invited to meet us – capital speeches made by Dickens and Charles Knight ... Tonight we act here for the first time, ... I shall most probably return on Sunday evening, when I hope I shall find you getting quite well again."

Note

1. WC performed the role of Shadowly Softhead in *Not So Bad As We Seem*. For Dickens' account of these proceedings, see Dickens to Mrs Charles Dickens, 13 February 1852: Dickens, *Letters*,VI, 598 and n.6.

To Edward Pigott, [16 February 1852]
MS: Huntington

17, Hanover Terrace | Monday evening

My dear Edward/

I send you the 3rd "Letter".[1] If you <u>can</u> let me see a proof of it, pray send me one. You shall have it back by return of post.

The paper looks admirably in its new <u>dress</u>[2] – the printing is really beautiful.

I don't see the distinction you mention, between the Portfolio part of the Leader and the other parts, and, if I did, I would not take advantage of it. I refuse my name <u>in principle</u>; and am by no means desirous of seeing it appear <u>under protest</u>, in a part of the newspaper specially set apart for protesting contributors! I always give it unreservedly – or I don't give it all.

As to what is "irreligious" or what is "heterodoxy", or what is the "immensity" of the distance between them, you and I differ; and it is useless to broach the subject. Nothing will ever persuade me that a system which permits the introduction of the private religious, or irreligious, or heterodoxical opinions of contributors to a newspaper into the articles on politics or general news which they write for it, is a wise or good system – either in itself, or in its effect on the various writers whom you employ. It is for this reason <u>only</u> that I don't desire to be "one of you" – simply because a common respect for my own religious convictions prevents me from wishing to ——— but <u>writing</u> on this subject is of no use. I hate controversies on paper, almost more than I hate controversies in talk – I'll explain myself as fully as you desire, when we next meet; and there's an end of it!

We have had a wonderful theatrical campaign. Even a Bristol audience is beaten in enthusiasm by the audiences of Manchester and Liverpool. They even laughed at a "[dimidum] me!"[3] We filled the Philharmonic Hall in Liverpool two nights following – Jenny Lind in the height of her vogue in the provinces was afraid to try what we have accomplished. <u>King Public</u> is a good king for Literature and Art!

affectionately yours | W.W.C

If you have no time to send me the proof, pray look over the article sharply as soon as it gets into the office.[4]

Notes

1. "Magnetic Evening at Home. Letter III – To G. H. Lewes", *The Leader* III; 100 (21 February 1852), 183–4.
2. By January 1852 Pigott was exercising full editorial control over *The Leader*.

3. Collins and Dickens toured Bath, Bristol, Manchester, and Liverpool with *Not So Bad as We Seem* at the beginning of 1852. For newspaper reviews of Collins's performance see Dickens, *Letters*, VI, 598 n.4.
4. This is written in the margin of the first leaf of the letter.

To Edward Pigott, [January–February 1852]

MS: Huntington

17, Hanover Terrace | Monday evening

My dear Edward/

Saturday evening, is the only free evening that I have in the week – Can you get [orders] for the <u>Marionettes</u>[1] on that occasion? I will call on you at the Office, at,[2] or <u>near</u>, 5 o'clock; and we will dine together. I shall not forget about Bentley; and, moreover, I have one or two things to say to you (quite <u>privately</u>) about certain doctrines of "<u>Leader</u>" <u>religio</u>n, which I wish to draw your attention to, [erased word] Very seriously – and which I ought to have mentioned to you long before –

ever yours | W. Wilkie Collins

If you would rather I called on you at your lodgings on Saturday, let me know.

My mother is better, thank you.

Notes

1. The Royal Marionette Theatre opened 12 January 1852 (cf. Dickens, *Letters*, VI, 592).
2. Doubly underlined.

To Edward Pigott, [20 February 1852]

MS: Huntington. Published K. Lawrence, "The Religion of Wilkie Collins: Three Unpublished Documents", *Huntington Library Quarterly* 52 (1989), pp. 394–6.

<u>Private</u> | 17, Hanover Terrace | Friday

My dear Edward,

You have not quite hit what I was "driving at", in my last letter. You seem to think that I wish to "impose restraint upon your absolute freedom of thought in Religion" – I want to do nothing of the kind; but I want to ask you what business Religion has in a newspaper, at all?

I say nothing about the rhymes on Acquinas – I may have my opinion about the necessity of connecting a belief in the ultimate salvation of the whole human race with a belief in the ultimate salvation of the devil – I say nothing about your friends' verses, but this: – They have no business in a newspaper. Admitting that the ultimate destiny of Satan is a useful and interesting subject for Christians to speculate on – how is that subject (made doubly grave by being coupled with Our Saviour's Name) presented to your readers? – "Cheek by jowl" with an article on puppets. Can any good be done, any purpose worth a farthing achieved, by such an anomalous coupling of the sacred and the profane – of "M" on Acquinas's aspirations for the salvation of the Devil; with "Vivian" on the history of Marionettes? Yet this animal you <u>must</u> have, if you introduce Religion into a newspaper.

It is not your freedom of religious thought that I wish to object to; but your license of religious expression – a license which is, to <u>me</u>, utterly abhorrent. I have never seen any religious <u>thought</u> in the paper – you have made your confession of political faith (and I agree in it, as you know) – but you have made no confession of religious faith. If you are to take a leading position in Religion as well as in Politics, let us know what your religion is, just as you have let us know what your politics are – What does the Leader believe in, and what does it disbelieve in? – Readers have a right to ask <u>that</u> question if a Journal which starts for the discussion of <u>religious</u> subjects, as well as political. Surely your mission is to <u>teach</u>, as well as to <u>inquire</u>. Surely you ought to teach us something definite in religion, just as you teach us something in politics, if you <u>must</u> have this "freedom of religious thought"? Why not let Mr Holyoake[1] write a series of articles on the advantages of Atheism as a creed? – his convictions have been honestly arrived at, miserable and melancholy as they are to think of.

But I repeat it, <u>religion</u> itself; is not a subject for the columns of a newspaper – <u>religious politics</u> (such as even described in that admirable article on the "Church in Distress") are fair game, if you please.

I honestly believe that if anything can prevent the Leader from achieving the great success which it bids fair to attain to – it will be the suicidal policy (as I think) of allowing the individual scepticisms of the different writers to appear in their articles on the affairs of the day. This is a course that has never been followed in any other system of political journalism that I am acquainted with. It tends to disunite contributors, who might otherwise be perfectly united. For instance, I go with you, in politics – I go with you (saving one or two exceptional cases) in social matters – I go with you in your judgment on Literature, but in regard to your mixing up of the name of Jesus Christ with the current politics of the day, I am against you – against you with all my heart and soul, I will expose and condemn as heartily as any of you the corruptions and abuses of Church Politics, as the inventions of man – but if one of the things you understand by "freedom of religious thought" be the freedom of mingling the Saviour's name with the politics of the day – I protest against that "freedom" as something irredeemably bad in itself; and utterly useless for any good purpose whatever.

Surely there is some difference between the "<u>orthodoxy</u>" which would keep you within the limit of this or that particular creed; of this or that particular church or community, and the "orthodoxy" which simply believes Our Saviour's name to be something too sacred for introduction into articles on the political squabbles and difficulties of the day.

You will ask, what does all this tend to? I will tell you, candidly. The lines on "Acquinas" and Thornton Hunt's "Political Letter" are written in a tone and spirit which I cannot subscribe to. Your letter, and the fact that these articles appear at a new era of the paper, show that the tone of which I complain will be continued as the established tone of the Leader literature, on religious matters. With that tone I cannot agree – it outrages my own convictions – and for this reason – <u>and this only</u> – I must beg that my name may never be appended to any future articles I may write for the Portfolio – to the story, for instance, of which you were talking the last time I saw you. If my name appears in the paper, the natural inference must be that I subscribe to the religious tone of Thornton Hunt's letter – that I am one of you in religion, as well as in politics. I make no claim to orthodoxy; but I dread such an inference as this – dread it <u>concientiously</u> – not from fear of "What the world will say".

What I mention here about my name does not apply in my reasons for keeping the Magnetic Letters anonymous. <u>They</u> would have been anonymous whenever I had sent them for publication.[2]

If with this restriction, you still wish to employ my pen – it is at your service. I will wish for y<u>ou</u>, my very best – I will give <u>you</u> all I fairly have to give of brains and time – I will give <u>your</u> work precedence over any other work any other man may ask me to do – but I will <u>not</u> give you my name, because I will not by so doing even <u>seem</u> to give in my adherence to the individual religious opinions which you allow your contributors to express in their political or literary articles. It might seem (to strangers) no very creditable way of "sticking to my principles" to continue writing in a paper, after I have in these [reactions] declined letting my name appear publickly <u>as one</u> of the contributors. You will know that I consider this inconsistency as a matter of friendship – from this wish to help you at a critical period – if I can be of help, <u>I</u> have no wish to withdraw from the paper, till it is well "set on its legs", and your interests are secure. I am neither a Protestant, a Catholic – or a Dissenter – I do not desire to discuss this [for: erased] or that particular creed; but I believe Jesus Christ to be the son of God; and believing that, I think it a blasphemy to use his name, as it is used in "Acquinas", and in the letter signed "Thornton Hunt".

I write these lines hastily, but candidly, and after some consideration. I ought to have expressed to you what I have now said, ere this; but a feeling of restraint which I cannot account for – and which I ought to have known you better than to have indulged – kept me silent. I thought I would wait, and see how this paper went on, how it started at its new era, before I spoke to you. This was uncandid and wrong – I am sorry for it – and I hope I have in some measure atoned for it, by the frankness with which I have spoken out, now.

But one thing more remains for me to say. The course I have taken is <u>my own course</u> – no one has prompted me to it – no one has attempted to give me any advice. I act under the dictates of my own opinion – <u>only</u> my own.

Yours affectionately | W. Wilkie Collins

To | E. F. Smyth Pigott Esqre

Notes

1. George Jacob Holyoake (1817–1906: *DNB*), atheist and radical.
2. "Wilkie ... wrote for *The Leader* a series of letters on the fashionable subjects of experiments in hypnotism and clairvoyance, 'Magnetic Evenings at Home', which appeared from January to April 1852 ... The letters ... were addressed to Lewes" (Peters, p. 109). Thornton Hunt (1810–1873: *DNB*) played a prominent part in the founding of *The Leader*: cf. K.H. Beetz "Wilkie Collins and *The Leader, Victorian Periodicals Review*, 15 (Spring 1982), 20–9; K. Lawrence "The Religion of Wilkie Collins: Three Unpublished Documents"; *The Huntington Library Quarterly*, 52 (1989), 389–402.

To Mrs Harriet Collins, [12 May 1852]
MS: PM

Hen and Chickens Hotel | (This is the true name!) | Birmingham

My dear Mother,

A rainy morning, and a little spare time give me an opportunity of reporting progress. We expected little from the Shrewsbury audience, and were most agreeably disappointed. More intelligent and appreciative people we have never acted to – The morning after the Play, we all breakfasted with Mr Clement[1], [the: erased] the gentleman who [erased word] took on himself the whole arrangement of the acting – A glorious old house – a magnificent view from the terrace – a grand champagne breakfast, and a roomful of Shrewsbury Ladies and Gentlemen [erased word] to receive us. What with the Champagne, and the compliments, and the Ladies breakfasting in gorgeous bonnets and shawls, I felt as if I had been at a wedding, by the time we started from Shrewsbury for this place. Here we found the ladies – and a very jovial and delightfully <u>ungenteel</u> evening we all had last night. Half the members of the Guild Company turned out, under "pressure of circumstances" to be very expert and astounding conjurors. Mr Coote[2] (the Duke of Devonshire's band-master) who is with us, accompanied on the piano-forte – in what, of all the successful impromptu parties that ever were, this [has: erased] was the most successful.

Tonight our first performance at Birmingham takes place – tomorrow the second,[3] – and, after that, on Friday morning, we go to Stratford on Avon and Kenilworth. I cannot say yet, what time we shall get back on Saturday – I dare say it might be by dinner time; but, if not, don't wait for me, and leave the door on the latch, when you go to bed. However, I will write again, and tell you something more definite before Saturday. With love to Charley

| ever yours | W.W.C.

Notes

1. William John Clement (1804–1870), surgeon: see Dickens, *Letters*, VI, 484, n.1. WC was touring with Dickens and the Guild Company performing Bulwer Lytton's *Not So Bad as We Seem*.
2. Charles Coote (1807–1879), musician and composer, the Duke of Devonshire's pianist: cf. *ibid.*, VI, 493, n.6.
3. For the contemporary reception of their performances at Shrewsbury and Birmingham see *ibid.*, VI, 673, n.2.

To Mrs Harriet Collins, [7 July 1852]
MS: PM

17, Hanover Terrace | Wednesday –

Summary:
Henry Bullar dined and asked her to go there. Mrs Bullar (who is now at Basset) would write. There is mail for her and Charley. "George Thompson is in town, and dines here today with Charles Ward." His wife is "still cheerfully waiting to <u>answer the bell when Nature rings</u>. The picture from Mr Thompsons (York Terrace) has come for Charley." He "got up this morning at a quarter to ten. I gave 'chops' a thrashing at half past, for trying to steal milk off the breakfast table."

To Mrs Harriet Collins, [25 August 1852]
MS: PM

Royal Hotel | Derby | Wednesday morning

Summary:
WC's "throat is very much better". Hardly feels the ulcer at all. "Not a good audience at Nottingham – except for the Farce". The parsons have been preaching against them. One "solemnly adjured his flock, all through last Sunday evening's services, not to compromise their salvation by entering" their Theatre. However, they have "a very fair audience of sinners and shall make money in spite of the saints".[1]

Note

1. Dickens plays down the opposition they met: cf. Dickens, *Letters*, VI, 745 and n.8.

To Mrs Harriet Collins, 1 September 1852
MS: PM

Royal Hotel | Manchester | 1st September 1852

Summary:
WC has "ten minutes before Rehearsal". His sore throat is "smooth again". "The Comedy has been brilliantly successful everywhere. Tonight we try the two new Plays."[1] The kindness of the Miss Brandlings during his stay at Newcastle was "beyond all acknowledgement. The eldest is the cleverest and the most agreeable woman I think I ever met with – all the elegance and vivacity of a Frenchwoman – and all the sincerity and warmhearted-ness of an Englishwoman. How it is she has never been married, is beyond all imagination." He goes to stay with Dickens at Dover, the week following.

Note

1. i.e., Charles Mathews' [(1803–1878: *DNB*), theatrical manager], *Used Up* and Dickens' and Mark Lemon's [(1809–1870: *DNB*), journalist, dramatist, actor], *Mr Nightingale's Diary*.

To Mrs Harriet Collins [9 September 1852]
MS: PM

10, Camden Crescent | Dover | Thursday

My dear Mother,

Forward all my letters to "care of Charles Dickens Esqre" at the above address. We received the kindest and heartiest welcome here. The house fronts the sea and is within a minute's walk of bath and bathing machines. I have had my first dip today, and feel all the better for it.

The sea air acts on me as if it was all distilled from laudanum. I was actually glad to go to bed last night at a $\frac{1}{4}$ past 10! We breakfast at 10 minutes past eight – after breakfast Dickens goes into his study, and is not visible again till two, when he is available for every pleasant social purpose that can be imagined, for the rest of the [erased word] day. Dinner at $\frac{1}{2}$ past 5 – and bed between 10 and eleven – Such is the life here – as pleasant a life by the seaside as it is possible to lead.

I shall get to work tomorrow, and finish and correct my book in a week, I hope. If good ideas are as infectious as bad, the end of the novel – written in this house – ought to be the best part of it.[1] Dickens anticipates a fortnight of the very hardest work to make up on our last trip. The visitors here are getting used to him now. But when he first came, they used to wait to waylay him every morning – and have a good long stare at the "Great man" as he went to his bath!

Write and tell me any news there is, and how Charley is going on. I am getting money here, as well as health, a six shilling "pool" passed into my fortunate pocket last night.

Affectionately yours | W. Wilkie Collins

Note

1. WC was correcting *Basil* and Dickens writing *Bleak House.*

To Mrs Harriet Collins, [16 September 1852]
MS: PM

10, Camden Crescent | Dover | Thursday morning

My dear Mother,

I have fixed Saturday next as the Day of my return – the hour I can't certainly inform you about. If I [return: erased] travel by the express, I shall not start till $\frac{1}{2}$ past 7 in the evening – and not get to Hanover Terrace till 11 o'clock at night. At any rate, don't wait dinner for me, and leave the door on the latch when you go to bed.

My excellent friends here have had an opportunity afforded them of showing me [erased word] even more than their usual kindness, by a bad attack of ear-ache and face-ache; which I suffered from pretty acutely all last Monday and Tuesday. Mrs Dickens's remedies – a little care – and a liniment from the doctor's, have set me up again today – I feel no pain, and am going for a walk in the sunshine.

Tell Ward, if you see him before Saturday, that I have no other excuse for not writing to him again, but excessive laziness. I hope he will accept the candour of my confession, as some mitigation of my epistolary short-comings.

You will have a glorious number of "Bleak House", on the last day of the month. Dickens read us the two first chapters as soon as he had finished them – speaking the dialogue of each character, as dramatically as if he was acting [it: erased] his own personages; and making his audience laugh and cry with equal fervour and equal sincerity. You will find a wonderful description of a death – terribly true and genuinely pathetic – [word erased] old Mr Turveydrop, too, is better than ever – Altogether, a famous number –

I have written to [Fribourg] and Treyer to send me some snuff, by way of securing a hearty welcome for my <u>nose</u>, on my return. Will you put it very tenderly into my Jar, as soon as it comes?

With love to Charley

Yours affectionately | W. Wilkie Collins

To Charles Ward, 16 September 1852
MS: Harrowby Mss Trust

10, Camden Crescent | Dover | September 16th 1852

My dear Ward,

In bed at $\frac{1}{2}$ past 10 – up at 7 – ten mile walk everyday – What do you think of that for W. W. C., of late-hours-and-no-exercise – notoriety? I am in a state of the rudest health and hardest fat, already!

Oh the "Dook" the "Dook"! How they <u>will</u> write about him! How they <u>have</u> written about him already! What sort of funeral will it be I wonder? Military I suppose – If they don't keep it simple, and free from all the damnable tomfooleries of plumes, black velvet, and undertakers – it will be a public failure with all of the public who are worth making an impression on –

I have done the book – <u>really</u> done it, down to writing the memorable word ["End"] – In a week more, I shall more likely be back to put the Mss in [to] Bentley's hands. [Novel] 2, will run to 350 pages, unless they print close.[1]

The walks about this place are really lovely, and more varied than any other walks by the sea side that I can remember anywhere. <u>Inland</u>, you get to copses, fields, lanes, downs, villages – scenery, in short, that looks as if it might be a hundred miles away from the coast. The views along the cliffs. I need say nothing about – they, as you may imagine, are all magnificent. We are going to the ruined monastery of S<u>t Radegonde</u>, this morning. What a place for <u>you</u> to wreak your antiquarian frenzy on!

The lunch bell has just rung – So I have my time to send my remembrance to Jane – to hope all the children are well – and to "undersign" myself

Ever truly yours | W. Wilkie Collins

Note

1. WC finished *Basil* on 15 September 1852 and delivered it to Bentley on 1 October 1852, who published it in 3 vols, of 300, 304, 302 pages respectively on 16 November 1852. The novel is dedicated to Charles Ward.

To Mrs Harriet Collins, [24 September 1852]
MS: PM

10, Camden Crescent | Dover | Friday night

Summary:
Dickens has persuaded him to stay till Wednesday next. They "have been to Canterbury today – walk there (15 miles) – back in a carriage, Cathedral white and brilliant against the brightest of blue skies – ... I don't know what I am writing about, I am so sleepy." Is "certain to be back on Wednesday".

To Edward Pigott, 25 June 1853
MS: Huntington

17, Hanover Terrace | Saturday 25th June

Summary:
It is months since he heard from him. Is he quite recovered? Write or drop in for dinner. He is much better. But "not strong enough to get to do more than 'toddle' out for half an hour at a time with a stick". His "illness and long confinement have muddled my brains dreadfully – I am still in very bad trim for anything that deserves the name of work."

To Mrs Harriet Collins, [7 July 1853]
MS: PM[1]

17, [Hendon Terrace] | Maidenhead | Thursday morning |
10 minutes to 9

Summary:

Has "begun the great reformation. Observe the hour above." He is "dressed, and <u>waiting</u> for the breakfast bell". He has "the bedroom which looks into the garden, with a literary table". He feels better already: "I take no beer and I stop short of his three glasses of wine." Has nothing more to say – "being too hungry for reflecting about anything".

Note

1. Envelope postmarked "MAIDENHEAD | JY 7 | 1853".

To Mrs Harriet Collins, 29 July 1853
MS: PM

Chateau des Molineaux | Rue Beaurepaire | Boulogne sur Mer |
July 29th 1853

Summary:

Got to Boulogne yesterday in two hours and a half, "rolling and pitching all the way". The company with about three exceptions were all sick the whole way across. "As usual, I escaped and enjoyed the voyage immensely." Mr & Mrs Dickens, Miss Hogarth, and Mr & Mrs Leech were all on the Quay when he arrived. "The house is full of quaint lively little rooms ... The Garden includes a Swiss Cottage, a rustic Chapel and altar, a Miniature Chateau (called the 'Chateau de Tom Pouce') and a 'Pavilion' near the house, which I inhabit." His "bedroom door opens at once into the garden". Tomorrow they go to Amiens and Beauvais. "Dickens will go to work again on Monday morning, and I shall follow his example. I have just read the new number of Bleak House, which contains ... some of the finest passages he has ever written. The better and nobler parts of Sir Leicester Dedlock's character are brought out with such pathos, delicacy, and truth to nature, as no other living writer has ever rivalled, or even approached in my opinion."

To George Bentley,[1] 6 August 1853
MS: NYPL (Berg)

Chateau des Molineaux | Rue Beaurepaire | Boulogne sur Mer |
6ᵗʰ August 1853

My dear Sir,

Your letter has followed me to this place, where I am rapidly getting well again as ever under the hospitable roof of Mr Dickens, who has been staying at Boulogne with his family for some little time past. I have fixed no time yet for my return to London; but I shall most likely be back in the course of next month and shall not fail to make a call in New Burlington Street as soon as I get home.

In the meantime, in case the project to which you allude should not be of a nature to admit of delay, I can only assure you that if you will write to me on the subject, at this place, I shall be happy to give it my best consideration, and to let you know the result as early as possible.

If I had had any personal experience of the clumsy jugglery which goes under the name of "Spirit Rapping", I should be very glad to assist in exposing it (if it has not already been exposed enough) in the Miscellany[2]— but I have never attended a "Séance", or exhibition of this last new Spirit of the Age, and I cannot write as I should write on that subject, or indeed any other, without some personal knowledge to draw from. However, I hope to be of some use to you later in the year. I am going to Italy in October, to review as many of my old local experiences as I can during a holiday of between two and three months. Any picturesque materials for short articles which I may pick up on my way, I shall be very glad to give you the refusal of for the Magazine.

I hope you get my card in return for the cards you sent me. The envelope was addressed to New Burlington Street. It is rather late, I am afraid, to offer you my best congratulations on your marriage; but I send them nevertheless, trusting that you will not think them the less hearty and sincere because they have been delayed.

With best remembrances to all the members of your family

Believe me | My dear Sir | Very faithfully yours | W. Wilkie Collins

I corrected the MSs of the Story adapted from the French (which I mentioned to you some time since as well fitted for the Miscellany) before I left London. It will be sent to you as soon as the author has made a fair copy from the corrected pages.

Notes

1. George Bentley (1828–1895), publisher, son of Richard Bentley.
2. *Bentley's Miscellany*, founded by Richard Bentley, to which WC contributed at least nine pieces.

To Charles Collins, 12 August 1853
MS: PM

Chateau des Moulineaux | Rue Beaurepaire | Boulogne sur mer |
August 12th 1853

My dear Charley,[1]

I have not much to write about, but I write [erasure] nevertheless for the sake of answering your letter. I scrawled a wild account of our visit to Amiens and sent it to Ward, telling him to forward it [erasure] to you, by way of sending you fresh news to me. Did he do so? We had no time for Beauvais. I don't believe in anything finer in the world than Amiens – which is said <u>in the</u> guide book to be the better of the two Cathedrals.

Since our little trip we have not left Boulogne. Dickens has been, and is still, hard at work; and I am hardly less industrious in my smaller way. We are to have great festivities, and rejoicings here the week after next, in honour of the completion of Bleak House. The publishers of the book, the illustrator, Forster, Lemon, and others are coming here. The grandest dinner is to be given that Boulogne can produce, and a picnic and a trip to Abbeville (to see the Cathedral [erasure]) are in contemplation to follow.

In the meantime, we content ourselves with such discussion after work as Boulogne affords. All Fairs are dull, but there is the dullest fair [erasure] now going on near us that I ever looked at. No shows or dancing – nothing but booths full of horribly – fragile merchandise – two "roundabouts" circling slowly, always to the same organ tune – and hosts of the worst-looking English people, staring about them, that our native country can possibly produce.

The Fêtes are much better. We have had plenty of Town Fêtes and country Fêtes, like those in and around Paris – and one <u>Fête des Enfans</u>, the prettiest and best of all. It began at $\frac{1}{2}$ past 3 and ended at twelve at night – and the admission was <u>five pence</u>!!![2] For this entrance fee we had provided an orchestra of 40 performers – thousands of variegated lamps to be lit as it grew dark – statues – flowers – amusements of every kind – racing in sacks, greased poles. Donkey races, balloons, fireworks and a grand lottery – The children danced on the grass with the grown people sitting round them – the trees were lighted with festoons of lamps – and round the palings outside, the general public who couldn't pay half a franc had a capital view of the proceedings within.

This Fête (which we might do [well] to imitate in England, if our stupid dignity would only let us) was set up by a Benevolent Society, the members of which are the briskest and pleasantest working doers of good actions, I ever met with. They were all employed with scarfs round their arms in directing the amusements of the Fête, the profits of which were to be given to the poor. One fat member who never ceased exerting himself, and welcoming everybody till he was in a profuse perspiration of public hospitality early in the afternoon – stood at the entrance as we went out at ten o'clock, bowing, smiling, pulling off his hat, and thanking us all [erasure] for having honoured the Society with [erased word] our company, as fresh and unwearied to the last, as if he had been a new man sent on duty – for the occasion.

There is a curious votive Chapel here – like a methodist meeting house outside – but different enough within. From the [erased word] ceiling hangs a perfect fleet of models of ships in an elaborate state of rigging, all presented by fishermen who have escaped drowning when their [erased word] boats have been out on stormy nights. Each man too presents a hideous coloured print of a saint or martyr – hundreds of which are stuck on the walls, in grimy little wooden frames. The smell in the place, produced by the mingling fumes of multitudes of burning wax tapers, and the fishy exhalations from the garments of worshipping women from the coast, was too much for my acute organ of smell, and drove me out into the fresh air before I had looked at half the sacred Roman Catholic frippery with which the inside of the chapel is decorated from floor to ceiling.

How is your leg? And is mother getting well and strong again? Ask her with my best love, how she got on in the great negotiation for [erasure] Peace, which she was about to attempt in the morning when I left home between those hostile clans – the Wards of Repton Park and the Wards of Fitzroy Square? Talking of hostility reminds me of marriage, and that of John Sleigh.[3] Send him my congratulations, and say I wish him long life and loads of children. He is one of those fresh-complexioned men with a low forehead and a sweet character, who always takes kindly to the institution of marriage. He will get domestic happiness, a large paunch, and a numerous family in the enjoyment of which advantages he will live respected and die happy. And there is an end for the respect of my friend Sleigh.

I must leave off and dress. We are going to dine today with Frank Stone,[4] who is here with all his family – in a comfortable country home at the top of a hill.

With love to Mother and best regards to Miss Otter

Ever affectionately yours | W. Wilkie Collins

The weather is lovely – glorious sunshine and cool air. I go on very well, except my legs, which are not as strong yet as they ought to be.

Notes

1. Above the salutation, WC writes "Thank you for forwarding the letters. They both wanted answers."

2. "ive pen" of "five pence" underlined twice.
3. Unable to identify.
4. Frank Stone (1800–1859), painter. See Dickens, *Letters*, VII, 100, n.2.

To Mrs Harriet Collins, 1 September 1853
MS: PM

Chateau des Moulineaux | Rue Beaurepaire | September 1st 1853

My dear Mother,

The festivities of our week of servicing are all over, and the guests all gone, except Wills[1] and his wife. We stuck to our gaieties in defiance of the incessant rain that tried to quench them – actually lunching one day in a high road in a heavy shower. I was <u>in the carriage</u>, Dickens and Miss Hogarth were walking, and our visitors and the young ladies were on horseback – the Stones[2] bringing up the procession with their carriage full, in the rear. We blocked up the whole road, and enjoyed our picnic in the rain, as much as you enjoyed yours in the sunshine. Marvellous to state nobody came down to breakfast the next morning with a bad cold.

"The grand-dinner" (which Dickens had pledged himself should be the best that Boulogne could supply) was a banquet to make a classical epicure's mouth water. The table was charming decorated with flowers, and a nosegay was placed by each guest's napkin. As for the dishes, I say nothing; having preserved my Bill of fare, as a memorable document for my family to peruse when I come home. Talking of dinners Miss Coutts has been here on her way to Auvergne. She and her "companion" and her "companion's" husband, and Sir James Kay Shuttleworth[3], who is travelling with them, all dined here; and we all dined [two erased words] with them at their Hotel the day after. Miss Coutts (if she did not possess a farthing) [erased word] I should write, and think, the same of her[,] is really, and not conventionally, a very "charming person" – I never saw a more gentle and winning manner than hers.

I have just heard some news which will shorten my letter, by changing my plans here. I shall be back earlier than I expected, to make my preparations for an Italian Tour. An important meeting of the Guild is arranged for Friday the 9th. Dickens will leave for London on Tuesday the 6th. Wills and his wife go also on that day; and I shall join the party. Instead of starting for Italy on the 20th of October, we shall start on the 10th. What day I shall return here, [several heavily erased words] before we set out on our journey, I don't know <u>yet</u>. But I think I can say safely that (wind and weather permitting) I shall be in Hanover Terrace on the evening of Tuesday the 6th – So if you and Charley are not in town then, you can write to the servants to tell them of my proposed arrival. If I am not home before their usual time of going to bed, they need not expect me; for the Train is due in London at a quarter past six P.M.

Under any circumstances I must have returned to Town – not only on on account of my passport and money – but also on account of Bentley – From whom I have had a letter about my new book, which will oblige me to settle matters about publication with him in New Burlington Street. I have not even done the 2nd volume[4] yet; but he has a new project for issuing his [future: erased] publications; and wishes to make a bargain with me for the future (that is, the winter) in reference to it, before he completes his plans and makes them public.

Shall you be back in London on the 6th or away at the Langton's or still at Miss Otter's? I should like to know your arrangements, [erased word] when I get back. [two erased words] Don't disturb them on my account, but only let me know what they are.

With love to Charley believe me | Ever affectionately yours | W. Wilkie Collins

I have all sorts of kind invitations here but can't settle, till I've seen Bentley.

Notes

1. William Henry Wills (1810–1880), manager and joint proprietor of *Household Words* and *All the Year Round*.
2. Frank Stone and probably his wife Elizabeth (cf. Dickens, *Letters*, VII, 69, n.5).
3. Angela Georgina Burdett Coutts (1814–1906), friend of Dickens who shared his philanthropic work. She inherited the controlling shares in Coutts & Co., where WC and Dickens had accounts. See Dickens, *Letters* I, 559, n. and Edna Healey: *Coutts and Co. 1692–1992: the Portrait of a Private Bank*, (1992). Sir James Kay-Shuttleworth (1804–1877), aducational reformer.
4. i.e. of *Hide and Seek*.

To Mrs Harriet Collins, [9 October 1853]
MS: Private Possession

Sunday morning | Boulogne

Summary:
They hope to be at Lausanne in a week. "We start for Pons at $\frac{1}{2}$ past 12, tomorrow, dine with Miss Coutts on Tuesday, leave Pons on Wednesday morning by railway for Strasbourg" then they go by rail to Basle, and carriage to Lausanne, "a three days drive".

"Do you remember, or did you ever know, a certain <u>Angus Fletcher</u>?[1] He dined here yesterday – a harmless madman, who was much with Dickens at Genoa, and began life as a sculptor. He knew Wilkie and my father well.

Mark Lemon is coming today to dine, and see us off on Monday. Dickens's new courier is a German, young" who "seems to know his business well".[2]

Notes

1. Angus Fletcher (1799–1862), sculptor, see Dickens, *Letters*, I, 514.
2. Dickens wrote to Mrs Charles Dickens, 13 October 1853: "So far, Edward has done very well indeed!" (*Letters*, VII, 163).

To Mrs Harriet Collins, 16 October 1853
MS: PM

Lausanne | 16th October <u>1853</u>

My dear Mother,

Today is Sunday – we only arrived late last night – and this is a Protestant place, so I can't tell whether there is any letter from you, [till: erased] at the Office, till tomorrow. In the meantime, I take this opportunity of writing home, in the hope that good news is in store for me [erased word] – Monday – from you and Charley.

To begin at the beginning: – We started from Boulogne on Monday last, as we had arranged – and found Paris literally overflowing with English travellers, and altered (in the <u>Tuileries</u> quarter) past all recognition by the commencement of a magnificent new Street, running from the Orlace to the Hotel de Ville![1] Old houses were being demolished, and new houses were [springing] up, over nearly a mile of space in the heart of Paris. The Street will be the broadest, longest, and grandest in the world, when it is finished. We dined in the evening with Miss Coutts, and met a certain [foreign: erased] French Prince, whose name I have forgotten, but who arranged our plans for getting into Italy, by telling us that we were liable to be turned back if we attempted to enter the Austrian dominions from Switzerland, because "political reasons" made these said Austrians suspicious of all travellers entering their part of the country from a Republic which is plentifully stretched, in this and the neighbouring Cantons, with liberal refugees. The only effect of the warning thus given to us will be to prevent our crossing the Simplon and to make us choose the St Gothard, or St Bernard Passes instead – by either of which routes we can enter Italy from the Sardinian dominions instead of the [Swiss].[2]

On Wednesday morning we left Paris for Strasbourg, by the best railway I ever travelled on – delightful carriages, excellent punctuality, admirable speed. The journey lasted over ten hours; but none of us were in the least tired by it. Thursday morning was spent in getting through the "sights" of Strasbourg. The oddest is certainly the famous <u>Clock</u> which exhibits a fantastic puppet show, every time 12 oClock strikes. Our Saviour is in a niche above the dial. At the first stroke, a procession of the twelve Apostles issues from a door and passes before him; each of the twelve stopping to receive his benediction – then passing out again at an opposite door of exit. St Peter's cock (big enough to eat-up fifty St Peters) flaps his wings, and crows mechanically three times, during the ceremony – the machinery in the inside of this Brobdinag bird creaking and rattling audibly while the automation goes through its performance. A cherub shakes an hourglass, and [our Saviour: erased] the puppet representing our Saviour, waves its hand to the right, and left, in token of general benediction – and this closes the exhibition of the clock, which is actually displayed in³ the magnificent Cathedral, to crowds of people, who all gape at it and laugh at it in the same breath!

Another sight of a very different kind is shown in the Church of St Thomas. In two glass cases are preserved the bodies of a "Count" and his daughter (aged 14) – Both were embalmed before burial, and the girl has the dress on which clothed her when she was put into her coffin, <u>two hundre</u>d years ago. The grave flowers are round her head – the lace is perfect over her bosom – the rings are on her fingers – nothing is decaying about her but her face; and that is falling away slowly into dust. It was a very touching and solemn sight.

On Thursday afternoon, we left Strasbourg for Basle – again by the Railway, which ends at that place. We got an excellent carriage, four horses and a postilion, as substitutes for Steam and were off again at half past eight on Friday morning, with a Strasbourg sausage, a bottle of wine, brandy, [and: erased] [Rirsch-Wasser], and plenty of bread to keep off hunger on the road. In a few hours we began to get into the real Swiss country. Immense masses of hill-woods blazing in the [erased word] sun with the most vivid autumn red yellow, and purple I ever saw – farm-houses with barn, granary, and stable, all under one immense overhanging roof – little fortified towns with streets and quaint gables and carved balconies – shepherds singing the Rauz der Vaches – cattle-bells chiming on every hill-side – roofed bridges and wild streams – all gave us assurance that we had already pushed our journey as far as Switzerland. On Friday night we slept at Berne; and leaving that place early on Saturday morning caught sight of the German Alps, just as we got outside the town. The mighty peaks rose dark and dim, with the sun behind them through masses of thick white cloud, rolling far <u>below</u> their summits, and far <u>above</u> the morning mists smoking up from the Valley's beneath. We left this sublime sight behind us and made for the Italian Alps. It was a clear moon-light evening, [and: erased] when the Lake of Geneva and the miles on miles of soaring mountains beyond it, burst into view from the [two erased words] high land above Lausanne. The cold mountain air was nestling solemnly in the pine forests on either side of us as we first looked on this unparallelled scene – a scene never to be forgotten and never to be described, either by pen or pencil!

We are staying here with Mr Townshend,[4] in a charming country house on the borders of the Lake. Our plans for getting into Italy are not yet settled, and cannot be, till we gain decisive information on Tuesday next at Geneva. Tomorrow we go to Vevay and the Castle of Chillon.

We travel in a state of mad good spirits, [erased word] and even play on our journey all through the day. I am Keeper of the Privy Purse for roadside expenses of an irregular nature, which are not included in ordinary travelling charges; and am in this capacity the purveyor of all the pic-nic eatables and drinkables, consumed on the way, between breakfast and dinner. Egg is constantly exercised in Italian Dialogue by Dickens. The Courier turns out to be a perfect treasure! He spares us all the troubles and minor anxieties of travelling. He packs our trunks, gets our linen washed, settles our bills, [erased word] procures our railway tickets, pays our postillions, and – most important of all – renders in his accounts fairly and rightly to a farthing. In short, he takes all the inconveniences of travelling to himself, and leaves all the pleasures to us.

The next place to write to me at will be Genoa (Poste Restante). Don't pay your letters – the foreign post offices being most to be depended on, when they don't get their money beforehand. Let me hear how you are, and what home news you have. Remember me to Ward, and other friends who may appear at Hanover Terrace. Send my love to Charley, and tell him that I have read a little of Jeremy Taylor – in accordance with my promise: a little because my present course of life is not favourable to theological studies, and Jeremy is rather involved and hard to understand after a day's [erased word] rolling over rough high roads in a travelling carriage.

If I have anything more to add, I will put it in a postscript tomorrow morning. It is too late tonight to write any more –

Ever affectionately yours | W. Wilkie Collins

Monday morning/

I have just received your letter, and delighted to hear that you and Charley are both well. I will write again from Genoa, when I have got your letter there/

Notes

1. For this and some other details in the letter cf. Dickens to Mrs Charles Dickens, 13 October 1853 (Dickens, *Letters*, VII, 163, ns. 2–5).
2. The unidentified Prince "was not correct, and they in fact crossed into Italy by the Simplon Pass" (*ibid.*, 163, n.4, and cf. Dickens to Miss Coutts, 25 October 1853: *ibid.*, 170–1).
3. Word is doubly underlined.
4. i.e., "Dickens' friend Chauncy Hare Townshend, who had taken holy orders, was a wealthy man who, perhaps fortunately, never practised his profession" (Peters, p. 133).

To Mrs Harriet Collins, 28 October 1853

MS: PM

Hotel de la Croix di Matte | Genoa |[1] 28th October 1853

My dear Mother,

Your letter has just been brought to me, and I am duly grateful for all the news it contains – especially the good news from home. [erased word] the letter which Charley is writing must be directed to me at the "Poste Restante, Rome". We go to Naples from this place on Monday by Steamer and thence to Rome, Florence, Bologna, Verona, and Venice. Sicily is [given] up, as impracticable in the short time we have at our disposal. And we hope to be back in England as early as the 10th of December – urged principally by economical considerations in forming this resolution. So much for the future – and now for the Past.

My last letter left us at Lausanne. We went to this place for the first night; but Mr Townshend hospitably insisted on lodging us all in his house the next morning. The arrival of Dickens produced a prodigious sensation in the English colony at Lausanne, which practically expressed itself by a grand dinner and a grand evening party. [erased words] All the resident gentlemen whom we consulted about the best route to take to get into Italy were unanimous in declaring that the "French Prince" who had solemnly assured us that we should not be let into Italy by the Austrians if we went by the Simplon Pass was utterly wrong – so by the Simplon we determined to go – and here we are without having experienced the smallest hindrance in crossing the dreaded frontier.[2] I shall never believe in a diplomatic nobleman again as long as I live.

We went to Geneva by the steam boat, and started the next morning by post at <u>four</u> o'clock for Chamounix. Soon after sunrise we began to toil up the mountain sides, which we had hitherto only seen from a distance. Rather more than half way to Chamounix we had to leave the carriage and got into a vehicle called a "Char". There were no springs to this said <u>char</u>, which was compounded of [frousy] leather curtains, and clumsy woodwork, and looked exactly like a rotten sedan chair on wheels. In this

extraordinary carriage, we continued our journey on such a road – or rather
<u>no</u> road, as never was seen before. When we were not up to our axle in mud,
we were jolting over the [bed: erased] dry bed of a torrent. How it was that
we were not overturned fifty times before we got to Chamounix I cannot
to this moment imagine. Somehow or other, our [mules] tore through
everything, our carriage bumped over everything, our driver yelled to his
beasts incessantly and we finished the journey, sore with jolting, but
otherwise uninjured. As to describing the scenery (especially when we got
near to Chamounix) it is out of the question. Imagine a thousand feet of
almost [erased word] perpendicular precipice and pine forest on either
side of you, with the gloom of night settling grandly on <u>miles</u> of weird rock
and gloomy foliage – imagine a torrent beneath you, sprawling, crashing,
and leaping in the dim light over a chaos of split [rock: erased] stone –
imagine a wild mule track winding about, and heaving up and down before
you, whenever the tossed up ground will allow it a few feet of tenable space
to continue its course – imagine, lastly, right in front the eternal snows of
[erased word] Mont Blanc, ghastly, and awful in the deepening twilight,
rising and rising ever into the [erasure] night only, till the great clouds
themselves looked earthly by comparison with it – Imagine all this, and you
will have some faint idea of the View we saw, when we left the carriage,
and walked up the last ascent, before going down into the Valley of
Chamounix.[3]

   The next day was devoted to the Mer de Glace. We went up the mountain
on mules – the beasts, as usual preferring the extreme edge of every
precipice all the way up. There is not the least danger however (except to
people whose heads turn giddy on heights), as long as you let them take
their own way, and leave the bridle on the pummel of the saddle. You
know all about the Mer de Glace from books. It is an enormous mass of ice
wedged in between two sides of the mountain; and looks less like a frozen
sea (in my opinion) than like a frozen city of pinnacles, [and: erased]
minarets, and obelisks. We descended a little way on to it, and looked
down into one of the <u>crevices</u> – an awful place, two or three feet wide, and
<u>three hundred</u> feet deep, with the ice-walls shining blinding green all the
way down. Beneath an invisible torrent of thawed water flows, with a
distant all-pervading, still sound, very [erased word] grand to listen to in
the frozen and silent solitudes of the mountain. The sun was shining
brilliantly, there was literally not a cloud in the sky, and the snow all round
us was dazzling in its purity, as we looked at the upward view of precipices,
[erased word] crags, and interminable icy wildernesses where even the
hardy alpine fir is unable to grow.

   From Chamounix we rode on mules to Martigny – the vast precipices,
and vast forests, ever increasing round us as we went until we gained at
last the topmost summit, and looked down into the renowned valley of

Martigny, bounded on the horizon by the whole chain of the Bernese Alps with the blue Rhone winding hither and thither through [the: erased] flat green pasture-lands. This day again was cloudless, from sunrise to sunset. You may have some idea of the overwhelming vastness of the scenery of Switzerland, when I tell you that we were occupied <u>three hours</u> in incessantly descending, before we reached the valley, and [got] to our Inn (an old Convent) for the night.

From Martigny we went to Buez, and from that place began the ascent of the Simplon – Napoleon's great road into the South, over the Italian Alps. At this place we left the Swiss Valleys, and left them (for a reason which I will presently tell you) without regret. All the magnificent scenery which I have been telling you of, the mountains, forests and lovely wooded hills are so many fatal courses of misfortune and misery to the human race. The beautiful valleys are nests of pestilence and the people who inhabit them are hideous with [idiotious] [erased word] disease, and deformity. The unbroken chains of mountains [obstruct] the air, and prevent the exhalations from the marshy ground about rivers and streams, from escaping. Every healthy breeze that comes from the snowy peaks is fatally tainted before it can reach the cottages in the valleys. [erased word] Many of the people are born idiots (Cretins) as a matter of certainty, if they are born in the valleys. The first of these miserable creatures that I saw was about the height of Ward's eldest child, had the face of a monkey, and could utter no articulate sound. I asked the Postillion how old he was, and was told that he was <u>twenty years</u> of age. There are hundreds and hundreds of creatures like this in all the Swiss Valleys we passed through.

Still more frequent is the hideous deformity called the <u>goitre</u> – a [erasure] bag of flesh growing from the throat, generally as large as a hat, often the size of a carpet bag, and affecting the women particularly. Some of them walk with the goitre actually slung over their shoulders and <u>we</u> heard of a boy (but I am glad to say did not see him) who trundles his goitre before him in a wheelbarrow. He is a renowned beggar in one of the valleys, and makes a good living by exposing his deformity.

All that we had seen before, grand as it was, was not to be compared with what we saw on the Simplon. How the men who made the road, were hung over the precipices, to cut the way out of the rock, and build it up above the ravine, passes all comprehension. The views grow literally terrific as you get higher and higher up. Towards the top of mountains all vegetation ceases, and perpetual ice and snow begin. Such is the danger here, in the winter time from snow storms and avalanches, that ice refuges are built for travellers to fly to over a space of a mile and three quarters. Some of these refuges are in the form of galleries hewn out of the living rock, numerous icicles hang at their sides and waterfalls pour over their roofs, the stream rushing over the windows which light the refuges, in one vast sheet of falling water. Lower down the sun at midday was still so powerful even amidst the snow, that it was a pleasure to lie down on a felled tree, and bask in its warmth, while looking miles [down: erased] away into the valleys-beneath. But towards the sunset, the real icy cold made itself felt, and nothing but brisk walking [erased words] in advance of the carriage really kept us warm. We descended the mountain through the famous Gorge of Gondo. You remember the Gorde d'Olivets when we were going to Toulon? Well the Gorge of Gondo is twenty times as long, ten times as high, and fifty times as wild and precipitous as that. We were in one continuous ecstacy of astonishment and delight all the way through it. All the landscape painters in the world might come to this place, and find subjects for pictures for the rest of their lives.

Our night's lodging after the Simplon was in Italy,[4] at [Domo] d'Ossola. Here were the vast rooms, and the dirt and the screaming servants with their pleasant Italian manners – all unchanged since I had last seen them. We set forth the next morning to pass from [Domo] d'Ossola to Milan – a long journey and a lovely day for it. Never was any contrast more remarkable than the contrast between this journey, and the journey over the Simplon. We were now driving, in the warmest brightest [indecipherable word] along the lovely shores of the Lago Maggiore. The great snow mountains, were far behind us, gently rising hills were on one side, with vines and mulberry trees, and pretty cottages and country-houses, dotted all about them. On the other side was the blue water, without a ripple stirring its surface – with its islands and [erased word] their palaces and terraced gardens all reflected in the bright stillness of the lake with boats stealing along far and near, covered prettily with bright awnings – in short such an Italian scene as one dreams of and sees faintly represented some times in what are called "poetical pictures".

We crossed the river into which the lake empties itself in a ferry. The sunshine was in all its rich afternoon glory – the view [erased word] beautiful beyond description or imagination – embracing almost the whole length of the Lake, with its islands, its boundary hills, and the mysterious lustre of the snowy Alps in the far distance. There was an old blind fiddler in the boat, who sang some Italian national songs, harshly and unscientif-ically enough, but with a certain [erased word] earnestness and spirit which made them very pleasant to hear. [erased words] I don't know whether it was the music which reminded me of old times in Italy, or the scenery or the gliding motion of the boat over the clear water, and through the lovely river landscape or the state of incessant excitement that I had been in for the last three or four days, that affected me – or whether it was all these things together – but I never felt nearer astonishing everybody by bursting out crying (!!!) than I did while we were ferrying over the river and listening to the blind fiddler's Italian songs. The poor old fellow said "Goodbye" in

English with immense unction as we stepped on shore. He had been forty years blind, had two blind children and depended for support on what he got for singing [from] passengers by the ferry boat. He made a good day's work of it with us, and sat down in [erased word] a corner [erased words], to wait for a fresh audience in great contentment and satisfaction.

The town at which we were now landed was on the Austrian frontier. What we did here and how we got to Milan, and from Milan to Genoa, I must reserve, however, for another letter, which I mean to write from the Steamer to Charles Ward.

Charley must send off his letter to Poste Restante, Rome, as soon as possible, after he receives this. Our next place for letters will be Florence (also Poste Restante). If you write to me there, despatch your letter, if you can, three or four days after Charley has despatched his. It will then be sure to arrive in good time for me.

With love to Charley and best regards to all friends,

Believe me | Ever affectionately yours | W. Wilkie Collins

I have bought you <u>another</u> bracelet of Genoa silver work and a snuff box for Charles Ward. I reserve getting Charley's present till I arrive at Naples, or Rome.

Notes

1. The "Pilgrim Edition" editors transcribe the address, "C. Dickens to Mrs Charles Dickens, 28 and 29 October 1853" as: "Croce di Matta, Genoa" (VII, 176 and see 2).
2. "I resolved to come by the Simplon – and did" (Dickens to Miss Burdett Coutts, 25 October 1853: VII, 170).
3. None of this is described in Dickens' letters home: cf. Dickens to Mrs Charles Dickens, 25 October 1853 (VII, 173). See also WC "My Black Mirror", *Household Words*, 6 September 1856, xiv, 171-172 (*ibid*, 173, n.4)
4. Underlined twice.

To Charles Ward, 31 October 1853
MS: PM

Genoa | October 31st 1853

My dear Ward,

If my mother has shown you my letters to her you will be acquainted by this time with our passage through France and Switzerland, as far as the frontier of Austrian Italy. My last letter home left off with our passage in a ferry across [erased word] river into which the Lago Maggiore empties itself. From that point, I shall now get in a little, in this present letter to you, as far as Milan, and Genoa too, if my paper gives me room enough.

The town at which the ferry-boat landed us, was all alive with the white Austrian uniform. If we were to be stopped and turned back at all (a calamity which certain reports in Paris had led us to look on as possible) this was the place at which our further progress would be barred. Dickens's servant took our passports to the Office, and we went away in some little suspense to the Inn where we enjoyed the loveliest possible prospect and ate the dirtiest possible dinner. Just as we had done, an officer entered and, very politely, begged our attendance before the examiners of passports. We found this dreaded official the very cream and pink of politeness. He only wanted us to answer to our names (pronouncing mine with a low bow, as "Wilkers Collers", and complementing me on my Italian) and was then quite ready and willing to let us go on. On we went accordingly to Milan, travelling [fast] changing the carriage at every third stage or so, and getting worse and worse vehicles, the nearer we got to our destination. Our last carriage was of the period of Louis the 14th and was so indescribably "fusty" that I lit a cigar in self-defence the moment I got into it. Before we started, the postmaster who was extremely attentive and drunk, assured us that the road swarmed with thieves and that unless we took some precaution, we might have our luggage stolen in the dark (it was then night) from the top of Louis the 14th's coach, while we were riding inside. [erased passage] We asked the postmaster what precaution he would recommend. "Tie three strings to each of the three trunks" said he in broken French, "and hold the end in your hands as you ride". This was actually done, and we held our three impromptu bell-ropes all the way to Milan. It was like sitting in a shower bath, and waiting to pull the string – or rather like fishing in the sea, when one waits to feel a bite by a tap at the [erasure] line round one's fingers. If you had only heard the noise that was made in starting us, with these string-detectors – the way in which the postmaster waved a tallow candle and howled at all the men in the yard, who crawled frantically about the top of the carriage entangling themselves with the rope, and howling at the postmaster in return – if you had only heard this, you would have imagined we were taking all the treasures of [Golconda] to Milan, and were perfectly certain to be attacked by bands of implacable robbers at every mile of our way. No such thing, however, occurred. Not one of us felt the nearest approach to a bite – and we got into Milan about half past ten with all the minutest atoms of our baggage still in their proper places on the roof of the fusty coach.

There is nothing characteristic about Milan as a <u>city</u>. It is a place of magnificent streets, and palatial houses; and might be a French town of the first class as far as outward appearances go. The Cathedral is one of the great sights of course. The façade is a compromise between the Gothic and the Classical styles; and like all compromises is unsatisfactory and feeble enough; but the interior is noble in its gloom and mystery. The body of St

Carlo Borromes (a really good man in spite of his being a Saint) is preserved in a crypt. They show it clothed in magnificent episcopal finery and jewels, encased in a crystal tomb. The roof of the crypt is of solid silver, with bas reliefs of the same metal in the cornices, jewels sparkle all over the tomb and in every available part of the saint's dress. In short, a more dazzling and beautiful mausoleum never was built. It is utterly out of harmony with the character of the good man who reposes in it, and whose motto "Humilitas" stares you in the face over his priceless jemmed coffin – but the Roman Catholics don't mind trifling little inconsistencies of this sort – and the sacristan gets 5 francs for [showing] the place – and strangers always admire it – and so everybody is pleased which is a great thing to attain by the exhibition of any man's dead body in this world.

There are several picture galleries at Milan – full of rubbish with here and there a good picture or two to keep the spectator from turning his back against the old masters in disgust. The best example of these glorious exceptions is Raphael's celebrated Sposalizio (the betrothal of the Virgin and [indecipherable word]) – a picture that really deserves its reputation. Nothing to approach the divine beauty and refinement of some of the [erased words] in the composition has been painted since Raphael's time. Copies from this picture, and prints, give no idea of it in its highest aspects.

But the so-called grand Art Sight of Milan is Leonardo da Vinci's "Last Supper". I have heard people who cant about Art talk in raptures of this picture. It is not a <u>picture</u>: it is the utter ruin of something which <u>was once</u> a picture. There is [erased words] a faint, very faint, reflection of the original majesty and beauty left in the face of Christ – but all besides is ruined – or worse – painted over in the most infamous manner by modern restorers. When the original faces have not been distorted by the clumsiness of the picture [erased word] – patcher – they are torn and frayed up, blotched, stained, or utterly rubbed out. The picture is in short, just recognisable as a picture with a great many figures in it – and that is all. Anybody who pretends to be able to see anything of Leonardo da Vinci's services in it now, pretends to achieve a downright impossibility.

Of course, we went to La Scala – the second largest Theatre in the world. As we[1] saw it, its size was its only advantage. It was miserably lighted, wretchedly dirty, mournfully empty, and desecrated by some of the very worst singers I ever heard, and some of the mouldiest scenery I ever saw exposed to gaslight. The Opera was Verdi's last and noisiest production –[2] the tenor was laughed at, and the Prima Donna was hissed – in short, the whole performance was utterly miserable and incapable, even for Italy – and that is saying a great deal in this present state of Opera here.

By way of being economical, we left Milan for Genoa by diligence – an awful and penetential vehicle, with damp seats, which ran at the rate of five miles an hour. We got a good dinner on the road, and a bottle of good wine for the night – and as everybody (horses included) was asleep at the post-houses, we had plenty of time for wayside refreshments of an indescribably composite character at every halting place. But by the time we reached the railroad from Turin after 20 hours of travelling over the worst high roads I ever saw, we were so utterly disgusted with our vehicle, that, when the carriages stopped at an unfinished station "four hours from Genoa", we relapsed into our old posting habits, and got a comfortable private carriage of our own. I got some cold meat from an Inn to carry us on (the landlord sprinkling salt over it with his own greasy and hospitable fingers) and we arrived at Genoa in the evening, as lively and fresh as if we had only gone through the fatigueness of a short journey.

Here we have been through the Palaces with their marvellous portraits by Vandyck and have attended mass in the wonderful churches whose ceilings [erased words] are all ablaze with gold. Dickens's Genoese friends have loaded us with hospitalities[3] and we leave tomorrow by the English Steam Boat, for Naples, with all sorts of amicable good wishes to bear us prosperously on our way. When you answer this, write to me at Poste Restante, Florence, three or four days after the receipt of my letter. I hope I shall hear that you have quite recovered, and that Jane and the children (to whom I beg my love) are quite well. I sent you various messages of condolence by your father, when I got my circular notes at Coutts's, – sore throat, and its accompanying miseries, being afflictions for which I can feel deeply from personal experience.

Beneath this, is an order [erased word] [on] Longman, for the money due to me, on the 4ᵗʰ of December. Will you tear it off, and send [part of leaf removed] account, as usual. I don't remember the exact sum to which I am entitled (it is £28 something, I think) – but I have no doubt the order as here written will obtain for me my "lawful rights".

I have got your snuff box and a brooch for Jane. The snuff-box you gave me, was stolen at Milan – by a pickpocket. There was no other way of accounting for the loss of it. I had every enquiry made by two different emissaries, but no good result followed. You may imagine my misery at losing such a [hinge] and a present from you. I have bought a box just like it (in tortoiseshell) here. It has a promising hinge; and that is my only consolation.

Give my love to my mother and Charley, when you see them; and say I shall write from Rome.

Ever Yours, | W. Wilkie Collins

Charles J. Ward Esqre

On second thoughts, you had better write and send off your letter to make sure of my receiving it as soon as possible after the arrival of this.

Notes

1. The word "we" is doubly underlined.
2. Dickens wrote to Georgina Hogarth, 29 October 1853: "We went to the Scala, where they did an opera of Verdi's, called 'Il Trovatore', and a poor enough ballet. The whole performance miserable indeed" (Dickens, *Letters*, VII, 181).
3. See Dickens to Mrs Charles Dickens, 28 and 29 October 1853 (*ibid*., VII, 177).

To Edward Pigott, 4 November 1853

MS: Huntington

Naples | November 4th 1853

My dear Edward

I have followed all the great stages in your fortunes in my letters to England, as far as Genoa in regular succession. The Neopolitan luck is now all that is waiting to complete the chain of our Travelling Events up to this present date – the Vigil (as you will see by the top of my letter) if [that Fate] [going] You may [hear] if you go to [Hanover Terrace], is to Charles Ward's [how] we got through France and Switzerland to [indecipherable word]¹ Genoa. You shall now hear if you will read my letter how we got to Naples this morning.

I always wish to be philanthropic but I cannot shut my eyes to the palpable fact that the travelling part of the human race wants thinning. We have encountered crowds everywhere. No Hotels are large enough, no coaches numerous enough, no post horses indefatigable enough to accommodate, hold, and [d-] the legions of tourists who are now overflowing the continent in every direction. Even the [indecipherable words] or old [indecipherable words] [1000] to [indecipherable words] and [indecipherable word] forever, [plying] from [two indecipherable words] calling at [indecipherable word] Civita Vecchia and Naples by this way teak – built copher fastened; and making 15 knots an hour, turned out to be an ignoble and utterly unfit receptacle for the number of passengers who wanted to go to [indecipherable word]. We went on [indecipherable word] board at Genoa at [half] past [ten] and found the deck thronged. A perfect fleet of boats was about the ship, one of them [indecipherable word] full of small [indecipherable word] singers from the opera trying to pick up a [indecipherable word] little extra salary by saluting us with shrill choruses from Verdi's operas. It was [worth] a [indecipherable word] to hear the English Club officer of the Valetta [shouting] to [these] [same] Minstrels [impersonated by shirtless for] [indecipherable word] with fiddles, and coffee-coloured women with guitars) to get out of our way as we began to heave anchor. "Hallo you Sir, you're in the way." "I say, Signora. sheer off

– Oh, d-n it,! Mademoiselle <u>will</u> you sheer off!" – [six] – [indecipherable word] was the symphonous accompaniment to "[two indecipherable words]" and the fiddles – and amid such noises, mingling with that sort of chaotic and [purposeless] [comical] screaming which constitutes the staple of ordinary Italian conversation did we steam out of the harbour of Genoa [? ing] the palaces [indecipherable word] of the [lovely] city glittering behind us in the sun and the hills beyond them lightly covered with white and purple clouds, rolling onward in calm processions before a pale North Wind.

Nothing could be pleasanter than the voyage as long as the daylight lasted. With some few exceptions presently to be noticed, our travelling companions were all really agreeable people – the sea was smooth – the offices of the ship all polite [indecipherable word] when night came, and beds were in demand [indecipherable word] we were rather more than twice two many [indecipherable word]. Berths in the Saloon (on the seats) had been kept for us but the atmosphere was so stifling, that we have attempted to occupy our impromptu beds – and determined to rough it with wrappers and sofa pillows on Deck. Just as we were comfortably asleep under an awning, down came the rain – <u>Italian</u> rain which pours like a waterfall. We retreated towards the cabin. Prostrate bodies of men and women in those distorted attitudes which only the bedless on board ship can assume, prevented entrance – the atmosphere was [emphatic] in short, the place was a nautical Pandemonium, sulphery with the fumes of past dinner and present human breath! So on deck we went again, and fell asleep at last in spite of the elements on the [cabin] sky light. I was kept awake for some time, by a <u>bore</u>, one of those who infested the ship. Neither rain, nor darkness, nor want of bed, quelled this conversational miscreant. He talked everywhere to everybody on every possible subject, in a [prose] cracked bass voice that almost always seemed close at my [ear]. You will have some idea of him when I tell you that he was describing the origin of the "Rejected [Add...rs]" and giving personal sketches of James and Horace Smith [taciturn] American, at three in the morning, with the rain [battering] on [deck] and the lightning flashing on the sea, when I fell asleep and heard no more of him.

The next morning we reached Leghorn. The ship being detained in port for certain "<u>Practique</u>" reasons which it is not worth while to explain. Dickens and Egg and I and [Sir] Emmerson Tennent and his family[2] and the Captain and Doctor, and the third officer, all went on shore to spend the day in seeing the sights of Pisa. At dinner at the Hotel Dickens, in his – own good [humoured] way, let off an incessant fire of jokes at the Captain (with a [indecipherable word] pointed meaning in them) all alluding to the misconduct of the [four indecipherable words] double [indecipherable word] number of people to take passage by the Valetta. These jokes were received in [ ] "good part" and they produced their effect. The next night we got beds.

Did you ever sleep in a Store Room? Egg and I slept on two dressers in the store room of the Valetta. I had a barrel of flour, a basket of apples, and a bed of bread under the outer edge of [indecipherable word] couch. Dinner of figs, bunches of grapes cannisters of spices were all around us – the smell as the smell of a clean chandler's shop. [two indecipherable words] we had the steward and an old gentleman, and [a ship's] cat in the store room; and well "pigged together" as the vulgar saying is, in the most amicable and comfortable manner imaginable. I never slept better in my life. Dickens had a share of a friend's cabin. In short, everybody had some sleeping accommodation – in unheard of parts of the ship, [except] the man who prevented us getting on deck under an umbrella (it rained again in the second night), and would not hear of being sheltered below on any terms. I was in hopes that this extraordinary deck-hermit among the passengers might be the 'bore' and that he might catch cold and lose his voice, for the benefit of the ship's company. But no! – it was somebody else. The man with the [indecipherable word] voice was in high preservation, when I went [indecipherable word], talking about Moore's `Melodies'; and [humming] [indecipherable word] with a mouthful of beefsteak, to his next [indecipherable word]. The second morning brought us to Civita Vecchia (a wretched, seaplace – infested by beggars and French soldiers) – and the third, after another [luxurious] night in the store-room, saw us fairly straining into the Bay of Naples. It was about seven o'clock – misty on one side of the view, brightly sunny on the other. The sea was of the real mediterranean blue – light wreaths of white smoke were curling up quietly into the fair morning [sky] from the Crater of Vesuvius – the Islands in the Bay showed their lovely forms with a soft indistinctness indescribably visionary and beautiful to look at – and the unrivalled scene of Naples itself, with its gardens, its lofty houses, and its grand forts, gleamed again right under the sunny portion of the sky. Every part of the view was familiar to me, though it is 15 years since I saw it last – But such a place as this (seen from the sea) is never to be forgotten, when you have once looked at it.

I must tell you, that we left the "bore" (who was bound for this place) complicating every arrangement, confusing the police officer who was calling our names, and getting into everybody's way, as we went over the ship's side. We thought we had at last fairly got rid of him, when the boat landed us. Vain hope! Just before dinner we were walking towards the King's Palace, and were stopping to look at some bag-pipers from the Mountains, when I heard a voice close at my ear, say "Calabrians – eh?" I looked round and there he was! We [bolted] directly; but bolting is no use. Unless some good Samaritan murders him tonight, I have a presentiment that he will be the first living creature I shall set eyes on, on going out of the Hotel tomorrow morning. I suppose men of this kind are created as a sort of moral <u>hair-shirts</u> for impenetential Protestants who won't "mortify" the flesh with any rougher discipline than a cold bath and a rub with a Turkish towel.

This is a rambling, scrambling, scrawling letter – but I can't write anything correct and regular, for I have not long done eating a very capital dinner, and washing down the same with copious draughts of Lachryma – and I am, as you know, one of that unhappy race who get particularly stupid after repletion. Will you send, or <u>take</u> this letter to my mother, when you have read it? It will give her some fresh news of me, since Genoa, which she will be glad to hear. Say also that I will write to Charley from Rome. Give my best regards to Lewes; and believe me

Affectionately yours | W. Wilkie Collins

Write to me as soon as you conveniently can, after receiving this and direct your letter to "Poste Restante, Venice". I met with a subscriber to the <u>Leader</u> at Genoa, who praised the paper with real sincerity and enthusiasm, and recommended it in all directions.

Notes

1. Sara S. Hodson, Curator of Literary Manuscripts at the Huntington has kindly examined this letter for us. She writes:

   the letter suffered much over the years before it came to the Huntington ... the ink has bled through extensively and has actually eaten through the paper in some parts, obliterating text. Also, bits of paper along the original fold lines have chipped away, leaving holes resulting in the loss of text ... Some portions of the text may never be legible and will have to be omitted or filled in from context alone. (letter to W. Baker, June 6, 1996)

2. Sir James Emerson Tennent (1804–1869), author and politician; Letitia Tennent, married Sir James in 1831 (d. 1883); William Emerson Tennent (1835–1876); "Eleanor or Edith" Tennent – see Dickens, *Letters*, VII, 183.

To Charles Collins, 13 November 1853
MS: PM

[Hotel des Iles Britanniques] | Rome | November 13th 1853

My dear Charley/
   Here I am actually in Rome again after an interval of no less than sixteen years. It may seem (and very likely <u>is</u>) egotistical enough – but nothing has astonished me more than my own vivid remembrance of every street and building in this wonderful and mournful place. Houses, fountains, public

buildings, shops even appeal to me as familiar objects, that I cannot help fancying I must have been in daily contact with, since my first introduction to them in the old bye gone time. All the other places we have visited in Italy have seemed more or less changed to me. This place seems, and really is, unaltered. I recognised, this morning, all the favourite [erased word] haunts on the Pincian Hill, that we asked to run about as little boys – I saw the same Bishops, in purple stockings, followed by servants in gaudy liveries – the same importunately impudent beggars – the same men with pointed hats and women with red petticoats and tightly swaddled babies that I remembered so well in England since 1837 and 1838. Not the least changeless object in Rome was our old house in the Via Felice. The Virgin is still in her niche – the cabbage stalks and rubbish are strewn about underneath – the very door looks as if it had never been painted since we left it. Genoa I did not know again, till I got to the great street of palaces – Naples I found altered in one or two important respects, as far as the town is [erasure] concerned – but Rome is what it was when we saw it. <u>Here</u>, I can hardly help fancying that I must have gone to sleep at fourteen years old, and woke up again at the comparatively mature age of twenty nine.

Such are my impressions of Rome – but I must go back a little, and tell you something of Naples, before I say anything more about what I have seen here. Pigott has a letter of mine, which I told him to send or take to you, describing our voyage from Genoa to Naples. Our occupations <u>at</u> Naples remain to be recorded. The first day after our arrival we went to Pompei with Sir Emmerson Tennent and his family – friends of Dickens's, whom we met on board the steam boat, and very delightful people. Many things have been excavated since our time – the day was lovely – we <u>picknicked</u> among the ruins – and did not get back till dark. The next day Egg and I, leaving Dickens to write letters and make calls, went to the Baiae side of the Bay – got on men's backs in the Sibil's Cave, and so splashed through much subterranean water by torchlight – wandered about temples and amphitheatres and saw the wretched dog tortured at the Grotto del Cane (I roared fiercely to the man to let him go before he became insensible, being unable to hear the howling of the poor brute as the mephitic air acted on him – and so stopped the experiment before it was complete). We saw quite enough, however, both at the Grotto del Cane and elsewhere to convince us that all the so-called "<u>sights</u>" on the Baiae side of the Bay are as nothing compared to the fine sight of Nature [erased words] – the [bells], the sea, the islands and the lovely sky, which cost not a farthing, require no guide, encourage no beggars and live longer in the memory than all the antiquities and chemical curiosities that ever h<u>ave</u> been discovered, or [will: erased] ever <u>will</u> <u>be</u>.

The next day was devoted to Vesuvius. Besides the Tennents (father, mother, son, and daughter) Layard of Nineveh[1] fame, was of our party. We reached the Cone (on horseback) about half past four in the afternoon. The [toil some] ascent on foot occupied us half an hour. The ladies were carried up on chairs. Egg and I were the last of the gentlemen who arrived at the summit – we discreetly rested, whenever we felt fatigued, and so got to the top quite fresh, and ready to enjoy the marvellous volcanic obstacle, without any [alloy] of the slightest sense of fatigue. The mountain was very quiet – [not: erased] no flame, no stones, no noise – nothing but thick clouds of sulphurous smoke. The last great eruption was in 1850;[2] and it has altered Vesuvius, past my recognition. <u>All</u> is crater now, the moment you get to the top – the hollow space we walked over when I visited it in 1838, exists no more. Dickens, Layard, Egg and I, went all round the mouth of the crater. I shall never, as long as I live, forget the view from the highest point, over Sorrento and Capri, with a blood-red setting sun gleaming through the hot vapour and sulphur smoke that curled up high from behind us, as we rested for a few minutes to look at the western prospect. The descent was as lively and as rapid as usual [erased word]. Our procession as we rode along by torchlight, with a young Italian moon shining above us, a perfect army of guides around us, and wild lava rocks on all sides of us – was a picture in itself, such a picture I am afraid as could never be painted –

We called on Iggulden[3] at his private house (he had previously left calls for Dickens and me at the Hotel). We did not see him however, until we went to his place of business to get money. [erased words] He was extremely depressed and gloomy, and [was: erased] surrounded by wretched pictures, on which he had been lending money, I suspect. He expressed himself as quite amazed that Dickens should still be a "lively man" with nine children – and grievously desired to know whether I was still going on "writing books", and whether I ever meant to "practise my profession". He asked after you and my mother with great interest, and then introduced me to a tall young gentleman with a ghastly face, immense whiskers, and an expression of the profoundest melancholy, who was casting accounts, and reckoning up dollars, in the outer office. Do you remember little "<u>Lorenzo</u>" who was the lively young "Pickle" of the family in our time? – Well! This was Lorenzo!!!! He asked me whether I had not broken my arm when I was last in Naples. I told him y<u>ou</u> had. He rejoined gloomily: "Galway's dead"[4] – and then waited for me to say something. I said, "God bless me! Is he indeed?" – And so we parted. I must not forget to say that Charles Iggulden – the pattern <u>goodboy</u> who used to be quoted as an example to me – has married a pretty girl w<u>ithout</u> his parents' consent – is out of the banking business in consequence – and has gone to Australia to make his fortune as well as he can. I was rather glad to hear this, as I don't like "well-conducted" young men! I know it is wrong! But I always feel relieved and happy when I hear that they have got into a scrape.

We had reserved our last day at Naples for a visit to Sorrento – but, after weeks of incredibly fine weather, the rain came at last, on the said day – They had not had a drop in the town in nearly two months before. We waited at Naples, accordingly – Went to the museum and the opera – and heard a prima donna at the San Carlo, who ought to make a great reputation in London [some] of these days, if managers have the sense to find her out. The opera itself was Verdi's last – Very poor – The theatre magnificent in its unrivalled size and sober, tasteful decorations.[5]

On the 10th we started for Rome by [Vetturino] – a good carriage and a jovial old driver, with a purple face, white head, and a [wall] eye. On the 12th we arrived at the luxurious and delightful hotel[6] in the Piazza del Popolo from which I [erased word] now write. This morning was devoted to the Colisseum and the Forum. The afternoon to Vespers at St Peter's. I was detained at the hotel, and started late, leaving Dickens and Egg to precede me to St Peter's. And, for once in a way, the procrastinating man was the lucky man of the party. As I was walking along the street which leads from the Ponte S. Angelo to St Peter's, two dragoons dashed past me, clearing the road at full gallop, two carriages came after, with cardinals inside – and next came a state coach with the Pope himself. Every creature near me fell on his or her knees. I stood up, of course, but pulled off my hat. The Pope (I suppose, seeing me the only erect figure out of a group of 30 or 40 people), looked straight at me as he passed – and bowed as he saw me with my hat in my hand. He looked care-worn, old, anxious, and miserable – I just saw his head sunk sadly on his breast as the carriage dashed by me. There was an idea among the strangers present that he would be in St Peter's at Vespers; but he never appeared. The Interior of the Church looked more sublime and overwhelming than I ever remember to have seen it. The Nave was grand with gathering darkness, while the high altar sparkled with hundreds of fantastically disposed lights. In the immensity of the building, the pealing of the great organ and the voices of the full choir, sounded faint – and mysteriously far off – it was impossible to follow the music note by note, [erasure] in the position which we occupied, or to see the ceremonies plainly; but the service was all the more impressive to me, on this very account – I mean, on account of the visionary uncertainty of all that we saw, and the alternate swelling and sinking of all the sounds that we heard!

On the 6th of December we hope to be at Turin, going round by [erased word] Venice and Verona, before we get there. On the 13th or 14th, we expect to be back in London, travelling by way of Lyons and Paris. When my mother sends her next letter (the sooner the better) tell her, with my best love, to direct it to Poste Restante, Lyons. I shall be able to write an answer, I hope, from that place, fixing certainly the day of my return.[7]

Now for other messages: – Tell Millais I will write to him from Florence (I got his letter in yours, this morning) – Remember me kindly to Ward and Bullar and any other friends you may see. I am very sorry [erased word] to hear of William Brandling's death – I only saw him once, but I carried away a [very: erased] pleasant impression of him, poor fellow, even from that short acquaintance. Remember me to Henry[8] when you see him next.

I [erased words] highly approve of Miss Otter's plan for pitching her tent near my mother's, in case they both move from their present residences. To begin in the country with a good neighbour in the shape of an old friend, seems as promising an entrance into a state of rural existence as could well be desired. But where are they and we to go? We must discuss that question when I get home. In the mean time I send best love to the Hanover Terrace household; and remain (too sleepy and tired to write anymore).

Yours ever affectionately | WWC

Notes

1. Austen Henry Layard (1817–1894: *DNB*), whose *Nineveh and Babylon* was published during the summer of 1853. Dickens wrote to Miss Burdett Coutts, 13 November 1853: "At Naples I found Layard – with whom we ascended Vesuvius in the Sunlight, and came down in the Moonlight, very merrily" (*Letters* VII, 189).
2. "Vesuvius had last erupted on 6 Feb[ruary 1850] for nearly a month" (*ibid.*, VII, 190, n.4).
3. William Iggulden (1794–1864), banker the Collins family had known in 1838. See Harriet Collins' diary in Victoria and Albert Museum, London.
4. Galway was the son of Captain Thomas Galway, UK Consul in Naples, and was blamed by Collins' mother for breaking Charles' arm in Naples. See Harriet Collins' diary, Victoria and Albert Museum and Clarke, pp. 39–40.
5. WC, Dickens and Egg saw Verdi's *Il Trovatore* with Rosino Penco (1825–1894), Naples-born soprano: "her performance in *Il Trovatore* in Rome this year was her greatest success ... She sang at Covent Garden 1859–62." Dickens wrote to Georgina Hogarth, 13 November 1853: "The night before we left Naples we were at the San Carlo, where with the Verdi rage of our old Genoa time, they were again doing the 'Trovatore'. It seemed rubbish on the whole to me, but was fairly done. I think ... the prima donna, will soon be a great hit in London. She is a very remarkable singer and a fine actress, to the best of my judgment on such premises" (*Letters*, VII, 192, and n.3).
6. i.e. the Hotel des Iles Britanniques.
7. They arrived in London on 11 December 1853 – a Sunday (cf. Dickens, *Letters*, VII, 225).
8. For Henry Brandling see WC to Charles Ward, 1 August 1850, n.1. William Brandling was probably a relative, a brother or possibly father, of Henry who was a draughtsman and topographical lithographer.

To Mrs Harriet Collins, 25 November 1853
MS: PM

Venice | November 25th 1853

My dear Mother,
   By the time you receive this, you will have seen my letter from Florence to John Millais, and will know what our plans are for returning. They are still unaltered. On the 12th or 13th of next month I hope to be at home again. If no future change takes place, this will most likely be my last letter, for we expect to arrive at Lyons at night, and leave again, straight for Paris, the next morning – so I shall have not time for writing in France. However if I discover at Paris, that the tides and their attendant trains will bring us late at night to London, of course I will warn you as early as possible. In the mean time, look out for me on the 12th or 13th – "till further notice".
   We left Florence in an excellent English travelling carriage with six horses and, posting all day and all night arrived in the morning at Padua, where the railroad took us to Venice in a little more than an hour. Thus, the journey which took ten days when we all travelled together "[Vetturino]", was performed in about eight and twenty hours by post horses and steam. I have no idea, as yet, whether the railway bridge has altered [erased word] the approach to Venice for the better or the worse. We stayed all day at Padua seeing pictures and churches, and travelled here in the dark. The Hotel Gondola met us at the Railway Station – we left our modern inventions, our comfortable carriages propelled by steam; and the next minute (while the engineer's whistle was still screaming above us) there we were on the dark water in a boat of the middle ages, rowing along streets of water that have not altered for the last [four] hundred years. It was the most bewildering "jumble" of the totally modern and the totally antique that ever I met with!
   Our Hotel is at the mouth of the Grand Canal, close to St Mark's. The first day [erased word] we were all anxiety to see how Venice looked. It was a lovely, sunshiny morning (we have only had <u>three</u> rainy days for the last seven weeks – how's that!) – it was a lovely morning, and the first object we looked at was our old friend the Church of San Salute with its huge white cupola glittering in the sun, almost opposite to us. Just below, at our right, we next saw the seaward side of the Ducal Palace and below was the Mole, with turbaned Turks and petticoated Greeks by dozens, diversifying the lively native Venetian crowd stretching away from us on either side as far as we could look.
   Here as at Rome, nothing seems to have altered for the last fifteen years. The glorious pictures look as superbly superior as ever to everything else in the Art of other schools. Coming fresh from all that the galleries of Rome

and Florence can show, I am more struck than I could have imagined possible, with a sense of the superiority of the Venetian painters – and especially of Tintoretto, [the: erased] to my mind the chief and greatest of them all. You remember his marvellous "Crucifixion" in the Scuola di San Rocco – but do you also remember well his <u>Paradise</u> in the Ducal Palace? This picture is altogether without a parallel in the world. It is <u>70 feet</u> long by thirty high. They have tried in Venice to count the figures in it, and left off in despair at <u>three thousand</u>!!!¹ Such is the wonderful genius of the painter, that there is really no confusion in this amazing picture – the longer you look at it, the <u>less</u> confused it gets. The whole Assembly of the (blessed) are all tending upwards towards God from every part of the picture. The grand general lines of the composition seem to have been taken from the lines of clouds – so that when you get to a distance from the picture the hundreds and hundreds of human beings and angels seem to be all circling together [erased words] below the "Mercy Seat", as clouds circle at midday below the sea. This seems to me to be the sublimest [erasure] pictorial idea of [erasure] representing Heaven, that ever entered into the head of any painter – and it is carried out with a victorious ease in every part of the picture that it absolutely bewilders one to look at. Charley and Millais [erased words] and Hunt, ought to come here if they go no-where else. These Venetians, employed as they almost always were, to represent conventional subjects, are the most <u>original</u> race of painters that the world has yet seen.

We lead the most luxurious, dandy-dillettante sort of life here. Our Gondola (with two rowers in modern footmen's [erasure] liveries!) waits on us wherever we go. We live among pictures and palaces all day, and among operas, Ballets and Café's [erasure] more than half the nights. Yesterday evening we went to hear Verdi's "Nabuco" in the Gondola – one of the Rowers going before us, [with: erased] as soon as we landed to light us upstairs into our box by means of a huge ship's lanthorn, which there was not the slighest occasion for, but which the gondoliers persisted in bringing as a proper assertion of our own magnificence.² This said "magnificence" by the bye, was of the most economical kind. We got the best box in the Theatre, on the Grand Tier for exactly seven and sixpence in English money – just the price which <u>each</u> person must pay in London for entering the pit of the Opera, without any security of finding a seat when he gets inside. Both the singing and dancing were very fairly and pleasantly done – and it was as satisfactory and as long an evening's amusement, as the veriest glutton of theatrical enjoyment could properly desire.

Here, we are already beginning to feel the cold which we shall soon have to encounter in its more Northern intensity, among the snows of [erasure] Mont Cenis, on our journey into France. The marble floors of the Academy were so chilly today that we could not comfortably stand still on them for two minutes together to look at the pictures – and the shrill North Wind is [erased word] blowing so freshly that our Gondola <u>really rocked</u> this afternoon at the entrance of the Grand Canal. Warned by these signs of evening frostiness, I have purchased a Venetian Capote – an immense long garment which [erased word] falls below my knees and is made of some hair cloth, thickly lined and renowned for its resistance to wind and weather. A Monk's hood is attached to the Collar, to keep the head and face warm in case of necessity – and the whole is sold for sixteen English shillings. With this, and my bulky British Wrappers, I can defy the elements – even when we come to sledges on the top of the French Alps.

How are you? and how is Charley? and how do the country plans go on? I shall have all these questions answered when I get back – as well as two others of an indignant nature which I mean to address to those two epistolary recreants Messrs Charles Ward and Edward Pigott. I told the first to write to me at Florence, and the last at Venice; and at neither place has the ghost of a letter appeared. I suppose they delayed writing their answers – though I gave them time enough in all conscience, in both cases – till it was too late. Catch me writing to them again – that's all!

I believe I have a great deal more to [tell: erased] write to you, but I cannot for the life of me tell where I ought to begin "fetching up my arrears", just at present. We travel at such a rate, visit so many places and see so many things, that reflection and remembrance appear to be [erasure] absurd impossibilities, until our [erased word] journey is fairly over. It seems seven months instead of seven weeks since we started from Folkestone. As for <u>notes</u>, I have not made one – they are all in my letters, and what is not in my letters must be reserved for our fireside. In the mean time, the waiter is laying the cloth for dinner, and my hunger is so sharply stimulated by the sight of the knives and forks that I am physically incapable of writing any more. So, with my love to Charley (for whom I have bought a Roman Crucifix!!!)

Believe me | Ever affectionately yours, | W. Wilkie Collins

Notes

1. "hree thousa" of "three thousand" underlined twice.
2. Dickens offered a slightly different description to his wife: "Imagine the procession led by Collins with incipient moustache, spectacles, slender legs, and extremely dirty dress gloves – Egg second, in a white hat and a straggly mean little black beard – Inimitable bringing up the rear, in full dress and big sleeved coat, rather considerably ashamed" (Dickens, *Letters*, VII, 215).

To Charles Ward, [15 March 1854]
MS: Huntington:[1] unheaded, undated

Summary:
His sentiments on the subject of the approaching Russian War, are dictated by the most disinterested feelings of Patriotism.

Note

1. WC postcript on a letter from Millais to Ward, accompanied by drawing of a sailing ship with figure at the bow and comment "Sir C. Napier | British Fleet".

To Edward Pigott, 16 May 1854
MS: Huntington

17, Hanover Terrace | May 16th 1854

Summary:
WC is delighted to hear he is getting better. What a "sad time" Pigott has had. His new book[1] comes out on the 25th, and he has 70 pages still to write, besides negotiations with Bentley. Hopes they will meet soon.

Note

1. i.e., *Hide and Seek*, published in three volumes by Richard Bentley.

To Mrs Harriet Collins, [early June 1854]
MS: Private Possession

17, Hanover Terrace

Summary:
"You will find inside letters from Millais and Charley and Miss Otter." Tells his mother "Old Mrs Dickinson[1] called to ask you to dinner, just as I was going to Miss Coutts's – so I went to Stratton Street <u>dry</u> and saved cab hire. A nice party – rooms palatial, especially the new one, which is one of the most beautiful things I ever saw – grand ... – plenty of famous people – Miss Coutts full of kindness and hospitality ... Opera the other night. Grisi[2] wonderful". WC got a seat from a Press friend in a private box.
"I have another letter from Bentley – <u>sanguine</u> this time. We have nearly sold half the edition. Not so bad in War times, and before a single review has come out, or people have had time to talk about the book[3] to each other."

Notes

1. Mrs Dickinson, widowed mother of Frances Dickinson (1820–1898), and family friend, see Dickens, *Letters*, VIII, 316 n.2., and Gasson.
2. Giulia Grisi (1811–1869), soprano. She "excelled as Bellini's Norma". Dickens also saw her in "Lucrezia Borgia". See letter to Mrs Georgina Hogarth, 22 July 1854: *Letters*, VII, 377, n.1.
3. *Hide and Seek.*

To [J. Marsh], [10 June 1854]

MS: University of Illinois, Urbana. Davis, p. 155

17, Hanover Terrace | Saturday

My dear Sir,

Did we settle that the <u>Globe</u> was to have a copy of Hide and Seek? I was asked whether a copy had been sent, last night, by one of the contributors to the paper, and not being certain what arrangement we had made, was guarded in my answer. I only write now to tell you of this, in case y<u>ou</u> think it desirable to let the paper have a copy. If you do not, we can allow the matter "<u>to be adjourned sine die</u>".[1]

The proper negotiations are in progress with Th<u>e Thunderer</u>. I hope to give a satisfactory account of them in a few days. As to the subscription – about which Mr Bentley wrote to me the other day in a very desponding tone – I don't care two straws whether it is large or small. Give the Press time to introduce the book to public notice – and give the readers time to [erased words] get through the story – and I have no fear about the result.[2] The booksellers and librarians are a parcel of apes, and the public voice is the stick that cudgels them into activity.

Faithfully yours | W.W.C.

Notes

1. *Hide and Seek* favourably reviewed in the *Globe and Traveller*, 24 June 1854, p. 3.
2. *The Times* did not review the novel.

To Richard Bentley, 10 July 1854

MS: University of Illinois, Urbana. Davis, p. 157.

17, Hanover Terrace | 10th July 1854

Summary:
Declines his offer for the copyrights of *Antonina* and *Basil*. Cannot afford to part with £200. Hopes that he may have another opportunity in future of making *Antonina* and *Basil* his own property.

To Richard Bentley, 12 July 1854

MS: University of Illinois, Urbana. Davis, pp. 157–8

17, Hanover Terrace | July 12th 1854/

Summary:

Thanks him for the modified offer for the repurchase of *Antonina* and *Basil*. But he has "no <u>certainty</u>[1] of being better able to pay the second £100 at the end of a year's time than" he has now. "If this war continues,[2] the prospects of Fiction are likely to be very uncertain."

Notes

1. WC doubly underlines "ertain" of "certainty".
2. The Crimean War.

To Mrs Harriet Collins, 27 July 1854

MS: PM

<u>Vi</u>lla <u>du Camp de Dr</u>oite | B<u>oulogne sur Me</u>r | July 27th 1854

My dear Mother,[1]

We are living here in such a state of Elysian laziness, that it is an absolute effort to me to write this letter. The cool sea breeze blows over us by day and by night without cessation. We are on the top of one of the highest of the hills above Boulogne. My bedroom windows look straight down into the valley, with buildings and gardens climbing up the opposite side of the hill, till they end under the ramparts and trees of the old town. This house is all doors, cupboards, and windows – the rooms are bright, clean, and lively beyond description – and when we want to be out of doors, we have a garden with pretty flowers and [turf] walks on one side, and a field with a haycock to lie under on the other. In this field we have just been playing at "Rounders" with the boys. If I had not had this game to stir me up, I very much doubt whether I could have summoned energy enough to sit down to this letter.

The camp is within easy walking distance – far enough off, however, to be no annoyance. We should not know here, as long as we kept within the grounds that there was a camp at all. Numerous numbers of soldiers are all about us nevertheless. Boulogne itself swarms with them. Drums and bugles are to be heard in every street. Our old locality – the market place had a whole regiment in it today with a real live <u>Vivandière</u> serving out drams to the men in the most operatic manner possible. You may be curious to know what was the dress of this Fille du Regiment. She had on a short glazed hat, stuck very much on one side – a tight blue jacket that fitted her without a wrinkle, an ample scarlet petticoat – ample as to breadth – that came to her knees – and scarlet trousers. Her hair was dressed in the regular feminine way – plain bands, with a knot or lump, or bunch, or whatever you call it, behind [and: erased]. Her small barrel of spirits was coloured with red, blue, and gold, and slung over her shoulder. She was a very passably pretty woman – was evidently treated by the men with great distinction – and appeared to be very glad to find that all the civilians in the market place were taking special notice of her. We have no [two erased words] women among us who wear the uniform of the regiment they serve and follow. So the Vivandière was a great sight for the British part of the population of Boulogne.

No plans about expeditions into the surrounding country have been settled yet. We are talking of a trip to a queer place in this neighbourhood – situated in a slough of black mud, which obliged the inhabitants of the village to wear a peculiar kind of [high] patten instead of shoes whenever they leave their [indecipherable] all the year round.

I suppose you are now staying at Maidenhead. Give my kind regards to my friends there. Also write and tell me any news there is, and say what Charley's plans are. Does he stay at home? Give him my love and believe me | Affectionately yours | W. W. C.

If Charley intends leaving home, you had better ask Charles Ward to call once a week and see if there are any letters

Note

1. Envelope with postmark. Alongside the address, WC writes: "Direct [to] me care of <u>Charles Dickens Eqr</u>".

To Charles Collins, 31 August 1854

MS: PM

Villa du Camp de Droite | Boulogne sur Mer | August 31st 1854

My dear Charley, [1]
  There is to be a "grand dinner" here on the 12th of September – Mark Lemon & Bradbury Evans are coming to it – and Dickens is hospitably resolved that I shall not go away till the furtive solemnity is accomplished. I am far too comfortable and happy [erasure] in this charming place to be ready to leave it – so I remain gladly enough for the dinner on the 12th and

my return home may therefore be considered as deferred till the middle of next month (September).

We have hardly had a cloud in the sky here for the last week – except at sunset, when fiery and purple clouds seem to rise and float towards us from the English shore. The airless heat in the morning is something indescribable – but every afternoon the <u>sea</u>-breeze rises, and our flags stream out gallantly above the haystack. We have increased the height of the mast, and have now got a <u>tri-color</u> three yards long floating over the Union Jack (of similar dimensions), in honour of the alliance between the two countries, and in special compliment to France the land of our temporary sojourn. When the morning breeze freshens to what the sailors call "half a gale of wind" we [erasure] bring out a mighty kite – jointly produced by the labour and ingenuity of Dickens and your humble servant – which is supposed to be capable of taking up more string than can ever be brought to accommodate it. For cool evenings we have a [<u>mammoth</u>] [Trap] Bat, and Ball, and play matches in which there is very little [erased word] science and a great deal of fun. So the time passes – as to amusements – inside the gates of this "Property".

Outside the gates, we have every sort of preparation [erasure] going forward for the military manoeuvres which are to take place as soon as the Emperor comes. The right Wing of the camp has now got its full complement of Four Thousand men. The tents and mudhuts of the soldiers [erasure] stretch out along the coast, literally for miles and miles as far as you can see. On the "Fete Day" of Napoleon, we went to see a military mass out at the camp. They made the loveliest little rustic Chapel with evergreen Gothic arches, and a soft floor of [indecipherable word] ferns. Flags floated all around it, and the sea (as blue on that day as the Mediterranean itself), murmured within a stone's throw of the back of the chapel. Ten thousand men were under canvas for the occasion. The regiments approached the chapel from all sides, all at the same time converging towards our common centre [indecipherable word] and threatening in the far distance, bright almost as the sun itself, with glittering fragments, and flailing swords, and gleaming cannon, as they approached and formed three sides of a square – an immense square – in front of the chapel. Then the General on a white horse, followed by a staff of thirty or forty mounted officers, came galloping to the front – pulled up suddenly – was saluted by a braying of trumpets and a rolling of drums – and then the mass began. It was accompanied by the military bands. When the flag was raised, the artillery fired their great guns & the ten thousand men presented arms – the bayonets and swords all floating up together into the sun. It was one of the grandest sights I ever saw.[2]

The service was performed by one meek-looking old <u>curè</u>, who came shambling in through all the magnificent military preparations with his nasty black Cassock trailing in the dust, and his green umbrella under his arm. He put on his vestments in a sort of ornamental cowshed – and after mass preached a sermon which had the great and singular merit of being only five minutes long. One noticeable point in connection with the secular part of this military mass, was the extraordinary civility of the officers and soldiers. When the general public got into wrong positions (which they did about a dozen times) they were not pushed about as at our reviews – but politely entreated with bows and smiles to move back a little. One officer made his band play to please us – and another sent privates off duty, scouring all over the camp for chairs for all the ladies – every woman in the place being included under this denomination. It is really a remarkable army, for good breeding and quiet behaviour.

The few men who get drunk on fête days, are only harmlessly exhil[a]rated. They dance, embrace each other, sing opera airs, and flourish their pocket handkerchiefs – but interfere with nobody. Charles Ward would be enchanted with the contrast they present to the British Grenadiers.

I intend this letter for Mother, when you have done with it. Give her my love and tell her to stop in the country as long as she can.

Affectionately yours, | W.C.

Notes

1. In the margin WC writes "I hope you will stick to a modern life subject. You did quite right in putting my name down for Brandling's book."
2. WC's sheet ends here. In the margin he writes: "Show this to C. Ward – till I can write him a letter for himself."

To Charles Collins, 7 September 1854
MS: PM

Villa du Camp de Droite | Boulogne sur Mer | September 7th 1854

My dear Charley,[1]

I brought no great coat here with me (thinking I should leave during the heats of August). Crossing the channel however, in the middle of September, as I shall most probably do – is not to be accomplished comfortably without "top-hamper" of some kind – as we say at sea. Will you be kind enough, as soon as you get this, to have my brown coat <u>with the wide sleeves</u> wrapped up in a piece of brown paper, and to send the parcel by the lad from the stables, addressed to <u>Mark Lemon Esq.</u> | Punch Office | 85, Fleet Street. | Lemon is coming here on Monday and will be at the Punch Office on Saturday. If you can manage to send the parcel on Friday afternoon (assuming that you get this Friday morning – tomorrow morning –) it will be sure to find him. I will write a note to Lemon, on the other side of this sheet, which you can put into an envelope and send with the coat by way of explanation.

About the public fêtes and military solemnities here the newspapers and popular talk in general will inform you. In regard to our private share in the present rejoicing, I have to tell you that we illuminated the house in the English way,[2] and astonished all Boulogne by the spectacle. The French illuminate outside their houses, with oil lamps in devices with which the wind interferes considerably. We shut all the front windows in the English way, and put candles in them. This house is all windows. We had <u>114</u>[3] candles burning, in 114 clay candlesticks, stuck on a 114 nails, [erased word] driven into the window sashes. When we were ready to light up, every soul in the house (except the children) was stationed at a window – Dickens rang a bell – and at that signal we lit up the whole <u>114</u> candles in less than a minute. The effect from a distance was as if the whole house, was one steady blaze of light. It was seen for miles and miles round. The landlord went into hysterical French ecstasies – the [erasure] populace left their illuminations in the town, and crowded to the Ramparts opposite our hill, to stare in amazement. We let off fire works besides – and to crown all, we had not the slightest alarm or accident. I shall have more to tell, when we meet.

Affectionately yours, | W.C.

Notes

1. WC writes in the margin: "I have not yet fixed a day for returning, but you may expect me, unless you hear to the contrary any day next week <u>after</u> the 12th. My love to Mother."
2. *The Times* of 6 September 1854 noted that "The Mayor of Boulogne, M. Fontaine, had invited every inhabitant to illuminate his house façade "in order to celebrate the Anglo–French Alliance and the arrival of the Royal Yacht with Prince Albert on board on Tuesday 5 September. He was met by the French Emperor (see Dickens, *Letters*, VII, 410, nn. 3,6).
3. "114" underlined twice.

To Charles Ward, 10 September 1854
MS: PM

Villa du Camp de Droite | September 10th 1854 | Sunday

My dear Ward,[1]

Thank you for what you have done about the Chronicle[2] and for what you mean to [erasure] try with Hood.[3] In relation to the latter negotiation,

if it should not succeed, I have only [three] words to say – <u>Try no more</u> –
or (if you like the form better) – <u>Hood be damned</u>.

I shall be back, I believe, next week – at the latter part of it. This smooth
existence of mine will soon become as ruffled as yours – though in a
different way. I have plenty of hard work in prospect – some of it, too, work
of a new kind, and of much uncertainty as to results. I mean the dramatic
experiments which I have been thinking of, and which you must keep a
profound secret from everybody, in case I fail with them. This will be an
anxious winter for me. If I were not constitutionally reckless about my
future prospects, I should feel rather nervous [two erased words] just now
in looking forward to my winter's work.

Two thirds of your depression of spirits come from want of change, and
will be cured by a holiday. The other third may be successfully combatted
by mild [indecipherable word] and dogged spirit – drinking every now and
then. As to what you shall do next month I have an economical suggestion
to make. Consider Hamilton Terrace as your headquarters and start off by
early-morning trains short distances into the country — [erasure] walk [s:
erased] about for hours wherever you please – dine cheap – and return by
the late train – sometimes, where the [indceipherable word] can be
depended on; sleep and return next evening. I have a map of the country
25 miles round London, [see: erased] which you can take possession of –
and whenever I can make a holiday, I will help you to assume the character
of Nature's housemaid and "<u>scour the plains</u>". If you want a cheap and
healthy holiday plan there you have it!

You know as much about our public festivities here, from the papers, as
I do. I saw the Victoria and Albert and the two attendant steamers enter
Boulogne harbour from the heights. It was a very pretty sight, and was fired
at by large guns and small with the noisy royalty proper to the occasion.
The reviews I have not seen – hating [just], knowing nothing of soldiering
and having already [assisted] at military manoeuvers [which: erased] before
the Emperor's arrival. The public concert was not loud enough for the
open air – but some excellent players helped to make what music there was.
The Fireworks were very grand – but we had fireworks of our own to let
off on the same night and did not pay them so much attention as they
deserved. Our illumination of this house was a veritable "blaze of
triumph"– ask Charley to show you my letter giving an account of it. The
public ball was not different from other public balls here – and was injured
by threatenings of rain. Now we are all quiet again, and the last days of the
English excursionists have drained off. I have much more to tell – but my
paper is exhausted, and I shall see you I hope this day week. In the
meantime keep up your spirits – give my love to Jane (whom I trust to find
better when I see her) and believe in | Ever yours | WWC

Notes

1. In the margin of the first leaf of writing paper WC writes "My love to my mother and Charley, if you see them – they know that they [may] expect me back towards the end of next week."
2. i.e. the *Morning Chronicle*.
3. Probably a reference to Thomas Hood (1799–1845).

To Mrs Harriet Collins, 13 September 1854
MS: PM

> [Villa du Camp de Droite | Boulogne sur Mer] | Wednesday evening
> | September 13th [1854]

My dear Mother,

There is a general break-up here on Friday next – so on Friday you may expect me at Hanover Terrace. The boat crosses at $\frac{1}{2}$ past 3 in the afternoon – and there is a train from Folkestone which starts at 7 in the evening, and reaches town about 10. If we get through the Customs House in time this is the train we shall travel by, and I shall most likely be home soon after eleven. Let the servants sit up, with orders not to despair of me until 12 o'Clock has struck – by which time if I do not ring at the bell they may conclude that I have been obliged to stay at Folkestone – or change my plans in some way. Leave me some cold meat, and a bottle of beer, I shall want nothing more. I hope I shall find you all right in your accustomed atmosphere of the Park. We are well out of the way of Cholera there, I should think. My love to Charley. All news I reserve till we meet.

> In haste | Affectionately yours | W Wilkie Collins

I have got the Morning Chronicle Review.[1] [Some] one sent it here. I will bring it for you in my trunk.

Note

1. Unidentified.

To Edward Pigott, [18 December 1854]
MS: Huntington

17, Hanover Terrace | Monday morning

My dear Edward,

Thank-you for the pains you are taking about my books. I have left "Basil" at the office today. Will you explain to M. Forgues that the first edition in 3 volumes is out of print? I am therefore obliged to send him the cheap edition.

Don't talk about having no home to go to – you know you are at home here. Come and eat your Christmas dinner with us – you will find your knife, fork, plate and chair all ready for you. Time six o'clock.

Millais is still staying with us. He has [moreover] got the most delightful rooms in a new <u>artist's house</u>, just behind the church with the extinguisher-spire in Langham Place. He has a noble painting-room – a large bedroom, a bath-room and the full use of a kitchen, for £50 a year! – nothing in Paris, as cheap, as that I suspect. How I should like to be with you! how I wish I could get out of the way of the <u>Patriots</u>! Nothing is left to send to the soldiers now – but Ices for next summer. Every man has his potted grouse flannel waistcoats of the finest [Cambravol], Bible prayer-book, and Butlers Analogy – (to wipe his a-se with). Our virtuous country women have been dancing with the Russian officers at a ball at Brighton – that is the last war news.

The paper goes on famously – I have done an article for this week on <u>Chaucer</u>, [apropos] of Bell's admirable edition.[1] The Christmas number of Household Words has made a great impression. It is thought the best – a, noble, and exquisite story by Dickens in it – a delightful sketch of two French children by Sala. <u>My</u> "poor Traveller" is a broken-down Lawyer – who has "given satisfaction", I am glad to say.[2] I am just putting the last hand to the Finale of my play – More, however of this, and many things when we meet.

Mind you come on Christmas day

Affectionately yours | W.W.C

There are no French works or plays I particularly want just now – or I should take advantage of your kind offer – give my respects to M. Regnier if you see him again, and if he remembers me.

Notes

1. "Chaucer" *The Leader*, V: 248 (23 December 1854), 125–6: a review of *Poetical Works of Geoffrey Chaucer*, ed. R. Bell (London: Parker and Son, 1854).

2. "The Seven Poor Travellers" published in *Household Words*, 14 December 1854. The first contribution was by Dickens, the second by Sala, the third by Adelaide Procter, the fourth by Wilkie Collins, the fifth by Sala, the sixth by Eliza Lynn, and the seventh by A. Procter.

To Edward Pigott, [December 1854]

MS: Huntington:[1] Published K. Lawrence, "The Religion of Wilkie Collins: Three Unpublished Documents", *Huntington Library Quarterly* 52 (1989), pp. 396–8.

Note

It seems to me that people who think this new Proclamation by the Pope of the Immaculate Conception of the Virgin Mary, likely to damage the Papist Church, take rather too hasty a view, and decide (as it appears to me) quite erroneously. Damage to the Papist Church can only come from the Papists themselves. If this new piece of sacred Tom Foolery shakes the faith of individual Romanists, or disunites congregations, down the Church may go in good time certainly. – If it does neither, the Church stands firm. That seems clear enough to begin with.

Now what shakes a man's faith? – an outrage on his common sense or rather a flat official contradiction to whatever is purely the result of the exercise of his reasoning powers. Such a contradiction to the reasoning power of any man woman or child in this world (not absolutely an idiot) may most certainly be found in this new Proclamation.

But how can that affect individual Romanists – or Romanist congregations. Does any Papist make use of his reason when he lets his Church give him his religion? Does not his Church expressly tell him he must give up his reason, and accept mysteries which outrage it, implicitly as matters of faith. Does not every good Papist who will not let his butcher, baker, wife, or children, rob him of one particle of his common sense if he can help it, voluntarily hand that common sense over altogether to the keeping of his Priest whenever his Priest asks him for it? If this be true – and I can't see how it can be otherwise than true – where is the common sense, where is the reasoning power, to be outraged and contradicted among Papist con-gregations by the Pope's new Proclamation? What is there in the Immaculate Conception to outrage millions of people who believe (if one may abuse the word by using it in such a sense) – who believe in "The Real Presence"? – when Smith, a lay Papist, believes that if he gives money to Jones a clerical Papist to pray his soul out of Purgatory, Jones will succeed if Jones prays fairly up to his terms, what in Heaven's name is there in the Immaculate Conception to stagger Smith? For these reasons I think that the new Proclamation will rather be popular than otherwise <u>inside</u> the pale of the Papist Church.

Outside it has outraged the independent thinkers (a minority) and the Protestant Party – another minority compared with dunderheaded humanity in general. Said Dunderheaded humanity when it falls to being religious, wants anything you please in a religion – except common sense. In an age where thousands of people join the Mormons, I cannot see, for one, why the Immaculate Conception should stand in the Papists' way in making new converts. If infinite weakness, eagerly swallows infinite nonsense at the hands of Joe Smith, why not at the hands of Pius the Ninth?[2] – I am not at all sure that this consideration has not weighed privately with the Sacred College – and that the theological physicians of long standing have not slily dropped a fresh infusion of nonsense into their great dogmatic dose, with the wise purpose of not letting even the smallest quack in the same line of business go too far ahead before them.

Notes

1. This note is separated from the WC holograph letter now at the Huntington to which it was originally attached.
2. Pope Pius IX declared on 8 December 1854 (the Feast of the Immaculate Conception), the doctrine of the Immaculate Conception.

Part III
Literary Activity:
Folkestone, Paris, London

1855–26 July 1859

LITERARY ACTIVITY: FOLKESTONE, PARIS, LONDON

Germs of situations, characters and ideas – later to surface in his novels – reveal themselves in his letters. A letter of 24 January 1855 notes Bentley issuing a second edition of *Rambles Beyond Railways*. One letter [14 February 1855] sees Wilkie enjoying himself in Paris with Charles Dickens. On his return to London Wilkie is involved with the affairs of the Garrick Club and with the production of his drama *The Lighthouse*. He refers in one letter [20 March 1855] to being "in doctor's hands again".

A percipient letter [2 July 1855] to Edward Pigott written on John Millais' wedding day expresses his wish that his friend may successfully consummate his marriage. Letters [August and September 1855] from Folkestone, where he is again staying with Dickens and his family, follow what has now become a routine of trips to Boulogne and involvement with the Dickens menagerie. On 2 September 1855 an activity which Wilkie was continually to return to emerges in a letter to his mother – yachting. It also refers to Thackeray, Kinglake, the working on a manuscript and observes that his "soul is sick of the seaside women of England".

The end of February 1856 sees Wilkie and Dickens in Paris. Wilkie writes ecstatically of his delight in his Parisian apartment, of his lost luggage and the publication of *A Rogue's Life*: Dickens is "delighted with the first chapter". In March 1856 Dickens returns to London and Wilkie stays in Paris. Subsequent letters to his mother and Charles Ward are full of requests for money, most of which he has earned from his writings – his mother having the only family bank account until he opens his own in the summer of 1860. Ill-health is not far from the surface. He writes from Paris of "sweating for four consecutive days". He tells his mother that he "read the sketch of [his] new novel to Dickens ... he was quite excited and surprised by it". This was *The Dead Secret*.

Wilkie is sufficiently recognized as an author to have his work included in the Tauchnitz series of English novels: in this instance *After Dark*. Mid-August and September 1856 see Wilkie with Dickens and his family in Boulogne again. In April 1857 he is corresponding with the publisher, Frederick Mullett Evans concerning payments and the publication of *The Dead Secret*. In a letter to Charles Ward [May 1859] there is an early mention of Caroline Graves who is to play such a crucial part in his life and with whom he sets up home. Indeed letters are written from different addresses – from Hanover Terrace and Clarence Terrace (where he lived with his mother) and New Cavendish Street (where he lived with Caroline). Immediately following his annual visit to Dickens at Broadstairs, Wilkie is searching for his own place nearby to write his next novel. He lights upon Church Hill Cottage on the Ramsgate road just outside Broadstairs, Kent.

To George Bentley, 24 January 1855
MS: BL

17 Hanover Terrace | Regents Park | January 24th 1855

My dear Sir,

   Yesterday, in clearing out one of my study-table drawers, I disinterred the enclosed account of the Second Edition of the "Rambles". Will you kindly hand it to Mr Marsh to make up to the present time, and to place among the expenses incurred the £10, which you obliged me by advancing to Mr Brandling?

   Our second edition has now been published three years! – and, for the sake of the novelty of the sensation, I should like to feel, <u>this</u> year, that it has returned something – however little – to the "owners on both sides". Will you, therefore, kindly send me a cheque, when your settling day comes, for whatever share of the profits I may be entitled to, up to the present time? As to the copies on hand, I am sure you will agree with me that any attempt to dispose of them <u>now,</u> would be perfectly useless. We must wait till better times. The war has certainly had a specially disastrous influence on us. I was privately informed, some little time since, that the <u>great Review</u> of "Hide and Seek" was actually in type, and that but for Sebastopol, the Thunderer's notice would have appeared some months ago. After this, you will not be surprised to hear that I side with Bright on the subject of the war!¹

Faithfully yours | W. Wilkie Collins

George Bentley Esq.

Note

1. Bentley published *Hide and Seek*, 6 June 1854. England entered the Crimean War on 28 March 1854. The novel wasn't reviewed in *The Times*. Bright opposed the Crimean War and overseas intervention.

To Mrs Harriet Collins, 14 February 1855
MS: PM

Hotel Meurice | Paris | February 14th 1855/

My dear Mother,

   We got here on Monday evening, with much less suffering from the cold than we had anticipated. The sea-passage was, for the time of year, an easy one, the greatest sharpness of the frosty air being on land, at Boulogne.

Here, the difference between the French atmosphere and the English made itself piercingly felt. Compared with French frost, our national frost seems to be always wrapped up in more or less of soft fog. We should have felt this difference unpleasantly enough on the railway from Boulogne to Paris – but for the excellent metal cases of boiling-water placed in each carriage, and renewed several times in the course of the journey. These kept our feet and legs warm, and made the air like the air of a room. Tell Charley, with my love, that we passed, [erased word] beyond Amiens miles of fields overflowed, and now covered with the smoothest perfectest ice, unmarked by the traces of a single skate.

We are settled here in a delightful apartment, looking out on the Tuileries, gorgeously-furnished drawing-room – bedrooms with Turkey carpets – reception room – hall – cupboards – passages – all to ourselves. Paris is almost snowed up. The Boulevard pavement is inches thick with snow and ice – the Cafés are filled with shivering Frenchmen who congregate round the stoves. It is the height of the gay season here, in spite of the Siberian state of the weather. The great masked ball at the Opera takes place this week. The two Theatres we have been to, [erased word] up to this time, proved to be well filled. In short Paris amuses itself as gaily as ever, and only talks occasionally on the [erased word] miserable subject of the war in the East.

The principal effect of the Alliance here seems to be shown in the great additional number of English inscriptions one sees [erased word] in the shop windows, and in the increase of the [erased word] once rare class who speak English. Shopkeepers, cabmen & waiters, [and: erased] if they only know two words of our language, let off these two words at our countrymen in the most vehemently persevering way. I suppose this is by way of practising for the Exhibition time. The building is externally nearly complete. The roof only is of glass – all the rest is stone-work of the solidest kind – evidently built to serve some permanent purpose quite unconnected with Sight-seers and Exhibitions.

I think we shall be away about ten days, dating from the day of our start. But nothing is positively settled yet. Put any letters that come for me, away in a drawer – and tell any inquiring friends, generally, that I shall be back towards the end of the month.

Mind you write me an answer to this, directing simply "Hotel Meurice, Paris" – and telling me how you and Charley are, and any home news there is. I shall most likely write again, and [tell: erased] warn you of the exact day of our return.

Ever Affectionately Yours | W. Wilkie Collins

I suppose my parcel has gone safely to Parkers by this time – and that Charley and Ward have settled the money-matters with my cheques – also that my packet of books went to Pigott.[1]

Note

1. In this letter WC makes no mention of being unwell; however, Dickens in a letter to François Regnier written the same day, 14 February 1855, writes: "Collins not being very well has seen Dr Olliffe, and the Doctor has given him some strong medicine, and has cautioned him not to go out in the snow for two or three days, except in a carriage and then well wrapped up" (*Letters*, VII, 537).

To Mrs Harriet Collins, 19 February [1855]
MS: PM

Hotel Meurice | Monday Feby 19th /

My dear Mother,

We propose leaving [Paris] tomorrow (Tuesday the 20th) – sleeping at Boulogne on Tuesday night, and crossing, weather permitting on Wednesday – in which case we shall be due at London Bridge at a quarter past nine on Wednesday night. The only delay which [can] take place may be occasioned by the state of the sea. If we find it blowing a gale we shall probably wait a day for calmer weather. But no such necessity will I hope occur. Under any circumstances, leave the door on the latch and a kettle with some warm water at the fire and some wine on the night table on Wednesday – for we may be after our time in consequence of the snow.

It has been three degrees colder here than in London. But we have been amusing ourselves in spite of the Polar state of the temperature. Did I tell you [erased word] before I started, that we meditated a further trip to Bordeaux? I think not. We have been obliged to give up this "mad" idea (as you would call it); the Railway traffic in the West of France having been literally stopped altogether by the snow.

We have escaped with only <u>two</u> dinner parties, and have had our time to ourselves, for the most part, from morning till night. I [must: erased] wait till I see you to tell you all our adventures – having neither time nor space to write about them now. With love to Charley | Affectionately yours | W. Wilkie Collins

To E.M. Ward, [20 March 1855]
MS: Texas: Coleman

17, Hanover Terrace | Tuesday | [20 March 1855]

My dear Ned,

I have ordered the <u>Athenaeum,</u> and shall read the article about you with the greatest interest. Mr Darvill's letter put me up to the facts of the case which are certainly disgraceful enough.[1] The whole question of protection of the interests of authors as well as artists in their own works, is coming before the public – in connection with the taking off of the Newspaper Stamp, which will enable any scoundrel who starts a low paper to steal articles from good papers – or <u>whole</u> <u>books</u> with perfect impunity, as the act now stands – just in fact as the scoundrel stole your name and sold his copy of your picture with it.[2] If nothing else will do, the authors must have a <u>League</u> and the artists must join them. Parliament and hereditary legislators don't care a straw about us or our interests – we must somehow make them care.

I will mention the case to Dickens of course the next time I see him – or, if I don't soon get well, – the next time <u>he</u> comes <u>here</u>. I am in the doctor's hands again – a long story which I will not bother you with now.

I hope Mrs Ward is progressing satisfactorily towards what some French author calls "<u>the sublime fact of maternity</u>". My love to the children – My mother has been laid up with influenza – and is only just out of bed. Charley goes on slowly – slowly – with his picture – We are all sick and sorry together – but as patient, as righteous Job – and as cheerful about "the good time coming" as Mr Henry Russell the eminent vocalist.[3]

My mother sends all kind messages – so does Charley – Millais has been ill in bed, to complete the <u>partie carrée</u>.[4] He has only just got to work again.

Ever yours, | WWC

Notes

1. Reports that one of the paintings of the brother of Charles James Ward, Edward Matthew Ward (Ned) (1816–1879) was copied and sold as an original appeared in *The Athenaeum* (10 March 1855). Ward's solicitor, Henry Darvill, proposed, in the same issue, that to stop fraud the government stamp all originals. The next issue of *The Athenaeum* (17 March 1855) contained an editorial section reviewing an extensive correspondence concerning the matter.
2. As Richard Altick relates in *The English Common Reader* (Chicago 1957), the Newspaper Stamp Act of 1819 was aimed at the radical press yet restricted the cheap press. The 4d tax on newspapers costing less than 6d attacked anti-government or anti-religious papers, but spared those which dealt in "matters of devotion, piety, or charity" (pp. 321–54). From March to mid-June Parliament debated and passed a bill to repeal the Stamp Act.
3. Henry Russell (1813–1900) tenor and actor (Boase). Ned's wife the painter Henrietta Ada Ward (1832–1924) had six children.
4. i.e., party of four.

To Edward Pigott, [2 July 1855]
MS: Huntington

17, Hanover Terrace | Monday

My dear Edward,

I am very glad to hear that Mr Galloway[1] will be able to attend at the office during the latter part of the week – the more so, as Dickens knows of no man sufficiently trustworthy and intelligent whose services could be had for a temporary period only.

Tomorrow is John Millais his wedding day. Luard[2] and Charles Ward and his wife dine here. Do come too (as one of Jack's friends) if you have no other engagements – We dine at six, and shall drink limitless libations. May he consumate successfully! and have the best cause in the world to lie late on Wednesday morning![3] (You see I am like that excellent parson and bulwark of the church, who married George) – I can't resist Priapian jesting on the marriages of my friends. It is such a dreadfully serious thing afterwards, that we ought to joke about it so long as one can.

Affy yours | WW.C.

We act the Lighthouse (in public) at the Campden House Theatricals. Tomorrow week.

No need to dress if you come tomorrow.

Notes

1. Alfred E. Galloway, on *The Leader* payroll in 1852 and its publisher and printer 21 October 1854–18 December 1858.
2. John Luard (1830–1860), painter and close friend of Millais.
3. "Millais married the still-virgin Mrs Ruskin in 1855 ... With Effie's encouragement Millais came through the marital ordeal triumphantly. `By George, Charlie, I am truly a favoured man,' he wrote to Charles Collins after the wedding night. `It is such a delight to feel a woman always about one part of oneself'" (Peters, pp. 125–6).

To Edward Pigott, 9 August 1855
MS: Huntington

3, Albion Villas | Folkestone | Thursday

My dear Edward,

I return the proof corrected. Why should you not come here for this next Saturday? or, if you can't manage that, make up your mind for Saturday fortnight – I am not certain, but I hope I shall be able to prolong my stay here until that time.

We made a great success on Monday of the trip to Boulogne. The ladies went with us. Blue sky and calm sea on the passage over – everything ready for us (in accordance with a Telegraphic message) at the Hotel des Bains. Tuesday we went to the Camp, and returned in the evening to Folkestone. A roughish passage – All sick except Miss Hogarth, Stanfield[1] and your humble servant. Such a contrast between the picturesquely martial look of the French camp, and the dreary unmilitary aspect of our camp over here at Shorncliffe – between the brisk jollity of the French Soldiers and the hangdog stolidity of the foreign legion![2] Five hundred of these wretched substitutes for a national soldiery were disembarked here yesterday, from a transport, for the Queen's inspection today. Such a set of dirty, ill-looking vagabonds, I never saw in uniform before. The <u>stench</u> of them, as they stood in line before befouling the fragrant sea air on the pier, is not out of my nose yet. If <u>these</u> (paid) allies don't disgrace us in the Crimea I give up appearances for ever. Falstaff himself would have blushed at the sight of them!

If it is convenient to you, any time next week, to let me have my cheque for MS, I wish you would ask Mr Galloway, to send it me in a Post Office Order, made payable at the <u>Office here</u>, to "<u>William</u>[3] <u>Wilkie Collins</u>" (3 Albion Villas, if they want want my address at Folkestone). I am obliged to give you this trouble, because my money shows signs of running short after the trip to Boulogne, and because, as <u>my</u> money is always put to my mother's account at Coutt's, I can't draw any of it without a cheque from her. She is, by this time, staying at Southsea – or I could get my "supplies" from Hanover Terrace easily enough.

<u>Do</u> come here – I know you would enjoy it so!

Affectionately yours | W.W.C.

Notes

1. Clarkson Stanfield (1793–1867) marine and landscape painter.
2. "On 22 August the Foreign Legion stationed at Shorncliffe and Dover assembled at Sandling Park, for a fête" (Dickens, *Letters*, VII, 696, n.3). This was a German legion created "to take over the duties of British Regiments sent to the Crimea ... The Queen had reviewed the camp on 9 Aug[ust]" (*ibid.* 692 n.2).
3. Underlined three times.

To Charles Ward, 20 August 1855
MS: PM

3, Albion Villas | Folkestone | August 20th 1855

My dear Ward[1]

We have just been out for a walk and have been driven back wet through by a squall rather before our usual time of returning — so I get a little leisure to write to you.

<u>Leisure</u> seems a curious word to use when I am [two erased words] supposed to be enjoying a holiday – but I am, in real truth, at work (beginning a new speculation) in the morning – In the afternoon we are taking prodigious walks and climbing inaccessible places – and, after a good dinner moistened with various good drinks, I leave you to imagine how utterly lazy I must necessarily feel all the evening considering the previous exertions of the day and the sleep-producing qualities of the sea air – My leisure time, in fact, is exclusively spent in smoking and sleeping – and I am getting fat in consequence, in spite of all the exercise.

I have no news to tell except that I meet George Smith nearly everyday – that we smile, nod, shake hands, exchange remarks about the weather, and are mutually and rapidly arriving at the end of our small talk. Wigan,[2] by the way (if Charley has not told you already) is unable to perform the Lighthouse[3] – his company not enabling him in the flourishing present state of the stage to "cast" the play. Dickens thinks I have had a lucky escape, and Charley (who went to see the actors at the Olympic [two erased words] foreboding that they might be actors in my drama) thinks so too. I <u>may</u> show the play to Regnier[4] when I go to Paris – but nobody else shall see it in London. The principal part really requires a first-rate serious actor – and where is he to be found, Anno Domini 1855, in this great and prosperous Kingdom of England? (Say nothing about this Olympic business, as Wigan might not like to have the real reason of his being obliged to decline the play generally [known].)

We have [erasure] had the Queen and Albert here, reviewing the Foreign Legion, and received by the local population with solid indifference. Said Foreign Legion is composed of the filthiest, clumsiest, drunkennest, ugliest set of unmitigated louts you ever looked upon. They are a disgrace to the country — The Worst of the Household troops is an elegant and [clean: erased] sober man by comparison with them.

So I hear that you have been made the happy father of another "Ogre"— the largest and stoutest baby ever borne. You lucky devil!

Will it be giving you any trouble if I ask you to send your Stationer or Porter to buy for me the following books: – ? 1. A secondhand copy of "Hide And Seek," advertised at <u>Mudies</u> for six shillings – (I can't ask Bentley in his present state to give me another copy if any are left). 2nd "Human Longevity" translated from the French. Published by Baillière. 3/- 3. "Magic & Witchcraft"[5] in Chapman & Hall's cheap "Series" price 1/-. Also, if any copies of the reduced "Mr Wray's Cash – Box", are still to be had at a shilling, or two shillings (I forget which) to get me two copies of the same – We have no copy of the book at Hanover Terrace. If you can keep these at the Strand for me till I come to town, I will send for or fetch them, when I reimburse you. But don't bother about these books, if it is any trouble.

Ever yours | W.W.C.

Notes

1. In the margin of the first leaf of writing paper WC writes "I shall most likely be back at the end of the month – but no day is fixed yet. Write and tell me how Jane is, and give her my love – and tell me any news you have."
2. George Smith (1824–1901). Publisher. Alfred Sydney Wigan (1814–1878: *DNB*), lessee of the Olympic, October 1853–August 1857.
3. First performed in a private production at Tavistock House, 15 June 1855.
4. François Joseph Philoclès Régnier (1807–1885), French actor and manager.
5. [George Moir], *Magic and Witchcraft*, reprinted from *The Foreign Quarterly Review*, 1852.

To Mrs Harriet Collins, 2 September 1855
MS: PM

3, Albion Villas | September 2nd 1855/

My dear Mother,

I ought to have written to you long ago, but I waited day after day until I could tell you something definite about my departure. Nothing was settled before yesterday, and then I made up my mind to get back this next week, towards the middle of it. There are some people I want to see and some things I have to do in London, before I leave again for Brockley Hall with Pigott – we are to start about the 10th, and, if we can manage it to include in the trip a ten days cruise in the Bristol Channel, sailing ultimately to the Scilly Islands. I shall not be back for good, most likely, before October – so much for my plans at present.

We have had a delightful time of it here – all alone, until the last week, when we had a little dinner company – Thackeray and Kinglake ("Eothen") among others; Thackeray pleasanter and quainter than I ever saw him before. Pigott came here, and slept a night, at the same time young Charles Dickens is now passing his holiday here, and Mark Lemon and his daughter arrived last night.[1] The boys have gone back to school and have thus helped to make room for the [accession] of Visitors.

I began to work at your M.Ss.[2] three weeks ago. After I had done fifty pages; leaving not many things and transferring others, but keeping as close as I could to the simplicity of your narrative, I began to have my doubts whether it would not be necessary (with the public) to make a story to hang your characters and incidents on. I had told Dickens, in confidence, the history of the Manuscript – and I now read to him what I had done. He thought it a good notion and well worth going on with, but felt as I did that without more story it would not do with the public. Strangers could not know that the thing was real – and novel-readers seeing my name on the title-page would expect a story. So I am going to [try back], and throw a little dramatic interest into what I have done – keeping the thing still simple of course and using a [two indecipherable words] of your materials. As soon as I have made the alterations and have started again, I will let you know [how] I proceed.

I shall most likely show "The Lighthouse" to Regnier when I go to Paris, to find out from him whether it is translatable and actable in French. As to trying anybody else in London it is useless. There is no actor on our stage capable of doing Dickens's part, Wigan was obliged to decline the play because he could not "cast" the part – that is, <u>act</u> it. If Macready had been still on the stage the play might have been performed – [erased word] any present English tragedian would make nothing of the part of "Aaron Gurnock".

This place is full – [erased word] troops of hideous women stagger about in the fresh breezes under hats as wide as umbrellas and as ugly as inverted washhand basins. The older, uglier, and fatter they are the bigger hats they put on – and the more execrably they dress themselves. My soul is sick of the seaside women of England. If I had not the bonnets of the ladies [erased word] in this house to look at, I should be in a rage from morning to night. Your story about the lady and the dentist is very good – but useless for book-purposes, because the public would not believe it. There would be the old cry of exageration – nevertheless it is very amusing.

Boating, fishing, and excursion-making have drained me of money (though I got five pounds from Charley) – and I have barely enough to take me back to town. If my calculations are right, I have £20 in your hands – left of the bill-paying. £10 I owe to you. Can you write me a cheque for the other £10, <u>cross it, "Coutts & Co"</u> and send it by post to [four heavily erased lines] <u>Charles Ward, at the Bank</u> (Coutts) telling him to keep the money till I call for it? If you have not got your cheque-book, you can write the draught on a blank sheet of paper. In any case, you must put a stamp on.

Why should you not go back to the Bullar's? Why not stop away until the end of October when it does you so much good? I should be at home all that month – and you know how well I can keep house. Forward me any letters you get from Charley – To Folkestone, if <u>before</u> Thursday – to Hanover Terrace, if after – I mean in case he is going at once to Perth.

Ever affectionately yours | W.W.C.

My kind regards to Miss Otter and Miss [Thompson]

Notes

1. Cf. Dickens, *Letters*, VII, 711, n.2; 712, n.9.
2. This is clearly a reference to the Manuscript his mother had written about her own life (now in HRC, University of Austin, Texas). The introductory part of *After Dark* attempts to use at least some of the ideas behind the MS.

To Edward Pigott, [4 September 1855]
MS: Huntington

3, Albion Villas | Tuesday

My dear Edward,

Dickens has persuaded me (as <u>this</u> week is his holiday time after finishing a certain preliminary division of the new book[1]) to stay here over Sunday. So that my arrival in town is deferred till Monday, when I shall return in the afternoon to London. If this is too late for you, by no means wait for me. I can follow you to Brockley on Thursday – or perhaps on Wednesday (the 12<u>th</u> or 13<u>th</u>) I shall be delighted to find myself at the Hall – but I must work every <u>morning</u>, having a new iron in the fire, which I will tell you about when we meet. Any books for the <u>Leader</u> I shall be delighted to do as well – and the afternoons can be consecrated to walks.

Now about the yacht trip – Everything very jolly, <u>except</u> the tremendous consideration of the <u>Equinox</u>. I find by my Almanack that it begins on the 23rd September. Surely we shall not have time for the Scilly Islands, starting only on the 18th or 19th? And as for returning in an Equinoctial Gale in a boat of 8 tons, with one able seaman on board, is that not rather "tempting Providence" by making a toil of a pleasure? Had we not better make a brief burst upon the Welsh coast, and get back before Boreas can overtake us?

If you should by any unforeseen cause be delayed in London, come and dine at Hanover Terrace at $\frac{1}{2}$ past 5 on Monday, (when I have <u>positively</u> settled to be back) – and we can talk things over.

Kindest remembrances from all here

The lunch bell is ringing!!

Affectly yours | W.W.C.

Note

1. Probably *Little Dorrit*: cf. Dickens, *Letters*, VII, 698.

To Edward Pigott, [October–December 1855]
MS: Huntington

17, Hanover Terrace | Wednesday

My dear Edward,

I will be at the office on Friday afternoon, and will do a <u>paragraph</u> about the R. A. – the hanging and the PreRaphaelites <u>alone</u> will take up a whole article, as I shall treat the subject – and this I must do for <u>next</u> week, working in the morning when I am fresh and have my wits about me. – I think a paragraph by way of preliminary will be quite enough, considering that we are going to treat the subject at full length this year – I have got the ticket. Forgues' pamphlet has not arrived yet.[1]

Of course I will undertake it.

I am glad the notice of Bohn is thought likely to benefit the publisher. I have written to say in defence of my low opinion of Boccaccio – except that I always was a heretic about him and always shall be.[2] My appreciation is all wrong on no end of literary subjects – and I can't for the life of me get it right excepting Falstaff and Dogberry, I think Molière a greater humourist than Shakespeare, and one of the most tedious books (to <u>me</u>) that I ever read in my life was <u>Tom Jones</u>. This is wrong, I know, but all men have their "cracked" points – and these are some of mine.

Langham Chambers would be a much better situation for you, as well as cheaper.

[Affectly] Yours | W.W.C.

We will go next week, and suffer under Cushman[3] – there is another of my cracked points!

Notes

1. "M Forgues on the Caricaturists of England", *The Leader* VI: 283 (25 August 1855), 823–4.
2. Probably a reference to an unsigned WC review in *The Leader*: see K.H. Beetz, "Wilkie Collins and *The Leader*", *Victorian Periodicals Review*, 15 (5 May 1982), 20–9.
3. Charlotte Cushman, (1816–1876) the American actress.

To Mrs Harriet Collins, 28 February 1856
MS: PM

No 63, Avenue des Champs Elysées | Paris |
Thursday Febry 28th 1856/[1]

My dear Mother,

Here I am safe, sound, and already better – in the quaintest and prettiest bachelor lodging that ever was built. I have a bedroom, sitting-room, dressing-room, and kitchen, all comprised in one little building – like a cottage in a ballet. Opposite to me is another cottage like mine in which the "concièrge" and his wife live – and behind me is a large mansion, with twice the number of windows that they would think of putting into a house of similar size in England. The whole group of buildings is shut in by smart green gates – outside of which the stir and bustle of the Champs Elysées goes on from morning to night. So much for my habitation. I only wish you could come over and see it.[2]

I got through the journey with less fatigue than I expected. But I began it under rather unpleasant circumstances. The cab selected by the wise and observant Jane, was, in regard to the horse the very worst that could have been picked up in all London, at any hour of the day or night. The lame, sickly and miserable cabman did his best, but the still more miserable horse, staggered at every fresh step as if he was going to drop down dead in the road. By the time we got into Tottenham Court Road, I was obliged to stop at the nearest cab-stand, pick out the best horse in another cab, shift luggage, [erased word] bribe the man to drive fast, and so do my best, in a state of unspeakable vexation, to catch the train. I succeeded with about three [seconds: erased] minutes to spare. We had a beautiful passage – but, owing to a change in the arrangements for labelling luggage, did not get to Boulogne in time to wait for the examination of the trunks there, and to catch the Paris train. I had thought, as the rest of the passengers did, that the baggage would pass the Boulogne Customs House immediately, and be examined at Paris. As it was, there was nothing for it but sleeping at Boulogne, or leaving [erased word] my trunk and hatbox in the care of a Custom-House Agent, to be forwarded [erased word] after me, today. Being resolved to sleep in my own Parisian apartment at any hazard I accepted the last alternative – had a<u>nother</u> scramble in a cab (shouting "Vite! Vite!" to the coachman every minute) – and, after a<u>nother</u> narrow escape of being too late, caught the train again. I found Dickens's [erasure] servant waiting for me – and Dickens himself h<u>ere</u>, all kindness and cordiality, with a supper for me at his house. – A fire in my bedroom and a dry and excellent bed, completed the arrangements for my comfort. I feel the journey a little in the shape of a headache this morning – but have profitted, in other respects, already, by the change of air.

The first chapter of my "Rogue's Life" is published today[3] – Dickens is delighted with it.

Tell Charles Ward, I have no time to see him at the Strand – but that I will write to him soon. Tell Mrs Dickinson[4] too of my safe arrival and say also that she have a letter.

With love to Charley | Affecty yours | W.C.

Notes

1. In the lefthand margin alongside the address, WC writes: "Write soon to the address below. If you have a chance of showing the Herricks some attention, after [erased word] their refusal to see '<u>W. Salter</u>' the other night, do."
2. In "Laid Up in Two Lodgings", *Household Words*, 13 (7 June 1856) 481–6, WC contrasts being "laid up" in lodgings in Paris and in London.
3. *Household Words* 1–29 March 1856: see Gasson.
4. Frances Vickress Dickinson (1820–1898), journalist: see Gasson.

To E.M. Ward, 8 March 1856
MS: Texas: Coleman

63, Avenue des Champs Elysées | Paris | 8 March 1856

My dear Ned,

I think this is the best title:[1] The Last Parting of Marie Antoinette and Her Son (<u>Scene: the Prison of the Temple. Persons present, the Queen, her son and daughter, the Sister of Louis the Sixteenth, and the Members of the Revolutionary Committee</u>).

I have underscored the tract in parentheses, because it must be printed in italics to distinguish it from the title. So <u>you</u> must underscore it in copying it out. If "Members of the Revolutionary Committee" is not the right phrase, of course you can alter it to something historically and recognisably expressive of who the men are in the left hand corner of the picture. Also, when you copy out the translation (which I am now about to add) put after it, "Translated from___" whatever the book is, which you don't mention in your letter.

The translation is on the other side [of the page].

At last, the Queen having collected all her energies, seated herself, drew her son near her, and placed both her hands on his little shoulders. Calm, motionless, so absorbed in grief, that she neither wept nor sighed, she said to him in a grave and solemn voice: "My child, you are going to leave us. Remember your duties when I am no longer near to remind you of them. Never forget the merciful God who has appointed you this trial, or your mother who loves you. Be modest, patient, and good, and your father in heaven will help you." She said those words, kissed her son on the forehead, and gave him back to the gaolers.

I have been obliged to make the above translation rather a free one, for it happens oddly that, short as the original passage is, it contains quite a cluster of idiomatic French expressions and forms of construction which it is difficult to render literally into English. However, I hope both the extract and title as they stand here, will be satisfactory.

I have got the most perfect little bachelor apartment. A "pavilion" like a house in a pantomime – and the most willing pleasant <u>concièrge</u> and wife, in the world, to wait on me. Here my luck has stopped. I caught a chill a fortnight ago, from which I have now recovered, but which while it lasted, seriously interfered with Paris pleasures and put me back sadly in some work I had to finish. Some things, however, I have seen of the interesting sort – two charming little plays at the Gymnase acted to perfection, and a very fine portrait of Dickens by A. Z. Scheffer.[2] I went expecting to be disappointed – and came away amazed. The picture is to be exhibited in the rooms of the corrupt institution to which you belong.

In the way of imposters, add to <u>our</u> prime experiences here the name of <u>Madam Ristori</u>[3] – the Italian actress about whom they have been going mad in Paris. Perfect conventionality of the most hopelessly stage kind – walk, attitudes, expression, elocution, all nothing but commonplace in a violent state of exaggerations. We saw her in a play of Alfieri's,[4] exhibiting the unnatural bestiality of a daughter in love with her own father, in long classical speeches. Virtuous females of all nations, sitting in balloons of crinoline petticoat, observed the progress of this pleasant and modest story with perfect composure.

I am to be taken today to see Mr Leighton's new triumph in art – Orpheus playing the fiddle.[5] Adelaide Kemble[6] is said to have been the model, more or less, for every man, woman, and child in the composition! Surely an amusing canvas "must be the result of this"!

With love to the "home Circle"

Believe me, | Ever yours, | Wilkie Collins

Notes

1. For one of Ward's historical paintings.
2. Ary Scheffer (1797–1858), historical and portrait painter.
3. Adelaide Ristori (1822–1906), highly successful Italian actress.
4. Vittorio Alfieri (1749–1803), Italian tragedian.
5. Lord Frederic Leighton (1830–1896: *DNB*), distinguished Victorian painter.
6. Adelaide Kemble (1814–1879), "one of the best English singers of the century" (Boase).

To Mrs Harriet Collins, 11 March 1856
MS: PM

63, Avenue des Champs Elysées | Paris | March 11th 1856

My dear Mother,

I must have expressed myself badly about my luggage. I left it, <u>knowingly</u>, in the hands of the official person (in uniform) charged with the business of sending passengers' baggage after them, when they have not time to wait for the Custom House examination. Of course both trunk and hat-box arrived quite safe by the first train in the morning.

As for women managing better than men, suffer me to remind you that it was a woman who fetched the wretched cab that was the cause of all my woes at starting. The [wrapper] I admit was not exactly the right article of baggage to leave behind – but Charley was right – I did not want it on the journey, the cold weather only setting in the day after my arrival here. As for the [pepper], (in the words of Captain Shandy in reference to his nephew's first [informative] work) "wipe it up and say nothing about it". Our [bottle] has been delivered with the other things, and Mrs [Nearrs] friends' stomach will be all the better for not having too much British Supper in it.

What I <u>do</u> want though is some more handkerchiefs, I have only <u>eight</u>. There must be some more at home. Can you make them up into a small parcel and send them, or take them in Mrs Gibbon's carriage, to Household Words office, addressed to me to Dickens' care. Dickens went to London on Sunday evening last, to stay a week – so Saturday will be time enough. Write on the parcel so that he may know what it is "handkerchief, for Wilkie Collins". Also, likewise send a note to [Fribourg & Treyer] telling them to pack up a quarter of a pound of their tobacco mixture for me, and send it addressed in my name to care of Charles Dickens Eqre. Household Words office, 16. W[a]llington Street North Strand, on or before Saturday next. If you have no other means of sending the handkerchiefs, ask Charley to take them on one of his night walks. If the office is shut, he has only to ring at the private door – one door nearer Waterloo Bridge, than the public door. So much for business.

As for myself, I have had the luck as usual to catch a chill (everybody does the same here in March) – Rheumatic pains and aguish shiverings but I am <u>all right again now</u>. The thing was taken in time, and I got up this morning with nothing to complain of but a little weakness left from judicious and necessary [flegsicking] and sweating in bed.

I dined out last week with the Dickenses, at a French party. Met the Editor of The Re<u>vue</u> Brit<u>anni</u>que[1] among others. My story[2] in Fraser's is translated into French in that magazine and the editor told me that Scribe (the famous Dramatist) had spoken of it "with enthusiasm". I have also been introduced to Ary Scheffer (the painter). He had done a wonderful portrait of Dickens, a [indecipherable word] is to be exhibited at Trafalgar Square. He was very kind and so was his wife.[3] Talking about Trafalgar Square, tell me, or ask Charley to tell me, how he is getting on with his picture. Also ask Charles Ward to send me the Athenaeum which has the review of "After Dark" in it[4] – He will know what is necessary to pay beforehand for postage – so send him my address, and tell him I would have written before – but my leisure has been occupied by work – the end of "A Rogue's Life". I shall have done in a day or two, and will write to him and Pigott and E. Ward. Tell them all so when you see them.

What about letting the house? If it comes to anything for Heavens sake leave all my books and things packed up out of harm's way. Write soon and tell me how you are, and your plans and so on. I am just going out for a turn in the sun.

With love to Charles, Affty yours | W.C

Notes

1. Amédée Pichot (1795–1877), editor and translator.
2. i.e., "Mad Monkton".
3. Sophia, whom he married in 1850, and who died in June 1856 (see Dickens, *Letters* VIII, 34, n.2).
4. Possibly a mistake for the *Examiner* which on 1 March 1856 contained a favourable review of *After Dark* (cf. Dickens, *Letters* VIII, 39, n.1).

To Mrs Harriet Collins, [16 March 1856]
MS: PM

63, Avenue des Champs Elysées | Paris | Sunday.

My dear Mother,

I have been writing to Wills to pay my money for the Rogue's Life into your account. It must be more than £40 – and more will be paid in, as I do other things for Household Words here.

I find by reckoning up my accounts, that you have advanced me £10 – send a cheque for [erased figure] £20 more to Ward to be paid into Lafitte's here for me. You will find they have advanced me £30, and you will have £40 to reimburse you at Coutts's at the beginning of April – to say nothing of what I gain further as the month goes on.

I have also told Wills that Charley will pay him the £2, odd, – he had better do it by a cheque from you, which can be charged also to me, if you like – No need [to] turn up your eyes – You won't advance more than I can already pay back, <u>before</u> you are put to it for money towards the middle of the year. I am obliged to ask for the £20 now, because I am obliged to pay everything here <u>in advance</u>. I am out of debt for lodging, attendance – at this moment, till the 11<u>th</u> of April.

Write and tell me when you have sent the money to Ward.

The Empress began her labour at 5 on Saturday morning, and ended at 6 this morning. 101 guns fired to announce a boy. Prodigious preparations for illuminating – Flags at an awful premium – Trumpeting and soldiering going on in all the streets – Crowds about the Palace. I am just going out to see more. My cold is almost well.

What about the Wards? I am going to write and give him a title for his picture tomorrow.

Love to Charley – they are waiting for me to go out, and I have no time to say more.

Why don't you or Charley write?

Affly yours | W.C

To Mrs Harriet Collins, 19 March 1856
MS: PM

63, Avenue des Champs Elysées | Paris | March 19th 1856

My dear Mother,

I have this instant got your letter. As for the last one, that is a mystery – I should have got it if it had been delivered here. The Post is desperately irregular – but, [indecipherable word] in case, it seems to have been downright untrustworthy as well.

Now about the new house – the news of the taking of which comes to me "like a clap of thunder". The situation seems an excellent one – But did, we have a surveyor to go over it? I see no objection that can be made, provided we are not committed to a long twelve year's lease – and this, I gather from your note, we need not be. Otherwise I don't think you could have done better than take the house. The quiet neighbour on one side is an invaluable attraction. But what do we save in rent for our ready money outlay of £150? £30; or £40, a year? Are the taxes reasonable? And about the drainage? I suppose that is all right. What does the back look out on? And, furthermore, what are you and Charley going to do from the 5th of April to the 5th of June? You are going about visiting, I suppose? And does he take a room? – Answer – all these questions. I shall most likely return to town at the middle of April – when I shall have Pigott to go to at Richmond, and Mrs Dickinson at Failey Hill – and lots of other friends if I like – so I am provided for.

I am very sorry to hear of poor Pigott's fresh trial.

I have [erased word] received the parcels, quite safe from Dickens. Thanks for the handkerchiefs and critiques – The Athenaeum is very kindly and skilfully done. Dickens thinks the machinery in which my stories are inserted very nicely imagined and executed – and he brings word that Miss Coutts (whom he saw when he was in town) was delighted with it. Look attentively at the 4th and 5th chapters of my Rogue's Life. I am rather proud of them. The last chapter was finished in spite of rheumatism. I am all right now.

I was introduced to Mr Leighton and saw his new picture of Orpheus yesterday. Here is my remembrance of it.[1]

A lady came in and asked where he got his notion of the figures. Mr Leighton smacked his forehead, and said "Here! Here!" – It is the worst life-size picture that ever was painted. "[indecipherable name]" is absolute perfection compared to it. But the young fellow has talent for small delicate pencil and water colour designs, some of which he showed me.

With love to Charley | Affectionately yours | Wilkie Collins

Is Charley's new painting room to be in the drawing room?

Note

1. Ink drawing by WC follows of four figures named "Prosperine", "Pluto", "Orpheus playing the fidle", "Eurydice", with the word "Hell" written in the centre between the first two and the second two figures. WC's reference is to Sir Frederic Leighton's "The Triumph of Music. 'Orpheus, by the Power of her Art, Redeems his Wife from Hades'". See S. Jones, et al. *Frederic Leighton 1830–1896* (1996), p. 108.

To Charles Ward, 19 March 1856
MS: PM

63, Avenue des Champs Elysées | Paris | March 19th 1856

My dear Ward,

Dickens, I hear told you of my illness. It came of course at the most unlucky time possible, just in the midst of the labour of writing the last longest and most difficult chapter of my "Rogues Life". Everybody here, natives, as well as visitors, has been catching cold. My particular experience of the general malady took the form of rheumatism. I cured myself by sweating – the only way of getting rid of such maladies that I believe in. My arms, legs, back, head, neck, and teeth were all rheumatic by turns. After relieving my mind by swearing and my body by sweating for four consecutive days, I came out victorious in the struggle. But it was rather trying while it lasted.

I have got a lodging that a man might live in for the rest of his life in comfort – and the heartiest pleasantest people in the world to wait on me. Paris is more magnificent than ever. The Rue de Rivoli is now in a perpetual state of illumination. In each arch of the area &c on the sides towards the street, is placed a brilliant gas light. The view from one end to another is as brilliant as Vauxhall in its best days. The Knave of the Louvre is all but completed – The matchless new street is in great part inhabited – And, you will be glad to hear, the old tower of St Jacques de la Boucherie which has been in a ricketty state for years past, is now restored with the most perfect taste. It looks far finer than it did, when surrounded by houses – for the simple reason that you have now room to see it. A new Boulevard is the next thing to be made – running at right angles to the new Rue de Rivoli – and joining the old Boulevard at the Porte St Denis.

We had an illumination here, on the day of the birth of the Imperial Infant who was created Prince of Peace and King of Algeria, as soon as he could squall and dirty his napkins. I went to the expense of <u>two Francs</u>! for coloured lanthorns for my own little window – and my illumination lasted out the night, which the rest in the Great House, at the side of [the: erased] which my Pavilion is situated, were all quenched by the rain. The Parisians however turned out in spite of the wet, engaged every carriage and thronged every footway. We had great [fanfaronading] with trumpets – quantities of soldiers everywhere – and 101 guns to announce the birth, not one of which I, (in the arms of Morpheus) was [erased word] respectfully wakeful enough to hear. As for news of the Peace Congress, we get it all from the English Journals.[1] Not one of the French papers has a line about it – Even in the way of mere gossip.

I have seen some perfect and some wretched dramatic performances here. Our great theatrical excitement now is about a forthcoming play on the subject of "<u>Paradise Lost</u>" at the Ambigu Comique! There has been great difficulty in getting a good Eve, with plenty of flaxen hair to flow over her innocent shoulders. The play is announced for Saturday next. I suppose "The Deity" and "The Devil" will be principal characters. Le Mal [Pheureax] Abel, and Le feroce Cain, ought to be made interesting – and will be, no doubt.[2]

I have just heard that my mother has taken a new house – a good situation near town. I see no objection, if we are not let in for too long a period of occupancy.

You will have received by this time a £20 cheque to be paid in to my credit at Lafitte's. Write as soon as the payment &c is made – and in the meantime with love to Jane and the children. Ever yours Wilkie Collins.

Notes

1. Probably a reference to *Galignani's Messenger*: "The Treaty of Paris was not signed until 30 March" and the War was unpopular in France (Dickens, *Letters*, VIII, 76, n.1).
2. WC went to the first night with Dickens, 24 March 1856. See Dickens to John Foster, [? 29–30 March 1856], (VIII, 78, and n.4).

To Mrs Harriet Collins, 5 April 1856
MS: PM

63, Avenue des Champs Elysées | Paris | April 5th 1856

My dear Mother

I like the situation of the house, so much that I am sure to like the house itself. As for money Wills has paid in for the <u>Rogues Life £50</u> to your account at Coutts's. So your advance to me is paid back, with a balance of £20 – which I shall increase by some more periodical work on my return. Talking about work, I read the sketch of the plot of my new novel[1] to Dickens a few days since. He was quite excited and surprised by it – and even <u>he</u> could not guess what the end of the story was, from the beginning. He prophesies that I shall get more money and more success with it, than I have got by anything else I have done. Keep all this a profound secret from everybody but Charley – for if my good natured friends knew that I had been reading my idea to Dickens – they would be sure to say when the book was published, that I had got all the good things in it from him. He found out, as I had hoped, all the weak points in the story, and gave me the most inestimable hints for strengthening them.

I shall come back about the middle of this month – having many reasons for not extending my stay here much beyond the six weeks I had originally allotted for it.[2] Of course you will proceed with all your arrangements for the country quite independently of me. I shall want nothing but the key which I left in the cupboard of your bedroom in an envelope, when I return. My strong box, and the long bureau on the little table in my room, remain I suppose, under the Ward dominion at No 17. As to <u>my</u> plans when I come back, they are at present in the clouds. If I take a fit of hard work, I shall probably settle down somewhere in quiet. Pigott offers Richmond – and [Stringfield][3] his study at Verandah House – So asylums for the homeless are not wanting. How long has Charley taken the lodging at Percy Street for? Does he stop in London after the pictures have gone in? Write next week, and tell me this. I thank Frith[4] for his invitation by this post. Tell Ward (E.M.) that Sir Joseph Olliffe,[5] was from home, when his letter to Lady Ely[6] arrived, but that it was forwarded to her, the moment Olliffe received it. Macready is coming on Sunday to stay a week with the Dickenses. There is to be a dinner party on Wednesday at which some great notabilities of Paris are to be present. I can't quite shake off my cold still – and feel occasional rheumatic twinges, which I allay by a vapour bath – Probably the change of air back to London will set me quite right again. Don't do too much – and <u>do</u> go away into the country as soon as you can. Let things take care of themselves. Don't you know the subject of Charley[']s picture yet? Give him my love and believe me

Affectionately yours | Wilkie Collins

I write in a hurry and [illegible word] I have forgotten some things I wanted to say

Notes

1. *The Dead Secret*, serialized in *Household Words*, January to June 1857 and published in two volumes, June 1857.
2. WC returned to London on 12 April 1856 "still ill, and took furnished lodgings at 22 Howland St Fitzroy Sq" (see the second part of his "Laid Up in Two Lodgings", *Household Words*, 14 June 1856, p. 517). "By June he had recovered sufficiently to go on a sailing trip in the Channel with Pigott and Pigott's brother" (Dickens, *Letters*, VIII, 95, n.1).
3. Unidentified.
4. William Powell Frith, R.A. (1819–1909: *DNB*), distinguished painter, studied with Charles Collins, close friend of WC and Edward Ward.
5. Sir Joseph Francis Olliffe (1808–1869), physician to the British Embassy in Paris.
6. Unidentified: cf. Dickens, *Letters*, VII, 376, n.11.

To Mrs Harriet Collins, 2 July 1856
MS: Private Possession

Summary:

[RYS Coquette, Torquay]
   "Charley's letter has been brought to me this morning, and I can't tell you how glad I am to hear that the War between you and Roberts is ended at last.[1] Now the house is your own, and the business is all done, you ought to be as well again by the time I return, as ever you were in your life.
   We got here from Cherbourg late last night, and are about to sail again as soon as possible for the Land's End. When we enter the Bristol Channel we are to be met by a fleet of boats from Weston with a band of music, [guns]of triumph, and <u>beef of course</u> (or it would not be England) in plenty

on board, to escort us to Weston. The Flower Show there, is to be on the 8th and I shall return either on the 9th or 10th ...

Our last port was Cherbourg – the French Portsmouth. They have a breakwater twice the length of ours at Plymouth ... But the town itself is a dull neglected place, full of the most intricately composite Continental stenches. There is a good Table d'Hote at the principal hotel (where we dined) – a pretty theatre ventilated (to which of course we went) and a whole population of women in high Norman caps, like this [2]

We have made acquaintance with a Cherbourg tailor who was employed to clothe the cook on board [–] a devout Papist believing in miracles &c &c, but otherwise an intelligent man. ... He introduced us to his father and mother (outfitters in the old part of the town) and we spent the evening with them and their two <u>bonnes</u> ! The young man showed us his library and gave us coffee and pipes in his bedroom. The old people walked a mile into the country to gather us nosegays and gave us such noyau and Claret, as I have seldom found equalled anywhere. There was no interested gratitude for much money spent, in all this. It was simply politeness and hospitality ... I bought <u>two</u> coloured shirts for rough wear for 2^s / 1^d each! ..."

Notes

1. "Harriet Collins moved into Harley Place in July, after protracted problems over the lease" (Peters, p. 166).
2. WC draws a Norman cap.

To Mrs Harriet Collins, 19 August 1856
MS: PM

Villa des Moulineaux | Boulogue-sur-Mer | Augt 19th 1856

My dear Mother,

I got here pleasantly enough on Saturday, and was at once installed in my comfortable Pavilion bedroom. Hitherto, the principle effect of the sea-air has been to make me inevitably lazy and sleepy. I have, however, contrived to finish my work as the enclosed leaves will testify. Please [string] them on to the leaves already in your possession (entitled "<u>The Family Mystery</u>") – take care that the pages follow each other properly – put the manuscript and the letter I enclose with it into an envelope, and direct the packet to

John Saunders[1] Esqre | 25 Essex Street | Strand.

—

If Charley is at home, and could take it on the day when you get it, so much the better – for it ought to have been sent in three days ago. If not, pray take or send it to Charles Ward, who will send one of the Bank porters with it – Only impress on him that it must not be delayed, or trusted to any but safe hands.

Write me a line to acknowledge, the safe receipt of my enclosures, and to tell me how you are, and when you go into the country. We have had some dinner company here – Jerrold, Shirley Brooks,[2] and the boys' schoolmaster – and the two Miss Powers (Lady Blessington's nieces)[3] are expected to stay, on Wednesday next. The Garden is beautiful – trees wonderfully grown – flowers in profusion. As for the town I have not been near it since my arrival. There is a fair on the opposite hill to ours with [erased word] wonderful shows, gingerbread and cheap jewellery. A lady staying here (Miss Boyle)[4] bought an emerald ring for a <u>franc and a half</u> which took in Townshend, who possesses the most magnificent real jewellery, and who admired the mock emerald as something quite priceless!

With love to Charley

Ever affectionately yours | W.C.

Notes

1. John Saunders (1810–1895), journalist and novelist who founded the *People's Journal* and ran the *National Magazine*, 1856–57. WC's "Uncle George or the Family Mystery" published in the *National Magazine*, May 1857.
2. Douglas William Jerrold (1803–1857), journalist. See Dickens, *Letters*, VIII, 202 n.2. (Charles William) Shirley Brooks (1816–1874), writer, editor of *Punch*, 1870–74. See Dickens, *Letters*, VII, 257, n.1.
3. Marguerite Power (1815–1867), writer, and Ellen, her younger sister. See *ibid.*, VIII, 84 no.8.
4. Mary Louise Boyle (1810–1890), writer. See *ibid.* VI, 169, n.2.

To Mrs Harriet Collins, 1 September 1856
MS: PM[1]

Villa des Moulineaux | Boulogue-sur-Mer | France | Monday

My dear Mother,

There have been some unexpected changes in our arrangements here, and I have only waited to write to you about our new plans until they were completely settled.

There has been an epidemic – (malignant sore throat) among the children here ever since June which the townspeople kept secret, of course, as long as they could, for the sake of their own interests. Being from out of the town we only heard vaguely about the disease, until last Saturday week, when Dickens received a letter from a Joseph Oliffe – Physician to the Paris

Embassy – entreating him to send all his children away from Boulogne. None of them were ill – our situation here being so healthy and so well away from the town – but Dickens, as a measure of precaution, instantly took Oliffe's advice – knowing the reliability of the man who offered it. All the boys were sent to London under their mother's care – those at school here as well as the youngest.

The next break-up was the departure for home of the two Miss Dickenses – Katie having a cough and loss of appetite which alarmed her father. We have since heard that Doctor Hastings[2] has pronounced [erased word] that nothing serious is the matter and that she is getting well in London.

Besides the gaps they made in our party – there has been a shocking catastrophe in the town. Gilbert à Beckett the writer and police magistrate has died of [brain] fever at a boarding house – and one of his children sunk just before him under a fatal attack of the epidemic. These deaths have cast a fresh damp over us – we all knew poor A. Beckett, and all hoped to the last that he would rally.[3]

Under these gloomy circumstances, Dickens gives up the house here – a month before the appointed time. Pigott arrived yesterday, and the two Miss Powers have been staying here for the last ten days. We all flit – on Wednesday or Thursday next. The youngest Miss Power goes to Paris the rest of us cross to [erased word] Folkestone. The ladies go straight to London, and Dickens and Pigott and I, if the weather is at all encouraging, walk back by short stages through the Kentish Hop Grounds – reaching home I cannot tell when to a day – but not earlier than the end of this week, or later than the beginning of the next.[4]

I hear from Pigott that you are going tomorrow to Maidenhead – All you have to do is to drop a line to the servants at Harley Place (I don't know their names) telling them that I am coming back, but am not certain to a day when. They will neither have to set up nor leave the door on the latch – for I shall arrange my return so as to be at home in good time. Above all things, you are not to think of hurrying from your [erased] visit at Maidenhead on my account – If you come back [erased words] before the right time, I shall take you to the railway and return you forcibly to the Langton's! I want you to get all possible good from the visit – and you know I can keep house as well as anybody. I am glad to hear Charley is with you. My love to him – and kind regards to the Langtons.

Don't get alarmed about me after all these accounts of illness and death, except that the damp weather makes my shoulders ache. I am perfectly well and taking such care of myself that my friends here hardly know me again.

Write and tell me how you are later in the week, addressing the letter of course to Harley Place.

Ever afftly [yours] | Wilkie Collins

Notes

1. Cf. Dickens, *Letters*, VIII, 178, n.4.
2. "J. Hastings, M.D. of 14 Albemarle St" (*ibid.*, VIII, 182, n.2).
3. Gilbert à Beckett (1811–1856), died on 30 August, his son Walter died on 28 August: cf. *ibid.*, VIII, 181–2, and n.2.
4. Dickens "left Boulogne with Collins and Pigott on 3 Sep, and they walked part of the way from the Kent coast, evidently reaching London on 6 or 7 Sep" (*ibid.*, VIII, 180, n.4).

To Frederick Mullett Evans,[1] 6 April 1857

MS: Bodleian

2, Harley Place | New Road | April 6th 1857

My dear Evans,

I saw Dickens yesterday. He is favourably inclined towards the notion of two volumes at a guinea – but advises that you should communicate with Mudie, and ascertain how many copies in the two volume form he would take, before we decide. This certainly seems the right course to follow "with all convenient speed", as the Dutch say.

I think, with the experience of "After Dark", to go by, we can hardly be wrong (especially if Mudie gives a satisfactory answer) in printing a guinea edition of 750, instead of 500.

With regard to the suggestion of terms, Dickens suggested that I should put it to you whether, on reflection, you would think one fourth of the profits, instead of one third a satisfactory advancement – considering that there is no risk of the book not paying its expense and that you have already an interest in "The Dead Secret" in its present form, as one of the Proprietors of Household Words. I need hardly say that I mention this suggestion in no spirit of bargaining – I merely leave it for your opinion, knowing that you will judge rightly and justly whichever way your decision points. I look forward with particular pleasure to the republication of the Dead Secret as the beginning of a connection with your house which I have long been anxious to form, and which I sincerely hope will go on in the future to our advantage on both sides.

Very truly yours, | Wilkie Collins

Note

1. Frederick Mullett Evans (?1803–1870), partner of William Bradbury (?1800–1869), printer and publisher. Dickens' publisher since 1854.

To Frederick Mullett Evans, 9 May 1857
MS: Bodleian

2, Harley Place | May 9th 1857

My dear Evans,

I leave with this, the title, Dedication, and corrected leaves of H.W. down to the "Part" of the Dead Secret which will be published on May 23rd. As there are many alterations, I should like (besides seeing proofs of the title and dedication) to compare the book proofs (when the chapters are set up) with the corrected leaves which I now supply. If both are sent to me together, I could see the effect of my alterations – which is all I want to do – in half an hour, while the messenger waited to take the proofs back.

The number for Saturday May 30th (which I finished and corrected last night) I will send as soon as I get it from Wills and have looked [at] it once again. The next number (for Saturday June 6th) which begins today, shall be the <u>last</u>, if I can possibly manage to get the conclusion of the story within the compass of a week's work. If not, it must run on to Saturday June 13th – which, as the number is published on the Wednesday previous, would give <u>June 10th, at the latest</u>, as the day for the publication of the reprint. If it is an object to save as much time as possible, before the Volume of H.W. comes out, we might then publish (as Dickens suggested on the Monday – that is to say on June 8th). I shall do my best to get done a week before this – but I have a terribly trying chapter to write and I can't feel sure of myself till that is done.

Wills wrote to me about [Dix and Edwards] and the supply of the mss of the last chapter. If the departure of the steamer and the conclusion of my work come neatly together – they can have sent to them a copy of the mss (which I will provide) as soon as the original leaves my desk for your office. If not, the fault is not mine. As I understand it, my claim on them for the £25 was established (quite irrespective of other circumstances), on the day when I wrote to refuse taking that sum from Messrs Harper. I did this on <u>their</u> account, and am a poorer man, at the present moment, by £25, than I might have been if I had served the interests of their opponents. It struck me, when I read their letter, that they took this view of the case. It is clearly the only just view. Perhaps, if I am not able to send the last chapter to America,[1] in Mss, before you send it in print, I had better write a line of explanation to [Dix and Edwards] to make sure of setting the matter right.

Ever yours | Wilkie Collins

F.M. Evans Esq

Note

1. *The Dead Secret* appeared in *Harper's Weekly*, 24 January–27 June 1857: Miller & Curtis of New York published it in one volume, 1857. [Dix and Edwards] possibly American literary agents.

To Frederick Mullett Evans, [21 May 1857]
MS: Bodleian

[Whitefriars] | Thursday Afternoon

My dear Evans,
    I have done!!!
    Those two blessed words, "The End" were written at $\frac{1}{2}$ past 3 today. The last chapter I have just given to Mr Gardener to set up and he will send it to me in proof tomorrow morning, to be corrected while the boy waits. This arrangement will, I hope, allow plenty of time for sending the slips of this final number to America, by tomorrow's mail. I understood from Wills that you would kindly undertake to do this. My corrections will all be done in the morning – so the number will be complete, I suppose, before noon.

Ever yours | Wilkie Collins

To Mrs Harriet Collins, 10 August 1857
MS: Private Possession

Monday night [2, Harley Place, W. 10th August 1857]

Summary:
    "The play has been a great success. The audience so enthralled by the story that they would not even bear the applause at the first embrace of Robson.[1] Everybody breathless. Calls for me at the end of the first Act. A perfect hurricane of applause at the end of the play – which I had to acknowledge from a private box. Dickens, Thackeray, Mark Lemon, publically appearing in my box. In short an immense success. I write this in the supper room in the midst of conviviality and applause. Charley is with us."

Note

1. Thomas Frederick Robson [Thomas Robson Brownhill] (?1822–1864), "became co-manager of the Olympic in 1857, and played Aaron Gurnock" in the first professional performances of *The Lighthouse* (Wolff, p. 270).

To Mrs Harriet Collins, 5 October 1857
MS: Private Possession

[2, Harley Place, Monday morning | 5th October 1857]

Summary:

"Don't make yourself nervous about nothing. My ankle gets stronger every day. I have been to Gadshill to talk over future work for H W[1] with Dickens, and I was overrun by all sorts of small occupations, or I should have acknowledged the receipt of your letter before – the cheque enclosed in which came quite safe.

Charley returns today. I was obliged to be back a day earlier. We shall have everything ready for you on Thursday. While the fine weather lasts you are quite right to stay away.[2]

Everything goes on smoothly here. Charles Ward comes to dine today ... Immense success of The Lighthouse. The other night the stalls were so full that the people had to be accommodated in the orchestra. Saturday last, I tried to get a private box for the Landons[3] and found they were all taken. Robson goes into the country for three weeks this month – When he comes back the run of the play is to be resumed. I have engaged to do then another."[4]

Notes

1. WC writes in a note inside the envelope flap: "All the mountain part in H.W. is mine." Probably a reference to "The Lazy Tour of Two Idle Apprentices", which WC wrote with Dickens, and which appeared in five parts in *Household Words*, October 1857.
2. WC's mother went to stay with her friends the Coombes.
3. Unidentified.
4. *The Red Vial* performed in October 1858 with Robson in the lead.

To Frederick Mullett Evans, 24 October 1857
MS: Johns Hopkins

2, Harley Place, | New Road | Oct 24 1857

Summary:

Thanks him for his kind note and the bill for £200 on account of *The Dead Secret*. Is disappointed that the edition is not all sold. Has made great progress with the public of other countries since he first began to write, but has made none, so far as solid results are concerned, with the public of his own country. Begs him to take any measures he pleases to make the book justify the advance he has been offered. If this means selling off the copies on hand for anything they will fetch and publishing a cheap edition forthwith, "by all means do so".

To Mrs Harriet Collins, [4 June 1858][1]
MS: Private Possession

Care of Wyndham Lewis Esq | Llanthettly Hall | Crickhowell | Breconshire

Summary:
WC has got safely to Wales. Back at Stringfields Tuesday next.
   "I sailed to Cardiff – or rather drifted in a calm to Cardiff yesterday." He is now staying at another of Mr Lewis's houses in Glamorganshire – then to Llanthettly Hall. WC has "seen a live <u>Bard</u> attached to this house – not a venerable man with a robe and white beard but a simple-looking middle-aged farmer, in corduroy trousers and a swallow tailed blue coat, who sat down at the word of command, and sang old Welsh songs, in a shrill falsetto voice, to the strangest plaintive wild savage tunes ... I was introduced as <u>Doctor</u> Collins as the only means of impressing the bard with a due idea of my literary importance. He was so struck with my title and beard that he offered to teach me Welsh in a month (the singing as well as the language) – and invited me to a solemn meeting of Bards in the autumn, on the condition of my making an oration if possible in the Welsh language!
   We have <u>nobody</u> here but my host and an intimate friend of his ... the pure air is still doing me worlds of good."

Note

1. Date from envelope.

To Jane Ward,[1] 1 December 1858
MS: Private Possession

2, Clarence Terrace | Regents Park | December 1st 1858

Summary:
Is sorry that he has drifted into an engagement on Christmas Day. Will atone for his shortcomings by being absent at their dinner, as well as hers, since he is "far from well" and sadly in want of another change. His lease on his house is up this Christmas, and he has no idea where to go to. Thinks

it quite likely that he may be in Paris, or by the seaside or in bed on Christmas Day. Asks why he may not keep Christmas Day, beforehand, quietly, with her and Charles, on either Monday or Tuesday next, at Clarendon Gardens.

Note

1. Jane Ward, née Carpenter (1826–1891). WC's favourite cousin who in 1845 married his close friend Charles Ward.

To Charles Ward, [May 1859]
MS: PM

2a, New Cavendish Street | Wednesday

My dear Ward,

I have today got a ticket sent me (for tomorrow night) to my friend [Rev] Townshend's box at Covent Garden. You won't mind my going away at eight o'clock – will you? – and leaving the engagement between us two on every other respect <u>exactly the same</u>. Dine at six – cigar afterwards – tea – I slip off – Caroline[1] keeps you company and makes your Grog – and you stay as long as you feel inclined. You will tell me when you come tomorrow – if you agree to this – and the dozen of wine shall be ready for you to take away.

Ever yours | (in haste) | W.C

Note

1. A very early reference to WC's relationship with Caroline Graves (c. 1830–1895), with whom WC lived, with the exception of two years, from c. 1858 until his death in 1889.

To the Rev. Chauncy Hare Townshend, 29 June 1859
MS: Wisbech & Fenland Museum

2, Clarence Terrace | June 29th 1859

Summary:
Has just called in Clarence Terrace and received the copy of his new poems. Will read the book[1] with very great interest. Has been staying at Gadshill and has now lost the opportunity to see him before departure. Ends his short note with "bon voyage" and "au revoir".

Note

1. An author's presentation copy to Collins of Townshend's *Three Gates* (1859) was part of lot 94 in the Puttick & Simpson, January 1890 sale of Collins's Library.

To Mrs Harriet Collins, 14 July 1859
MS: PM

2a, New Cavendish Street | Portland Place. W. |
Thursday July 14th 1859

My dear Mother,

I got back on Tuesday – saw Charley on Wednesday – and heard that you were at Maidenhead. I am so much better at Gadshill, and so much worse when I come back to London, that I am going away again, next week and am charged by Dickens to [erased word] take Charley with me. He has accepted the invitation, and as he will be away from Clarence Terrace next week, it seems a pity that you should come back. Charley tells me you thought of going on from Maidenhead to Oxford. Write and tell me what you think of doing and how you are. The heat of the streets, I can tell you, is all but insupportable, after the comparative freshness and coolness of the fields.

We have been very quiet at Gadshill. No company but Mrs Procter and Miss Procter.[1] Nothing settled yet about Dickens's trip to America, except that he will lose a fortune if he does not go. So his departure sooner or later seems inevitable.

I can't make up my mind yet about what seaside place to go to next month. My notion of trying the Isle of Man has been discouraged by a competent witness who has been there, and who says that nobody can live in lodgings, for the simple reason that good food is not to be got in the Island except at [erased word] two Hotels. The wine at both these places is execrable – so living [erasure] at the hotels seems as hopeless as living in lodgings – in the case that is to say of a man who can't drink beer, which is unluckily mine. I suppose I shall have to fall back on Broadstairs again, but I would much rather go to a new place.

It is so hot, at this moment, that I must stop here. I have been vainly trying to work – and now I find it just as hopeless to attempt to make this letter any longer. Remember me kindly to the Langtons and believe me

Ever affectly yours | W.C

[PS: erased] We don't go to Gadshill till Tuesday or Wednesday next – so there is plenty of time for you to drop me a line.

Note

1. Mrs Procter, née Anne Skepper, wife of the poet Bryan Waller Procter (1787–1874: *DNB*) –
    to whom WC dedicated *The Woman in White*. Their daughter Adelaide Anne (1825–1864)
    was also a poet.

To Charles Ward, 19 July 1859
MS: PM

2a, New Cavendish Street | 19th July 1859

My dear Ward,

I have nothing particular to record but the history of my own doubts. At this moment I don't know where I am going to in August. My last idea of the Isle of Man has been discouraged by [erased word] competent authorities who tell me I should be starved there if I went into lodgings and poisoned with execrable wine if I try the Hotels. I had a notion of trying the Freshwater side of the Isle of Wight – and have abandoned it again in despair. Today, I am going to run down to Gadshill, and go on doubting there. On Saturday I propose investigating the <u>old</u> town of Hastings. I hear it is picturesque and I know that it looks out on a fine open sea. Perhaps, I shall settle – there – or perhaps, at Broadstairs again – possible I may dart into Wales, and it would not surprise me if I drifted to the coast of Yorkshire. In short, I don't know what I am going to do, and I feel certain of nothing but my own powers of emitting perspiration, which seem to be perfectly inexhaustible.

There is no news in London except that we are to pay our little patriotic additions to [erased word] our beloved income tax, and that people are most unwillingly, beginning to give up believing in Louis Napoleon at last. In literature, the topic is the amazing and inconceivable badness of "Once A Week".[1] The friends of that unfortunate publication are even louder against it than the enemies – and the great gun, Tennyson (price £100) – has flashed in the pan. The cheap edition of <u>After Dark</u> is just published — (I have not seen it yet) – and my new book is sauntering through the press so slowly that we have not got to the end of the first volume yet.

Charley continues to spin madly in the social vortex, and is still trying hard to talk himself into believing that he ought to be married. Pigott is cultivating Zoological tastes in the verdant seclusion of South Bank. When I last saw him he had a bull-terrier puppy, a parrot, a squirrel, a goldfinch, and a wild black cat – together with the privilege of inhaling the odour of his neighbour's pigs, and hearing the continuous howling of his neighbour's big dog. My mother has been staying at Maidenhead, and has now gone to Oxford. Charley joins me at Gadshill this week – and that is all my news.

I will write again as soon as I am settled somewhere. Where shall I write to? You say nothing about your plans. Do you spend all your holiday at Sidmouth with Palk Hussey? Or do you go and seclude yourself with Padley? Or do you come and end your trip with me when I get a place?

Caroline sends you her kindest regards – and I must go up and put <u>another</u> shirt on!

Ever yours | W.C.

Note

1. *Once a Week*, a new journal published by Bradbury and Evans after the "winding up of Household Words" in 1859: "if the payment of £2,000 a year to Tennyson for contributions is any standard, its rate of pay was far higher than either of Dickens's periodicals" (R. L. Patten, *Charles Dickens and His Publishers*, Oxford, 1978, p. 270).

To Charles Ward, 25 July [1859]
MS: PM

2a, New Cavendish Street | Monday July 25th

My dear Ward,

I have just come back from Broadstairs, where I have taken a half-detached cottage all to myself, on the Ramsgate road with nothing between me and the sea but the open down. We go in on Wednesday August 3rd, and if you like to come and finish your holiday with us, by all means do so. We shall be settled in a day or two with our own servants here, and we have got a spare bedroom. So if you come on the 5th or 6th you are sure to find us ready.

Direct to me, <u>after</u> the 3rd August, | at Mr Wayhall's | Church Hill Cottage | Broadstairs | No time for more before the post goes out.

Ever yours | W.C.

P.S. I suppose I am right in believing that your holiday does not end before the middle of August.

To Mrs Harriet Collins, 26 July 1859
MS: PM

2a, New Cavendish Street | Portland Place. W. | July 26th 1859

My dear Mother,

Charley is still at Gadshill, and likely to remain there for the rest of this week, at least. I left on Friday morning last, travelled on Saturday (in despair of finding another place to suit me) to Broadstairs, and consulted the hotel-keeper there, who is an old friend of mine. The result is that I have got [erased word] one of two little cottages standing, unconnected with other houses, outside Broadstairs on the Ramsgate Road. Between me and the sea there is nothing but the smooth down in front of the house and fields and gardens behind it. I am to take possession (the day after the present lodgers leave) on Wednesday the 3rd August, and have got the place for six weeks from that time. Here I must begin my long serial story for All The Year Round[1] – and here if quiet <u>can</u> be got in this world for any man whose fate it is to create noises all around him by trying to write books, quiet seems moderately likely to be attainable. Lodgings were still to be had on the "Esplanade" – but pianos and children surrounded them – and it was cheaper for <u>my</u> purpose to pay a little more and have a place to myself. Talking about pay, I must have some money to start with. Have you got your cheque-book – or can you borrow a Coutts cheque of anybody? If not it can be written – Mr Combe will show you how – on a blank half sheet of paper: I want £25, out of the £40 which I paid into your account [erasure] a little while since. <u>Cross the cheque</u>, "<u>Coutts & Co</u>",[2] and send it to me, any day this week, addressed to care of | Charles Dickens Esqre | Gadshill Place | Higham | near Rochester. | I shall most likely go to Gadshill tomorrow to bid them good bye, and stay [erased word] till the following Tuesday.

The R.A. Ticket was forwarded to <u>me</u> at Gadshill last week. And I sent it by post to Mrs E.M. Ward – so "F.G." will see the pictures and the company – and if the company is not better worth looking at than the pictures, I, for one, pity "F.G." from the bottom of my heart.

My book is getting slowly through the press. The first volume is nearly printed, and the whole is to be published in September. Do you see All The Year Round? Look out a <u>fortnight</u> hence for an article called "The Bachelor Bedroom", in which I have taken off some of the guests at Gadshill, myself included. The cheap edition of "After Dark" is announced for immediate publication, price 2/6.[3] No more literary news about <u>me</u>.

As they all like Tennyson at Oxford, they may like to hear what he said about himself to a friend of mine, who repeated it to me. "My misfortune is," said the great T. – "that I have not got anything <u>in</u> me. If I had only got something <u>in</u> me, I could write as well as Shakspeare." yours ever, afftly | W.C

Kind regards to the Combes. I looked in at Clarence Terrace yesterday. No letter for you. All going on Well. I saw the tail of Miss Smith's gown on the staircase, and I thought Mary looking rather yellow.

Notes

1. i.e., *The Woman in White*.
2. "Coutts & Co" doubly underlined. WC and his brother Charles continued to use their mother's bank account at Coutts until the following year when WC opened his own account following the success of *The Woman in White*. See Clarke, Appendix C ("Wilkie Collins Bank Account"), pp. 228–9.
3. WC's *The Queen of Hearts* was published in October 1859, his "The Bachelor Bedroom", *All The Year Round*, 6 August 1859. *After Dark* first published in 2 vols in February 1856.

Part IV
The Woman in White, No Name and *Armadale*

7 August 1859–1865

THE WOMAN IN WHITE, NO NAME, ARMADALE

At Church Hill Cottage with Caroline, with "nothing between us and the 'great water'" [7 August 1859], and "shut up" daily at his desk "from 10 till 2 or 3, slowly and painfully" Wilkie launches his "new serial novel" [18 August 1859]. For six weeks, in spite of "suffering torment with a boil between [his] legs" [30 August 1859] and percipiently observing "I seem destined, God help me! never to be well", he labours on *The Woman in White*. Serialized in *All The Year Round* from November 1859 to August 1860, its composition absorbs Wilkie. By 11 December 1859, he has completed just over a third of the novel which, he hopes and believes, "<u>will</u> be the best I have written yet" [7 August 1859].

Commissions to Charles Ward abound. They include requests to pay cheques for contributions to *All the Year Round*, to secure books, such as copies of a five-volume set of Voltaire, and to negotiate with Tauchnitz for rights. Wilkie's rejection [13 January 1860] of a £500 offer from Smith Elder for *The Woman in White* demonstrates his continued desire to maintain control over his own literary property. By March 1860 he has moved with Caroline from New Cavendish Street to rooms at 12 Harley Street, still tied to *The Woman in White* by a "petticoat string, like a dog to his kennel" [23 July 1860]. Finally he writes triumphantly to his mother [26 July 1860] that at 5 p.m. he finished the novel. A celebratory dinner with Egg, Hunt, Lehmann and others follows on 9 August.

At no time in his letters to his mother is Caroline mentioned. On 17 July 1860 his brother Charles marries Kate, the younger daughter of Charles Dickens. Wilkie becomes a sought after guest by literary lionizers. He leaves with Pigott in September on his friend's new boat along the Bristol Channel to the Irish coast. At the end of October 1860 he responds to *The Times* critic about chronological errors in *The Woman in White*.

The year 1861 witnesses diverse activities. *The Woman in White* is translated into French. In the early summer Bentley re-publishes *Rambles Beyond Railways* and the cheap edition of *The Woman in White*. Wilkie writes to his mother that he is "slowly – very slowly – building up the scaffolding of [his] new book" [24 May 1861]. The as yet un-named *No Name* is to pre-occupy him for the next year or so. In spite of liver problems and back pains he still manages in June and July to get to Broadstairs and in August goes with Caroline and "Carrie" (Harriet) to Whitby.

Financial and literary success is now realized. In a celebratory letter of 31 July 1861 he tells his mother that Smith Elder has offered him the enormous sum of five thousand pounds for a "work of fiction a little longer than *The Woman in White*". Once he has completed his present commitments he will be able to leave writing for *All The Year Round*. By December 12 1861 he is "slowly getting to the end of the 1st volume" of what is to be *No Name*.

All The Year Round begins serializing *No Name* [16 March 1862]. The novel preoccupies Wilkie who makes perpetual requests of Charles Ward for specific dates, voyage times and postal timings. He takes Dickens' old house at Broadstairs for four months from early July until the third week of October. In the company of Caroline and "Carrie" he writes and takes sailing trips with Pigott and Bullar, finally returning "sadly fagged" [14 October 1862] to London. He writes to his mother that he has accepted three thousand pounds from Lowe for his novel which, with receipts from *All The Year Round* and America, adds up to four thousand six hundred – "not so bad for story telling" [12 August 1862]. He begins corresponding with Nina and Fred Lehmann and his physician Frank Beard; he will continue to write to them until his death.

A word which is to occur frequently in his letters surfaces on 15 January 1863: he writes to Charles Ward "for the last three days the gout has confined me to my chair". Wilkie's friend, Augustus Egg, dies suddenly in Algiers. From April until the end of June 1863, Wilkie travels with Caroline and "Carrie" to the spas in search of a cure. He writes lengthy letters home to his mother and Charles Ward, full of descriptive details and characterization. Back in England in July he goes sailing with Pigott but writes to his mother that he has "tried the sea experiment and it has failed" [4 August 1863].

Accompanied by Caroline and "Carrie" he visits the Isle of Man and in October he sets off with them for the Continent.These journeys form the basis and provide the background for *Armadale*: "ideas are coming to me thicker and thicker for a new book", he writes to his mother [4 December 1863]. During the trip to Italy "the two Carolines [suffer] sea martyrdom" [4 November 1863]. In Rome and Naples he revisits old places and "old Neapolitan friends" from a quarter of a century earlier [13 November 1863]. Letters to his mother and Charles Ward, written in January 1864, tell of his shock at Thackeray's death, of his sighting of the Pope and the loss of a faithful servant. He is constructing the framework for his new story and by 4 April 1864, is back in London.

Preoccupied with *Armadale*, on 19 July 1864, Wilkie tells his mother of his plan to go to Norfolk to study for the fourth number of its serialization. He is to be accompanied by his friends Pigott and Charles Ward. The last week of July 1864, sees him in Winterton and Great Yarmouth where he probably meets Martha Rudd, soon to be the mother of his children. By 9 September he is back in Harley Street and goes to Gadshill to "see if the Kentish air will relieve [his] muddled head". He is, as he tells his mother, "dreadfully shocked and distressed by" the death of his friend, the painter, Leech. During this period Wilkie has been accumulating legal and other details for *Armadale* which eventually runs in *The Cornhill* from November 1864 to June 1866. Wilkie is in Paris in February 1865, and by March he and Caroline have moved to a new address in Melcombe Place.

To Charles Ward, 7 August 1859
MS: PM

Church Hill Cottage | Broadstairs | August 7th 1859

My dear Ward,

I have waited to answer your letter and to tell you how sorry I am that you can't come and stay with us here, until my reply could find you at Coutts's. I certainly thought when I wrote that you would be able to pass the last week of your holidays here. Hot as the sun is, there is a fresh breeze flowing in from the sea all day long. There is nothing but the down between us and "the great water" – we are on the Ramsgate road, just outside Broadstairs – and we have got the cottage all to ourselves. Can't you manage, some time in the course of the next six weeks, to get here from Saturday to Monday? You did this, last year. Why not try it again? I wish you had never gone to the Devonshire coast. That picture of the hotel in your last letter, made me perspire to look at it.

You will receive two enclosures with this. The <u>small</u> note addressed to "Mr Holsworth"[1] is an order for the payment of my salary to Bearer until further notice. Can you send a porter with it, every <u>Wednesday</u>, beginning from <u>next</u> Wednesday <u>the 10th</u>? And will you keep the accumulation of money for me in your desk, till I want it? You will receive it ready done up in little paper packets containing £6..6..- each. The porter can call at any time that is convenient on Wednesdays – the later the better perhaps, as Wednesday, <u>morning</u> is publication morning.

The second letter is to T<u>auchnitz</u>, about my new book.[2] Will you put it into an envelope, address it to | Le Chevalier | Bernardt Tauchnitz | Leipsig | Germany | <u>and pay the postage</u> (which I will refund), and send it at once with your letters? Have I spelt Leipsig properly? or is it <u>Leipzic</u>, or Leipsig, or how the devil <u>is</u> it spelt? Y<u>ou</u> know best, and can correct my errors. I am not even sure whether <u>Bernhardt</u> is right – I know it ought to have an "h", but I am doubtful about the final "t". Then again, is it Germany or Saxony? I protest I know next to nothing about it!!!

If you will kindly do these two things for me [erased word] I hope I shall not trouble you with any more commissions. Do think about coming here. Give my love to Jane and the children, and believe me Ever yours W.C

Caroline sends you her kind regards.

Notes

1. George Holsworth of the *Household Words* office, sometimes written Holdsworth as in C. Dickens to W.H. Wills, 3 April 1858 (<u>Letters</u>, VIII, 541, n.4).
2. i.e., *The Woman in White*. Published on the Continent by Tauchnitz: see Todd and Bowden, item 525, p. 130.

To Charles Ward, 18 August 1859
MS: PM

Church Hill Cottage | Broadstairs | Thursday 18th Augt 1859

My dear Ward,

I pay my landlord here, week by week, and I have dwindled to my last five pound note. The necessary consequence is a modest demand on you for a driblet of <u>fifteen pound</u>s to hold up my tottering credit. My salary of Wednesday the 10th and Wednesday the 17th [erasure] (now in your hands I hope) amounts to £12..12..- and my salary of next Wednesday the 24th, which raises it to £18.18. will, by that time, more than square our accounts.

Can you <u>bring</u> the money yourself on Saturday next? Caroline and Charley and I will all be very glad if you can, and you and I will go out and hold divine service on the ocean, on Sunday. If it is still too soon after your holiday to manage this, I suppose the best way will be to send me a registered letter with three five pound notes in it, on the day you get this – if you can do so without inconvenience. Tell me when you think you can get a day's leave at the end of the week, and I will endeavour to [erasure] [humour] my <u>next</u> necessity for money (Good God! how rapidly those necessities follow each other!) so as to make it occur when you come.

We are very quiet here. No visitor but Charley. I am shut up at my desk everyday from 10 till 2 or 3, slowly and painfully launching my new serial novel. The story is the longest and the most complicated I have ever tried yet – and the difficulties at the beginning of it are all but insuperable.

Broadstairs is quite full – and is laboriously gay today in honour of the annual Regatta. The whole tribe of extortioners are enjoying their meridian glory of swindledom. – and the weekly bills make my hair stand on end. I used to disbelieve in Hell. I believe in it now, because I know of no other place, after this life, which will be hot enough to do full justice to the British tradesman.

Caroline and Charley send kind regards. My love to Jane and the children.

Ever yours | W.C

To Charles Ward, 30 August 1859
MS: PM

Church Hill Cottage | Broadstairs | Tuesday Aug 30th 1859

My dear Ward,

My last five pound note stares me lamentably in the face again. Will you send me, by <u>Registered</u> <u>letter,</u> <u>fifteen</u> pounds more, so that I may receive the money, if possible, on Thursday morning? By tomorrow (Wednesday the 31st) you will have received <u>four</u> weeks salary (Aug 10th, 17th, 24th, and 31st) amounting to £25.6.– and you will have sent me (counting this second £15) Thirty pounds. My salary for September 7th will therefore in a week's time, set me on the right side of the account again.

I have been suffering torments with a boil[1] <u>between</u> my legs, and write these lines with the agreeable prospect of the doctor coming to lance it. I seem destined, God help me!, never to be well.

Don't forget that we leave [here], unless some fresh misery happens to lay me up, on Wednesday September 14th – So try hard for the Saturday before. The six weeks for which I took this place will be expired by that time,

I can't write anymore[2]

Notes

1. The "oil" of "boil" underlined, and the "oi" of "boil" underlined twice.
2. Signature cut away.

To Mrs Harriet Collins, 2 September 1859
MS: PM

Church Hill Cottage | Broadstairs | September 2nd 1859

My dear Mother,

Charley wrote to you (I hope with a better pen than mine) the day before yesterday. On that day also Dickens arrived. He stays at the Hotel – dines here one day, and we dine with him the next – and seems to enjoy the change and the seeing his old haunts once more. He goes back to town next Monday (the American trip, by the bye, is postponed for this year at any rate) and Charley goes back with him, supposing Mary to have returned on Monday next. Benham[1] is coming on Saturday. Pigott I have heard nothing of. As for myself, I still stick so resolutely at my work, that my life is as uneventful as yours. The more I can get done [erasure] now the less trouble and worry for me when the story appears in All The Year Round.

I shall return to London when my time is up (on Wednesday the 14th) – literally driven away by the extortions of the Broadstairs people. No moderate income can cope with their demands. A skinny little chicken is three and sixpence – meat equally dear – vegetables three times the London price – my landlord won't draw me a bucket of water without being paid for it – the cook I have engaged (an excellent servant I must fairly own) sends me up my dinner and breakfast at the small charge of ten and sixpence a week, and her keep, tea, and beer besides – and I was in great luck to get her at that, through the intercession of the landlord of the Hotel here. And the Broadstairs people complain of the shortness of their season! It is a wonder they have a season at all. You will not be surprised, after reading this lamentable statement, to hear that I shall want some money before I can leave. I have fifteen pounds of my own, in your account – will you put ten more to it, and send a cheque for £25 – <u>crossed Coutts & Co</u>[2] – to Charles Ward, directing to him at the bank – Messrs Coutts & Co, Strand, London. W.C. This will clear me, and send me back to London, I hope, not quite penniless. I shall have more driblets of money coming in soon from the foreign reprints of "The Queen of Hearts" – which will soon be published. My kindest remembrances to the Bullars – I hope old Mr Bullar is better – tell Henry to come here if he possibly can. How long you have been away! and what a [several words erased] weary time it seems since we have seen each other! Ever your affectionate | W.C.

Charley sends his love, and he wants to know the exact day of Mary's return.

Notes

1. Charles Benham, solicitor of Benham and Tindell, of Essex Street, Strand, London.
2. Doubly underlined.

To Charles Ward, 7 September 1859
MS: PM

Church Hill Cottage | Broadstairs | Wednesday Sept 7th 1859

My dear Ward,

I am very glad to hear you are coming at last. Your course, on arriving at Ramsgate, is simplicity itself. You merely inquire for the Broadstairs' bus (which meets every train) – get <u>on</u> it, or <u>in</u> it, which you please – and tell the man to set you down at this place. Unless some new catastrophe overwhelms me, I shall be in the garden waiting to see you drive up. We look on to the high road by which you arrive, and are just the sort of house which nobody can possibly miss. I would come on to Ramsgate to meet you – but, although my incision is much better, I am hardly up to a long walk yet.

No commission, thank you, except the eternal commission to bring me money. I want you to bring a heavy purse this time, including (by anticipation) my salary of this day week the 14th – the last, I need give you the trouble of drawing for me. On the other leaf is <u>my</u> statement of our account. If it agrees with yours, then stow away in a safe pocket £32..14..6, making up that sum with one Ten pound note, four fives, and the rest in precious metals. I <u>hope</u> I shan't want so much as this but it is best to be on the right side – so please bring it.

Caroline's kind regards. Ever yours | W.C

Don't spoil your dinner on Saturday. We shall not dine till a quarter to seven – so you will have plenty of time.

Account

Ward receives, Salary at £6-6- a week,	Ward sends to Broadstairs two
From | August 10th – 6,, 6,,—	Registered letters containing
17th – 6,, 6,,—	fifteen pounds each— £30,,-,,-
24th – 6,, 6,,—	pays for registering— ,,1,,
31st – 6,, 6,,—	pays for stamp to Leipsig ,,-,,6
Sept 7th (today) <u>6,, 6,,=</u>	30,,1,,6
£31,,10,,—	
Add Salary of Sept 14th— <u>6,, 6,,=</u>	Ward brings with him
37,,16,,—	to Broadstairs <u>32,,14,,6</u>
Add cheque for <u>25,, -,,=</u>	£62,,16,,0[1]
<u>£62,,16,,</u>	

Note

1. WC draws a vertical line between the two columns.

To E.M. Ward, 7 January 1860
MS: Texas: Coleman

2a, New Cavendish St. W. | 7 January 1860

My dear Ned,

Your kind letter was left waiting for me two days at Clarence Terrace before I called for it – and my answer has been unfortunately delayed in consequence.

I am honestly glad to hear you like the opening of <u>The Woman in White</u>, because I know that you have an eye for detailing what is really genuine and good in literary workmanship. I do hope and believe the story <u>will</u> be the best I have written yet. It is on a much larger and much more elaborate scale than anything I have done hitherto – and, as far as it has gone, it has certainly made itself felt pretty strongly not only in England, but in America as well. The effort of keeping it going week after week is (in the reporter's famous phrase) "More easily imagined than described". When I approach the glass in the morning to brush my hair, I am quite agreeably surprised to find it has not turned grey <u>yet</u>!

Give my kindest love to Mrs Ward and the children, with a warm return on my part of all their good wishes, and a special kiss for my god-daughter.

Ever truly yours, | Wilkie Collins

To Richard Griffin & Co.,[1] 11 January 1860
MS: BL

2a, New Cavendish Street. W. Jany. 11th 1860

Mr Wilkie Collins presents his compliments to Messrs Griffin, and begs to return them the memoir[2] revised and corrected in compliance with their request.

2.a. New Cavendish Street. W.

Jany. 11th 1860.

He was educated at a private school, and passed a considerable time in Italy. His biography of his father, the late William Collins RA, is remarkably interesting not more as a life of the man than as a kind of history of English Art. "Antonina or the Fall of Rome" (his first novel)[3] became popular at once. His other works are "Rambles Beyond Railways", "Basil", Mr Wray's Cash-box", "Hide and Seek", "After Dark" and "The Dead Secret". Although roughly handled by many critics, those who have studied the works of Mr Collins will bear testimony to their distinctness of plot and incident and their clearness and simplicity of Style. His earlier works were, no doubt, tinged with the colours of exaggeration but with time came mellowness, and when he does write now he writes well and vigorously.[4] One of his[5] latest productions is the drama of the "Frozen Deep" written for the Author-Amateurs, and commanded by the Queen. Mr Collins is independent of literature, and may therefore write what he will without suffering much from a failure, except by the <u>amour propre</u> being wounded.

His latest work of fiction is "The Woman in White," which is now appearing, in weekly parts, in the columns of "All the Year Round".

Notes

1. Minor London publishers. See Dickens, *Letters*, IX, 202 ns1,2.
2. Printed cutting pasted to the handwritten memoir reads as follows: "COLLINS, Wilkie, son of the great painter, a distinguished biographer and novelist, born in London in 1824".
3. "his first novel": WC's holograph addition to the memoir. However, this should more accurately read "his first published novel". *Iolâni* had been written, but not published, before *Antonina*.
4. "rigorously" changed by WC to "vigorously".
5. "one of his" replaces "His".

To Charles Ward, [11 January 1860]
MS: PM

Wednesday | 2a, New Cavendish Street

Summary:
Thanks him for the Eau de Cologne. His weekly race with the press is beginning to weigh heavily on him. Asks him to come on Sunday to taste a new Stilton cheese. Is bargaining with the publishers for *The Woman in White* and may have some results to tell him on Sunday.

To Smith Elder & Co., 13 January 1860
MS: NLS

2a, New Cavendish Street W. | January 13th 1860

Dear Sirs,

I beg to acknowledge the receipt of your letters, offering me the sum of Five Hundred Pounds[1] for the copyright of "The Woman in White".

I thank you for making me this proposal; but I cannot avail myself of it, because it requires me to part with the copyright of my book. The offer previously made to me, purchases nothing more than the right of reprint for three years (in one form), on terms with which I have every reason to be satisfied. With that offer and with these terms, then, I have closed, after waiting till I had received and read your letter.

With thanks once more for your proposal,

I remain. | Dear Sirs. | Faithfully yours, | Wilkie Collins

Messrs Smith, Elder & Co.

Note

1. George Smith, II (1824–1901: *DNB*), of Smith Elder, the London publishing house, offered the £500 before he realized the current success of the serialization. He later admitted that he would have paid tenfold and still made "a large sum" had he known (*House of Smith Elder*, ed. Leonard Huxley (1923); and Robinson p. 131).

To William Henry Wills, 15 February 1860
MS: PM

2a, New Cavendish Street | W. | Feby 15th 1860

My dear Wills,

If I don't knock up, go mad, or die, the last number of The Woman in White will appear on Wednesday the 18th or Wednesday the 25th of July [1] next, in A.Y.R. This is as nearly as I can calculate it, at present. I may be a week over the mark – but I am not likely to be a week under. If you tell Lever[2] to put the pot of inspiration on to boil at the beginning of June I think you may be sure of giving him a good six weeks' notice. Ever yours | W.C

Notes

1. WC doubly underlines "Ju" of "July".
2. Charles James Lever (1806–1872: *DNB*), Anglo-Irish novelist, author of *Jack Hinton* (1842), and *Charles O'Malley* (1841), among other works. In 1858 Lever was appointed to a consular position in Spezia, Italy. In 1867 he became consul in Trieste where he died. His *A Day's Ride; A Life's Romance* began in *All the Year Round*, 18 August 1860 and ran until 23 March 1861.

To Charles Ward, [June 1860]
MS: PM

12, Harley Street. W. | Friday

My dear Ward,

Has Caroline written to ask you to come here and take pot-luck on Monday at six? I don't know – she has gone out. Come on Monday – and please bring with you a £10 note, a £5 [pound: erased] note, and five sovereigns – which I will exchange for a £20 note, which is no use to me in its present form – Also look at the Voltaire[1] next to the fire-engine place in Chandos Street – and tell me what you think of it.

Ever yours | W.C

I am <u>slaving</u> to break the neck of The Woman In White – and get done in 5 numbers more – I shan't have finished the number I am now doing till Sunday night.

Note

1. A 70-volume set of Voltaire, *Oeuvres Completes*, with a life and plates by Moreau ([Kehl], 1784), bound in rubbed calf, was in WC's library at his death (Puttick and Simpson *Catalogue*, 20 January 1890, item 206).

To Mrs Anne Procter, 23 July 1860
MS: Princeton

12, Harley Street, W. | Monday July 23rd

My dear Mrs Procter,

Except the day of the Wedding (when I was tied to my sister-in-law's petticoat string) I have been tied to The Woman in White's petticoat string, like a dog to his kennel. The reward of this solitary confinement under a female turnkey is not [erasure] far off. I hope and believe I shall finish the book (by dint of writing double numbers at the end) this week! So I accept your kind invitation with the greater pleasure, in the firm faith that the strain of the last ten months will have been taken off me, when I sit at your table on Monday the 30th.

ever yours | Wilkie Collins

The Wedding was a pattern wedding in two things – nobody made any speeches and the bride and bridegroom had to go away before the breakfast was over. There was also only the most moderate allowance of tears, at the last moment – and <u>they</u> were shed to the accompaniment of cheerful howling from Forster[1] and a shower of old shoes flung after the married pair as they fled into the carriage. They have gone to Calais[2] and they find that intensely dreary town quite delightful. Such is Love!

Notes

1. John Forster (1812-1876: *DNB*), close friend of Dickens, to whom WC dedicated *Armadale*.
2. "Calai" of "Calais" is doubly underlined. Charles Collins married Kate, Dickens' younger daughter, at Gad's Hill, 17 July 1860.

To Mrs Harriet Collins, 26 July 1860
MS: PM

12, Harley Street, W. | London | Thursday, 26th July 1860 |
five o'Clock. P.M.

[=]

Hooray ! ! ! ! !

I have this instant written at the bottom of the four hundred and ninetieth page of my manuscript[1] the two noblest words in the English language
—— The End[2] ——
and, what is more, I have wound the story up in a very new and very pretty manner. We shall see if the public are of my opinion.

Send me a line to say how you got to Maidenhead – and give my kindest remembrances to the Langtons[3] – and tell me if you are better.

I can't write any more – I must go out and walk off the work and the excitement of winning the battle against the infernal periodical system, <u>at last</u>.

Ever affectly yours | W.C[4]

Notes

1. i.e., *The Woman in White*: the draft 490 leaves printer's copy for *All the Year Round*, with holograph note dated 4 October 1860, giving the composition date as 15 August 1859, is now at PM. MA 79.
2. The letter "h" and "n" of "The End" underlined twice.
3. Old friends of Mrs Harriet Collins.
4. The signature is scored on top of the "W" and underneath the "C": a practice which remains constant with WC from this period onwards.

To William Holman Hunt, 1 August 1860
MS: Huntington

12, Harley Street, W. | August 1st 1860[1]

My dear Hunt,

I have done my book. We dine here (in celebration of the event)[2] on <u>Thursday August 9th at 1/2 past 6</u>. I hope you will be in town then and able to come. Send me a line to say Yes.

Ever yours | Wilkie Collins

Holman Hunt Esq.

Notes

1. Above the Gothic printed address, WC writes: "No dressing – or ceremony of any kind".
2. Among the guests at the celebratory dinner were Holman Hunt, Augustus Egg and Edward Ward.

To Charles Dickens, 7 August 1860
MS: Johns Hopkins. Text: Dickens, *Letters*, IX, 568

12, Harley Street, W. | August 7th 1860

My dear Dickens,

I beg to accept the renewal of my engagement with "All The Year Round" on the conditions proposed to me, which I understand to be as follows:

The engagement is to be for two years, dating from the 31st of July 1860

My salary, for those two years, is to be seven guineas a week.

I am to receive, during the same period, additional remuneration equivalent to one eighth share of the whole annual profits of All The Year Round paid me by cheque, at the time when the profits are regularly divided between the partners.

For this additional remuneration and for my salary, I am to write for "All The Year Round" during my two years engagement, one serial story of about the same length as "The Woman In White". The copyright of that story, on the completion of its periodical publication, to be my property.

I am also, when not engaged on the serial story, to write articles (the copyright of which is conceded to me) for "All The Year Round", as I can, and to suggest, as I can, and to assist you in any joint periodical production of which I may feel myself able to undertake a share.

I am to have five unoccupied months to prepare my serial story, before it is wanted for "All The Year Round".

I am not to write, during the term of my engagement, for any other periodical.

These are the conditions on which I renew my engagement,

Ever yours | [WILKIE COLLINS]

To Mrs Anne Procter, 8 August 1860
MS: Trinity College, Cambridge

12, Harley Street, W. | August 8th 1860

Summary:
Thanks her and her husband for their kind notes. Is delighted that the "Dedication"[1] should have been so well-timed. Has had two very friendly notes from Mr Milnes,[2] inviting him to Yorkshire and is attempting to find a few days to go. Mr Milnes proposes that he travels with her and Miss Procter on the 15th – which he would have liked, but he has a dinner engagement on that day. He is going to try for the 16th, and will write to Mr Milnes the moment he can feel certain about it. He says his only complaint of his host is against his handwriting. He is told that the station is "[ProBingley]" and that the house is "Fryston". "These two proper names are fac-similes (!)" Will she charitably translate them and, in addition, tell him at what hour the express leaves King's Cross.

Notes

1. To *The Woman in White.*
2. Richard Monckton Milnes (1809–1885: *DNB*). See 1 p. 248 n.

To Charles Ward, 14 August 1860
MS: Private Possession

12, Harley Street, W. | 14 August 1860]

Summary:
WC is just back from Gadshill, and then off to Yorkshire to Milnes's. *The Woman in White* "is done to the last fragment of correction, and will certainly be finished this week.

The book can't be worked too much in all ways – for it has been chosen (as being a noticeable novel) to become the pivot of a strike of all the libraries against Mudie. The libraries said as much to Low. They had been waiting for a popular book to try the question – and mine is fixed on. They declare they won't subscribe for a copy except on the same terms as those granted by the trade to Mudie. Cawthorn[1] said he would take <u>50 copies</u>, on the Mudie terms – and not one on any other. When I last saw Low he was firm, and declared that the public pressure should force the libraries to our terms ... I have not seen him since my return – and I feel disposed to trust the public too. We are just coming out at the crisis of the trade attack on Mudie's monopoly – and how it will end, nobody can say. In the <u>country</u>

we sold 200, on the first appearance of the advertisements ten days ago – and all the agents in provincial England, say the demand for the book is very large. An early notice in the Times will certainly help us in advertising the <u>fact</u> of the book's publication – and that is an important point.

I shall be back on Tuesday the 21st – and shall come to the Strand, when I shall have more news.

Charley and Katie are <u>still</u> at Calais! in lodgings! They think it a delightful place. Such is love ...

If you will pay the [account] I can settle with you when I come back – You must taste the wine. It is very genuine and good – but, to my taste, rather <u>thin</u>.

Pigott and Benham and I go a sailing on the 15th September. We think (on the rule of contraries hitherto observed by the seasons of 1860) that the equinoctial gales will bring us lovely weather.

Caroline sends her kindest remembrances. We have another servant – a hybrid white-[haired] young person engaged to help Mary – <u>going</u>! The hybrid and Mary don't agree. I am sorry to lose the hybrid. She sees me into the water-closet and out of it <u>regularly</u> – and tries the door every time I make water. I have reason to believe that the hybrid must have seen <u>My Person</u>!

I wish you had dined here on the 9th. The Genoese cook <u>really did wonders</u>. I never ate a more perfect dinner in Paris."

Note

1. Cawthorn, Hutt and Son, 34 Cockspur St, Circulating Library. For Charles Edward Mudie's Lending Library see Gasson. Sampson Low published *The Woman in White*.

To Nugent Robinson,[1] 28 August 1860
MS: Taylor Collection, Princeton

12, Harley Street, W. | August 28th | 1860

Summary:
"'Marian Holcombe' is 'no abstract personification of my own ideas'. The first conception of her character originated in my own observation of many women who personally, morally, and mentally resemble her. In delineating her, I have had these 'living models' constantly present to my mind, and have drawn from them, now in one way and now in another, to make the complete picture which I am happy to find has so much interested you. A character in fiction can only be made true to the general experience of human nature, by a principle of selection which is broad enough to embrace many individuals who represent, more or less remarkably, one

type. There are many 'Marian Halcombes' among us and <u>my</u> Marian is one of the number."

Note

1. Unidentified.

To Mrs Harriet Collins, 12 September 1860
MS: PM

12, Harley Street, W. |[1] September 12th 1860

My dear Mother,[2]

I got back from Stroud yesterday – a pleasant visit – wonderful kindness and attention from everybody, beginning with Gregory,[3] who lives in the most delightful old-fashioned house, just outside the town. The whole country more beautiful than I had supposed possible. Grand hills valleys and woods – the finest scenery of the kind, I ever set eyes on.

All sorts of good news still reaches me about The Woman In White. It is soothing the dying moments of a y<u>oung</u> Lady – it [erasure] is helping (by homeopathic doses of a chapter at a time) to keep an o<u>ld</u> lady out of the grave – and it is the first literary performance which has succeeded in fixing the attention of a deranged gentleman in his lucid intervals!! The other day I reckoned up what I have got by it thus far. One thousand four hundred pounds – [and: erased] with the copyright in my possession, and the disposal of all editions under the extravagant guinea and a half price, in my hands. Cock-a-doodle-doo! The critics may go to the devil – they are at the book still as I hear, but I see no [news: erased] reviews. Low talks already of dealing for cheaper editions – but we have settled nothing yet, for when I last heard of it, the Sale of the book in the expensive form was going on.

I return Charley's letter. My own unbiased opinion is that he and Katie are labouring under temporary insanity. When two people adopt the slowest possible mode of travelling in the ugliest part of France – when they eat and sleep in dirty places for the sake of "an idea" – and when they saddle themselves with a horse and carriage to take care of, and enjoy the botheration of it – what is to be said? As I before remarked, "temporary Insanity".

I shall keep this letter open till I go tomorrow to Clarence Terrace to see for letters. We are in the thick of fitting out for our cruise. On Friday we go to Bristol and to stay the night with Edwin Fox[4] – on Saturday by Steamer to Newport, South Wales – on Sunday sail from Newport (wind and weather permitting) in our new vessel. The best of the three men who went with Pigott and [me] to Scilly, goes with us this time – and the ex-captain of Pigott's father's yacht, supplies the other two men of the crew. There seems to be every prospect of fine weather. We are going to Ireland, if the wind will take us there.

Very glad to hear you keep so well. Forster [erasure] (whom I saw yesterday) sends you his best love. My kind regards to the Bullars. No more at present from

Yours ever affty | W. C.

Little Sydney Dickens has passed his examination and arrived in London yesterday in his uniform of a Naval Cadet. He had a glass of Champagne, and we took him to the Theatre immediately, by way of encouraging one of our naval heroes. Talking of heroes, I met one of Garibaldi's sons at Monckton Milnes's. A remarkably stupid boy!!

Notes

1. Above the Gothic printed address, WC writes: "I send The Spectator by this post. Look at page 864. A review of The Woman in White answering The Saturday Review" ["The Saturday Review" is underlined twice]. *The Woman in White* unfavourably reviewed in *The Saturday Review*, 25 August 1860, pp. 249–50. A rejoinder in the form of a favourable review appeared in the *Spectator*, 8 September 1860, p. 864. On the envelope flap WC writes: "Saturday. No letters at Clarence Terrace. Only Mr Wilson's receipt which has been given to Miss Smith. No callers. All right. W.C."
2. In the left margin of the first leaf of the letter WC writes: "Thursday. I have just heard terrible news of poor George Thompson. He has died at Melbourne (or near it) by his own hand. The fatal drinking-mania brought on delirium [tremens] – he was left with a razor within reach for a few minutes only and he cut his throat. The act was not immediately fatal – but his constitution was gone, and the doctors could not save him. He recovered his senses at the last, and died penitantly and [resignedly]. I heard all this from Ward." We have been unable to identify "George Thompson".
3. Probably a relative of Harriet Collins: one of the Carpenters who lived near Stroud and Salisbury.
4. Possibly Edwin Fox (1820–1891), auctioneer and land Agent (Boase).

To Mrs Harriet Collins, 3 October 1860
MS: Private Possession

12, Harley Street | October 3rd 1860

Summary:
WC got back from cruise on Sunday. "Only two days of steady rain, all the time – plenty of wind, sometimes rising to a gale – grand waves – a capital safe boat (though not quite large enough in the cabin accommodation) and

a crew of the pleasantest and best men I ever sailed with. We kept to the Bristol Channel – getting as far as Milford Haven on one side, and Clovelly on the other." Was a great success and they will get a bigger boat next year.

"Have you heard that Charley has bought another horse, and that he is going to drive himself to Lausanne? Ha! ha! ha! Across the Alps in a one horse chaise. They have to harness bullocks to pull four horses up those passes – what can be done with one? I am going abroad next week (probably). Only to Paris and first class all the way, with my own sitting-room at the best hotel when I get there – and every other luxury that the Capital of the civilized world can afford. No horseflesh for me – unless in the form of cookery in which case (with a satisfactory sauce) I see no objection to it.

Another edition of The Women in White published while I was away! A new edition of The Dead Secret proposed – and a new edition of Antonina announced."

WC "called at Clarence Terrace yesterday".[1]

Note

1. His mother was at Tunbridge Wells.

To Charles Ward, 10 October 1860
MS: PM

12, Harley Street, W. | 10th October 1860

My dear Ward,

I forget whether I told you that I wanted the bill discounted, and the money put to my account, tomorrow, or Friday (if possible). Bradbury & Evans are to have my cheque on Saturday – and unless my balance is fortified in time, I may (as well as I can calculate) be drawing it all out! Thank God I have no more heavy cheques to write, after B & E are satisfied.

Ever yours | W.C

Change your mind, and come to Paris. Only £4 – there and back 1st class. £4 more for expenses – and there you are. Sell a child – terms, £10 – down! Slawkenbergius[1] would fetch more, if disposed of by weight – but I think him too amiable to be parted with. Try the baby – and let us devour the proceeds at the Trois Frères.[2]

Notes

1. "In Sterne's *Tristram Shandy* Slawkenbergius is the author of a treatise on noses" (Peters, p. 233 n.).
2. Dickens' "favourite restaurant" in Paris (*Letters*, VIII, 28 n.4).

To Edward Marston,[1] 31 October 1860

MS: Princeton

12, Harley Street, W. | 31st October 1860

My dear Sir,

I am just back from Paris – and just away again tomorrow (for three or four days) to Devonshire. If any fresh impression of <u>The Woman in White</u> is likely to be wanted immediately, stop the press till I come back. The critic in the Times is (between ourselves) right about the mistake in time.[2] Shakespear has made worse mistakes – that is one comfort. And readers are not critics, who test an emotional book by the base rules of arithmetic – which is a second consolation. Nevertheless we will set the mistake right at the first opportunity. I will call in Ludgate Hill the moment I get back.

Very truly yours | W.C

The Tauchnitz Edition in Paris is out of print – not a copy of the book was to be had there for a week for love or money. They are going to dramatize the story at The Surrey Theatre – and I am asked to go to law about <u>that</u>. I will certainly go and hiss – unless the manager makes a "previous arrangement" with me.

Notes

1. Of Sampson Low & Co. (1797–1886), London publishers.
2. The review in *The Times* of 30 October 1860 revealed a crucial discrepancy in dates: "We could easily show that Lady Glyde could not have left Blackwater-Park before the 9th or 10th of August. Anybody who reads the story, and who counts the days from the conclusion of Miss Halcombe's diary, can verify the calculation for himself. He will find that the London physician did not pay his visit till the 31st of July, that Dawson was not dismissed till the 3rd of August, and that the servants were not dismissed till the following day."

To Charles Ward, 30 January 1861

MS: Private Possession

[12, Harley Street, W. | 30 January 1861]

Summary:
WC asks Ward to order book at once for him: "If I only get <u>one</u> good suggestion out of the six volumes, it will be cheaply purchased at £2.2.4 not of present use to me, it is sure to be of future use. I only hope it is not out of print ... I have only two words to say about that ball dress, and the

charming person in it – they are the words of the immortal Fielding: – 'My Arse in a Bandbox!'"

To William Holman Hunt, 2 February 1861
MS: Huntington

12, Harley Street, W. | February 2nd 1861

Summary:
 "I hear you took up the noble art of skating, last frost. If there is any more ice this winter, let us meet, and tumble in company. The whole secret of skating consists in not being afraid of perpetual sprawling at full length. When Charles and I learnt, as lads, we had a bottle of '[spodelds]' – stripped after a morning's practise – and anointed each others' bruises by the fireside. Thirty tumbles apiece, was one morning's average, in learning the 'outside edge' and 'the [three]'."

To Mrs Harriet Collins, 24 May 1861
MS: PM

[12, Harley Street W.] | Friday May 24th 1861

My dear Mother,

If you receive a copy of <u>The Daily Telegraph</u> which I have posted to day (to Basset) and if you look at the Report of The Newsvendors' Benevolent Institution, you will find that I have come out in a new character as Chairman at a Public Festival. The report is wretchedly meagre – but it is better than nothing – and I may tell you privately and personally that I really achieved a great success – and was followed out of the room (at the end of the proceedings) by the applause of the whole company, who stood up to cheer me. I "prepared" myself for only o<u>n</u>e toast – the toast of the evening – left all the rest to the spur of the moment, and, to my own profound astonishment, found myself speaking with the smoothness and composure of an "old hand". I said nothing about my inexperience till the end of the evening when they drank my health and thanked me – and then I told them I would confess, when I had fairly won their approval, what I had been resolved not to acknowledge <u>until</u> I had won it – that this was my first public appearance as Chairman of a Meeting. This brought down a prodigious burst of cheering – and Webster (of the Adelphi)[1] who sat at my right hand, and "supported" me in the kindest manner "booked" me as Chairman at the next public solemnity that <u>he</u> might be concerned with. I tell y<u>ou</u> all this because you will be glad to hear it – the practical upshot of it is, that this newly-discovered knack of mine may really help my books, by occasionally bringing me before the public, in the speechifying capacity which Englishmen are so unaccountably fond of admiring. So there is an end of that matter.

Let me know beforehand when you come to Clarence Terrace. I am slowly – very slowly – building up the scaffolding of the new book.[2] Egg has come back – but I have not yet seen him (having been out when he called). We had (The Dickenses, Forster, &c-) a capital day on the river, in a private steamer, with Scott Russell,[3] on Wednesday. Charley and Katie were "indisposed" and did not go with us – nothing very particular that I could hear of being the matter with either of them – except a cold of Katie's. No more news. Kind regards at Basset, and congratulations on the prospect of Mrs Bullar's return –

Ever afftly yours | W.C

Notes

1. Benjamin Webster (1797–1882), actor, proprietor, manager of the Theatre Royal Adelphi during the 1860s.
2. i.e., *No Name*.
3. John Scott Russell (1808-1882), civil engineer, shipbuilder "Railway editor on *Daily News* under CD ... Published several books on shipbuilding and naval architecture" (Dickens, *Letters*, VII, 351, n.4), cf. VIII, 47, n.2 concerning his financial difficulties and also George S. Emmerson, *John Scott Russell* (1977).

To Charles Reade,[1] 4 June 1861

MS: Mrs Juliet Noel (née Reade)

[12, Harley Street, W. | 4 June 1861]

My dear Reade,

I am sincerely glad to hear that you have got some rest and change. You have the work of a writer to do in this world, as well as the work of a reformer – and you have earned (and more than earned) the right to turn your back on the annoyances, delays, and disappointments of litigation,[2] and to take breath again in a higher and purer atmosphere both for body and mind.

I entirely agree with you about the shipless sea at Brighton.[3] My usual sea-side resort of late years has been Broadstairs alternating hard work at a new story, with short trips to sea in the roomy old English luggers of my friends and allies the boatmen. If you could come on one of those trips, we might make a pleasant time of it. I assume – after "Love Me Little, Love Me Long" (Vol 2nd)[4] – that you and the sea understand each other thoroughly, and never disagree under any circumstances however stormy! I like Margate too … as for my present proceedings, I am slowly putting up the scaffolding of the book which is yet to be built[5] … Give my kindest regards to Robson.[6]

Except short trips of a day or two, I shall be in town (probably) till the end of July – If you are ever near here, between this time and that, come and "report yourself" to your very truly | Wilkie Collins

Notes

1. Charles Reade (1814–1884: *DNB*), dramatist, journalist, novelist. See Gasson.
2. Reade wrote to WC from Margate, 31 May [1861]: "My complaint was relaxed uvula brought on I believe by the worry and anxiety of Reade v. this thief and Reade v. that rogue and Reade v. the other swindler." (Princeton: cited Clareson, p. 108).
3. Reade wrote to WC "that Margate was far superior to the 'shipless sea' of Brighton" (*ibid.*; p. 108).
4. Published in two vols, 1859.
5. *No Name.*
6. Reade wrote to WC "that Frank Robson was recuperating … at Margate" (Princeton: cited Clareson, p. 108).

To Nina Lehmann,[1] 12 June 1861
MS: Princeton

12, Harley Street. W. | Tuesday June 12th

-

Three Letters

-

Letter I

To Mrs Lehmann

Forgive me for being the innocent cause of your putting your foot in it. It was very kind of [erasure] you to try the experiment. I will prove my gratitude by doing everything you tell me. In one respect only, I have been the worse for the delightful party at Hallé's[2] – the "Great Kreutzer Sonata"[3] has upset me about classical music. I am afraid – I don't like classical music, after all – I am afraid I am not the Amateur I once thought myself. The whole violin part of "The Great K.S." appeared to me to be the musical expression of a varying and violent stomach-ache, with intervals of hiccups.

W.C

Letter II
To the Lady described as "my sister Ella" (supposed to be Mrs Priestley???)
=

Pray accept my best thanks for the double invitation. I will do my best to slip away in good time from a dinner-engagement for Friday – on which occasion we will unite our efforts (if Doctor Priestley and Mr Lehmann see no objection) with a view to "getting Mrs Lehmann's foot <u>out</u> of it" – if we possibly can.

Letter III
To "A.[G]." (supposed to be [Bondinella]???)

Yes. I think it <u>is</u> a great shame. In your case, I should take an opportunity of speaking privately on the subject to Chorley.[4]
   W.C
   I remain, Ladies, your obliged and devoted servant

Wilkie Collins

Note

1. Nina Lehmann, née Chambers (1830–?), wife of Frederick Lehmann (1819–1905) and close friend of WC, who referred to her as "Padronna".
2. Charles Hallé (1819–1895: *DNB*), who conducted the Manchester orchestra.
3. Beethoven's Sonata for violin and piano no. 9 in A, op. 47.
4. Henry Fothergill Chorley (1808–1872: *DNB*), music and literary critic of *The Athenaeum*.

To E.M. Ward, 27 June 1861
MS: Texas: Coleman

12, Harley St. W. | Thursday | 27 June [1861]

Summary:
His old enemy, "Liver", has been attacking him again and he has concealed it from his doctor.[1] Went to bed on Tuesday night with a bad pain in his right side, when he ought to have been enjoying himself at their party. Is going into the country tomorrow to try a change of air.

Note

1. i.e., Francis Carr (Frank) Beard (1814–1893), WC's long-time personal physician and close friend.

To Mrs Harriet Collins, 11 July 1861
MS: PM

Albion Hotel | Broadstairs | Isle of Thanet | July 11th 1861

My dear Mother,

I came here, last Friday, and propose staying till next Thursday the 18th – when I must get back to London for a week or so to collect all my literary goods and chattels for the writing of my new book. You will be glad to hear that I <u>tried</u> the outline of this said story upon Dickens, that he was immensely struck by it, and that he gave such an account of it to Wills in my absence, that the said Wills's eyes rolled in his head with astonishment when he and I next met at the Office. If I can only write up to my design, I think I can hold the public fast, with an interest quite as strong as in <u>The Woman In White</u>, and with a totally different story.

I should like to have told you all this instead of writing it – but after hours of bewilderment over Bradshaw, I have discovered that the trains from Ramsgate only give me two chances in the day, one too early in the morning and one too late [at: erased] in the afternoon. I must get down from London, and see you again, if I can, in that way, after leaving this place. In the meantime, write as soon as you can and let me know how you are, and whether the farmhouse is as pleasant as ever, and when Charley and Katie are expected in your neighbourhood, and how you get on for company. The only doubt I have, on reflection about your present place of retirement is that it may be a little <u>too</u> secluded and that you may feel lonely, now and then. Tell me how this is.

The fine weather is tempting people to the seaside everyday – and Broadstairs is filling already. Things go on just as they did two years since – the flight of Time leaves no mark on this British watering-place. Here are the middle-aged ladies again, with the youthful strawhats, placidly unconscious of their own absurd appearance, and their own [erasure] disclosure of lean old legs through the fine exhibiting medium of crinoline. Here are the Gentlemen looking through telescopes, the children digging perpetually in the sand, the fat-faced young English ladies reading cheap novels, the nursemaids giggling, the boatmen idling, the old women knitting, and the Shop Keepers cheating – all apparently unchanged since I was here last. I have excellent rooms in the hotel, and the wide sweep of the sea confronting me, when I look up from this paper. Where I shall go for my autumn work I have not yet settled. Sometimes I think of staying here – Sometimes, of going to Scarborough – Sometimes of exploring the unknown Suffolk coast, and [resting] [erased word] quietly at Lowestoft. When I next write to you, or see you, I suppose I shall have settled something. For the present, my budget of news is at an end.

Let me have a [erased word] speedy answer to this – for I am really anxious to hear from you – and believe me | ever yours afftly | W.C

To Mrs Harriet Collins, 31 July 1861
MS: PM

[12, Harley Street W.] | July 31st 1861

My dear Mother,

Here I am still in town, having been kept by literary business of a totally unexpected kind. Prepare yourself for an immense surprise – Go out on the lawn, and take a good gasp of fresh air before you turn this page – Endeavour to consider me (if life and health last) in the light of a wealthy novelist – are you ready, after all this preparation? – Then "read, mark, learn, and inwardly digest": –

First, Smith & Elder have <u>bought</u> me away from All The Year Round under circumstances which <u>in Dickens's opinion</u> amply justify me in leaving. The said Smith & Elder offer me (<u>in writing</u>) for a work of fiction a little longer than The Woman In White – which work of fiction is to follow the story I am now going to write for "All The Year Round" – the sum of

———————

Five Thousand Pounds[1]

! ! ! ! ! !

Ha! ha! ha!

=

Five thousand pounds, for nine months or, at most, a year's work – nobody but Dickens has made as much.

I am giving Low, as a mere formality, the right of bidding for this future new book, without (of course) telling him the sum I am offered. He is certain not to approach the amount which Smith & Elder propose – so the affair is (if all goes well) as good as settled.

The Story I am going to write for All The Year Round will be bid for by three other publishers – and Smith & Elder will again outbid <u>them</u> to get it. The second story to follow – namely, the Five thousand pounder, – will in all probability be published as a separate serial work. So I now stand committed (if I can manage it) to a work of fiction to be published (after appearing in All The Year Round) as a book in 1862, and to another book of fiction to be published as a separate serial story, in 1863 & 4 – So that, if I live & keep my brains in good working order, I shall have got to the top of the tree, after all, before forty. Keep all this startling intelligence a profound secret from everyone but Charley – in case you see him shortly or write to him. It is very important that nobody should know it, until the agreements are signed and the whole business completed in relation to both books.

Have you found a house? How are you? Does the solitude of that farmhouse begin to tell [erased word] on you? Send me a line by return of post, directed here – I shall not start for Whitby till Monday next – so, if the man doesn't forget to call for <u>this</u> letter there will be plenty of time for you to write before I go.

Ever yours affty | W.C

Note

1. WC writes this out in large bold letters.

To Mrs Harriet Collins, 7 August 1861
MS: PM[1]

Royal Hotel | Whitby |[2] Augt 7th 1861

My dear Mother,

I am at last established here, in excellent rooms, and in one of the finest places in England. Three large bow windows (on one side of the sitting-room) show me the German Ocean, the pier, the cliffs, and hundreds of fishing-boats, deep-laden with herrings. On the other side of the room, two more windows look out over the town, and the ruins of Whitby Abbey (celebrated in "<u>Marmion</u>") on the cliff above.[3] The approach to this place by railroad is unique in its beauty. The line follows the windings of a valley with the Yorkshire Moors rising on each side of it. Woods heath and a rocky stream (the Esk) [erasure] kept me looking out of the carriage windows in increasing astonishment and admiration [all: erased] for the last hour and a half of the journey. Everything in and about this place is on the grandest scale – it is like [erasure] journeying into another world, after the spick-and-span prettiness of the Southern Watering Places. You would be enchanted with Whitby – and I only wish you could come here, and enjoy it with me.

The five thousand pound negotiation is settled.[4] I signed the agreement on Saturday morning. The first monthly part of the new book to be delivered in manuscript on the 1st of December 1862 – the fifteen remaining parts to follow regularly each month – and the five thousand pounds to be paid, as the novel is written, in monthly instalments – no bills at long dates, and no difficulties, or complications of any kind. Smith & Elder have dealt with me like princes – and they are also to have the [book: erased] story I am now going to begin for <u>All The Year Round</u>, at the <u>highest price</u> that may be offered [me: erased] by the other publishers, for its republication in book form. So here I am "let" (if I [may] for the next [two: erased] three years, [and a half at best[&]: erased]. Keep all this <u>a profound secret</u> from everybody – for fear of false reports about me and "All The Year Round" getting into the papers – and also to keep Low in the dark about the sum offered to me – he has not <u>said</u> anything but I have reason to believe that he is finely exasperated at losing me.

Upon the whole, I think I am glad to hear of your change of abode – it takes you more into "the world", and more within reach of friends. Whatever you do, get a comfortable place where you settle – in a good high airy situation. You live so cheaply in [manuscript breaks off]

Notes

1. MS incomplete.
2. Address underlined twice.
3. See Sir W. Scott, *Marmion*, Canto 2, (ll. 9ff. where "The Abbess of Saint Hilda" is glimpsed).
4. "is settled" underlined twice. *Armadale* did not begin in the *Cornhill* until November 1864. *No Name* began 15 March 1862 in *All The Year Round*.

To Mrs Harriet Collins, 22 August 1861

MS: Private Possession

Royal Hotel Whitby | Augst 22nd 1861

Summary:
"I assume that the project of which I heard from Charley of your taking a house in a kind of partnership with your present landlord is abandoned? Upon the whole I think this is as well – because it leaves you freer of responsibility. When you return in October I shall be able to see for myself how you are lodged."

WC has completed the first weekly part of his new story. "Name of the two heroines – <u>Norah</u> and <u>Magdalen</u>. Will that do for the women? It was no joke getting back, after my hand had been out so long, to writing fiction. I made several false starts – but have at last fairly [bowled] off, to my own sufficient satisfaction."

He plans to get back the first week in September. The "Hotel is comfortable but noisy. Magnificent rooms, but ... You may imagine how the children interrupt me when I tell you that among the British matrons established in the Hotel is a Rabbit with <u>fourteen</u> young ones. She doesn't look at all ashamed of herself – nor her husband either!"

To Charles Ward, 22 August 1861
MS: PM

Royal Hotel | Whitby | Augt 22ⁿᵈ 1861¹

My dear Ward,

Am I right in supposing that you are back at the Strand? I think so – and write accordingly. Years seem to have elapsed since I last saw or heard of you.

We came back from Broadstairs on the 18ᵗʰ of July – stopped in town till the 5ᵗʰ of August – then came here. This is one of the most magnificent places in England. We see the ruins of a twelfth-century Abbey out of our sitting-room windows – a picturesque lively fishing town – a superb sea – lovely inland walks and rivers in endless variety – such is Whitby.

This Hotel is terribly noisy – but otherwise excellent. We are lodged in the most magnificent of all the private-rooms, and enjoy the services of an excellent man cook. I have started my new story, and am just at the end of the first weekly number.

Talking of Stories, I have news that will astonish you. After this book is done, I leave (with Dickens's full approval) "All The Year Round". Smith & Elder have signed agreements to give me <u>Five Thousand Pounds</u>,² for the copyright of a new work,³ to follow the story I am now beginning and to be published either as a <u>separate</u> serial, or in the Cornhill magazine, as they please. No living novelist (except Dickens) has had such an offer as this for one book. If I only live to earn the money, I have a chance at last of putting something by against a rainy day, or a turn in the public caprice, or any other literary misfortune. Smith & Elder are also (as is only fair) to have the refusal of the republication of my [erasure] story now on the arrival at the highest terms offered for it by any other publisher. <u>Keep</u> all these changes and future projects <u>a profound secret from everybody</u>. Otherwise, misrepresentation of my withdrawal from All The Year Round might get about – and Low is so exasperated at losing me, that I want also to keep <u>him</u> in the dark about my new publishers' names and the price – of both which facts he is now ignorant.

We shall (please God) return probably the first week in September – to get me on with my work which I can pursue more quietly at home than here. Perhaps, we may be back earlier. In the meantime, write here and tell me all your news. Also, please look at my account and tell me 1ˢᵗ what my present balance is? 2^ndly whether my Life Insurance Premium was paid for the National Provident[4] in July last!

How are Jane and the children? My mother is going to visit the Langtons & the Combes & afterwards to see Mrs Dyke – to return to Tunbridge Wells and settle in the best unfurnished apartments she can find. Charley & Katie are at Gadshill. Caroline sends you her kind regards – she is getting great benefit from this fine air – and so ends my budget.

Ever yours, | [W.C]

Notes

1. Alongside the date WC writes: "You will see why this is 'Private' on the next page."
2. Double underlined.
3. i.e., *No Name*.
4. WC took out an insurance life policy for £400 in July and took out one for a further £200 in 1862.

To Mrs Harriet Collins, 6 September 1861

MS: Private Possession

12, Harley Street [6th September 1861]

Summary:

"After leaving Whitby I went to York, Huntingdon, Cambridge, Ipswich, & Aldborough before coming back." WC "studying localities for my new story".[1] He got home on 2 September: "the advantage of the quiet of my own room to my work, after the distractions of English watering-places is not to be told in words. I am nearly at the end of the second weekly part – the story, this time, being particularly hard to squeeze into the periodical instalments. It will get easier I think as I go on – and I have plenty of time before me. If I can get two more numbers done before the end of the month, I hope to go sailing for a few days with Pigott, and I <u>must</u> pay Sir F. Goldsmid[2] a visit in Kent – ... When I am once immersed in my work I don't care where it is as long as I am quiet. I will never try it in an hotel again. On board a yacht, or in a detached house down a by-road, will be my next scene of composition.

I saw Mrs Dickinson's[3] death – Domestic troubles, solitude, opium and mercury, all successfully defied till 75 is not a constitutional achievement that everybody can compass. I suppose your mind was running in Cavendish Square when you directed your letter to me. I enclose the envelope for your perusal. It is lucky that I am pretty well known, or I should not have got your letter ...

I hear from Dickens that Charley and Katie are flourishing at Gadshill – and mean to stay through the month. I suppose Mrs Vickress will come back at once. Pigott desired his love. Hunt is staying at Monckton Milnes's – one of the places I have been asked to, and obliged to give up. I am going to dine with Egg on Sunday – he is still poorly."

Notes

1. WC set the seaside scenes of *No Name* at Aldeburgh.
2. Sir Francis Goldsmid (1808–1878), Anglo-Jewish philanthropist and MP.
3. Old family friend.

To Charles Ward, 11 September 1861
MS: PM

12, Harley Street, W. | September 11th 1861

My dear Ward,

I am too hard at work to get to you in time, this week.

Will Coutts's old books, or old <u>anythings</u>, help you to solve this problem for me?

What d<u>ay</u> of the <u>week</u> was the 4th of March 1846?

I want the information for my story.[1] If the 4th March 1846 was a Sa<u>tu</u>rday or a Su<u>n</u>day, it won't do for my purpose. Of course it will turn out to be one or the other! But [erasure] we may as well be certain.

What days next week (I don't dine at home tomorrow or Friday) will suit you to come and take pot-luck? Our new cook comes on Monday.

Ever yours | W.C

Note

1. i.e., *No Name*.

To Mrs Harriet Collins, 12 December 1861
MS: PM

12, Harley Street, W. | Decr 12th 1861

My dear Mother,

You ought to have had a letter from me long since – but I have been to Sir F. Goldsmids', I am only a few days back, and I am up to my eyes in work. The Goldsmids gave me the kindest welcome – I found the house

enormous, a park stocked with deer, & all the other luxuries and magnifi-
cences of wealthy country life, including a valet to wait on me, of twice my
height and ten times my dignity. On my return home, I change the valet
for the "printers devil" – my story is being set up in type, so that I may see
clearly what I have done. I am slowly getting to the end of the 1st Volume
– I say slowly, because I am writing with the greatest care and putting into
this new book all that I have got in me to put. I think it is my best work, so
far. No title fixed as yet. I have several to choose from – but I think better
may be found.

Yes: Mr Heavysides in the Christmas number (I mean "Waifs at Sea") is
my doing.[1] Did it amuse you. It made me laugh in writing it – which is what
my own fun seldom does.

People write to me from the four quarters of the earth. I enclose one letter,
the mystery of which you may be able to solve. I found it at the Garrick,
waiting for me, and addressed "Mr Wilkie Collins, Author, London". Who
the deuce is my fair correspondent?[2]

"Terrible Company" in the Christmas number is by Miss Edwards.
Charley's story about the Shadows you know. Dickens's introduction you
will recognise. The long American Story is by a new hand – a young man.
"Miss Kimmeens" – Dickens – and the conclusion, Dickens.[3] Now you are
informed.

The French translation of The Women in White is published in two
handsomely printed Volumes. – and The French critics are very civil – so
are letters from French readers. You like a title, don't you? What do [you]
think of a French Duke, writing to me in raptures? Ha! ha! ha!

I think my country visit did me good. At any rate I am less ailing than
usual – and in better spirits than usual. I have been directed by Beard to
some wonderful Turkish Baths, with excellent shampoos and great care in
the attendance. I don't overdo the Baths – I only take them once in ten days.

Here is enough about myself even to satisfy you. The extract beneath is
from this day's Times obituary.

On Tuesday, the 10th inst., at 7, York-Terrace, Regent's Park, William
Dodsworth, in the 64th year of his age. R.I.P.[4]

Is this our poor old pompous Doddy? I suppose so. Twenty years ago
would you ever have thought of seeing R.I.P. after his name?

If you like your present life at Southsea, I can say nothing against it. But
it sounds to me, lonely – and I would rather hear of you at Miss Otter's.
When does she come back? You don't say. Write as soon as you know, and
tell me.

The printer is after me again – I must shut up my letter, and correct his
proofs.

Yours ever afftly | W.C.

Charley & Katie both well – I saw them a day or two since. Walker called today. He and all his house have been ill – but have turned the corner. Mrs [Stringfield] has been dangerously ill – and is still in a very delicate state.

Notes

1. Appeared in *Tom Tiddler's Ground*. The extra Christmas number of *All The Year Round* for 1861, under the heading "Picking Up Waifs at Sea".
2. Letter not at PM.
3. Dickens' contribution to *Tom Tiddler's Ground*, the 1861 Christmas number of *All The Year Round*, was in three chapters: "Picking Up Soot and Cinders" (Chapter 1); "Picking up Miss Kimmeens" (Chapter VI); "Picking Up the Tinker" (Chapter VII). Charles Allston Collins' contribution was "Picking Up Evening Shadows" (Chapter II); that of Amelia Ann Blandford Edwards, "Picking Up Terrible Company" (Chapter III); John Harwood's was "Picking Up a Pocket-Book" (Chapter V).
4. Printed extract from *The Times* affixed to the letter. Dodsworth was "The spellbinding Tractarian" whose congregation Harriet and William Collins joined in the 1840s (Peters, p. 38).

To Mrs Harriet Collins, 4 February 1862
MS: Private Possession

[12, Harley Street, W. | 4th February 1862]

Summary:

"The whole first volume of my new story is <u>printed</u>. You shall read it, if you like, when you come to town.[1] Dickens, Wills, the Procters, Charley, Katie and Pigott have read it. The opinion is unanimous. Dickens <u>perfectly certain</u> it will make a great hit. Wills sat up past 1 in the morning, and couldn't sleep after it. The Procters (though <u>The Woman in White</u> was dedicated to them) like this book better. So do Charley and Katie. Pigott ... says the 'female interest' is the strongest he ever met with. All these individual opinions represent th<u>ousands</u> among the public ... the book is (what I have tried to make it) the better book of the two. Dickens says in the strongest terms that there is no sign of The-Woman-in-White success influencing this story, which is utterly unlike the other. I lay great stress on my originality this time – for the first element of success is not to repeat the other book.

But the title – the terrible title – is not decided on yet! It <u>must</u> be settled tomorrow. Here are some few, out of many.

1 <u>The Forbidden Fruit</u>
2 <u>Man and Wife</u>
3 <u>Nature's Daughter</u>
4 <u>The Beginning and the End</u>
5 <u>Behind the Veil</u>

6 <u>The Pitfall</u>
7 <u>Our Hidden Selves</u>
8 <u>Magdalen</u>
Which do you like? Don't let this letter out of your possession, and don't say anything about the titles ...
  My five thousand pound job for Smith & Elder is known right and left everywhere.
  I only went to Dover for a sight of my old, old friend the sea – had two lovely days – got plenty of exercise – and am now back to begin vol 2."

Note

1. Harriet Collins was staying with Miss Otter at Southsea.

To Charles Ward, 17 March 1862
MS: PM

12, Harley Street, W. | March 17th 1862

Summary:
WC forgot to ask Ward a question yesterday. If he writes "a letter today (March 17th 1862) to <u>China</u>[1] – say to Shanghai, or any other settlement of mercantile Englishmen in those parts – <u>when</u> does the letter reach its destination?" And if his correspondent in China writes back by the next mail, "<u>when</u> does the answer reach London? ... how of<u>ten</u> does the mail <u>to</u> China go" and how often that from China? Once a month, once a week or what? Hopes he was no worse this morning, after the dinner.

Note

1. In the fourth scene, chapter 13 of *No Name*, "Kirke's little nephew['s]" uncle has gone to China (*All the Year Round*, 11 October 1862, p. 100).

To Unknown Recipient, 21 March 1862
MS: Princeton. Text, Parrish.

12, Harley Street | Cavendish Square | London | March 21st 1862

Dear Sir,
  Absence from home has prevented me from sooner thanking you for your kind letter.

The published biographical notices of me, in England, are all more or less incorrect. I think I shall best show my sincere appreciation of the honour which you propose conferring on me and my books, by enclosing in this letter a statement written expressly to assist you. Any further information which you may require, I shall gladly place at your disposal on hearing from you to that effect.

You will find my little autobiography – like this letter – written (in accordance with your kind permission) in English. Though I am a constant reader, and hearty admirer, of French literature, I am sorry to say I can only write, and speak, the curious Anglo-French dialect which my countrymen in general have invented for their own use on the Continent. If I ever have the pleasure of making your personal acquaintance, I shall not hesitate to trust to your indulgence for all the mistakes I may make in "gender", "number", and "case". But in writing – and especially in writing to a critic – I shrink from taking those innocent liberties with the French language which so often disturb the grammatical entente cordiale between your country and mine!

Believe me, Dear Sir, | Very faithfully yours | Wilkie Collins.

P.S. Some few years since, an article relating to my earlier works, and written by my friend, M.E.D. Forgues, appeared in the Revue des Deux Mondes.[1] Some of the facts mentioned in that article may possibly be of service to you.

MEMORANDUM, RELATING TO THE LIFE AND WRITINGS OF WILKIE COLLINS.

(1862)

I was born in London, in the year 1824. I am the eldest son of the late William Collins, Member of the English Royal Academy of Arts, and famous as a painter of English life and English scenery. My godfather, after whom I was named, was Sir David Wilkie, the illustrious Scottish Painter. My mother is still alive.

I was educated at a private school. At the age of thirteen, I went with my father and mother to reside for two years in Italy – where I learnt more which has been of use to me, among the pictures, the scenery, and the people, than I ever learnt at school. After my return to England, my father proposed sending me to the University of Oxford, with a view to my entering the Church. But I had no vocation for that way of life, and I preferred trying mercantile pursuits. I had already begun to write in secret, and mercantile pursuits lost all attraction for me. My father – uniformly kind and considerate to his children – tried making me a Barrister next. I went through the customary forms (with little or no serious study), and was "called to the Bar" at Lincoln's Inn. But I have never practised my profession.

An author I was to be, and an author I became in the year 1848.

I had, in the year 1847, completed the first volume of a classical romance, called "Antonina; or, The Fall of Rome" – when my father died. I put aside the romance, to do honour to my father's genius, to the best of my ability, by writing the history of his Life and his pictures. This was my first published book. I then returned to my classical romance, completed it in three volumes, and found a publisher for it. The success (in England) of "Antonina" decided my career. I became, what I am now, a writer by profession.

These are the only events worth noticing in my life. My father's position as a painter made my early home-circumstances easy ones. He left his family (his widow, myself, and my brother) with an income to live on – which, though not the income of rich people, was sufficient for all their wants. Apart from my books – my life presents no events which have any claim on the public interest, or on your attention.

Works of Wilkie Collins. With the dates of publication.

1. Memoirs of William Collins, R. A., (1848)
2. Antonina; or The Fall of Rome. (A Romance) (1850)
3. Basil (A story of Modern Life) – (1852)
4. Hide and Seek. (Story of Modern Life) – (1854)
5. After Dark (A collection of short stories) – (1856)
6. The Dead Secret (A novel. Translated by E.D. Forgues.) – (1857)
7. The Queen of Hearts (A collection of short stories) (1859)
8. The Woman in White ("La Femme en Blanc") (1860)
9. No Name (now appearing periodically in "All The Year Round", and advertised to appear, in French, in Le Temps newspaper. This novel, when finished, will be of the length of "The Woman in White". I am now (March 1862) about half way through it.

An account of "Antonina", "Basil", and "Hide and Seek", with translated extracts, appears in the Revue des Deux Mondes.

Besides my Novels, I have written a great number of Essays, Sketches, &c &c in the periodical conducted by Charles Dickens, called "Household Words" – and also in "All The Year Round". These I have not yet corrected and republished.

I am also the author of three Dramas: –

1. The Lighthouse
2. The Frozen Deep   } None of these three have been printed.
3. The Red Vial.

"The Lighthouse" was first acted by Amateurs, at the house of Charles Dickens, who played the principal character. It was afterwards acted in public at The Olympic Theatre.

"The Frozen Deep" was also acted by the same amateurs, before the Queen, and afterwards in public for a charitable purpose. This play has never been performed by professional actors.

"The Red Vial" was performed at The Olympic Theatre. It was not successful with the public, though greatly liked by the actors. I have written no other Drama since, and my literary success has been entirely won as a novelist. If I had been a Frenchman – with such a public to write for, such rewards to win, and such actors to interpret me, as the French Stage presents – all the stories I have written from "Antonina" to "The Woman in White" would have been told in the dramatic form. Whether their success as plays would have been equal to their success as novels, it is not for me to decide; But if I know anything of my own faculty, it is a dramatic one.

Note

1. "William Wilkie Collins," *Revue des Deux Mondes*, 2e série 12 (October–December 1855), 815–48.

To Charles Ward, 15 April 1862
MS: PM

12, Harley Street, W. | April 15th 1862

My dear Ward,

Here I am, wanting something more. Can your stationer who gets books trade price, get | "Childhood And Youth" | Translated from the | Russian of Tolstoï | Bell & Daldy, price 6/6 | And when the book is got, can you send it, by foreign book-post to | Monsieur E.D. Forgues | 2 Rue de Tournou | Paris | If this is any worry [erased word] don't do it – I only write [under the idle: erased, followed by one other erased word] because I am under friendly obligation to M. Forgues (my translator) who is kindly assisting me in a dispute with a former French publisher of translations of mine – and because M. Forgues particularly wants the book. If you look in on Sunday we can settle the question of expenses. But if you are hard at work, and this is an interruption tell me so.

Caroline and I are going to Broadstairs on Tuesday in Easter Week – to see if I can find a quiet place to finish my book in.

Ever yours | W.C

To Charles Ward, 30 April 1862
MS: PM

12, Harley Street, W. | 30th April 1862

Summary:
Thanks him for note, and sends Caroline's thanks for the present he proposes making to her. They can get no such Eau de Cologne as his. Asks whether he will come in on Sunday. He has taken Dickens' old house (The Fort House) at Broadstairs for four months – and leaves town at the end of June.

To Frederick Lehmann, 28 July 1862
MS: Princeton

The Fort House | Broadstairs | July 28th 1862

My dear Lehmann,
   Here is a line to wish you most heartily a safe voyage out and a prosperous return. I need not tell you, I am sure, how sorry I am to miss the chance of having you here – and how glad I should be to hear, even at the eleventh hour, that the American voyage was put off – for Mrs Lehmann's sake as well as for yours and for mine. But I suppose there is no hope of this.
   The one chance for that miserable country on the other side of the Atlantic is, that these two [erasure] blatant impostors Lincoln and McClellan[1] will fail to get the 300,000 men they ask for. If I thought it could be the least use, I would go down on both my knees, and pray with all my might for the total failure of the new enlistment scheme. But the devil being the ruling power in American affairs, and I not being (as I venture to hope) on particularly good terms with him – it seems hopeless on this occasion to put any trust into the efficacy of fervent aspirations and cramped knees.
   All I do most [seriously] and earnestly hope is – that you will come back with all personal anxieties in the American direction, set at rest. We will then drink confusion together to your customers for light steel and my customers for light reading. I have hundreds of American correspondents but no friends there. If you want anything special in the literary way tell Harper of New York you are a friend of mine and he will be gladly of service to you. So would Fields (of the firm of Ticknor & Fields) Boston.

Goodbye my dear fellow – and once more may you have the best of voyages out, and the speediest of voyages back again!

Ever yours most truly, | Wilkie Collins

Pray thank Mrs Lehmann for her addition to your letter. I am not a good correspondent generally – but if she will write to me, in these long evenings, I promise to write back. We are in nearly the same situation – She shut up with her boys, and I am shut up with my book.

Note

1. George B. McClellan (1826–1885), Union general during the American Civil War.

To Mrs Harriet Collins, 12 August 1862
MS: PM

The Fort House | Broadstairs | August 12th 1862

My dear Mother,
I have delayed answering your letter, until I had some news to tell you. I have only today completed the sale of the copyright of "No Name". Low has outbidden everybody – and has offered the most liberal price that has ever been given for the reprinting of a work already published periodically – no less a sum than Three Thousand Pounds!! Add to this, [word erased] the receipts from "All The Year Round" and from America, and the amount reaches Four thousand, six hundred. Not so bad, for story-telling! I have had some worry and anxiety in the course of the negotiations, with the dire necessity of working all the time. It is an immense relief to have got it over – and I am on many accounts glad that Low is the successful man. Not a hope of the story being done before the end of the year!
We have had some fine, and some furiously stormy, weather here. The place is full of the usual seaside people.
Write soon, and tell me how you are at Basset. I am scribbling this after a long day's work – and I must get out and walk it off. Give my kind regards to the Bullars.
When you leave Basset where do you go next?

Ever yours affly | W.C.

To Mrs Harriet Collins, 1 October 1862
MS: PM

The Fort House | Broadstairs | October 1st 1862

My dear Mother,

I am glad to hear there is an end of your lonely occupation of the house, and a prospect of your paying another country visit. Give my love to Charley & Katie, who are back by this time I hope safe and sound. If it is any consolation to you, after the weather in London, to know that even here – in this house on the very edge of the sea – the atmosphere, until yesterday, has been [erased words] the atmosphere of a vapour-bath – take that consolation. Three nights since the whole eastern horizon was ablaze with sheet lightning – no thunder, no rain, and not a breath of air.

They are going to begin printing No Name in book form already! Low writes me and that there is a magnificent opportunity found in December and entreats me to enable him to publish by that time. I mean to try what I can do. My own anxiety to finish the story is as eager as Low's anxiety to publish it. I have a letter from Dickens about the 2nd vol, which I will keep to show you. If I was the vainest man alive, I could not have written of the book or thought of the book, what <u>he</u> has written and thought of it.[1]

I am a little headachy and tired – and I am going out to have a <u>tepid</u> salt-water bath. I swear by tepid salt-water baths – they soothe while you are in them, and they invigorate afterwards.

Goodbye for the present. Let me hear how you get on at Lady Lilford's.[2]

Ever yours affly | W.C.

Notes

1. Dickens wrote to WC, 20 September 1862: "I have gone through the Second Volume [No Name] at a Sitting, and I find it <u>wonderfully</u> <u>fine</u>. It goes on with an ever-rising power and force in it that fills me with admiration. It is as far before and beyond <u>The Woman in White</u> as <u>that</u> was beyond the wretched common level of fiction-writing" and so on (Dickens, *Letters*, X, 128).
2. See WC to Mrs Harriet Collins 18 November 1862, n.2.

To Charles Ward, 14 October 1862
MS: PM

The Fort House | Broadstairs | Oct 14th 1862

Summary:
Enquires about payments from Low. Wants to be sure before he pays for the Fort House. Is sadly fagged with his work – he "hopes to God I will finish in six weeks time". They will probably meet in London next week.

Sorry he could not come last Sunday. He lost nothing: "it rained incessantly – and the sand and sewage retired in the morning". He "never saw so low a tide".

To Mrs Harriet Collins, [6 November 1862]
MS: PM

12, Harley Street | Thursday

My dear Mother,

I had taken no news for good news and had hoped you were away at Lilford. I am very sorry to find how matters really are. On Saturday, I dine with Egg – and will call and see how you and Charley are on my way. The weather has upset <u>me</u> as well – I am no exception to the family – cold in the head, cold in the throat, cold in the chest – internal upset as well – ha! ha! ha! I am getting used to it – and I laugh like a fiend over my own maladies. There is only one true friend to the afflicted in body – and his name is Brandy And Water – and he comes with particular healing in his wings when he is <u>Hot</u>. Lay this advice to heart, and tell Charley to ponder it too.

Goodbye till Saturday. Get better.

Ever your affty | W.C.

Look out for a drunken Scotch coachman in my next number.[1] I think he will make you laugh.

Note

1. A coachman "preceded by a relishing odour of whisky" acts as a witness to a Will in the *No Name* instalment appearing *All The Year Round*, 15 November 1862, pp. 220–2.

To Mrs Harriet Collins, 18 November 1862
MS: PM[1]

12, Harley Street | W. | Novr. 18th 1862

My dear Mother,[2]

I have nothing to say, and no time to say it in. But I must just write to tell you I was very glad to hear of your safe arrival at Lilford Hall. You are well out of London this month – and you are much stronger I hope by this time.

As for me, my history is a total blank, filled up with scribbling over sheets of paper all day, and marking and countermarking on printer's proofs all night. Another three numbers I hope and trust will see me at the end. And what I shall do then – whether I shall go mad with the sudden emptiness of head, caused by having nothing to think of, or whether I shall go to Paris and forget myself and my book in that city of dissipation, or whether I shall go to Cowes and look over all the Yachts, which the winter-time gives me my pick of them, with a view to future cruising – is more than I can say. Sufficient for the day is the evil thereof.

Nothing stirs the stagnation of London but Bishop Colenso.[3] A bishop who doesn't believe in Moses and who writes a book to say so, is [considered: erased] an Episcopal Portent which makes clergy and laity stare alike. I have not read the book – but the sale is said to have been prodigious.

The Lehmanns are going to Paris. Ward's boy has come back from his first voyage with an excellent character. Egg has departed for another Winter at Algiers. Charley I have seen nothing of, and you probably know more about him than I do.

Write again, and tell me how you are, and how long you remain at Lord Lilford's. My kind regards to Lady Lilford & Henry and Miss Laura.

Notes

1. Letter incomplete.
2. Letter addressed to: "Mrs Collins | Lilford Hall | Oundle | Northamptonshire".
3. John William Colenso (1814–1883), Bishop of Natal. His *The Pentateuch and Book of Joshua Critically Examined*, appeared in parts 1862–63 and stirred up a lively press controversy.

To Francis Carr Beard, 24 December 1862

MS: Princeton

[12, Harley Street, W.] | Tuesday Decr 24th 1862

My dear Beard,

You will be almost as glad as I am to hear that I have DONE![1] – for you have had no small share in the printing of the book. I ended at two o'Clock this morning. I suppose you dine at home on Christmas Day? We are going to dine at Verrey's at six (Pigott with us). As you are a "family man" I dare not say – "come too!"

I shall be at home tomorrow if you are passing this way before three o'Clock. I feel dreadfully fagged.

Ever yours | W.C

Note

1. *No Name* was published in 3 vols, 31 December 1862. It was dedicated "To Francis Carr Beard; (Fellow of the Royal College of Surgeons of England) In Remembrance of the Time when the closing scenes of the story were written".

To Charles Ward, 15 January 1863
MS: PM

12, Harley Street, W. | 15th January 1863

Summary:

The information about the Hotel du Louvre is everything he wanted. The only difficulty is knowing when he is going to Paris. For the last three days the gout has confined him to his chair. It is as much as he can do to get up and down one flight of stairs. He got a letter from his mother on Monday begging him "not to go to Oxford until she got better or worse". So he remained (anxiously enough) at home. Since then he has had better news. She is still too weak to leave her bed, "but the more alarming symptoms are abating". As soon as his foot will let him, he will go to Oxford.

To Mrs Harriet Collins, 16 January 1863
MS: PM

[12, Harley Street, W.] | 16th January 1863

My dear Mother,

I need hardly tell you how glad I am to hear the good news that you are beginning to get a little better at last. The beginning is everything. If you can get sleep, and if you can only take nourishment with some regularity, you will now, I hope and trust, make daily advances nearer and nearer to recovery. The great [two words erased] object is to help you in gaining strength, by every possible means – and this I am sure will not be forgotten by the doctor, and by the good friends who are nursing you.

You would have seen <u>me</u> instead of my letter – but for the Gout![1] It has caught me at last in the right foot, after threatening me, as you know, for many years past. When I have got over it, the doctor declares I shall be infinitely better in health than I have been for a long time back – the suppressed[2] mischief being what has done me harm on former occasions. It is not a violently inflammatory attack. The pain in the foot is easily kept under by a simple poultice of cabbage leaves covered with oiled silk – and

I am getting the better of it already. The only real inconvenience is the present impossibility of wearing anything on the gouty foot or of [indecipherable word] it which necessarily keeps me from Oxford, and keeps me at home. But this will be over I hope in a few days more.

In the meantime, if you find yourself in the course of the next three or four days able to write, literally only three or four lines, without inconvenience – you know how glad I shall be to hear that you are making further progress on the way to recovery.

Ever affly yours W.C

Notes

1. The "out" of "Gout" is underlined twice.
2. Word is doubly underlined apart from the last letter which is singly underlined.

To Francis Carr Beard, 30 January 1863
MS: Princeton

12, Harley Street. W. | 30th Jany 1863

My dear Beard,

The sight of your handwriting again is the pleasantest and most reassuring sight I have seen for many a long day past. That expression of your opinion of the prescription shall be held sacred. It does not in the least surprise me. He[1] is so kind and good, and so full of sincere sympathy for both of us, that it pains me to say it – but the words must be spoken. He has done and can do nothing for me.

Today, the gout has seized in my left foot, without leaving my right. I am so utterly crippled that I cannot even get down stairs into the dining room. Both feet in pain – both feet nearly helpless. Elliotson came here today. I told him this – I said "I am so weak, I have no writing power left in me – give [me] a tonic – I must have strength." [He] has prescribed simple "Wormwood", the other medicine to be taken with it, if it agrees with me – to be left off, if it does not. Caroline to Mesmerise my feet, and to mesmerise me into sleeping so as to do without the opium!

I must be carried to you in a day or two, if my feet get no better. In the meantime, I can only keep my strength up as well as I can, by taking nourishment, at short intervals. I am doing this with fair success, and am stronger today. There is nothing else to be done.

You say nothing about yourself – but your being able to write is a good sign. Is the [Erysipelas] abating? I hope and trust it is. Don't exert yourself, don't move (even to a chair) too soon.

Ever yours | W.C

Note

1. John Elliotson (1791–1868: *DNB*), Professor of Medicine, University of London, a pioneer of medical hypnosis, who saved Thackeray's life in 1849.

To Charles Ward, 18 February [1863]
MS: PM

12, Harley Street | W. | 18th Feby

Summary:
"Today or tomorrow, Low will pay in the fourth and last instalment of the purchase-money for the American advance sheets of <u>No</u> N<u>ame</u> – which" will raise his credit to close on three hundred pounds. With Christmas Bills "all paid, this is plenty". He writes in bed – with his right foot plaguing him "this time by way of a change". His mother "is safe at Bournemouth. Of course,[1] as the Collins family were travelling on the line, the engine broke down, and the train was three hours late – but Charley was with" his mother and she "appears to have borne the accident and the delay pretty well". Sends "thanks for Miss Acton[2] from Caroline".

Notes

1. WC doubly underlines "Of course".
2. Unidentified.

To Mrs Harriet Collins, 19 March 1863
MS: PM

12, Harley Street | W. | March 19th 1863

My dear Mother,

I am glad to hear you are going to the Bullars in April – for you will want a little "company" after your seclusion at Bournemouth, and you will be staying with friends at Basset Wood who have a real regard for you.

As for me, I have been picking up information about German Baths from a visitor to the Baths who knows them by experience. My present idea is to go next month (when I am strong enough for the hateful railway travelling, which disgusts and depresses me even when I am in health) to Brussels, and thence to Aix-la-Chapelle, where there are famous Baths for rheumatic unfortunates – an excellent hotel – and a thoroughly competent doctor to advise about the bathing – when to bathe, how long, and so on.

If Aix La Chapelle does not suit me, I shall go farther on to Wildbad in the Black Forest, and try a famous spring there. I shall take a German travel-servant with me, supplied from Coutts's own register of couriers, for I am in no case to fight with the small worries of travelling – and I propose being away until the beginning or middle of June, travelling the latter part of the time, I hope, for <u>pleasu</u>re as well as for health. Such are my plans at present. Before I go, I shall come to you at Bournemouth. My friend (and doctor) [erased word] Mr Beard will go with me – he wants to see Bournemouth, in order to be personally familiar with a place which he is constantly sending his patients to – and he will take all possible care of me on the road. We should like to put up at the hotel – have two good bedrooms – breakfast and dine in the coffee room. While Mr Beard is walking about, I shall be with you. We shall get to Bournemouth I hope either Saturday the 28th or Saturday the 4th April, and stay till Monday. I will write again when the day is fixed. If I give you three days notice, will it be enough to secure beds at the Hotel? We don't want to go into lodging. Write and tell me about this. Ever affly yours W.C

The Smith & Elder book is put off <u>again</u> – not by any means given up. They have behaved most kindly and considerately about it.

To Charles Reade, 31 March 1863
MS: PM

12, Harley Street | W. | 31st March 186[3]

My dear Reade,

First and foremost accept my congratulations on your start in "A.Y.R".[1] Very fresh and individual – clearly and suggestively written – and the characters <u>living</u> creatures. You have begun excellently. Bravo, Bravo, Bravo! There is my criticism.

Secondly, read the enclosed extract. The writer of the original letter, my friend (and translator) M.E.D. Forgues – 2 Rue de Tournou, Paris – has written to another friend of mine – Mr Pigott (formerly of "The Leader"-now of "The Daily News") – with a message from a French publisher about your books. As Mr Pigott does not know you personally, he applies to me – and hence the roundabout manner in which this foreign overture reaches you. If I can give you any information, I am to be found here be<u>fore</u> two – or <u>after</u> six. Between these hours, I take a drive in the fresh air, and a dip in "Dr Caplin's Electro-Chemical Bath" – out of which I hope I am getting strength enough to go abroad on Monday week, April 13th . If you think it worth while to entertain the proposal, strike for Cash – It is "Very

Hard Cash" to be got. But even a Frenchman yields if you only squeeze him hard enough. As for my friend Forgues – who as you will see is only [an] ambassador in this matter – he is a gentleman, an admirable English scholar, and a translator who has not his equal in France. But the question of the proposed abridgement is another matter – and as M. Forgues says himself, a very difficult and delicate one. I can only say again – if I can be of the least use, come here and talk it over.

Ever yours | Wilkie Collins

Charles Reade Esqre

Note

1. Reade's "Very Hard Cash" serialized in *All the Year Round*, from 28 March 1863, for forty instalments.

To Francis Carr Beard, [4 April 1863]
MS: Princeton

12, Harley Street. | W. | Saturday

My dear Beard,

My back is painful again – and I had a restless night. But I managed to walk a quarter of an hour yesterday on the high road, and I shall try again today. I will call at Welbeck Street at or a little before four o'Clock this afternoon on the chance of seeing you before I go to the Bath.

I have been dreadfully shocked and distressed [erased passage] by news which I am sure you will hear with sorrow. Your opinion at Broadstairs of poor dear Egg, was only too well founded. Last night, Holman Hunt brought me the news of his death at Algiers.[1] It is in the Times Obituary this morning. Nothing can replace the loss – he was a man in ten thousand. It is [erasure] a calamity, in every [erased words] sense of the word, for everyone who knew him.

Yours ever | W.C

Note

1. On 26 March 1863. cf. Dickens to WC, 22 April 1863 (*Letters*, X, 237–8).

To Mrs Harriet Collins, 21 April 1863

MS: PM

Aix La Chapelle | April 21ˢᵗ

My dear Mother,

I got your letter – and was very glad to get it – today. Since I wrote from Dover, here is the narrative of my proceedings.

On Tuesday (the 14ᵗʰ) I crossed to Calais – a perfectly calm sunshiny passage – and met Edward Cooke,[1] the painter on board. Went on the same day by railway from Calais to Lille – a flourishing French manufacturing town, with picturesque streets and a few old buildings – a good hôtel, and no drawback but a fiercely-snoring Frenchman in the next bedroom at night. The next day; Wednesday, to Ghent – steady rain falling – slept at Ghent – went on the next morning to Liége, another manufacturing town, famous for cutlery & ironwork. I hobbled out here to see the [erased word] "Prince Bishop's Palace" (celebrated in <u>Quentin Durward</u>) – [erased word] not very interesting outside, but the inner courtyard one of the finest [erased word] pieces of ancient architecture I have seen for many a [day: erased] long day past. From Liége (on Friday) to this place.

There is only one drawback to Aix la Chapelle – it is down in the bottom of a Valley, shut in on all sides by hills. Otherwise, a fair and prosperous city – making cloth & needles & looking glasses, in factories some of which are actually buildings architecturally pleasant to look at. Beautiful drives all round the neighbourhood – carriages & horses which would pass muster perfectly in England – and two of the best hotels in Europe, both belonging to the same proprietor. As for your eldest son, he is as well known here as in London. [erased word] German readers, French readers, American readers, – all vying in civilities and attention. I am already engaged to be photographed by the local artist, and have promised autographs in all directions. Keep this to yourself – it would look like vanity to other people, but I know you will like to hear it, and therefore it slides into my letter. On Saturday last – after [an: erased] a visit from the local physician – I tried my first bath. The water at 98 Degrees, and <u>cooled</u> down to that from the temperature in the earth – the smell of sulphur unmistakeable – the taste like a decoction of rotten eggs. For the first day, no remarkable effect followed. But on Sunday, Monday, and today, I was allowed to take the <u>Douche</u>, and to have the warm sulphurous water poured on my weak back & leg & foot in a continuous stream. The result has been decidedly satisfactory even after three times trying only. My back is stronger – my flesh is firmer already – and with perseverance, I really hope these springs will prove, in my case as in the cases of hosts of others, to have been well worth the visiting. I drive out every day to the hills – and exercise my feet on the highest ground where the road is dry, and the air bracing. The length of my stay here of course depends on the progress I make towards recovery. I have no present intention of leaving, and my address until further notice is; – | Monsieur Wilkie Collins | Nuellens Hotel | Aix la Chapelle

I hope some of the Bullar family will soon return to Basset – for I don't quite like the notion of your being left alone, in that large house: it sounds dreary. However, I am glad to hear that your neighbours and our military namesake (who seemed to me to be a pleasant good tempered man) don't forget you – and I am equally glad to know that the Slough offer was promptly refused. Ladies who [erased word] take in boarders, under the pretence of "their homes being too large for them", are bores I don't believe in. Write again soon, and I will write again soon on my side. Ever affly yours W.C. P.S. The courier does admirably – an attentive competent servant, who saves me worlds of trouble.

Note

1. Edward William Cooke, R.A. (1811–1880: *DNB*), painter and etcher of marine subjects and architectural views.

To Charles Collins, 22 April 1863
MS: PM

Aix La Chapelle | Wednesday April 22nd 1863

My dear Charley,

I got here last Friday and began bathing on Saturday – after an interview with the local Doctor. So far, the process seems to be certainly doing me good. The baths are strongly sulphurous, and come so hot out of the earth that they must be cooled before use. I get into the water, up to my middle – an amiable elderly German gets in with me – [too: erased] puts the nose of a gigantic watering pot on to the end of a pipe which communicates with a cistern at the top of the bath house – turns a cock – and lets a mitigated stream of hot sulphurous water down on my back and legs, [all:erased] shampooing both with great dexterity. We shout to each other in the French language – our only means of communication – and after ten minutes under the falling water, he leaves me for another ten minutes to sit down in the warm bath and compose myself, after which another man wraps me in a scorching hot linen toga – and the process is ended. Besides this, I drink in bed, every morning before breakfast, a tumbler of the water from the spring – it is steaming hot, perfectly bright, and clean, and in taste like the worst London egg you ever had for breakfast in your life. Strange to say, it does not make me sick – and, stranger still, half an hour afterwards it leaves me with a very respectable relish for my breakfast. This completes the curative process. The doctor [erased word] (senior physician at Aix La Chapelle) proposes no medicine. He is a jolly German with a huge pair of gold spectacles, and a face like an apple – and he smokes his cigar with me every morning after breakfast, like a man who thoroughly enjoys his tobacco. He allows of <u>all</u> wines, provided they are of the best vintages (and my landlord here has not a drop of liquor that is not excellent) – all cookery provided it is thoroughly good – "Snacks" and luncheons, provided they don't come within less than two hours of the bath, are included in his large toleration. Upon the whole, he is a model physician – and where I really want his advice (in the matter of the Baths) he has twenty years experience to offer me.

This place is a strange mixture of new and old. A Cathedral in which Charlemagne was buried – and [indecipherable word] which might have been built yesterday. Wide clean streets, with prosperous, private houses and about a musket shot away from them, [a] [erased word] lonely old German-moated Grange. It is not a [gay] place – and it is down in a hollow with hills all around. But if I can only get well in it, I am willing to think it Paradise. My stay is of course uncertain – but I shall be here long enough to receive your answer, at any rate. Write and tell me how you are, and what you think of doing – and address the letter | Monsieur Wilkie Collins, | Nuellans Hotel, | Aix La Chappelle. | I have heard from Mother, who reports you better. Send her this letter when you have read it. I have written to her but have not said so much about the bathing as I have said here.

My best love to Katie | [WC]

To Nina Lehmann, 29 April 1863
MS: Princeton

Nuellens Hotel, Aix la Chapelle | April 29th 1863

My dear Mrs Lehmann,

Under any circumstances, I should have written to tell you all my news, and to ask for all your news in return. But a letter from my brother telling me that you too have been ill, puts the pen at once into my hands. I gather from what Charley says that you are now better – but I want to hear about you and yours from yourself – and I am selfishly anxious for as long an answer as you can send, as soon as you can write it. There is the state of my mind, expressed with the most unflinching candour!

As for me, I am all over sulphur, inside and out – and if ever a man felt fit for the eternal regions already, I (in respect to the sulphurous part of the Satanic climate) am that man. The invalid custom here is to rise at seven in the morning – to go out and drink the water hot from the spring – and to be entertained between the gulps with [erased word] a band of music on an empty stomach. You who know me, will acquit me of sanctioning by my presence any such uncomfortable proceeding as this. I have an excellent courier, [and: erased] I send him to the spring with a stoppered bottle, and I drink my water horizontally in bed. It was nasty enough at first – but I have got used to it already. The next curative proceeding discloses me, towards the afternoon, in a private stone pit, up to my middle in the hot sulphur spring – more of the hot water is pouring down on me from a pipe in the ceiling – a worthy German stands by my side, directing the water in a continuous shower on all my weak points, with one hand, and shampooing me with the other. We exchange cheerful remarks in French (English being all Greek to him, and German all Hebrew to me) – and oh don't we massacre the language of our lively neighbours. In mistakes of gender, I am well ahead of the German – it being an old habit of mine, and of my love and respect for the fair sex, to make all French words about the gender of which I feel uncertain, feminine words. But in other respects my German friend is beyond me. This great creature has made an entirely new discovery in the science of language – he <u>does without Verbs</u>. "Trop fort? Bon pour vous fort – Trop chaud? Bon pour vous chaud. Promenade aujourhui? Aha! Aha! bon pour vous promenade. Encore la jambe – encore le dos – frottement, ah, oui, oui, frottement excellent pour vous. Repos bon pour vous – a votre se[r]vice, Monsieur – bon jour!" What an excellent method! Do think of it for your boys – I would practise it myself if I had my time to begin over again. The results of all these sulphurous proceedings – to return to them for the last time, before I get to the end of my letter – are decidedly encouraging in my case, so far. I can't wear my boots yet – but I can hobble about with my stick much more freely than I could when I left London – and my general health is benefitting greatly by the change. As for the rest of my life here, it is passed idly enough. The hotel provides me with a delightful open carriage to drive out in – contains a cellar of the best Hock and Moselle wines I ever tasted – and possesses a Parisian cook who encourages my natural gluttony by a continuous succession of entrées which are to be eaten but not described. My books have made me many friends here – who supply me with reading and make me presents of excellent cigars. So upon the whole I get on well enough – and as long as the Baths do me good, so long I shall remain [here: erased] at Aix la Chapelle.

Here is a nice egotistical letter! But what else can you expect from a sick man? Write me another egotistical letter in return telling me about yourself,

and Lehmann, and Lehmann's time for coming home, and the boys – and
believe me,

Ever most truly yours, | Wilkie Collins

To Mrs Harriet Collins, 21 May 1863
MS: PM

Address – Monsieur Wilkie Collins | Hotel de l'Ours | Wildbad |
Wurtemburg |
May 21st 1863 | Germany

My dear Mother,
    Here I am, in The Black Forest! A mountain stream rushes by my window
– huge, precipitous hill-sides, clothed with impenetrable fir-trees to the very
top, shut in the view. More hill-sides rise opposite to them – and the
[erasure] narrow [erasure] green valley, and the rushing little stream, wind
in [out: erased] and out, for miles and miles together, with a village of
quaint gabled cottages scattered here and there by the water-side to enliven
the native solitudes of the Forest. Wildbad is one of these villages – with
all the luxuries of civilisation added to it, in the shape of Baths and Hotels.
Here are [erased word] gorgeous drawing-rooms, accomplished French
cooks, Banquets, and ornamental Bills of Fare. Here is a strident brass
band which plays God Save The Queen perpetually in homage to British
Strangers. And, most important of all, here is a Bath House, as big as
Buckingham Palace, and infinitely superior to it in architectural beauty. It
is strange to see all this magnificence, side by side with the unpretending
picturesque little native village – and stranger still, to think that some of
the acutest forms of human misery, represent the dismal foundation on
which the luxury and the grandeur are built up. Paralysis comes here, and
pays the bills which encourage the enterprising landlord to add to the size
of his [erased word] palace of an hotel. Rheumatism puts its aching hand
in its pocket with a groan, and justifies the Town-Council in Keeping up
the Splendour of the Bath-House. It is only the beginning of the season now
– but oh dear me! the number of people I have seen already halting on
crutches, hobbling on sticks, rolling silent in smooth Bath chairs! The only
place in which I have not had my felt shoes well stared at, is this place. They
are used to felt shoes, to pale faces, distorted figures, and [erasure] crippled
walkers. A well-dressed stranger, with the free use of all his limbs, would
be the right man to astonish the natives of Wildbad.

I got here yesterday, and tried my first bath this morning – after a good night's rest, the first for many weeks. The difference in the water here, and at Aix la Chapelle, is as complete as difference can be. At Aix the water was turbid – here, it is clear as glass. At Aix, it stank (of sulphur) – here, it is without odour of any kind. You lie down on a bed of clean delicious sand, and the hot spring bubbles up under you – [erased word] bubbles so fast, that the whole water of the bath is calculated to be changed every five minutes. Scientific men [so: erasure] disagree, as usual, about the curative quality in the water. Some think the earthy fire that warms the spring communicates an electric influence to the water. Others decry the electricity, and set up theories based on the scientific (or chemical) analysis of the springs. I know nothing about it – except that the bath is clean and warm and comfortable, that it has certainly cured many bad rheumatic cases, and that I mean to give it a fair chance of curing <u>me</u>. If I don't find myself better after a fortnight, I shall leave Wildbad, and come back to England about the middle of June. If I advance, and discard my felt shoes – which is <u>my</u> criterion of a cure – I shall probably make a longer stay. In any case, I have [a: erased] got a good doctor here – and my general health is excellent. My miserable feet still "kick" at any extra exertion, and my rheumatic muscles still indicate the changes in the weather with the most deplorable accuracy. Otherwise, I have nothing to complain of. The local physician examined me in bed this morning, and declared all my "organs" to be as healthy as could be wished.

Let me hear from you, by <u>return of post</u>. In these wild regions – far from railways – the post is, I suspect, uncertain. I shall be anxious for news as soon as I can get it, of you and your goings on. Tell Charley I will write to him [soon: erased] in a day or two. Ever afftly yours | W.C

To Mrs Harriet Collins, 2 June 1863
MS: PM

Hotel de l'Ours | Wilbad | Wurtemberg | June 2nd 1863

My dear Mother,

My plans for returning are [erased word] settled at last. The doctor directs me to take [erased word] twenty four Baths in all. More than this would do me harm, and less would not give the waters a fair [erasure] trial. I am more than half way through my baths today – and the last of them will have been taken on the 13th of this month. I shall leave immediately afterwards, and, if all goes well, I shall be back in London on the 17th or 18th.

Therefore, I have felt all the inconvenience – I might say the actual pain – produced by these extraordinary waters, on first attacking the constitution, and none of the benefit. But there are signs and tokens that the reward of my martyrdom is at hand. You may imagine how welcome it will be, when I tell you that my back has been quite as bad as it was when I left England – and that my feet are still troubling me as they troubled me two months since. Every lurking ache and pain (which I believed to be an ache and pain cured), has been roused and forced to alert itself. The result of this [erasure] bodily revolution – for it is little less than a revolution – will be, the doctor hopes, and thinks, to make a new man of me. I shall be obliged he [erased word] says to return to Wildbad next year to let the waters complete their [and: erased] work – and it is quite possible that I may have a short, sharp, and roaring fit of gout which will [erasure] be of inestimable benefit to me, if I will be a good patient and grin and bear it. In the meantime, if I don't go away relieved of my present troubles, I shall feel the relief a fortnight or three weeks later. Such are the doctor's prognostications. I may as well feel the benefit of the baths in England as not – and I must see Mr Smith (Smith & Elder) on the subject of the new book. So I return at once – to stay no very long time in London, but to try my old friend the sea, both for bathing and sailing, and a "supplement" to the Wildbad Waters which my medical adviser strongly recommends. [erasure] There are my plans and prospects, so far as I know them. We shall see what the future brings forth.

I think I should have proposed returning here, if the doctor had not suggested it. The beauty of the place, the interest and variety of all the walks and rivers, the comfort of the hotel, [and: erased] the extraordinary kindness and civility of all the people with whom I am brought in contact, the bracing delicious freshness and purity of the air – are some of the attractions which make Wildbad irresistible. There is occupation of the literary sort too for a rainy day – a snug little library, with four thousand volumes of English and French books, and The Times, All The Year Round, and the Illustrated London News into the bargain. There is a linen draper who sends for the summer fashions to Baden-Baden – and who combines a haberdashery department and cigar department as well – all in one little shop. There is a local shoemaker who is a man of genius, and has made me a pair of soft slippers, adapted to tender feet, which fit to a miracle. As for my landlord, whatever I ask him for, he produces as comfortably as if we were in Paris or London – and when I want money, he turns banker in a trice and becomes Coutt's correspondent at Wildbad as well as the host of the principal Inn! Half the people in this hotel, are people who have come here for the second time – and, after a fortnight's experience of the place I, for one, don't wonder at their returning to it.

[erasure] Send [erased words] Charley [erased words] this letter, so that he may know my plans for returning – and give my kindest remembrances to the Bullars. If you don't hear from me again, conclude that I am safely returning and that you will get a letter from Harley St next. There will be time for you to write to me again, before the 13th, if you write soon. It is close on ten o'clock, and I am so sleepy, I must say goodnight. I hope I shall get to Basset soon after I return.

Ever your affly | W.C.

Charley's letter from Gadshill reached me safely.

To Mrs Harriet Collins, 18 June 1863
MS: PM

Hotel de la Ville de Paris | Strasbourg | Thursday, 18th June 1863

My dear Mother,

Here is another "Report", to announce that I have got thus far on my homeward journey. After I wrote to you, my arrangements for leaving Wildbad were altered by the doctor, who strongly recommended me to take four baths more than [erased word] than the number at first prescribed, to make sure of the after-effect, and to give the waters the utmost possible chance of routing the Gout from its last lurking-places. Of course I submitted – and here I am, after twenty eight baths, unquestionably better, and on the road, I hope, to recovery at last. It is impossible to say for certain, just yet, how the Wildbad experiment will end – for I am still feeling the severe curative process of the Baths. The curative result, [may: erased] cannot be expected to absent itself completely for another fortnight or three weeks – but the doctor when I parted from him spoke of my prospects in a tone of cheerful certainty which was encouraging to say the least of it. I am to go back next year for five weeks – and there, for the present, is an end of Wildbad.

I go on to Nancy (not a woman, I beg you to understand – but a place!) tonight. Thence to Paris – then to Boulogne – then to England – and I hope to be back in London on Monday or Tuesday next, when you shall have news of my return.

I have had a most kind and friendly letter from Mr Smith (of Smith & Elder) allowing me until the 1st of December next to send in the first number of the new story for the Cornhill – and, what is more, for that same story, I have Got an Idea![1] So if the summer sees me [erasure] on my legs, the autumn will see me [erasure] (and God knows how I long for it) back at [erasure] my work – but taking that work easy, as the popular phrase is, in the strictest sense of the word. If the sympathies of my readers at Wildbad can help me to get well, I ought to be a marvel of health. Visitors of all sorts and [heavily erased passage] conditions showed me extraordinary kindness. Whatever the critics may say, [the: erased] readers are certainly grateful for a story that interests them. So don't mind what the Quarterly Review,[2] or any review says. Or rather, do as I do – don't waste your time in reading them.

Ever affty Yours | W.C

Notes

1. WC doubly underlines "t an Id".
2. Probably a reference to comments on *No Name* made by H.L. Mansel in his anonymously published "Sensation Novels", *Quarterly Review*, 113 (April 1863): 495–7.

To Mrs Harriet Collins, 2 July 1863
MS: PM

12, Harley Street. W. | July 2nd 1863

My dear Mother,
    Enclosed is a letter thanking old Mr Bullar for his interest in me. I am tied to no time for beginning – all am asked to do is to tell Smith & Elder whether they may advertise [me] in October next, as ready to begin with the new year. I am to say Yes, or say No – exactly as I think best – and which of the last two answers I [erased word] shall give, I don't know myself at present – I am waiting for the after-effect of the Baths.
    One result has already come – I can walk better. If other good results follow, I may venture to work again. If not, I shall be obliged to say "No" – [and: erased] for any sacrifice is preferable to the sacrifice of another break-down. I don't say all this to old Mr Bullar – for he is evidently persuaded that, well or ill, I must take my own brains out of my head, for a year, and supply the vacuum with the brains of a phlegmatic man who has not passed the last ten years of his life in a condition of constant mental activity. This is simply impossible. All I can say, and all you must say to other people, is that I am not bound to begin by any given time, and that I will not begin until I feel myself fit for it. I walked yesterday to the Serpentine – rested – and walked back again! An amazing achievement for me. If I can keep it up "Tony Lumpkin will soon be his own man again."[1]

Here are my plans for the summer and autumn. I am going next week to Gadshill for a few days – then perhaps if the Lehmanns are at their country house, I may go for another day or two, and see them. Next, if all goes well, I think of going with Pigott to Cowes, and trying to find a roomy comfortable vessel to hire for a month. Before I leave Cowes, I shall of course come and see you at Basset. My next "pitch" (as the strolling players call it) will be the <u>Isle of Man</u> – [erasure] where I want to look at the scenery &c with a view to my next book. The Isle of Man will bring me (especially if I sail there deliberately in my own vessel) to the September time, when I am to say Y<u>es</u> or <u>No</u> to Smith & Elder. If Y<u>es</u>, I shall necessarily be well enough to face the English winter. If my health forces me to say <u>No</u>, I shall fly South, with my honest and excellent Courier who is heartily attached to me.

All this part of my plan is [sufficiently: erased] in the clouds as yet – I can settle nothing positively until the next two months are past. In the meantime, I am decidedly getting better – and that is enough for the present.

As for yo<u>ur</u> plans, of course you must do what you really like best. But wintering at Basset, alone in that large house, requires a little consultation and consideration. We shall have time for this when I see you.

You say nothing about Lady Lilford. If you are going there, write and tell me when. Of course, I will write again, before my trip to Cowes. It will probably take place in this month – about the middle.

Is old Mr Bullar, "<u>The Reverend</u>"? If he is, destroy my envelope and redirect it for me. <u>My</u> address, as you will see, is simply "John Bullar Esqre".

Charley was here yesterday, looking tolerably well. He had no message but his love.

Ever aff Yours | W.C

Note

1. A character in Goldsmith's *She Stoops to Conquer.*

To Mrs Harriet Collins, 4 August 1863
MS: PM

12, Harley Street. W. | Augt 4th 1863

My dear Mother,
Another disappointment! I have tried the sea-experiment, and it has failed. All my nervous pains and susceptibilities to changes in the temperature increased as soon as I left the shore. For ten days a<u>nd</u> nights I

stuck by the vessel in spite of them. But time did nothing to acclimatise me to the penetrating dampness of the sea-air – and yesterday Pigott and I left the vessel together. [The: erased] A better yacht of his size I never sailed in. All the accommodations below perfectly comfortable – high winds and high seas now and then, but not a drop of rain – an excellent captain and crew – in short, everything right and good except my obstinate beast of a back, which registered (in pain) every shift of the wind to North or East all through the voyage. We sailed along the Dorsetshire and Devonshire coasts and back, touching at Swanage, Weymouth [erasure] Teignmouth, and Torquay – and got back to Cowes last Sunday morning. There is the history of the cruise, and there the result of another useless attempt to take "the short cut" on the road to health.

The next thing to be done is to run for it before the winter sets in. I shall try Naples first, and Sicily if Naples won't do – and I shall get away by the beginning of October, I hope, at latest, taking my papers with me so as to work if I am well enough when I once get settled. In the meantime, I am going to the Isle of Man to look at certain localities which I may want to turn to literary account one of these days. When I get back I shall come and see you – some time in September most likely. Keep me informed as to your movements (if you leave Basset) so that I may know what to do – and let me have a line to say how you are as soon as you get this.

[erased word] Don't be downhearted about me. I sleep better than I did, and I am not at all out of spirits. Doctor William Bullar has got well again with time and rest – and I must follow his example. Nothing shakes my resolution to pull myself through this mess – and you will see I shall do it. If the sea-experiment had succeeded, I might have been tempted to get to work again too soon. As it is, I shall give myself more time, and shall have all the better chance when I <u>do</u> begin. I am not forty yet – and I can afford to wait.

My kind regards to all at Basset. Write this week. Next week will see me on my way to the Isle of Man – to immerse myself in local superstitions and to study the habits of the famous tailless cats of Manx birth and breeding.

Ever your affly | W.C

To Charles Ward, 29 August 1863
MS: PM

Fort Anne Hotel | Douglas | Isle of Man | Saturday, August 29th 1863

My dear Ward,

Here we are at last! I had to send a special commissioner from Liverpool to engage apartments – and he has found them in a damp house, with an Eastern aspect. To complete the favourable circumstances under which I am beginning my investigations in the Isle of Man, the air is bitterly cold – and my miserable back suffers in consequence.

I can tell you nothing yet but that the island is very grand from the sea – and that we see the fine Bay of Douglas from our windows. My first excursion is to be made tomorrow – and as soon as I have seen what I want for my purpose I shall come back. It is too late in the year to be visiting northern islands in my rheumatic condition. C. and the child well – passage from Liverpool raining for half the way across, but calm. Crowds in the steamer, crowds here – all Lancashire goes to the Isle of Man, and all Lancashire is capable of improvement in looks and breeding.

About that business of the Frenchman and the bill. If it is necessary for me to draw the bill, and if you get this letter in time to answer it by Tuesday's post, send me the bill to sign – for I shall in all probability not leave there certainly before Thursday. If time fails us, perhaps you will kindly write to Hetzel[1] and say that circumstances have compelled me to be absent from London for a few days since I wrote to him, and that immediately on my return I will attend to his letter. If he has paid the money into Lafittes well and good. If he makes "a statement" instead, keep it till I come back. If he has taken no notice – damn his eyes, and wait till I [get back: erased] return!

Ever yours | W.C

N.B. No antiquities in Douglas. Every third shop a spirits shop, and every second inhabitant drunk.

Note

1. French publisher.

To Mrs Harriet Collins, 1 September 1863
MS: PM

Fort Anne Hotel Douglas | Isle of Man | September 1st 1863

My dear Mother,

It is, I believe, perfectly easy to travel to Jericho, Hong Kong, or the Sandwich Islands. The one inaccessible place left in the world is the Isle of Man. I think I told you that the landlord of one of the hotels here never answered my letter, and that the communication by electric telegraph with this place is at an end through the breaking of the submarine cable. These were the London difficulties. The Liverpool difficulties came next. [Where I go: erased]

I had to send a special messenger from Liverpool to see if apartments were to be got anywhere – the hotels being literally crammed with thousands of rough & ready visitors from the manufacturing districts. The man went one day by steamer – and returned the next, three hours after his time, in consequence of a gale of wind. There was only one [place: erased] house which could receive me – a house with a bitter cold Easterly aspect. Away I went the next day, in the most horribly crowded passenger-steamer I ever sailed in. Rain half the way across – and no room below, if I had been inclined to venture there. Tide out when we got here – disembarkation in boats – fearful noise and confusion – an old lady tumbled into the water and fished up again by her venerable heels. I waited – as I always do in these cases until this hubbub was over – bribed a sailor – and got myself and my baggage comfortably into a boat. Mounted a rock by a slippery path – passed through a staring line of Lancashire [sailors] – found myself here. Nothing that I wanted (in the literary way) at this place. Consulted the landlord – and drove off to a remote quarter of the island. Crowds here again – landlord distracted – got rooms at last – and next day started in a boat for the place I wanted to see – the Calf of Man separated from the Island by a Sound. Boat a dirty little fishing boat – crew a man for one oar, and two boys for the other. Pulled out of the bay and found a heavy sea and a smart south west wind. Valiant crew just able to keep the boat's head to the sea, and no more. I saw we should be wet through, and should take hours before we got to our destination. Ordered them to return – and consulted the landlord. "Can't do it landlord." – "I thought not, sir." "Can [we get: erased] I get near the place by land?" "Yes sir." "Have you got a carriage?" "Got a jaunting car, sir." [erased words] "And a horse?" "Yes, Sir." "Put the horse [to] then." Out came this car with an Irish boy to drive. Set off at a gallop – mounted a hill – descended again by a road [erasure] all rocks and ruts – I had to get down and walk from sheer inability to bear the jolting. At last we reached the place – wild & frightful, just what I wanted – everything made for my occult literary purposes. I forgave the Isle of Man on the spot – and today I have returned to this hotel. A day or two's rest after all this exertion, will bring my stay here to an end – and I shall be back in London, if all goes well, next week. Direct your answer therefore to Harley Street – and tell me when I can come and see you before the end of this month. A time when there are no visitors will be best – and a time when I can see Henry, if he is with you. Let me know about this – and tell me also whether you have got the copy of my father's will. I shall not be leaving England until the end of the month – so there is plenty of time to make our arrangement. You shall hear all about the Isle of Man when I see you.

Ever aff yours | W.C

To Mrs Harriet Collins, 24 October 1863
MS: Private Possession

[Savona Saturday Oct. 24 1863]

Summary:
[Change of plans] ... "I gave up the voyage from Marseilles to Civita Vecchia, in doubt of the weather which did not incline me to commit myself two days beforehand to taking a cabin and paying an exhorbitant sum of money for it. So I decided on travelling to Genoa by vetturino, and following our old route when we were in Italy. Everything is changed since that time – except the lovely scenery. The old Comiche road of our experience is replaced by a new highway infinitely less dangerous and quite as interesting as our route in my father's time. Nice is no longer recognisable. Immense hotels have sprung up, fronting the sea – a public walk has been made along the shore – and the town is three times the size ... My first stage, after Nice, was to Mentone, and my next to San Remo. I wanted to see both these places, and to ascertain whether they would suit me, in case of disturbances in South Italy driving me northward again in the winter. Of the two, San Remo pleased me most – but both are so like little "gardens of Eden" that it is hard to choose between them. I saw them at the best time, under every possible advantage – the lemons and olives ripening close to the sea, the sky cloudless, the air so soft and warm that the opening of all the windows became a matter of absolute necessity. Two hours before I descended to Mentone, I had been shivering in the bitter wind on the tops of the mountains – and here I found people sleeping in the sun on the kerb-stone of the public street. But the position of San Remo is even warmer ... At San Remo tropical palm trees grow in full luxuriance

– and the town climbs a hill side in a succession of winding streets every one of which is a picture in itself. There is a new and a very good hotel ... out of the noise of the town, looking over olive groves and the Mediterranean – ... [At Naples] there is nothing threatening as yet – but in a newly-established kingdom, and with a lazy population which is being <u>forced</u> by a conscription to serve in the Italian army, there may be disturbance lurking in the future. We shall see.

In the meantime, here I am – at the last stage of my vetturino journey – in this ancient city and sea-port, with Genoa visible out of my windows in the blue distance. I am giving the horse (and myself) a day's rest; and I go on tomorrow to Genoa. Thence, if the present delicious weather continues, I shall take the steamer along the coast to Leghorn – and from Leghorn I shall coast it again to Civita Vecchia, which the railway has put within two hours reach of Rome. My stay at Rome will not be a long one. About the 5th or 6th of November will probably find me on my way to Naples. [Addresses Poste Restante Rome, c/o Messrs Iggulden, Naples] ...

... the mild climate is certainly doing me good. I walk up the hills on the road, faster than the horses can walk after me – and I don't get into bed at night, with the infirm deliberation of a man of seventy or eighty years old. My principal annoyance has been ... from the <u>mosquitos</u>. But I have set my invention at work, and have found out a protective night dress for the face and hands. I have got a small muslin <u>balloon</u> – which ties under my beard, and encloses my whole head and face – without touching nose eyes or mouth, and I have had the sleeves of my night-gown sewn up with a couple of old cambric pocket-handkerchiefs. In this extraordinary costume, I can hear the mosquitos humming all round me with the most supreme indifference. When I wake, in the grey of the morning, I see them crawling over my muslin balloon and my cambric mufflers, trying hard to find a way in – failing at every point – stopping to consider in 'indignation meetings' of twos and threes – expressing their sentiments in a sound like a very small wind at a very great distance – and then flying away in disgust."

To Charles Ward, 4 November 1863
MS: PM

Hotel des Iles Britanniques | Rome | November 4th 1863

My dear Ward,

By yesterday's post, I sent you a line or two, enclosing a cheque dated Nov. 22nd, 1863, and addressed to you or <u>order</u>, for £25–. If you don't get the cheque in due course, <u>stop</u> the document, and let me know – and I will send another.

You did quite right to accept Tauchnitz's offer – which I consider to be a very fair one. Thank you also for writing to Trubner & Co about that American proposal. I will communicate with them from this place leaving the thing open – for I must not commit myself before a line of the new book is written. The unfortunate lady must have her reply as well. It is my next book she wants to translate (not The Woman in White). Let me produce the book first – "piano! piano!" as we Italian travellers say.

Since I wrote to you from Mentone, the hardships of travelling have given us a taste of their quality. We got to Genoa most prosperously – from Genoa by sea to Leghorn, and still nothing to complain of – from Leghorn to Pisa (to wait for the French boat to go on to Civita Vecchia) and still all was sunshine. But at Pisa the weather changed. The sirocco brought rain, fog, damp – and the pangs of Sciatica wrung me in both <u>hams</u> at once. It was the turn of my fellow-travellers next – when we got on board the boat for a night-voyage to Civita Vecchia. As ill-luck would have it, the wind got up. It blew fresh – and the two Carolines suffered sea-martyrdom. Caroline Junior[1] had a comparatively easy time of it, and fell asleep in the intervals of retching – but Caroline Senior was so ill that she could not be moved from the deck all night, and she has hardly got over the effect of the voyage yet. The sea (as usual) did <u>me</u> good – but I have registered a vow to take my companions on no more night-voyages.

We are in great comfort here – An excellent "apartment" of five rooms on the first floor – a good cook – and a comfortable carriage to drive out in, make our Roman sojourn pleasant enough. But the weather – on which I depend so much that I can't keep perpetually talking about it – still has a grudge against me. Rain and thunder – have given place today to a cold North-East wind. The model climate which is to cure me, is not found yet. My foot still troubles me – but the sciatica is gone, so I don't complain. This wonderful place is just what it has been ever since I can remember it – the Ruins, the Churches, the Streets, the very house I lived in with my father & mother twenty five years ago – all look as if I had left them yesterday. I see no change any where except on the Pincian Hill – and there it is a change for the better, the public garden and park being greatly improved in the laying out. The one [great: erased] annoyance of Rome (to my mind) is the French garrison which makes incessant martial noises with drums and bugles all over the quiet old city. Two ferociously-conceited little warriors were marching briskly about the sacred neighbourhood of the Colosseum yesterday, practising [erasure] bugle-calls with might and main, and enjoying their own noise as only Frenchmen can – and, not far off, an awkward squad was actually being drilled under the very arches of the old Temple of Peace. Nothing is serious to a Frenchman, except soldiering – and nothing astonishes him but the spectacle of his own bravery.

We are going to the Opera tonight. I have got the best box in the theatre big enough to hold six people – for £1 –!!! No ticket delivered – the key of the box is handed to me by the box-keeper when I pay the money in the morning at the office – and we walk in at night when we like and open the box door for ourselves.

I have made so many plans already, and then unmade them again (is <u>unmade</u> grammar? I think not) that I hardly like to write positively about the future. But I think I am certain to be here until Monday next at any rate. After that, the chances are that I shall be on my way to Naples. So when you next write, address to me "care of Messrs – Iggulden & Co, bankers, Naples" – and I shall be sure of getting the letter. In the meantime, I have no new commissions to trouble you with. The "Miscellanies"[2] represent the only business-transaction I have left behind me – and this you are already kindly prepared to look after when the time comes. Give my best love to all at home, and tell me when you next write that [Coosey] is strong and well again.

Ever Yours, | [W.C]

Notes

1. Harriet Elizabeth (Carrie) born to Caroline Elizabeth Graves, 3 February 1851. Married Henry Powell Bartley, 1878. Died 1905. See Gasson.
2. *My Miscellanies*, two volumes of selections from WC's non-fictional essays in *Household Words* and *All the Year Round*, dedicated to Henry Bullar. WC left the publishing details to Charles Ward.

To Mrs Harriet Collins, 13 November 1863
MS: PM

Hotel d'Angleterre | Chiaia | Naples | November 13th 1863

My dear Mother,

I got your letter, addressed to me at Iggulden's, yesterday. I also received your other letter (from the Poste Restante) at Rome. From Rome I wrote to Charley and told him to send my letter on to you. So much for the family correspondences, to begin with. As far as I know, none of our letters have missed [us].

And now, what have I got to write about? Nothing but the weather. It is tiresome in the last degree to be perpetually dwelling on this one subject – but everything I do is decided by the state of the [erased word] atmosphere, and all my worst existing difficulties are difficulties set up by the rain and the wind. My letter to Charley will have told you what the weather did with me at sea. At Rome, I found the sun again – [erased word] heat, boiling [hot: erased] heat, on one side of a street, and deadly chilling damps (in the

shade) on the other. For a [erasure] week, I waited in expectation of a shift
of the wind from the north-east quarter in which it obstinately hung. Out
every morning, [erasure] in the track of the sunshine – bathed in perspira-
tions – back again as fast as I can, to shift my clothes and rub myself down
before I get chilled – out again in a carriage to avoid more perspiration –
drive into the Campaqua to get all the sunshine without any mixture of
shade – clouds to windward, & showers following each other in great
sheets of [erased word] moisture – back again to the hotel – [She] comes
out once more – tired of driving, tired of walking – go and look at a church
– driven out by the damp – go and look at the Colosseum, driven out by
the damp – so home to dinner – shut the windows, on account of the
evening chill – an hour later, atmosphere insupportably heavy, open the
windows again – shut them again – and so on till bedtime. [After: erased]
A week of this was enough for me – and left Rome. Severn[1] called on me
before I went away – and I called on him – and both times we missed each
other. Mr and Mrs Rudolph Lehmann I met in the street – and heard from
them of Janet Chambers' death.[2] I saw no one else before my departure.

And how did I get to Naples? Of course I got to Naples in the rains.
Furious, drenching, tropical rain – and no shelter whatever for anybody at
the terminus. And here I am, in splendid apartments looking out on the sea.
And what have I seen? Squalls of rain and wind, with watery glimpses of
sunshine between whiles – Capri appearing and disappearing in mist – the
Mediterranean leaping in white angry waves – Vesuvius shrouded in inky
clouds – men-of-war steamers (assembled here to be reviewed by the King)
making for the harbour, with their topmasts struck and their bows pitching
furiously into the furious sea. A public ball was given last night in honour
of the King's presence. I was offered a ticket and wisely declined. Why
wisely? Because it blew a hurricane and it was doubtful if the watchman
& horses could have faced the storm. Hail battered like musket shots against
the windows! Lightning illuminated the whole seaward view from Sorrento
to Baiae! What woke me this morning? My worthy travelling-servant's
knuckles on the door??? [Pooo! Puh!] Thunder.[3] What do I find <u>inside</u> my
window, on getting up? – A pool of rain-water. What am I in at this
moment? <u>Another</u> perspiration. The rain is over, and a faint sun is shining,
and a hot damp Sirocco wind is blowing. Are my legs <u>on</u>, or off, my body?
They feel <u>off</u>, and I haven't energy enough to care about looking for them.
I am going out as soon as I have done this letter – and I have just laid a dry
flannel waistcoat across the chair, in anticipation of my return. Who is to
help writing about the weather under such circumstances as these?
Everybody says nothing like it ever happened before. Everybody says –
"Wait, and the climate <u>must</u> recover itself." Well, I <u>will</u> wait, as long as my
flannel-waistcoats hold out. When they are all drenched together, it will be

time to [erased word] go on, and discover an opportunity of drying them in some other [erased word] part of the globe.

Doctor Strange[4] called on me today, and sent you all sorts of kind messages. He is very little altered. I asked after Mrs Strange. Dead! [erased word] Just as I had made up a miserable face, and said I was very sorry – The doctor informed me he [was: erased] had married again! So I made up a jolly face, and said I was very glad. The doctor has given up practice. He too says the weather is without precedent – and he warns me against Palermo, which he declares to be [relaxing]. So that refuge is taken away, and there is really nothing left for it but to wait here in the hope of a change for the better.

The Igguldens[5] I have not yet seen. But Doctor Strange reports them to be all alive and hearty – except the youngest son, La[u]rence, who died some time since of consumption. I am going to the bank – the Igguldens' bank – to get some money – and I will keep this letter open, so as to tell you any news I hear from our old Neaplolitan friends.

I have just come back from the bank. Years have told on Iggulden – he looks shrunken, and he speaks feebly. All his children are away in England – he and Mrs Iggulden are left the Darby and Joan of Naples. [erased word] Many friendly messages to you and Charley. I have promised to call on Mrs Iggulden and on Mrs Turner (whose son is a partner in the bank). Upon the whole, raking up these ashes of old friendships is melancholy work. Iggulden was (to my astonishment) struck by <u>my size</u>, which he appeared to associate in some way with the success of my books. He gave me some orange-blossoms – and we parted very tenderly.

Naples – as far as the rain has allowed me to see it – is not much changed. The Villa Reale is twice the size it was in your time, and the Toledo is lit with gas. But the hideous deformed beggars are still in the streets (though the Government professes to have removed them) – [Punch] [squeaks] and rootle-tootles all over the city – vagabond cabmen drive after you go where you may, grinning and shouting and insisting on your getting into their mangy – little vehicles – no two members of the populace can meet in the street and talk about anything without screeching at the tops of their [erased word] voices, with their noses close together and their hands gesticulating madly above their heads. – Here are all the old stinks flourishing – all the fruit-stalls and iced-water stalls at all the old corners of the streets – here are the fishermen with the naked [mahogany] legs – here are the children with [erasure] a short shirt on, and nothing else, and here are their fond mothers hunting down the vermin in their innocent little heads. Political convulsions may do what they please – Bourbons may be tumbled down, and Victor Emmanuels may be set up[6] – Naples keeps its old cheerful dirty devil-may-care face in spite of them.

When you next write – and don't let it be long before you do – address to me at this hotel. It was a great pleasure to hear that you are so comfortably settled, with so many friends about you. Your letter satisfies me that you have done the right thing in settling where you are. Go on and prosper, and believe me your ever affly W.C

P. S. I am getting ideas – as thick as blackberries – for another book. But say nothing about it yet, my general health is infinitely improved – and my rheumatic twinges are only what I must expect while the damp weather lasts. I really hope and believe I shall come back [erased word] well.

Notes

1. Joseph Severn (1793–1879), artist, befriended the Collins family in Rome in the 1830s.
2. Rudolf Lehmann (1819–1905), portrait painter, older brother of Frederick Lehmann. In 1861, he married Nina Lehmann's sister, Amelia Chambers; Janet Chambers was the mother of Nina Lehmann.
3. "Thunder" underlined once: "hunde" underlined twice.
4. The English doctor called in to treat William during the 1838 family visit (Clarke and Harriet Collins' diary, Victoria and Albert Museum, London).
5. The English banker the Collins family had known in 1838, (*ibid.*).
6. Victor Emanuel II (1820–1878), excommunicated by Pius IX in 1859.

To Mrs Harriet Collins, 22 November 1863
MS: PM

Hotel d'Angleterre | Naples | 22nd Novr 1863

My dear Mother,[1]

Some news for you. Naples does <u>not</u> suit me, and I am going to leave it on Tuesday or Wednesday next, for Rome, on my way to Florence. After having made all my arrangments for wintering here – liking this part of Italy and this scenery as strongly as I do – it would be idle to say that I am not [erased word] disappointed by the change which is forced on me in my own plans. There is no help for it. I have remained long enough to <u>know</u> that this place is doing me harm instead of good. For the last week, the weather had not merely improved – it has been lovely – and day by day in [erasure] spite of the blue sky and the soft air I am getting weaker. The climate is too relaxing for me. My appetite is beginning to fail me – I don't sleep so well as I did – and my foot, which accurately follows the state of my general health, is getting stiff and painful again. It was impossible to foresee this – it was impossible to know how the experiment would turn out until the experiment was tried. The knowledge is gained now – South Italy won't do for me.

Will Sicily do? No – the medical men here (who are <u>not</u> in attendance on me, mind) say that Palermo is <u>more</u> relaxing at this time of year than Naples. A friend of Holman Hunt's – a Scotch physician who has been four years at Naples – tells me composedly to turn my back of Europe altogether, and go to Cairo – where the air is <u>dry</u>[2] and exhilirating,[3] and where the temperature keeps (in winter) at one cool medium for months together. I dare say, this is good advice – but there are many reasons why I can't take it just now. My own idea is to try Florence – because it is inland, because it is (I hear) well drained – and because I feel that I want stringing-up with a little brisk bracing cold air. Of course, if I find such a winter there as <u>we</u> found when we were [erased word] in Italy – I shall leave again. Florence is on the way, from this, to Mentone and San Remo, where I am sure of a mild atmosphere. But my confidence in mild sea-side atmospheres is shaken – and I am determined to try a cold place next. I am not afraid of <u>simple cold</u> – it is cold complicated by damp and fog that hurts me. You shall hear how I get on when I reach Florence. I shall stay three or four days at Rome, and one or two more at Sienna – and take it very easy on the road. If you have not already written to me before you receive this, direct your letter to <u>Poste Restante</u>, <u>Florence</u>. If you <u>have</u> written I am sure to get your letter, forwarded by the landlord here. Don't suppose I am likely to be laid up again. I am not giving Naples time to lay me up – I am going before the enervating climate can fasten its hold and get me down.

I have very little news. Driving out, and sitting out in the open air – the air poisoned with the infernal stinks of Naples – walking a little and talking a little [erasure] represent my present existence. I dined with Doctor Strange[4] and his second wife – very cordial and pleasant. I have also seen Mrs Iggulden[5] who sends you many kind messages. She doesn't look a year older, and she received me as if we had parted yesterday. Her conversation was almost exclusively devoted to her own latter end. She lives for Mr Iggulden, and as soon as she has settled him properly in his grave, the only prospect she can look to with the least satisfaction is the prospect of her own death. Such are the sentiments of this excellent woman! Sophy (the tall daughter) is dead as well as Laurence – and the youngest daughter is sent to England to keep her out of a Neapolitan love [erasure] entanglement. I suppose these family misfortunes have soured good Mrs Iggulden about herself and her destiny. I persisted in making bad jokes all through the interview – and I think I did her good.

Yours ever afty | W.C.

Notes

1. Alongside the address WC writes: "I suppose you have got 'My Miscellanies' by this time. Charles Ward writes me word that the first edition was all cleared off on the day of

publication." *My Miscellanies*, reprints WC's stories from *Household Words* and *All the Year Round*, 2 vols published by Sampson Low, 1863.
2. "dry" doubly underlined. The name of Holman Hunt's physician friend eludes us.
3. "lir" of exhilirating" doubly underlined.
4. Treated WC's father in 1837.
5. Whom the Collins family had known in 1838.

To Mrs Harriet Collins, 4 December 1863
MS: PM

Hotel des Iles Britanniques | Rome | December 4th 1863

My dear Mother,

Here is another report, in case you are anxious about me, to say that I am better in Rome, and that in Rome I mean to remain – on the profoundly wise principle of letting well alone. I felt the change beginning as I approached this place in the railway. The horrible Neapolitan exhaustion and depression, seemed to be oozing out of me like the valour of "Acres" in the Rivals[1] – and a brisk cold atmosphere stole refreshingly into its place. The North wind was blowing at the time – in other words, there was just the dry, sharp cold in the air that I wanted. My spirits, my appetite, my capacity to sleep, all rallied – and my foot got better exactly in proportion as <u>I</u> got better generally. I still feel my rheumatic pains – but I also feel the strength to battle with them. So while the "cold weather" lasts, I shall certainly stay in Rome. If there is a change to relaxing, rainy South winds, and if the change seems likely to be permanent – I shall have to go northward again to Florence or Turin. But for the present my address is at this hotel – and I have written to Florence to have my letters (which have been forwarded from Naples) forwarded back here. This uncertainty about my [forward address: erased] own plans and movements is inconvenient enough – but there is no help for it. Now the Neapolitan scheme has failed, I can make no plans beforehand. I must stop in a place while it suits me – and go on when it suits me no longer – and my letters must dodge me as well as they can. For the present, there is no doubt about Rome being the place for me.

I have no news. Thus far, I have kept myself <u>to</u> myself – and I doubt if anybody in Rome knows I am here. Ideas are coming to me thicker & thicker for a new book – and while I am putting them down and considering and <u>re</u>-considering them "company" only distracts and worries me. I think I am going to hit on a rather extraordinary story this time – something entirely different from anything I have done yet.

Rome is positively crammed with English. I hear our national language, I see our plump clear national physiognomy everywhere, the Theatres are all shut in anticipation of the Carnival – but a band plays on the Pincian, and a caravan of wild beasts is exhibiting in the Piazza del P[o]polo just outside my window – and with these "Gaieties" Rome is contented until the New Year comes.

If you have written to Naples, or to Florence – I shall probably get your letter sent on from Florence in a day or two. If you have <u>not</u> written lately, let me have a letter here. Ever yours afft^{ly} | W.C.

I will write and tell Charley my <u>last</u> change of plans (!) by tomorrow's post.

Note

1. Bob Acres in Sheridan's *The Rivals* who, when he finds that his rival is his friend, his courage is "oozing out at the palms of his hands".

To Mrs Harriet Collins, 8 January 1864
MS: PM

Hotel des Iles Britanniques | Rome | Feast of St Collins |
(8th Jany 1864)

My dear Mother,[1]

If your reckoning is right – which I have a melancholy satisfaction in doubting – I am now writing to you at the mature age of <u>Forty</u>. Mercy on us! Who would ever have thought it. Here is "forty" come upon me – grey hairs [erased word] springing fast, especially about the temples – rheumatism and gout familiar enemies for some time past – all the worst signs of middle-age sprouting out on me – and yet, in spite of it all, I don't <u>feel</u> old. I have no regular habits, no respectable prejudices, no tendency to go to sleep after dinner, no loss of appetite for public amusements, none of the melancholy sobrieties of sentiment, in short, which are supposed to be proper to middle age. Surely, there is some mistake? Are you and I really as old as y<u>ou</u> suppose? Do review your past recollections, and see whether you are quite sure that there is no miscalculation and no mistake.

I have got all your letters. Your last reached me yesterday. Don't suppose I am in any want of money – I am not the less obliged by your proposal, but I have a thousand guineas at Coutts's, and if I can only go on, as I am going on now, I shall soon make some thousands more. No fear at present of my being [erasure] worried by want of "means". As to the photograph, get it copied (if you like) by a photographer at Tunbridge Wells. Sending to Aix la Chapelle would be expensive & troublesome, and would probably lead to some absurd mistake. If you will take my advice, however, you will wait till I come back – when I <u>must</u> sit again to Cundall & Downes.[2] All the "negatives" of the photographic portraits in The Woman In White are exhausted by the large sale – and, this time, I will take care that some really good likenesses are [erased word] produced. But when am I coming back? Well, I hope in March next. I shall probably – but mind nothing is certain in relation to <u>my</u> movements – leave Rome towards the close of this month, and saunter back by Florence, Bologna, Parma, Milan, Turin, and so over Mont Cenis into France. My stay at Florence will be long or short as I find the place suit me. I have dreams (between ourselves) of beginning my new story there – I mean beginning to <u>write</u> it, after I have constructed the framework here. But all this is pure speculation. All I can say <u>now</u> is that I see no reason why I should not be back in England in March.

The weather here is simply perfect. Now and then a day of damp South or West Wind – but generally dry cold bracing frosty north breezes. Last Sunday snow fell, and actually remained unmelted on the roofs of the houses. The circumstance was extraordinary enough to be noticed in the official report of the Roman Observatory! As early as nine in the morning, the Pincian Hill was [erasure] crowded with the Romans, surveying the amazing spectacle of snow all round them – and showing the whitened church cupolas to their children who had never seen them whitened before. Day after day of crisp air and cloudless skies has followed the snow. Invigorated by the blessed dryness of the atmosphere, I can walk for two hours at a time, and can "bully" my foot at last, in return for the "bullying" which my foot has inflicted on <u>me</u>. On the day of the snow, I went to one of the churches here, and found <u>children preaching</u> – children of five six and seven years old, who had learnt their little sermons and little gesticulations and genuflections and crossings, and let them off at the congregation with perfect solemnity and composure. As each child ended, the congregation cried "Bravo!" – and the next child (male and female indiscriminately) popped up into the temporary pulpit like a Jack in the Box. I ventured on asking a Priest near me (I am on excellent terms with the Priests as we all take snuff together) – what it meant. He said – "You read the New Testament my dear sir? You remember the passage: <u>Out of the mouths of Babes and Sucklings &c&c</u>? Very good! There <u>are</u> the Babes and Sucklings! And what have you got to say against that?[3]" I had nothing to say against it – and I cried "Bravo" with the rest of the congregation.

I have been answering your last letter but one – but not your last, telling me of Thackeray's death.[4] I had seen the news some days before in "Galignani" and had tried hard to hope it was a false report – but the next day's paper cut the hope from under me. I am heartily sorry for his poor children and for Charley and all his intimate friends. I, as you know, never became intimate with him – but we always met on friendly and pleasant terms. He has left a great name most worthily won, and he has been spared the slow misery of a lingering death-bed. These are the consolations for his loss – which his family and his old friends will feel when Time has helped them. I can say no more.

While I write of this great loss to English literature, I am reminded of a little loss to myself which has happened since I last wrote to you. [indecipherable name] Nidecke, my travelling servant, died in this hotel about a fortnight since. A week after he took to his bed (under an attack of gastric fever) he was no more. I did all that I could have done for a relative of my own. The English clergyman, the English Doctor, and the landlord of the hotel all helped me. He sank so rapidly that there was no time to speak to him about his friends or his affairs. The law of Rome obliged us to bury him (in the Protestant Cemetery) four and twenty hours after the breath was out of his body. His nearest relative has been discovered since by examination of his papers and has been written to. And so I have lost a faithful servant, who was really attached to me. I was with him a few hours before his death, and almost his last coherent words in this world were words which thanked me for the care I was taking of him.

When I go on to Florence I can engage a well-recommended man from this place. Until that time – as I don't care to have a stranger about me – I decline all offers from travelling servants of all nations.

I keep out of [erasure] the so-called "Gaieties" of Rome – dinners, balls, & so on. When I want evening amusement, I can get a numbered stall in the best operatic theatre for two shillings English. No infernal [dress] and expense and evening costume – and very fair singing and dancing – a good orchestra – & Verdi's music. I am a constant member of the audience, and bless my stars that I am in Rome, and not in London, where they won't let me into the Opera unless I spend a guinea and put on a pair of black trousers first. I see Severn and Rudolph Lehmanns (Mrs Rudolph has just had another girl quite successfully) – and I exchange cards with polite residents – and plead illness when there is a threatening of anything more serious than cards, and so manage to lead my own life at Rome in my own way. I leave you to whirl in the vortex of Society and to represent your vagabond eldest son [erasure] among Persons of Quality. Joking apart, I am really delighted to hear that you are so comfortable and happy and so well surrounded by friends at Tunbridge Wells. I hope it won't be very long now before I am able to [come: erased] judge of all your little [erasure] luxuries for myself. And goodbye for the present. My love to Charley and Katie. Let Charley know you have heard from me. | Ever yours aff^{ly} | W.C

Notes

1. Alongside the address WC writes: "P.S. | When you write again – if you write towards the end of the month – I think it will be safest to address me at Poste Restante | Florence."
2. Photographers in New Bond Street, London. They produced in oval format the frontispiece for the one volume Sampson Low edition of *The Woman in White* 1861, a real tip-in photograph, the only one used in his novels.
3. "hat" underlined once, and "a" of "that" underlined twice.
4. Thackeray died on 24 December 1863.

To Mrs Harriet Collins, 14 January 1864
MS: PM

Hotel des Iles Britanniques | Rome | Jany 14th 1864

My dear Mother,

Only a line to say that on second thoughts I think you had better continue to write to me <u>here</u>. I doubt if I shall lay the foundation of my new book – a very difficult job this time – soon enough to leave for Florence this month. The bright cold weather continues – and I go on getting steadily stronger. So consider my departure put off for the present. If any serious change in the weather does drive me away, the landlord here will carefully forward all my letters. But while the dry air lasts I shall stick to Rome. No other news. Love to Charley.

Ever your affly | W.C

To Charles Ward, 14 January 1864
MS: PM

Hotel des Iles Britanniques | Rome | January 14th 1864

My dear Ward,

Your letter, enclosing my second Letter of Credit for £500, reached me safely this morning. A few days previously, I also received the snuff and my bereaved nose has been in a state of placid cheerfulness ever since. There was some trouble (all taken off my hands by Freeborns)[1] in finding the precious canister, in consequence of nobody knowing exactly where it was – not even the people who wrote to tell me that it had arrived, and who could not produce it on demand accompanied by payment of the money! The administration of salt and tobacco had not got it – nor the custom [indecipherable word] – nor the office, at last it turned up (God knows how) at the railway station, and nobody could account for its being there when it did turn up. This is how we do business in Rome. No matter – I have got it. Take my blessing for sending it!

As to Poole, don't trouble further in this matter. Let it rest until I get back. No bill came into my hands – but it <u>may</u> have been lost in the unutterable confusion of my departure from England. I can't swear to anything under these circumstances – and I am sorry you have had the trouble of sending a second time and copying an extract from my letter. Damn all money matters! I wish we paid as the patriarchy did, with a drove of oxen or a sack of corn. The currency here – but for my excellent friend the Ercole Junior at Freeborn's – would drive me distracted. There is one price for the Pope's gold, and another for Victor Emmanuel's, and another for Louis Napoleon's and another for silver – and I have opened an account with Freeborn, and have got a primitive Roman cheque book – and when I don't make mistakes (which I generally do) I get paper money to pay in, and paper money is at par, and I save I don't know how much, and there is my financial statement for the present session!

My little domestic landscape begins to look brighter at last. Caroline is very much better – able to walk out, and beginning to show some faint signs of colour in her cheeks. She wants to be at home again (how like cats women are!) – and bids me to tell you with her kind regards that she wishes she was pouring you out a glass of dry Sherry on a nice gloomy English Sunday afternoon. Caroline junior has had a dirty tongue – but we threw in a little pill and fired off a small explosion of Gregory's powder – and she is now in higher spirits than ever, and astonishes the Roman public by the essentially British plumpness of her cheeks and calves. As for me, I go on thriving in the cold – and I am at work again constructing my story. If I know anything about it, I have got a fine subject this time – something entirely new at any rate. And so the Times is beginning to pat me on the back – is it? Well, we shall see what they say to my next book if [they listen to: erased] I live to write it!

I encountered the Pope yesterday, in the Trastevere on the other side of the Tiber in a street about the width of Cranbourn Alley. An outrider in green came clattering by to drive all vehicles out of the way, or the state coach could not have got by at all. He was followed by a fat member of the Guardia Nobile, with his legs almost bursting out of his blue breeches, and his cheeks quivering like jelly as the horse shook him in the saddle. These two dragoons – then the state Coach, an amazing vehicle of the period of two hundred years since – the Pope smiling at the window with the most perfect good humour, and comforting himself with a pinch of snuff. I had just closed my own [box] – and I felt a sympathy with his holiness which no words can describe.

How you would enjoy this place! Can't you get sent on some commercial mission while I am here? The same day I saw the Pope, I saw a church founded in the year 224 (what do you think of that for antiquity?) – with splendid preserved Mosaic pictures six hundred years old – and with the stone exhibition (a [spanker], I can tell you!) that was hung round the neck of St Calixtus before the Pagans pitched him head foremost into a well. The Columns of the church were of red granite from an old temple, and the ceiling of gold was designed by Domenichino. It was dim and solitary – a mysterious awful and ancient place. I said to myself, "if Ward was here, I should never get him out again?"

I was shocked by coming suddenly on the news of Thackeray's death in Galignani. It is a terrible loss. We can only remember, as some consolation <u>now</u>, that he lived long enough to do the work of a great writer, and to leave to his children and his country a great name.

Today's post brought me also a letter from Nidecker's brother saying he had heard of the death through "Messrs Coutts", and thanking me for what I did to try and comfort and save the dead man. I am glad to have got the letter and to know that his nearest relative approves of my conduct. The rest is now in the hands of the Swiss Consul, to whom the [brother] has communicated through the Swiss Confederation.

The note below, is only a line to my mother to tell her, on second thoughts, that she had better send her next letter here, instead of to Florence as I had told her in my last. Since I wrote, I have found so much to do in sketching the outline of my book, that I doubt whether I shall have done in time to go to Florence as early as I had planned. If there is any serious change in the weather to drive me away (of which there is no prospect at present) the landlord here will forward all my letters. So write to this address till further notice – and cut off and enclose the scrap below to my mother, or ask one of the girls to do it if you are busy. My love to them, and to their mother. No other commissions for you but this.

Ever yours W C

Note

1. English bank in Rome.

To Mrs Harriet Collins, 20 April 1864
MS: Private Possession

[12, Harley St. | 20 April 1864]

Summary:
"I have waited to write until I had actually begun. After much pondering over the construction of the story,[1] I positively sat down with a clean sheet of paper before me, and began to write it on Monday last. So far my progress is slow and hesitating enough – not for want of knowing what I have to do, but for want of practice. After a year and a half of total literary abstinence, it is not wonderful that my hand [should] be out. Patience and time will I hope soon give me back my old dexterity – and meanwhile it is something to have begun.

I am going to drop the dinners gradually. Talking of dinner there is one I can't drop which you may like to hear of. The Royal Academy have woke up at last to the knowledge that your eldest son is a literary man – and have asked him to their grand Dinner this year. I shall go some hours before the time – and see the Exhibition, with no crowd in the way.

Charley I saw last night – and thought him looking better, though he is still a little troubled by his cough. They have had visitors to see the house, but no formal proposals to take it yet. I have read Charley's book[2] – and have really liked it. There are excellent things in it – I hope and trust the sale will encourage him to go on, and do better still. When I next see Mr Smith I will ask about the sale. I sent you a very fair notice in a rising paper called 'The Reader'[3] and Ward has sent you another in 'The London Review'."

Notes

1. *Armadale.*
2. *The Bar Sinister. A Tale.* 2 vols, published by Smith Elder, 1864.
3. *The Reader* ran from 3 January 1863 until 12 January 1867.

To Mrs Harriet Collins, 19 July 1864
MS: PM

12, Harley Street. W. | July 19th 1864

My dear Mother,

It is all very well for you to talk of heat – but if you only felt the difference between Tunbridge and London! I am writing in a profuse perspiration, with the window open, and without an idea in my head. What have I done since [erasure] we went to Hastings? Well – I came back to a heap of dinners – the last of the season. Also, to a proof of my second number which I had to pull to pieces again – and which it took me two days to set right. Next came number 3, which I am nearly half way through already. When it is done, I go to Norfolk to study for number 4. Pigott and Charles Ward go with me, and we shall get some sailing. Then I go for a day or two to Lord Houghton's[1] in Yorkshire – then come back to some quiet seaside place (if there is such a thing to be found) on the East Coast to go on with my work – And these are my plans, so far as I know them. I shall try hard to get a day with you before I go to Norfolk – but I can't tell yet when I shall have done the number. You shall hear when I am near the end of it.

I met the Dickenses on Saturday at Wills's – and Miss Hogarth[2] told me Charley was [erased word] certainly better for his stay at Gadshill.

[Erased word] Danger on railways from murdering men is nothing – if you don't carry a banking bag. But danger from virtuous single ladies whose character is "dearer to them than their lives", <u>is</u> serious. I won't travel alone with a woman – I promise you that. "The British female" – judging by her recent appearances in the newspapers – is as full of "snares" as Solomon's "Strange Women" – a mixture of perjury and prudery, cant and crinoline – from whom (when we travel in railways) may the [erased] Guard deliver us!

Write again soon – and, if you feel hot, try a bottle of Sauterne from Hastings – four pinches of snuff – and a mild cigar.

Yours ever affly | W.C.

Notes

1. Richard Monckton Milnes (1809–1885: *DNB*), Lord Houghton, poet, editor, and friend to many writers.
2. Georgina Hogarth (1827–1917), sister-in-law of Dickens: she edited his letters.

To Mrs Harriet Collins, 26 July [1864]
MS: PM

12, Harley Street | W. | Tuesday July 26th

Summary:
Thinks he will be able to come for the day, "on Thursday next – travelling by the same train as usual". He and Pigott go to Yarmouth on Saturday – and he wants Friday for preparations. He has "done the hardest chapter" in his book. His mind is made up to go from Harley Street. He has "lost at different times, four working days since" he saw her, "through nothing but pianos at the back of the house and organs, bagpipes, bands and [Punches] in front. There is nothing for it but the Temple."

To E.M. Ward, 6 August 1864
MS: Texas: Coleman

Victoria Hotel | Great Yarmouth | 6 August 1864

My dear Ned,

I have only just heard from Charles – who is here with me – that Mrs Ward has been seriously ill, and that you are still in some anxiety about her. If it is any trouble to you to write, ask Fanny[1] to send me a line to say – I hope and trust – that Mrs Ward is going on favourably. This is Charles's inquiry as well as mine – and you have his sympathy as well as mine, under a domestic anxiety which we both hope to hear has now ceased to be an anxiety any longer.

I am down here cruising at sea, and studying localities (inland) for my new book.² On Wednesday I go away for a short visit to Yorkshire – but return here on the Saturday following.

> With best love, | Ever yours | Wilkie Collins

Notes

1. i.e., the Wards' housekeeper.
2. *Armadale.*

To Charles Dickens, 8 September 1864
MS: Yale

> 12, Harley Street. W. | Thursday Sept 8

My dear Dickens,

I shall never get to Gadshill at all, if I wait for a proper opportunity. Have you got a bedroom empty (in which I can do a little work) on Saturday next? And, if so, may I come on that same Saturday – by the 4.5 Express to Gravesend – for two or three days? I have got a "move" before me later in the month, and I have not the least idea where I shall go or what I shall do next.

> Ever your afft¹ y | W.C

To Mrs Harriet Collins, 9 September 1864
MS: PM

> 12, Harley Street. W. | 9ᵗʰ Sept 1864

My dear Mother,

I am not surprised to hear that St Leonards didn't agree with you. After our Hastings experience you never ought to have gone there. I am glad you are back again in your own bracing air. But how strange that you should be in a<u>nother</u> hotel. You are becoming a perfect commercial traveller! Will you notice, while you are at [two indecipherable names] whether it is quiet. Any [indecipherable word] [audience], dogs, children, musical instruments, snorers next door to your bedroom, and so on? I might do a little writing there, later in the year if it was quiet.

In the meantime, I am going tomorrow to Gadshill for a few days, taking my work with me. [Their: erased] The oppressive atmosphere weighing on us, just now, as you know never agrees with me. I must see if the Kentish air will relieve my muddled [erased word] head – and besides I have long owed Dickens a visit. I shall be back about the middle of next week – and the week after, I hope I shall have finished the number, and be able to make some arrangements for having a day or two with you.

Charley was here the other day, in better spirits and I think looking better. He and Katie are to be at Gadshill to say goodbye while I am there. Whether the dull [erased word] little watering-place in central France to which he is going will do for him, I doubt, simply because it is dull. But, being so far on the way, he can go on to Nice, which is lively – or to San Remo which is beautiful. It is a great thing to have got the responsibility and expense of that miserable house off his shoulders. The [for: erased] mere freedom from that anxiety is I think sure to do him good.

Write and tell me when you are back in your own cottage. I am making my own flesh creep with what I am writing just now of the new book.[1] Whether the public flesh will follow my example remains to be seen. Millais can't do the illustrations – but a very good design for the first number has been done by Mr Thomas.[2]

Ever yours affly | W.C.

At the end of this month you will have the remaining numbers of the book to read, all corrected and complete.

Notes

1. i.e., The wreck episode, and Allan Armadale's dream.
2. George Housman Thomas (1824–1868; *DNB*), wood engraver and illustrator.

To Edward Pigott, 24 September 1864
MS: Huntington

12, Harley Steet. W. | London | Saturday Sept 24th | 1864

My dear Ted,

I can only write a few lines in answer to your kind note – and knowing your affectionate regard for me, I am afraid I shall disturb you. My illness declared itself on Monday last – the Gout has attacked my brain. My mind is perfectly clear – but the nervous misery I suffer is indescribable.

Beard has no fear of the attack proving absolutely dangerous – but he cannot yet decide when I can work again or what is to be done about the Cornhill. With Smith away, and the first number made up on the 1st of next month, the disaster is complete – unless I take a turn to the better, in the next few days.

For the present, keep all this <u>a profound Secret</u>, on the chance of my rallying back to my work. If I <u>can</u> conceal my condition from my mother, I <u>must</u>, I <u>have</u> concealed it so far.

Come in when you get back and say goodbye, if you can. If not, God bless you.

Ever yours affy | W.C

To Mrs Harriet Collins, 19 October 1864
MS: PM

The Lord Warden Hotel | Dover | October 19th 1864

My dear Mother,

Here is a little report of me since I left you. I got to this hotel on Saturday – and found Dickens and Miss Hogarth established in the best rooms in the house, with another equally good room reserved for me. The sea is close under the windows, and the [sea: erased] wash of it in my ears at night has had the effect of [erased word] giving me such nights' rests as I remember having when I was a boy – but very seldom since. I keep perpetually out in the air – take tepid warm salt-water baths – do nothing but idle, when I <u>am</u> indoors – and, as a necessary result of all three sanitary proceedings, feel very greatly the better for my trip to Dover. But it won't do to stay here too long. The relaxing effect of all these Southern Watering-places, always tells on me as soon as the first influence of the change is over – and I am going back to Harley Street tomorrow (Thursday) while I [erased word] have yet my benefit from Dover, without drawback of any sort from the softness of the air. [Do: erased] My next move will be probably (as you know) to Sir F. Goldsmid's – and then I must get back to work.

Talking of work, Dickens has read my proofs, and is greatly struck by them. He prognosticates certain success. Miss Hogarth couldn't sleep till she had finished them – and (to quote quite another sort of opinion) Mr Smith tells me that the Printers[1] are highly interested in the story. I set equal store by getting the good opinion of these [two words erased] latter critics

– for it is no easy matter to please the printers, to whom all books represent in the first instance nothing but weary hard work. [indecipherable word] the whole, therefore, "Armadale" seems to promise fairly enough at starting. I have lost my blotting paper, and am obliged to shift my paces to suit my wet ink. But there is not much more for me to say. Not many people here – the winter season not having yet begun. No public news, and many of [my: erased] our friends still away from London. By-the-bye (if you have not heard again from Charley since I left) Miss Hogarth has heard from Katie of their safe arrival at Wiesbaden – with their next proceedings in the clouds as usual. They were vibrating, between Cannes a<u>nd</u> Palermo(!) in considering their future plans, when Katie wrote.

Shall I find a letter when I get back tomorrow to tell me how you are? If not, write to Harley Street soon, [erasures], and don't forget what I told you about driving out & getting the air. I may bring a Brougham and Coachman with me next time, if you, don't employ that basket carriage a little oftener!

Ever your afftly | W.C.

Note

1. "rinter" of "Printers" underlined twice.

To Mrs Harriet Collins, 3 November [1864]
MS: PM

12, Harley S^t. W. | Thursday | Novr 3rd

My dear Mother,

I have only a moment to scratch a few lines, and to enclose a letter for Charley from Miss Thackeray[1] for you to forward to Charley's next address. It is too late to send it to Geneva. He seems to be going on well – that is one comfort.

As for me my [erasure] digestion is out of order, and my head suffers accordingly. It is not eating & drinking – but the horrible East wind stopping up my skin, and by so stopping it, collecting my bile. But I get on with my work – approaching the middle of the new number already. I am glad you like the look of the 1st number and illustration. It is too early yet to know how it has done – I have seen nothing but a favourable mention of my start in todays Mor<u>ning</u> Post.

I have been dreadfully shocked and distressed by poor Leech's[2] death. I heartily liked him and we <u>had</u> many nervous troubles in common. My doctor [erased word] thinks I had better <u>not</u> risk attending the funeral. I will call and ask after poor Mrs Leech, the next day. Charley will be grieved to hear it, I know.

No more [train] – paper – or news. Write again soon.

Ever yours afftly | W.C.

Notes

1. Anne Isabella Thackeray, later Lady Ritchie (1837–1923; *DNB*).
2. John Leech (1817–1864; *DNB*) illustrator and artist.

To Mrs Harriet Collins, 18 December 1864

MS: Private Possession

[12, Harley Street, W. | Sunday Dec 18 1864]

Summary:
    "Those giddy symptoms that I told you of rather increased after I saw you. My friend Beard himself suggested consulting Doctor Radcliffe[1] – the great authority now on brain and nerves. The doctor came yesterday – and to my great relief arrived at the same conclusion as to what was the matter with me which Mr Beard had reached ... He declared there was <u>not the least reason for any alarm about my work</u>. I was suffering he said from 'gouty irritation' which had upset the nerves for a time only. He assured me, and afterwards privately assured Mr Beard in consultation that there was nothing whatever seriously wrong with me. I am put under a 'new treatment', with a change, to help it, in all my habits. Dine lightly at <u>two</u> – work from four to 7 or 8 o'clock – go out – come back for supper at $\frac{1}{2}$ p. 9 or 10. Bed between 11 & 12. Light breakfast – read and idle between breakfast and two o'clock. Eat light ... poultry-eggs, farinaceous puddings – <u>no lean meat</u> – claret and hock to drink – and for the present no exciting myself with 'Society' and dinner parties ...
    I propose, if all goes well, moving on Wednesday to No 9 Melcombe Place, Dorset Square, (for the time being) ... Most of my things have gone before me – and the move is being accomplished without trouble."

Note

1. Dr Charles Radcliffe (1822–1889: *DNB*) "one of the earliest investigators ... of the electrical physiology of muscle and nerve".

To Mrs Harriet Collins, 6 February 1865
MS: Private Possession

[9, Melcombe Place | Tuesday Feb 6 1865][1]

Summary:
   "Between work and evening engagements I am living rather in a whirl just now – but it seems to agree with me. My friend Beard has hit on a fortifying compound of drugs, Quinine, Acid, and Dandelion, that has done me infinite good. Seven and twenty pages of No 18 are done and in the printer's hands – but I must extend the number to three pages more, to leave myself elbow room in 19 & 20. So much for 'Armadale'." WC hopes to get to visit his mother on 12th–17th February. He "must get back for dinner at Sir F. Goldsmid's ... Another of my plans (still in the clouds) is to go to Paris again with Lehmann towards the latter part of the month ... I certainly want a <u>change</u> – and I think it would give me a fillip for the last two numbers.
   I called on Charley & Katie a week ago, and found them both, not only well, but <u>Fat!</u>[2] Charley had not then heard from Chapman and Hall. He promised to let me know when something was settled – and I have received no news from him yet." They will meet at dinner party at Highgate.

Notes

1. WC uses Athenaeum paper. Envelope addressed to ["Mrs Harriet Collins | Elm Lodge | Mount Ephraim | Tunbridge Wells"].
2. WC underlines "Fat!" twice.

To Mrs Harriet Collins, 27 February 1865
MS: PM

Hotel du Helder | Rue du Helder | Paris | Monday. Feby 27th 1865

My dear Mother,
   There is only one thing to say about the journey here – it could hardly have been easier and pleasanter if it had been a journey in the summer. The passage across was one of the calmest passages I have ever made – nobody sick anywhere on board. We got to this excellent hotel after a slow and safe railway journey from Calais in time for an [erasure] excellent dinner. It is one of the small hotels in which the landlord looks personally after the comfort of his guests, and the servants wait on you as if you were at home. If you ever alter your mind and come with me to Paris, we will stay here.

They have some Brandy fifty years old – will <u>that</u> induce you to come some day?

The weather is not very cheerful – the air damp, the sky overcast, and the streets muddy. But Paris looks as crowded and as [a: erased] vividly animated out of doors as ever. Our places at the theatres are obliged to be taken some days beforehand – and the restaurants and cafes seem to be fuller than ever of people with nothing on earth to do but to dine, smoke, talk, and drink coffee.

I have been here too short a time to have anything else to say about Paris – except that the change has done me good already. My book is as entirely off my mind here, as if my book was done.

Write as soon as you can, and let me know how you go on at the new house, and how y<u>ou</u> feel, y<u>our</u> change of place. Everything seems to have begun so well at Elm Lodge that I am in hopes we both did a very wise thing when we entered Mr [L]eaman's doors. Are there any noises? I ask this with a view to my work, when I come back.

We have settled at present to return on the 8th of March. You shall hear again, if we keep to that day – my impression is that we shall.

Mind you write soon.

Ever yours aftly | W.C

The last <u>I</u> heard of Charley (from C. Ward) they were still at Mentone.

To William Holman Hunt, 22 April [1865]
MS: Huntington

9, Melcombe Place | Dorset Square N.W. | April 22nd

My dear Holman,

Have I the face to write to you? Yes – for it is not my fault I have removed from Harley St to the address above, I only got your letter [word erased] today. When I am in town, I am here and always glad to see you. At other times I am with our dear old mother at Elm Lodge, Mount Ephraim, Tunbridge Wells where you will be also always welcome, as you know. [word erased] Sunday I go to Slough to dine. Monday, I go to Elm Lodge to stay till Saturday. Saturday, I come back to town to the [Pitt] Dinner (if the gout doesn't trip me up). These are my present engagements. Shall I be too late to see <u>the</u> picture on Sunday <u>week</u>? I am afraid so. Is it too late to help in finding the title. Write to me at – or come to, which would be much better – our little snuggery at Tunbridge Wells next week – and if the title is not yet found I will cudgel my brains till it <u>is</u> found.

I saw your "Afterglow in Egypt"[1] – and thought it magnificent. Really a noble picture mentally <u>and</u> technically. I have asked after you perpetually. The answer has always been "He is down in the country <u>at</u> a portrait." Our mother has your photograph, but never expects to see <u>you</u> again.

Charley is certainly better, and is coming back next month. He writes in good spirits and has finished a new novel.

Ever yours | Wilkie Collins

Address next week
 Elm Lodge Mount Ephraim | Tunbridge Wells.
 Come down if you can and chose your own day. <u>Bed</u> if you like.
 On and after <u>this day week</u> (Saturday) address 9 Melcombe Place

Note

1. Now in the Southampton City Art Gallery.

To Mrs Harriet Collins, 2 May [1865]
MS: PM

9, Melcombe Place | N.W. | Tuesday May 2nd

My dear Mother,[1]

Here is news of Charley with a vengeance! He will be at Tunbridge Wells by the latter end of the week, I should think. If he is, give him (& his wife if she comes) <u>my</u> room – for I am afraid I shall not be able to get away this week and I have written my apologies to Mrs [A. Pott] accordingly. As to next week, if Charley is still with you (which I hope he will be) give <u>me</u> the little back room. I want nothing but p<u>illow</u>s, and I won't have you turned out of y<u>our</u> room. My hope is that I shall have got the number done, and shall come on Monday next for a holiday. The rain in the air [erased word] [excites] my rheumatism but I am otherwise going on famously. No harm from the Academy Dinner. Many inquiries after y<u>ou</u>. Old Pickersgill[2] made quite a scene about me and my books – wrung my hand a dozen times across the table – and implored me to come & see him! Exalted Functionaries sitting near us, stared till I thought their eyes would drop out. I left directions here (being in a violent hurry) to send you the Times report[3] of the dinner, and I hope you got it. An excellent exhibition.

Write and tell me how you feel about Charley. Don't excite yourself – take it easy. I am just going to work.

Ever yours afly | W.C

Notes

1. Envelope postmarked: "LONDON – NW | 1 | MY 2 | 65".
2. William Pickersgill (1782–1875; *DNB*), portrait painter.
3. See *The Times*, 1 May 1865, p. 6a.

To Lady Louisa Sophia Goldsmid,[1] 15 May 186[5]
MS: Private Possession[2]

9, Melcombe Place | N.W. | May 15th

My dear Lady Goldsmid,
Many thanks for the card "to remind" which you have kindly sent to me. This time, I will be worthier of your indulgence. If I am alive, it [will appear: erased] is needless to say how gladly I shall take my place at your table. If I am <u>not</u> alive, be so good as to look towards the conservatory, when the butler comes round for the first time with the Champagne. You will receive a Luminous Appearance – with an empty glass in one hand, and a blessed rosary for Miss Jekyll[3] in the other. That will be <u>Me</u>. Vy truly yours | Wilkie Collins

Notes

1. Wife of Sir Francis Goldsmid.
2. WC uses water-marked paper: "JOYNSON | 1865".
3. Gertrude Jekyll, (1843–1932; *DNB*) gardening author and society journalist.

To Alice Ward, 14 June 1865
MS: Private Possession

9, Melcombe Place | Dorset Square. W. | June 14th 1865

My dear Alice,
Will you accept a small pair of earings – as some assistance to you in "renouncing the ... and vanities of this wicked world" at your first ball on Monday next, offered by Your affectionate Godfather | Wilkie Collins
P.S. – The jeweller has promised to send the earings to Kent Villa today.

To Mrs Harriet Collins, 17 August 1865
MS: Private Possession

9, Melcombe Place | [17 August 1865]

Summary:
   "The number is done <u>at last</u>, and I must go on tomorrow and begin the next, or lose one of my three months of advance, which I want to get if I can help it.

   I am better – but there are certain small derangements about me which are not quite set right yet." – WC hopes to get to his mother – "but nothing can be fixed because of backwardness in work.

   London is not so bad in August. It is wonderfully quiet – all the people who interrupt me are away and the post is delightfully slow in bringing letters. Charles Ward is back, and Pigott is here tied to the paper. All our other friends are away and I roam the empty streets and inhale the delightful London air (so much healthier than those pretentions humbugs the seaside breezes!) and meet nobody, and come back with the blessed conviction that I have <u>not</u> got to 'dress' and go out to dinner, and feel that London in August is London under a most attractive aspect.

   My love to Rosa. I had hoped she would have got stronger in your bracing air. If only she would write a serial story, she would find it impossible to be ill long – the printers would not allow it!

   Talking of printers, Charley's new title[1] is certainly not a good one. But I don't think it matters. Any title will do – if a book suceeds – and <u>no</u> title will do if it doesn't.

   I hope you have been to the theatre at the Wells, and taken Rosa there with you. A civilised example of that kind is much needed by the pious barbarians in your parts."

Note

1. *At the Bar: A Tale*, 2 vols, 1866.

To Reverend Dr Deems,[1] 5 October 1865
MS: Fales Collection, NYU. Published Coleman

Elm Lodge – Mount Ephraim | Turnbridge Wells | England. |
Oct: 5th 1865

Dear Sir,
   I have had no earlier opportunity than this, of replying to your letter.
   I think I can give, what is called, a practical answer to the question prompted by your kind interest in my book. Neither "The Woman In

White", nor any other of my Serial Stories, [erasure] were completed in Manuscript, before their periodical publication. I was consequently <u>obliged</u> to know every step of my way from beginning to end, before I started on my journey.

To make this plain, by an instance. When I sat down to write the seventh <u>weekly part</u> of "The Woman In White", the first weekly part was being published simultaneously in "All The Year Round", and in "Harper's Weekly".[2] No after-thoughts in connection with the first part, were possible under the circumstances – and the same rule applied of course week after week to the rest of the story. I had no choice, but to know what to do before hand throughout the whole story – and months before a line of it was written for the press, I was accumulating that knowledge in a mass of "notes" which contained a complete outline of the story and the characters. I knew what Sir Perceval Glyde was going to do with the marriage-register, and how Count Fosco's night at the opera was to be spoilt by the appearance of Professor Pesca, before a line of the book was in the printer's hands. The minor details of incident, and the minuter touches of character, I leave to suggest themselves to me at the time of writing for [a: erased] publication. But the great stages of the story, and the main features of the characters, invariably lie before me on my desk before I begin my book. In the story I am now writing ("Armadale"), the last number [erasure] is to be published [erasure] several months hence – and the whole close of the story is still unwritten.[3] But I know at this moment who is to live and who is to die – and I see the main events which lead to the end as plainly as I see the pen now in my hand – as plainly as I see the ground laid, months since, in the published part of the story, for what (if I am spared to finish it) you will read months hence. <u>How</u> I shall lead you from one main event to the other – whether I shall dwell at length on certain details or pass them over rapidly – [erased words] how I may yet develop my characters and make them clearer to you by new touches and traits – all this, I know no more than you do, till I take the pen in hand. But the characters themselves were all marshalled in their places, before a line of "Armadale" was written. And I knew the end two years ago in Rome, when I was recovering from a long illness, and was putting the story together.[4]

Such is the best explanation I can offer of all that is explainable in the mental process which produces my stories. I beg you will accept it as an acknowledgment on my part of the interest you feel in my books, and as some small repayment (made through you) of the debt of obligation which I owe to my American readers.

Believe me | Dear Sir | Faithfully yours | Wilkie Collins

To | The Revd Dr Deems

Notes

1. Charles Force Deems (1820–1893), Methodist minister, founder of the Church of the Strangers in New York, 1868. Author of *Life of Jesus* (1872) and *A Scotch Verdict in Evolution* (1885).
2. 29 November 1859.
3. *Armadale* began in *Cornhill* November 1864 and ran for 20 months until June 1866.
4. WC was in Italy between the winter of 1863 and the spring of 1864.

To [Mrs E.M. Ward], 6 December [1865]
MS: Texas: Coleman

9, Melcombe Place NW | Wednesday | 6 December [1865]

[no salutation]

I have been here – Syren of the Pianoforte[1] – with my back tied up in knots by neuralgic rheumatism, ever since I last saw (and heard) you. I am going tomorrow to comfort the old lady at Tunbridge Wells.[2] And, if I am not utterly crippled, I will come back by Sunday next at seven.

My own hope is that the change of air may do me good. But the infernal damp is mischief to a wretch of my constitution – and I sometimes doubt if I shall be able to tide over the English winter, unless the frost comes. Well is the typical Englishman nicknamed "John <u>Bull</u>". The nervous system of a bull, is the necessary nervous system for any man who lives in this island. Oh my country, between November and February, how I hate you!

Yours affectionately, | WC

Notes

1. A reference to WC's friend Henrietta Ward. In *Heart and Science* WC describes Le Frank's technique: his "pianoforte-playing resembled the performance of a musical box" (Chapter 23).
2. i.e., WC's mother.

Appendix:
Unpublished Letters

As indicated in the Preface, letters which have not so far been published in full or in a summarized form, are included in this Appendix, in date order, with an indication of the present source.

Date	Recipient	Topic	Source
1847			
May 20	George Richmond	Seeks details for father's biography	Princeton
1848			
May 4	Robert Peel	Seeks dedication for biography	Texas
22	Benjamin Disraeli	Seeks subscription for biography	Bodleian
June 26	George Richmond	Seeks prospectuses of biography	Texas
Aug 3	Alaric A Watts	Asks for proofs of biography	Notts Arch
[August]	Alaric A Watts	Discusses proofs	Unknown
1849			
Jan 10	William Etty	Sends copy of biography	Private
June 18	WC Macready	Sends copy of biography	Kansas
[mid-June]	Miss Clarkson	Invitation to rehearsal	PM
Nov 12	Richard Bentley	Sends last sheets of *Antonina*	NYPL
26	Richard Bentley	Accepts terms for *Antonina*	Illinois
Dec6	Richard Bentley	Name change for *Antonina*?	NYPL
1850			
Early July	Richard Bentley	Complains about advertisement	Princeton
Feb 28	Richard Bentley	Has sent *Antonina* for Review	Illinois
March 2	Richard Bentley	Misunderstanding on book order	Illinois
25	Octavia Blewitt	Cannot act as steward	Royal Lit Fund
May 21	Richard Bentley	Discusses 2nd edition of *Antonina*	NYPL
Nov 14	Richard Bentley	Seeks Brandling's illustrations	Private
Dec 28	Richard Bentley	Discusses *Rambles beyond Railways*	Illinois
[1850]	Mrs Richardson	Declines invitation	Private
1851			
Jan 4	Richard Bentley	Accepts invitation	Illinois
Feb 18	Richard Bentley	Asks about free copy of book	NYPL
28	Charles Ward	Asks for reviews of *Rambles*	PM
April 29	Octavia Blewitt	Declines dinner invitation	Royal Lit Fund
[pre-July]	J Marsh	Opening galleries to public	Illinois
Oct 23	Richard Bentley	Idea for Christmas story	Illinois
Nov 5	Charles Dickens	Performance of play in Bristol	PM

Date	Recipient	Topic	Source
22	Edward Pigott	Is "seedy barrister". Sends proofs	Huntington
Dec 8	Richard Bentley	Advertisement for *Mr Wray's Cash-box*	Illinois
24	J Marsh	Delete preface to *Mr Wray's*	Illinois
[late 1851]	Edward Pigott	Will he accompany to play?	Huntington
[late 1851]	Edward Pigott	Sends *Leader* copy of Xmas book	Huntington
[1851]	Edward Pigott	WC unable to call on him	Huntington
1852			
Jan 1	J Marsh	Requests book for *The Leader*	Illinois
7	J Marsh	Requests review copy.	Illinois
9	J Marsh	Reminds him to send copy to *Frazer's*	Illinois
13	J Marsh	Requests copy of *Rambles*	Illinois
March 3	Edward Pigott	Discusses contents of *The Leader*	Huntington
11	J Marsh	Wants space in *The Leader*	Illinois
[March]	J Marsh	Millais has not received payment	Illinois
April 1	J Marsh	Asks when article will be published	Illinois
19	George Bentley	Declines invitation. Has to rehearse	NYPL
July 14	J Marsh	Will bring article	Illinois
Sept 16	Edward Pigott	Regarding *Leader*	Huntington
Oct 1	Richard Bentley	Discusses terms for *Basil*	Illinois
[pre-Nov 16]	Richard Bentley	Sends Vol I of *Basil*	Illinois
[1851–52]	Edward Pigott	Cheque has not been received	Huntington
[1852]	Edward Pigott	Discusses wedding invitation	Huntington
1853			
Feb 4	Edward Pigott	Requests more books	Huntington
5	EM Ward	Asks about portable gas	Texas
March 5	Frederick O Ward	Discusses French translation (*Basil*)	Rylands
April 27	Mrs Tennent	Declines dinner invitation	Mrs Clarke
June 25	Edward Pigott	"Toddles out with a stick"	Huntington
August 17	George Bentley	Discusses terms for *Hide and Seek*	NYPL
[1850–53]	Edward Pigott	Suggests ways to get *Antonina*	Huntington
[1850–53]	Edward Pigott	Gives advice. Suggests visit Academy	"
[end 1853]	Unknown	Request for autograph	Unknown
1854			
Jan 14	George Bentley	Offers articles on Italy (rejected)	NYPL.
[Feb–Mar]	Edward Pigott	Asks about article for *The Leader*	Huntington
March 20	George Bentley	Hopes to bring "major opus"	NYPL
June 1	SC Hall	Wants copy of *Art Journal* for bearer	Royal Lit Fund
[June]	Edward Pigott	Asks about opera and theatre	Huntington
July 21	E M Ward	Going with Dickens (to Boulogne)	Texas
Sept 25	Mrs Henry Bullar	Send Dickens signature	Yale
[Late 1854]	Charles Ward	Asks for *Tales of First French Revolution*	PM
[1854	Edward Pigott	Glad to see French actor	Huntington
[1854]	Edward Pigott	Discusses reviews of *Hide and Seek*	Huntington
[1854]	Edward Pigott	Discusses troubles of *The Leader*	Huntington
[1854]	Edward Pigott	Discusses *Leader*	Huntington
1855			
Jan 21	Edward Pigott	Introduces West Indian friend	Huntington
30	Edward Pigott	Discusses articles	Huntington
[Jan–Feb]	Edward Pigott	Asks him to second Luard at Garrick	Huntington
Feb 3	Edward Pigott	Discusses duplication of reviews	Huntington
5	Edward Pigott	"Delighted to hear about George"	Huntington

Date	Recipient	Topic	Source
Feb 9	George Bentley	Acknowledges cheque for *Rambles*	BL
22	Edward Pigott	Back from Paris. Regnier's message	Huntington
Mar 16	Peter Cunningham	Seeks support for Luard at Garrick	Princeton
March 28	EM Ward	Discusses letter to Athenaeum	Texas
April 21	Edward Pigott	Avoiding Shakespeare dinner?	Huntington
30	WH Wills	Thanks for payment for article	PM
June 7	Mr & Mrs Spiers	Declines invitation	Princeton
28	Mark Lemon	Discusses terms for *The Lighthouse*	Princeton
[mid-July]	Edward Ward	Declines visit to Doctor Diamond	Unknown
[July]	Edward Pigott	Sends article	Huntington
Sept 2	Edward Pigott	Discusses details of yachting trip	Huntington
3	Edward Pigott	George's wedding. Oysters & port wine	"
Oct 31	JW Parker	Thanks for cheque	PM
Nov 1	Thomas Hodgson	Copyright of *Hide and Seek*	Texas
[1855]	Edward Pigott	Party. "Returned in maudlin state"	Huntington
[1855]	Richard Bentley	Proof corrections for *Rambles*	Princeton
[1855]	Edward Pigott	Discusses showing play to Wigan	Huntington
[1855]	Edward Pigott	Problem of getting theatre seats	Huntington
1856			
May 9	Peter Cunningham	Has given prospects to editor	Princeton
June 5	Rev Chauncy Townshend	Sends his brother's address	Wisbech
18	Bernhard Tauchnitz	Accepts offer. Suggests *Hide & Seek*	Unknown
26	Charles Collins	Reports details of yachting trip	Private
Aug 15	Richard Bentley	Requests sales details of *Rambles*	Illinois
23	Bernhard Tauchnitz	Pleased with editing of *After Dark*	Unknown
Sept 20	Richard Bentley	Discusses remuneration for *Rambles*	Illinois
1857			
Jan 30	WR Sams	May not make appointment	Huntington
March 30	FM Evans	Estimates for reprinting *The Dead Secret*	Private
June 4	JJ Oakley	Cannot write for him	Princeton
8	Albert Smith	Wishes to borrow French book	Private
12	FM Evans	Asks for six copies of *Dead Secret*	Bodleian
July 25	Richard Bentley	Thanks for novel *Anne Sherwood*	Illinois
[summer]	[Miss Agnes]	Ill and unable to come to dinner	Unknown
Sept 26	Walter Herrick	Discusses articles	Princeton
Oct 17	J Palgrave Simpson	Discusses *The Lighthouse*	Princeton
Nov 10	Miss Browne	Pleasure in complying with request	Private
1858			
Jan 15	Charles Kean	Thanks for putting name at Princes Theatre	PM
March 20	Herbert Watkins	Requests three copies of "profile" photo	Texas
April 13	James Lowe	Is ill. Cannot meet. Sends books details	Texas
24	Herbert Watkins	Thanks for photographs	Kansas
26	FM Evans	Encloses pamphlet for printing	Private
27	FM Evans	Has communicated with Townshend	Bodleian
June 15	Phillips Sampson	Acknowledges £24. Should be £32	Princeton
July 10	R Monckton Milnes	Thanks for loan of pamphlet	Trin Cam
16	R Monckton Milnes	Declines invitation. Returns pamphlet	Princeton
Aug 12	EF Underwood	Extra £8 – thanks. Mentions new story	Harvard
Nov 5	Unknown	Refuses proposal to publish his play	Huntington

Date	Recipient	Topic	Source
1859			
Jan 13	EM Ward	Suggests Judge Jeffreys as picture	Texas
Feb 9	Mrs Harriet Collins	Will be back in London tomorrow	PM
10	Richard Bentley	Requests annual accounts for *Rambles*	Illinois
23	Mrs Henry Bullar	Declines party invitation	Princeton
24	WS Emden	Encloses possible one-act farce	Unknown
April 21	WSF Mayus	Declines to write contribution	Sydney Lib
27	E Nelson Hazell	No representations of The Lighthouse	Princeton
[May]	Charles Ward	Suggests Caroline entertains him	PM
[May]	Charles Ward	Delays wine delivery	PM
Oct 27	Charles Ward	Get *Queen of Hearts* for Forgues	PM
Nov 8	Charles Ward	Delighted Jane's confinement over	PM
Dec 11	Edward Pigott	Thanks for article in *Daily News*	Huntington
24	William & Norgate	Encloses lost addressee to Customs	Unknown
[1859]	Charles Ward	Asks him to "take pot luck" tomorrow	PM
[1859]	Charles Ward	Thanks for money	PM
[1859]	Charles Ward	Asks him to pay subscription	PM
1860			
Jan 1	Mrs Henrietta Ward	Thanks for present for god-daughter	Texas
11	Sampson Low	Discusses offer for *Woman in White*	Princeton
11	George Smith	Discusses other offer for *Woman in White*	Texas
March 26	Mrs Anne Procter	Has been moving	Princeton
April 13	Sampson Low	Details of pages of *All The Year Round*	Private
19	Holman Hunt	Arrangements for seeing Dickens	Huntington
25	Rev Chauncy Townshend	Accepts dinner invitation	Wisbech
May 5	WH Wills	German translation of *Woman in White*	Hopkins
15	Miss Chambers	Fate of characters in *Woman in White*	Texas
31	Henry Blackett	Introduces his brother	Private
[June]	Charles Ward	Will call on him	PM
July 5	Charles Ward	Pay insurance. Invites to dinner	PM
11	Charles Ward	Orders claret. No need of champagne	PM
27	Rev Hely-Hutchinson Smith	Discusses poem	Private
Aug 3	EM Ward	Finished *Woman in White*. Party invite	Texas
6	Richard Bentley	Promises a future story	Illinois
7	Charles Dickens	Renewal of terms: *All The Year Round*	Hopkins
7	R Monckton Milnes	Hopes to pay him a visit later	Trin Cam
22	Mrs Harriet Collins	Reports sales of *Woman in White*	PM
27	Charles Ward	Invites to dinner	Private
Oct 2	Charles Ward	Invites to dinner. Republishing 2 novels	PM
5	Charles Ward	Asks him to call after church	PM
8	Unknown	Colonial copyright	Huntington
13	FM Evans	Encloses cheque	Private
13	Sir James Tennent	Will see him on return from Paris	Private
[Nov]	Edward Marston	Discusses reprinting of his novels	Unknown
Nov 14	Sir James Tennent	Promises to be at Board of Trade	Private
21	Edward Marston	Explains decision about reprinting	Unknown
Dec 3	Richard Bentley	Discusses future of contract	Illinois
5	Charles E Mudie	Accepts dinner invitation	Illinois
18	Charles E Mudie	Sends apologies	Illinois
19	Charles E Mudie	Arranges to meet to see new hall	Illinois
[1850–0]	Edward Pigott	Invites him to dinner	Huntington
[1860]	Charles Ward	Can't make Friday. Asks him to call in	PM
[1860]	Charles Ward	Invites him to try claret	PM
[1850–60]	Richard Bentley	Thanks for delivery of book	Illinois

Date	Recipient	Topic	Source
1861			
Jan 1	Sampson Low	Views on six-year leasing copyrights	Private
9	E M Ward	Can't visit : "Carrie" has measles	Texas
12	Sampson Low	Thanks for agreement	Private
Feb 13	R Dionis	Gives authority for French translation	Princeton
18	Herbert Watkins	Not to publish photograph – yet	Texas
March 5	R Monckton Milnes	Accepts invitation	Trin Cam
25	WH Wills	Invites to dinner	Princeton
26	Holman Hunt	Invites to dinner	Huntington
April 13	Émile Forgues	Discusses Balzac and Forster	Princeton
16	Charles Ward	Invites to dinner with Caroline	PM
17	Edward Walford	Corrects biographical details	Columbia
18	R Monckton Milnes	Is delighted at election to Committee	Trin Cam
[April ?]	Charles Ward	Invitation to dinner	PM
22	Charles Ward	Has paid bill	PM
May 8	George Bentley	Says *Rambles* has not reached him	BL
20	Ludwig Loffler	No to translation offer	M/c Cen L
30	EJ Soundry	Agrees to mention with poem	Private
June 12	Herbert Watkins	Thanks for portraits	Kansas
14	Lady Goldsnid	Gives advice about copyright	Texas
July 14	Mrs EM Ward	Cannot join theatre party	Texas
Aug 7	George Gregson	Likes Whitby	Yale
19	Mrs Monckton Milnes	Cannot join them as hoped	Trin. Cam
26	Charles Ward	Hotel noisy. Going to York	PM
Sept 2	Sampson Low	Proofs. Dedication to *Hide & Seek*	Unknown
13	Charles Ward	Invitation to dinner	PM
18	Miss ML Wrigley	Autograph. Glad *W in W* pleased her	Princeton
Oct 10	EB Neill	Discusses possible offer	Princeton
10	Sampson Low	Asks to check *Queen of Hearts* terms	Texas
21	Mrs Anne Procter	Discusses possible publishing offer	Camb Un
Dec 12	JB Brown Jr	Promises show pictures of his father	Illinois
13	Charles Ward	Encloses cheque & letter for translation	PM
[1861]	Charles Ward	Requests 10 sovereigns	PM
[1861]	Charles Ward	"Come and take pot luck"	PM
[1861]	Charles Ward	Asks to be picked up	PM
[1861]	Charles Ward	Requests money	PM
1862			
Jan 8	C Whiting	Sends parts for *All The Year Round*	Unknown
28	BC Tauchnitz	Ready to receive any proposal	Unknown
28	John Watkins	Arranges appointment	Private
Feb 6	Sir James Tennent	Declines second invitation	Unknown
[Feb]	Charles Ward	Asks for two sovereigns	PM
March 8	Mrs EM Ward	Offers two dates for dinner	Texas
17	Charles Ward	Asks about timing of mail to China	PM
April 1	EM Ward	Discusses their reactions to *No Name*	Texas
June 15	Charles Ward	Requests another cheque book	PM
30	Francis C Beard	Invites him to Broadstairs	Princeton
July 3	Charles Manby	Will sit for photograph on return	Texas
9	Charles Ward	Asks about marriage licence & mails	PM
13	Charles Ward	"There is a bed for you here"	PM
17	James Richter	Encloses proofs of *No Name*	Private
Sept 1	Sampson Low	Discusses US mailing of *No Name*	Private
11	Charles Ward	Requests review and German translation	PM
12	Charles Lever	Introduces Pigott who is going to Italy	Harvard

Date	Recipient	Topic	Source
Oct 6	Charles Ward	Asks mailing time from Dumfries	PM
30	AG Carlier	Declines French translation offer	Un B'ham
Nov 13	Nina Lehmann	Sends a promised autograph	Texas[copy]
21	WH Wills	Discusses M/s from William Bernard	PM
Dec 17	CA Calvet	Declines proposal for *Red Vial*	Huntington
1863			
Jan 5	Richard Bentley	Discusses future literary co-operation	Illinois
15	John Hollingshed	Cannot accept his proposal	NYU
16	Charles Ward	Requests money & new cheque book	PM
Feb 23	William Wright	Complies with request for autograph	Private
March 3	WP Frith	Returns Mrs Frith's album	V & A
12	Henry Morgan	Sends proof of portrait from *W in W*	Unknown
April 6	John Millais	Requests he support him at club	Texas
July 11	Sampson Low Jr	Discusses illustrations for *No Name*	Yale
Aug 21	TH Hills	Asks for prescription to be made up	Melbourne
22	Sampson Low	Confirms terms for *My Miscellanies*	Unknown
Sept 27	Mrs Harriet Collins	Attack of gout. Going to Continent	Private
29	Mrs Harriet Collins	Leaving for Rome on Saturday	Private
Oct 8	Holman Hunt	Planning to go to Rome & Naples	Huntington
Nov 2	Charles Ward	Discusses money for Rome	PM
[1863]	Charles Ward	Back again. Invites to dinner	PM
1864			
April 4	Frederick Ouvry	Details of marriage licence	Texas
5	Frederick Ouvry	Discusses plot of *Armadale*	Texas
5	Charles Ward	Thanks him for second certificates	Harrowby
20	Whittaker Collins	Thanks for re-directing letter	Texas
21	Routledge, Warne etc	Returns proof of *Men of the Time*	Unknown
May 4	John Watkins	Will make appointment for photo	Private
June 11	Mrs Harriet Collins	Sends four autographs and photographs	PM
28	Henry H Bemrose	Request for autograph	Private
July 27	R Monckton Milnes	Accepts invitation to Fryston	Trin Cam
Aug 6	R Monckton Milnes	Will be at Fryston next Wednesday	Harvard
6	EM Ward	Mrs Ward's illness. Cruising at sea	Texas
Sept 16	WH Wills	Will second him for Garrick	Private
Nov 8	Mr & Mrs Frith	Delighted to accept dinner invitation	V & A
1865			
Jan 4	Mrs Harriet Collins	Asks to lunch at the Bullars	Private
12	Printers of *Cornhill*	Has lengthened March number	Princeton
Feb 2	Mrs Harriet Collins	Will bring *Cornhill* & M/s of *Armadale*	Private
6	Richard Bentley	Requests accounts of *Rambles*	Illinois
21	HF Chorley	Unable to accept invitation	Kansas
21	Frederick Enoch	Requests "revises of Part 7"	PM
March 8	George Bentley	Requests details of *Rambles*	Illinois
8	Mrs Harriet Collins	Back from Paris. See her next week	Private
9	Unknown	Received proofs	Un B'ham
11	George Smith	Membership of Garrick. *Armadale*	NLS
16	Elizabeth Benzon	Accepts dinner invitation	Private
April 4	Unknown	Makes appointment	PM
13	Mrs Harriet Collins	Reports his chairmanship of meeting	Private
15	Unknown	Leaves corrected proof of last no	Private
21	Printer	Thanks for "revises" of *Armadale*	Yale
June 25	Mrs Mitchell	Hopes to see them for dinner	Private

Date	Recipient	Topic	Source
26	Benjamin West Bell	Thanks for extract from *The Times*	Texas
July 1	Mrs Harriet Collins	May go sailing at Yarmouth	PM
Aug 17	Charles Ward	Asks about credits in his accounts	Harrowby
Sept 21	J Elliott	Introduces Mrs Slade	Private
Oct 28	Mrs Harriet Collins	Encloses manuscript from Newcastle	Private
Nov 30	JH Nightingale	"Strange deaths on board 'Armadale'"	PM
Dec 9	Unknown	"A few lines, signed as you request"	Yale

The index appears at the end of Volume 2.